Shadows of Betrayal

SL Harby

Cover Art by
Gilbert Arthur

Shadows of Betrayal is dedicated to each and every one of my readers. Your support and encouragement keep me writing. Your enjoyment inspires me to continue creating and bringing these worlds to life.

I owe special gratitude to my wife and biggest fan, Jessica, without whom these stories would have remained untold.

Contents

Part One

Part Two

Part Three

Cast of Characters

Earth

Jillian Allen – The heroine of our story
Marisol Diaz – Jillian's best friend
Hector Thompson – Plague Man's reflection, drug dealer
Cyrill Nephus – Jillian's school friend
Stephen Moses – Hollis's comatose reflection
Veronica Moses - Stephen's ex-wife

Taerh

Hollis the Slender – The hero of our story
Asaege – Jillian's reflection, revolutionary leader
Aristoi – Hollis's closest friend and comrade, Songspear
Seran Ash – Hollis's mentor, thief
Plague Man – Hollis's sworn enemy
Mika – Hollis's former comrade, murderer of his friends

Gods and Goddesses of Taerh

Olm – God of Justice, Creation, twin brother of Umma, known as the Father of Justice, Lord of the Dawn
Umma – Goddess of Nature, Knowledge, twin sister of Olm, known as the Mother of the Forest, Lady of Light
Sharroth – God of Shadow, Deception, younger brother of Olm and Umma, known as the Master of Beasts, Father of Lies, Bringer of Shadows

Cast of Characters

Kern

Hollis

Gods and Goddesses of Pine

Part One:

Shadows of the Past

"The brighter the light, the darker the shadow."

-Carl Jung

Chapter One
A Bitter Journey

Hollis saw the baleful eyes a split second before the massive snow bank exploded, showering him with frozen detritus. Rolling to the side, he felt the creature's wedge-shaped head pass within a handsbreadth of his fur-wrapped body. The thief's vision was obscured by a sinuous, shaggy form, but he heard a sharp snap as its fanged mouth closed on empty air. As he scrambled back on heels and hands, Hollis saw Aristoi spin around, her spear already raised before her.

Between them, coiling for its next strike, was a monstrosity thankfully limited to the far north of Taerh. Known as a furred serpent, the creature more than lived up to the horrendous image its name had conjured in Hollis's mind. The creature's true length was hard to judge among its sinuous coils but the thief guessed it must have measured at least sixty feet long and reached more than three feet around at its thickest point. Never a fan of snakes of any size, Hollis faced something out of his nightmares in the furred serpent. No matter how quickly he scrambled, his supine position offered him limited options to dodge the creature's next strike.

A sudden, wordless shout broke the snow-muted stillness, attracting the monster's attention for a split second. Behind its bulk, Hollis saw the burnished iron head of Aristoi's spear glint for an instant in the clear northern sun before it sank into the mass of the serpent's coils. The creature recoiled, turning its attention to the Songspear and allowing the thief to scramble to his feet. He was almost swept from them again as the monstrosity shifted to face the new threat. A thrashing tail struck him in the thigh with the force of a hammer, but the thief gritted his teeth and retreated a few stumbling steps. Once out of range of the twitching appendage, Hollis drew his Wallin Fahr and began circling the serpent.

Aristoi held her spear at chest height, its tip tracing lazy figure eights in the air. The creature slithered forward almost imperceptibly, curling its body into an s-shape. Its head followed the path of the Songspear's weapon as if they were connected by an invisible fiber. Without warning, the serpent lashed out, its mouth opening well past what should have been possible. In the same movement, the creature launched its coils forward, advancing its bulk towards her in an instant. For a split second, his position permitted Hollis a brief glance of the cavernous maw, lined with two rows of short curved teeth. All of them were angled towards the slimy abyss that was the serpent's gullet. Aristoi danced backward with a deft pair of steps. At the same time, she dropped the head of her spear and extended it towards the incoming monstrosity. The weapon's tip entered the serpent's head just under the jaw but the creature was able to cut short its lunge quickly enough to pull back with only a scratch along its fur-covered hide.

Like water over stone, the serpent's body oriented itself more directly in front of Aristoi. The thief took advantage of the beast's distracted focus, lunging forward with his Uteli blade. Its thick fur and the resilient skin dulled most of the weapon's bite, but the Dwarven steel sword still left a long crimson wound in its wake. As the creature's head snapped around to strike at Hollis's renewed threat, he danced back out of range.

Before the serpent could shift its attention back to her, Aristoi drove her spear into it just behind those deadly jaws. As it turned on her again, the Songspear leapt backwards, the iron blade of her spear stained dark with the beast's blood. The beast's bulk shifted again as it tried in vain to keep both of its no-longer-easy-meals in sight. Aristoi's feet slid across the snow-covered ground in an attempt to make that impossible.

As the furred creature turned its eyes from him, Hollis leapt towards it, a powerful upper-cut aimed at the underside of its massive head. It had not lived long enough to grow to such a size without gaining cunning in equal measure. Its gaze snapped back towards the

2

lunging thief. The serpent pulled its head out of the sword's deadly path, coiling its body for a counter strike against its off-balance opponent. Tucking his shoulder, Hollis turned his ill-fated charge into a clumsy roll. He prayed that it would carry him far enough away from the fang-filled jaws of the beast.

As it turned out, his plea proved unnecessary. Aristoi's spear met the serpent's throat mid lunge, its own momentum adding to hers. Despite being impaled on two feet of sharpened iron, the creature shifted its massive body forward. Before she could react, the Songspear was carried to the ground. Hollis pivoted smoothly as he came to his feet, watching as his friend was buried beneath a heap of undulating furred coils.

Held above the writhing mass, still transfixed on six feet of dark wood and polished metal, was the serpent's head. The struggling beast's jaws snapped ineffectually at the air as its powerful body thrashed in an effort to pull itself from the spear. Its unreasoning struggle was most likely the only thing that saved Aristoi. The entirety of the serpent's strength was devoted to pulling itself free rather than crushing the life from the woman trapped below it.

The thief dashed forward, using one of the heavily muscled coils as a stepping stone to gain enough height to bring his sword down across the beast's raised neck. This time, furred coat and leathery skin proved no match for Dwarven steel. His blade bit deeply into muscle and bone. Concerted struggle turned to agonized flailing in the space of a breath. A thrashing coil cast Hollis aside with astonishing ease. The shock of hitting the ground knocked the sword from his hand. The thief's eyes scanned the ground for the blade as he rolled to his feet, but it was lost in the snow.

Drawing his thick-bladed dagger, a gift from a departed companion, Hollis swore he would not add the Songspear to that ever-growing list. The serpent's struggles must have wrenched the spear's butt free from where it had wedged itself because its half-severed head no longer rose above the forest of flailing, blood matted coils. As he approached, doubt fell upon the thief's heart like cold water. He could see no sign of Aristoi amid the writhing mass.

Closing his eyes for a second, Hollis drew upon the gifts granted him by the Well of Worlds. A soft cloak of serenity draped itself across his shoulders, driving from him the frigid fingers of uncertainty. When he opened them again, it was with new eyes. Although the heap of coils continued to conceal anything within their depths, it was clear that in their midst was a section that undulated less vigorously. Therein lay his comrade.

3

Pushing aside his deep rooted trepidation of snakes, the thief reached into the rippling nest and grabbed hold of a furred loop. He slid his dagger beneath the pulsing mass and pulled with all his might. The weapon's keen edge parted skin and muscle, cutting it cleanly in two. Ignoring the hot wash of blood and viscera against the skin of his exposed hands and face, Hollis captured another coil and repeated the exercise.

The thief wasn't sure when the serpent ceased to struggle, but it was quite dead by the time he pulled Aristoi free of the embrace of its quickly cooling body. Laying back in the snow, he closed his eyes and tried to catch his breath. He heard the Songspear doing the same nearby. Between gulps of air, Hollis muttered to himself, "Fucking snakes."

*****

The two friends sat in silence, only the intermittent snapping of the fire between them breaking the stillness of the night. Spread before them was the remains of their sparse evening repast, a humble meal of roasted snake and hardtack. Winter came early to the Rangor Wastes and held it firmly in its skeletal claw. The serpent's attack on them was proof that easier prey had already migrated south and made any hope of further fresh meat a distant possibility.

When Hollis finally spoke, his voice cut the silence like a midnight church bell. "Explain to me again how we are to find your friend. There is nothing but permafrost and tundra as far as the eye can see."

Aristoi looked over the thief's shoulder into the darkness. "I find the desolation very calming after even a short time in that rat's warren you call a city."

He raised an eyebrow but let her comment pass. "Calming or not, it does not lend itself to locating one man among its vast acreage. It is less a case of a needle in a haystack and more one of a needle in an onion field."

"I missed your colorful, if not overly dramatic manner, North-erner." The Songspear shrugged. "As to finding Valmont, we must rely upon him finding us. My hope is by not hiding signs of our passage, he will do just that once he comes across them."

Hollis squinted into the night. "As deserted as the wastes seem to be, are you certain that he will be the only one to come across our trail?"

She nodded. "We crossed into Bone Dog territory at some point yesterday. These lands were avoided by most other Rangor clans before the Dogs were wiped out months ago. Their destruction did

4

nothing to diminish the rumors of the curse that hangs over it."

His head snapped around, a hard glare hanging in his eyes. "Curse? Why am I just hearing about this now?"

"Would you have come if you had known?"

Hollis shrugged. "Most likely."

"Then what does it matter?"

"And if I said no?"

Without missing a beat, Aristoi replied, "That would have been justification for not telling you." The small smile coloring her lips took a good deal of the sting out of her words.

The thief made a wordless sound of displeasure but found her grin infectious.

She continued, "Please do not tell me that Hollis the Slender, Child of the Well of Worlds and Slayer of the Walker, is afraid of ghost stories and whispered superstitions."

He grumbled, "It just would have been nice to have been told is all."

The Songspear put her hand behind her ear and leaned in dramatically. "What was that?"

Hollis sighed softly, the frown on his face evaporating. "I would dearly like to hear a few of these ghost stories."

She winked at him. "Now, that is the spirit."

He chuckled before growling, "Make with the 'once upon a time.'" When she cocked her head, the thief amended, "It is an Earth saying … tell your tale, Songspear."

"Your language is so peculiar," she commented before launching into her story. "During the Age of Legends, when the First King and his descendants ruled the Cradle, the ancestors of the Rangor had already been following the same seasonal path for centuries. Where the Grand Kingdom found the Sibling Gods in the words of the Heralds, the so called 'northern barbarians' read their desires in the howling wind and driving rain."

"Both of those things certainly leave a great deal to interpretation," Hollis interjected.

Aristoi nodded. "That they do, but no more so than the written word, as both of us can attest from our mutual experience in Oizan."

"You make a fine point." The thief's mind returned to his part in the ongoing revolution within the city he still called home. Although he was not directly responsible for the death of the Hand of Light, Olm's chosen on Taerh, there were many who sought to put the blame squarely in his lap. In truth, his part was more a matter of coincidence than anything else. A chance meeting within the Great

Library led to a grass roots rebellion among people nourished for too long on too many promises and too little respect.

At the center of the maelstrom that had coalesced into a movement was the figure of the Prophet. She brought light to lives previously dominated by ignorance and darkness. This intellectual illumination took the form of the words of the Father of the Dawn, Olm himself. Called *Dialogues of the Chalice*, the words found within sparked the fires of uprising against the forces of the status quo. Although most called her Prophet, Hollis knew her simply as Asaege.

With her name, the image of the woman he had grown to love formed in his mind. The soft curves of her face brought a smile to his lips like a sweet spring breeze. However, it wasn't her beauty alone that had captivated the scoundrel known as Hollis the Slender. He had known many pretty faces, but none had captured his heart as Asaege had done. Beneath the surface of the academic she showed the world, was an intensity that put some of the finest warriors he had known to shame.

Had she turned her formidable will towards politics or riches, there was no doubt in the thief's mind that Asaege would have found success beyond even his own imagination. The only goal on her razor-sharp mind, however, was leaving the world a better place than she was forced to live in. Exiled from the Great Library for the crime of bringing knowledge to those who could not afford it, she took to the alleys and tenement walls to spread her message. Although he had a hand in that portion of her crusade, in his mind the success remained hers alone.

Hollis felt a sharp, bittersweet knife plunge into his heart as he thought of his dearest Asaege carrying on alone while he was half a world away. Although she had grown up in Oizan, just as he did, she has always seen her city in the sun. The thief's world had always been viewed by the gauzy light of the moon. No fool by any measure, Asaege had not been privy to the true depths to which humanity could sink when its way of life was threatened. He hoped that she could depend on those in her closest circle: Rudelph, Toni and Seran, but a life lived on the streets of the Ash had eroded most of the trust Hollis possessed in the motivations of other people.

The thief looked up to see Aristoi staring at him with patient eyes. "Where did you go?" she asked. Before he could push an answer past the worry that had taken up residence in his chest, she said, "She will be fine, Northerner. She has a strength for which I do not believe you give her credit."

6

"It is not her strength that I doubt," he growled. "As long as the Binders or Guild benefit from her movement, she has nothing to fear from them. My concern is with when their interests no longer intersect."

In a gentle voice, Aristoi prompted, "Do you not believe she knows that? She, too, is a child of two worlds; she will never be alone."

The truth did nothing to assuage the dread in his heart, but Hollis nodded. Looking out into the night, he prompted, "You were telling me about the Rangor during the Age of Legends ..."

She studied him out of the corner of her eye for a second before continuing. "The messages those early people read in the world around them shaped their lives and those of their descendants, even to this day." She gestured at the land around them. "This was called Kukardisch. It loosely translates to *the valley of graves*."

Hollis raised an eyebrow. "The entire valley is a graveyard?"

Aristoi nodded. "They believed that just as the souls of the departed must journey to their place of judgment, so too their companions must travel to put them to rest. For thousands of years, the Rangor have come here to bury their dead beneath snow, stone and soil. Legend has it that in ages past, the floor of the valley had been as flat as a still pond."

The thief squinted into the darkness, rolling hills spread out as far as his eye could see. "Each of these swells are ..." He searched for an appropriate term.

She provided it. "A collection of cairns, some holding thousands of fallen Rangor."

He slowly shook his head. "Amazing."

"None can tell when the wolves appeared, prowling among the mounds. Their tawny-white coats, the color of aged bone, were seen as a sign. These Baenulf or Bone Wolves were believed to be guardians of the dead. Supposedly, the Baenulf could travel between the lands of the living and dead with impunity. In addition to guarding the cairns from grave robbers, they would accompany the souls of properly buried Rangor into Umma's sight, defending them from any who sought to interfere with their travels."

"Are you saying that the entire valley is haunted by some sort of ghostly guard dogs?"

"That is what the Rangor believe. They are so revered that every year or so, every clan bring their children here to remain in the creatures good graces. One child born to each tribe that year are left among the cairns. If the tribe has the Baenulf's favor, they accept

7

the child as one of their own. But if the clan has done something to offend the guardians or too long has passed between sacrifices—"

"Wolves need to eat," Hollis finished, his voice low and dangerous.

"Wolves need to eat," the Songspear agreed. "Those claimed by the Baenulf formed their own clan, taking the protection of the valley onto themselves."

"The Bone Dogs?"

She nodded. "The same. It has been this way since the Age of Legends ..."

The thief watched his friend carefully. When she paused, he frowned suspiciously. "Until?"

"Until the Snow Queen came. She declared that the practice of sacrificing children to the Bone Wolves was barbaric."

"She may have had a point," he muttered.

Ignoring his words, Aristoi continued, "The Dogs objected, saying that the Baenulf were as much a part of Rangor life as the elk or the tundra itself." She met Hollis's gaze. "She had them hunted down to the last man, woman and child. Her route toward bringing civilization to the Rangor involved slaughtering an entire clan of their own people."

"Your friend, Valmont?"

"The Bone Dogs were not the only clan to draw the ire of your former comrade, Mika. There were others that wanted no part of her new way of life. Those, however, she only murdered until the rest came around to her way of thinking."

The thief shook his head, "Mika would not do this ... she was intense, sure ... but you are talking about tyranny on a level of which she is not capable."

The instinctual denial within Hollis warred with the haunting knowledge Asaege had gleaned from the journals of his own mentor, Silvermoon. He and Mika had traveled back into the Rangor Well alone, but Mika alone emerged. Although the memories the thief had of the Mantrian swordswoman were of a staunch ally, logic told him that she was most likely responsible for Silvermoon's death.

"Of which she *was* not capable," Aristoi amended.

He opened his mouth to protest but his companion raised her finger. His words died in his throat as he searched the darkness beyond their campfire. He could just make out shadows as they moved among the mounds.

"We are not alone," the Songspear warned.

"Baenulf?"

She shook her head, "Our visitors are of the two-legged variety." Hollis saw her swallow hard, as if she could push down a fear for which he had not explanation. "They carry cold iron."

The thief's gaze snapped to his friend's face. "How can you tell?"

Aristoi muttered the only two words that would have brought his protests to an abrupt end at that moment. "Trust me."

His trust in the Songspear, forged on many roads, was such that he simply nodded, taking her word for truth. He breathed deeply through his nose, searching for the calm place he had come to call the "Understanding". Just as when they fought the furred serpent, everything around him snapped into clarity.

Over Aristoi's shoulder, he counted two shapes moving in the darkness. "A pair behind you," Hollis warned.

"At least that many lay in the opposite direction. They have cut off our escape; we may need to make our stand here."

*****

The first of the figures charged into the flickering perimeter of firelight as Hollis leapt to his feet. Hurdling over the small campfire that separated them, he moved past Aristoi and stood at her unprotected back. The scruffy, bearded figure pulled up short as his unaware target suddenly proved itself less so. Behind him, Hollis heard his companion rise as well. Although the scenery was foreign to both of them, the thief and the Songspear fell into old habits.

He felt a light tap on the outside of his left calf, courtesy of Aristoi's spear. Smoothly, Hollis rotated to his right, a third pair of opponents appearing in his peripheral vision. "Six," he hissed. He didn't need to see the Songspear to sense the terse nod of her head in the dim night.

The other intruders entered the feeble ring of illumination, Hollis noted that they shared their comrade's unkempt appearance. Behind them in the darkness, he could make out several more shapes. Mirroring the first man's caution, they held dark metal spears before them. In contrast, the thief's Dwarven steel Wallin Fahr gleamed like the moon itself. Held in both hands, he allowed its tip to sway in a slow figure-eight, like the tail of an agitated cat.

"If we do not get to work soon, Southerner," Hollis remarked over his shoulder, "this situation is likely to grow beyond our capabilities fairly quickly." He caught motion out of the corner of his eye. "Right," he snapped as he rotated again. Faced with the prospect of the thief's burnished blade, the warrior cut short his advance. "Perhaps a rousing tune?"

9

Silence hung in air where Hollis expected the Songspear's response. When the expected reply came, her voice held a flutter that didn't bolster his confidence. "I do not think that would help matters."

Resisting the temptation to turn on his partner, Hollis snorted his displeasure. The frigid tundra air turning his breath into a cloud of condensation before him. "In another few seconds, there will be little that will." The thief pulled upon the "Understanding" as he watched the four men before him. Based on the nervous shuffling of his feet, the overzealous warrior seemed torn between remaining at his present distance and closing on Hollis. While the man should have had confidence in his weapon's superior reach, trepidation colored his every movement.

"Move," Hollis called as he lunged forward. His sudden charge took the warrior by surprise, allowing the thief to get past the spear's sharpened head. Releasing his sword with his left hand, he fastened it around the shaft of his opponent's weapon. The warrior had to make the split second decision to cut short his withdrawal or continue it without his spear. He made the appropriate choice, leaving Hollis with six feet of ash and cold iron clutched in his fist.

Behind him, he heard the scraping of Aristoi's boots against the permafrost. Satisfied that his comrade was on his heels, the thief pressed the temporarily weaponless warrior before he could draw the axe on his belt. Launching a clumsy overhand stab with the spear, Hollis kept the man at a distance. In his peripheral vision, he saw the remaining intruders closing around them. *Our only chance is to break free of the group and outrun them*, he thought. Hoping that the Songspear would follow his lead, he braced for another charge.

A voice cut the building din of conflict. The words were foreign to him but their meaning was unmistakable: *Stop.*

Chapter Two

A Renewed Accord

The warriors surrounding the pair fell back cautiously, their spears pointed inward. One of their number growled a question to the unseen speaker. Both the query and answer were incomprehensible to the thief.

Hollis drove the spear in his left hand into the ground and shifted to a two handed grip on his Wallin Fahr. Keeping it between him and the ring of enemies, he asked, "Any chance you speak any of the local dialects?" The question was low and pleading.

"A few," Aristoi responded. Her voice still contained a quiver that the thief found equal parts unusual and disconcerting. "They have been tracking us for the better part of the night."

"Is it too much to hope that all of this is a misunderstanding?"

The Songspear didn't respond. Instead she called into the darkness. "Valmont? Is this any way to greet an old friend?"

A boy barely into his teens stepped into the light, an iron tipped spear held casually at his side. Not yet grown into his lanky frame, Valmont stood just under six feet tall. Hollis's first impression of him was all sharp angles and shaggy black hair. The gifts of the Well told another story. His piercing blue eyes held a combination of intensity and distance that is only earned by witnessing terrible things. Around him, men twice his age clenched their spears in white-knuckled grips, unvoiced terror plain in their faces. Valmont's expression was one of weariness, as if there were no horrors before him that could contest with the ones that haunted his memories.

Greeted with silence, Aristoi continued, "I came north at your request, why is it that I do not feel welcome?"

A small, sad smile bloomed on the boy's lips. "Hospitality is in short supply these days, Songspear."

She raised an eyebrow. "Your Trade Tongue has improved."

Valmont nodded. "When the honor of my clan was torn asunder … when the Snow Queen crushed the Furred Serpents beneath the heel of her boot, I was forced to learn some hard lessons. Your language was among the easiest of them."

Hollis squinted at Aristoi.

The Songspear whispered, "His clan took their name from the creature." As the thief nodded, she turned her attention back to the boy. "I am sorry to hear about your people."

Valmont turned his head and spit into the snow. "I wish I could say that the Serpents resisted to the last man, woman and child. Once the real fighting began, most of my clansmen chose to serve on their knees rather than dying on their feet." His mouth twisted as if tasting something bitter.

Aristoi's eyes darted to the ring of cold iron in the center of which she and the thief stood. Although it had paled, fear still colored her expression. Hollis could see that Valmont noticed; the boy's eyes narrowed as he glanced between them and the weapons.

The thief spoke up. "If we are all friends here, I would consider it a kindness if you could pass that along to your comrades. Even in short supply, hospitality should never be served with bared steel." Hollis's words snapped Valmont out of his reverie. He hoped they also interrupted any chain of thought as well.

"Of course," the boy said before turning to his warriors. A few clipped phrases in their language was enough to convince the men to stand down. Again, the thief was impressed by the level of respect the grown men afforded Valmont.

"My thanks." Hollis's words were for the boy, but he continued to study the Songspear beside him.

After barking another order to his people, Valmont gestured into the darkness. "Our camp is not far. I can not offer much beyond elk stew and goat cheese but hopefully a warm fire and company will make up the difference."

"That is more than generous," Aristoi said.

The thief nodded in agreement. "Let us stamp out our own fire

12

and we will take you up on that." He closed his fingers around his companion's shoulder before leaning in to whisper to her. "I realize those cold iron spears were not meant for you specifically, my friend. All the same, I have an inkling that your trepidation has something to do with an explanation, too long delayed."

*****

"It is complicated," Aristoi began. Valmont and his men lead the way across the permafrost, presumably towards their camp. Twenty yards ahead of the pair, they seemed content to let the thief and his companion have their privacy.

"I assumed as much," Hollis said, watching the figures ahead of them. "After the situation in the Great Library courtyard, I had suspicions." When both their lives and the fate of Asaege's revolution perched upon a razor's edge, Aristoi had called upon potent magic to drive fear into the hearts of the forces opposing them. In the moment, the thief had assumed it was another bit of her song-magic.

That assumption had rung false, even in that moment. As time passed, his mind kept returning to it, like a bit of sand caught beneath a fingernail. Those grains kept pulling his thoughts back to that night. Through the "Understanding" he was able to remember the events as if they occurred seconds prior, rather than weeks. The same gifts that granted him extraordinary powers of perception and recollection also rendered him resistant to most magic. The mournful sound of that wordless song was no exception, however it hit him differently than any other experience he'd had with Thaumaturgy before that night. Although each time he was exposed to the arcane syllables that were the language of magic, the words themselves were instantly forgotten, Hollis could always feel their power in his chest. The howling sound engendered nothing but dread in his heart.

The thief could see the trepidation in his friend's eyes. "I remember a time, not so long ago, when I had an equally complicated story to tell."

The Songspear nodded.

"Do you remember what you told me?"

"I said I could not possibly believe your story if you did not share it with me."

"The only way we can begin to uncomplicate things is for you to share them in the first place."

Aristoi opened her mouth and then closed it again, a deep frown creasing her lips. For his part, the thief waited patiently as he walked beside her. A tense silence hung in the air for longer than he would have liked, but Hollis continued to wait for the Songspear to find her words.

"You are aware that this is not my first visit to the Wastes."

He nodded.

"A few months before we met in the Emir's dungeons, I had traveled north in search of a rumored Well of Worlds among the Rangor. Although my search ended in disappointment, the extinguished Well was not all I found."

The thief turned to regard his friend, trying to keep the devouring curiosity from his face. "From what I have seen, there is not much to be found besides ice and snow."

The Songspear paused, a debate clear on her face. She took a moment to come to a decision before continuing. "As payment for allowing me access to the Well, the chief of the Furred Serpents demanded that I deal with a creature that had been hunting his people."

Hollis nodded. "Can I assume that this creature had a particular distaste for cold iron?"

Aristoi gave a brief nod but her expression spoke volumes. She was struggling to get through her explanation and his questions were not making the process any easier. "Have you heard of the gwyllgi?"

The thief frowned and shook his head.

"Churchyard beast?"

Again he shook his head.

"Black dog?"

That term awakened a memory from Hollis's reflection before they had become one. The black dog legend persisted throughout much of Stephen's world in one form or another. Always taking the form of a large black canine, they were often portents of death, if not the purveyors of it themselves. Authors such as Doyle and Bronte fixed the black dog in the popular culture of that world.

Aristoi must have noted the recognition on the thief's face. "Its true nature is lost in legend and exaggeration, but I assure you the beast is indeed very real ..." The woman's eyes grew distant, as if she watched events shrouded within her memories. Hollis continued to walk beside her, offering his support through respectful silence. One moment stretched into several as the pair's only companion became the crunching of permafrost beneath their boots. An uncertainty that the thief was unused to seeing in her face colored her expression. "... very real indeed."

The Songspear closed her eyes and shook her head slowly. When she opened them, her voice was calm and sure, as if her momentary doubt had never been. "The black dog had been stalking the clan for much of the autumn, driving them from the safety of their seasonal home and deeper into the tundra. I suppose they saw me and my Long Walk as a convenient way of bringing either the gwyllgi or my inquires to an end." Through gritted teeth, she hissed, "My impression was that they were ambivalent as to which outcome came to pass."

Hollis rolled his eyes. The gesture carried the understanding gleaned from two lifetimes. "Witness my lack of surprise," he muttered.

"A difficult choice placed before me, I allowed an undeserved confidence in my skill with spear and song to drown out common sense."

The thief tilted his head, watching something more than simple fear cross his companion's features.

"When I finally faced down the beast, I found both my faith and ability insufficient for the task. If it had not been for Valmont, the creature most likely would have devoured me as it had done so many members of the boy's clan." The Songspear growled, "Some nights, I almost wish he had been too late."

Hollis frowned at her. "You can not mean that." The haunted look in Aristoi's eyes made him doubt his words.

"The gwyllgi legends are a mess of superstition and half-truths, but the one thing on which they all agree is the fact that there is a sickness in their souls. Depending on the source, it is said to be a spiritual disease or a shard of Sharroth himself. Those that fall victim to the beast's jaws but do not perish are infected by a measure of their corruption."

A cold wash of dread swept through Hollis's veins.

"Like a wasting sickness, it eats away at one's very soul until there is nothing left but malevolent cunning and joyful brutality. When they can resist the wicked siren's call of their own inner darkness no longer, the victim's body twists into a profane amalgam of wolf and man. Another gwyllgi is born."

The thief reached out a hand, laying it gently on Aristoi's shoulder. He felt her wince beneath his fingertips. "In the courtyard of the Great Library —"

"— To this point, I have been able to pull upon a measure of the darkness growing inside of me without surrendering completely to its influence."

"So when you were injured at the Well of Worlds? When Plague Man ran you through beneath the Ivory Cathedral?"

"Even the most dire of sicknesses have their advantages."

"Were you infected when we met?"

15

"The Emir was less concerned with any crime with which I was accused than the side effects of my curse. It was a small blessing that his inquisitor did not turn to cold iron in his experiments."

"But the spears carried by the Bone Dogs .... there is no way they could know."

The Songspear shook her head. "Although, their cold iron would kill me as surely as any of my reluctant brethren, it is not truly meant for me." Her next words struck Hollis to his core. "Another gwyllgi stalks the wastes."

*****

True to their word, the Bone Dogs' hospitality included a warm fire and simple meal. Amid the wash of dirty faces and suspicious eyes, Hollis counted no more than two dozen men, women and children in the broken clan's camp. He thought he would feel uneasy, surrounded as they were by strangers, but something else filled his heart as the flickering flames highlighted the desperate faces around them. Pity.

Sitting tailor-style close to the fire was a figure wrapped in a great furred cloak. A slight swelling at chest and hip indicated that she was female, but any other feature was lost in the depth of the garment. One of the Bone Dogs they met on the tundra crouched next to her, offering a weathered, wooden bowl. A reverence was clear in his posture.

Between mouthfuls of thick stew, the thief asked, "Is this all the folks you have?"

Next to him, Aristoi elbowed him sharply in the ribs.

He shifted his eyes to her, a questioning glance hanging in them before turning back to regard Valmont. "I can not imagine you asked us here for a reunion. If this Snow Queen is who my comrade suspects her to be, you will need more than this motley smattering to stop her." The expressions around the fire turned dangerous. Hollis amended, "No matter how stalwart their hearts." Although it didn't completely salve their indignation, the anger surrounding him cooled somewhat.

In contrast to the emotion surrounding him, Valmont's face remained stoic. "We are not so foolish as to believe that our few can stand against her many."

The kid has a good head on his shoulders, the thief thought, gaining another measure of respect for the young Rangor despite himself. "Perhaps you can enlighten us as to your purpose bringing us so far north?"

The Songspear spoke up, her words for Valmont but her hard

16

glare directed at Hollis. "Although I object to my friend's approach, I do not find fault with the root of his inquiry."

The boy shook his head slowly. "It is not the Queen against whom we war. It is the malaise in the hearts of our brothers and sisters that is our real foe. She simply takes advantage of the fear and resentment that was sown much before she came to reap it for her own purposes."

"Where then do we factor into your plans, Valmont?" Aristoi's voice was gentle but held an undercurrent of forged steel. "Two strangers, products of the very south that the clans resent, will not exactly help you win hearts and minds."

"The Dread that Walks has returned." His words seemed to pull the air from the bodies of the men and women around him, replacing it with a razor taloned tension. Hollis could see that even the boy's shoulders slumped under the weight of his declaration. To his credit, Valmont pushed through his fear. "And its kin have followed it north."

"Black Dog?" Hollis asked beneath his breath. The Songspear nodded, mirroring the uncertainty around her. His unfamiliarity with the creatures caused the thief to frown. *I am missing something*, he thought. Thinking better of dismissing something of which he had only minimal understanding, he left any further objections unsaid.

"How many?" Aristoi asked.

Without the advantage of the "Understanding", Hollis doubted that anyone could have detected the slight quiver to her voice.

"At least a half dozen. It is because of them I have called due your debt to my people."

Her words knife-edge sharp, the Songspear said, "It was you alone who pulled me from the jaws of my enemy. It was you alone who nursed me back to health. My obligation is to you alone." She took a shallow breath. When she spoke again, her tone was again conversational. "If it is your wish that I discharge it for the benefit of your clan, I would not deny your right to do so."

Something hung in Valmont's eyes; Hollis was unsure if it was fear or regret. "That is my wish."

Half bowing her head, Aristoi kept her gaze locked on the boy as she said, "So shall it be." She turned to the thief.

Hollis spoke before the words could form on his friend's lips. "You do not even need to ask. Your debt is mine."

The Songspear mouthed, *Thank you.*

The thief smiled softly, letting the expression be his only response.

17

Aristoi turned her attention back to Valmont. "Tell me."

"I swore to keep the Furred Serpents safe, even from themselves. At the time, I had no idea that the last part would prove to be the more difficult. Hlruf, the chieftain with which you made your agreement—"

"—the one to kill the beast in exchange for something he knew was of no use to me?" she interrupted.

The boy nodded, a touch of guilt coloring his features. "Yes. If it makes a difference Hlruf died having never allowed the secret of your agreement pass his lips. He was betrayed by one of his shield brothers, a coward by the name of Knud." Valmont turned his head and spat onto the frozen ground beside him.

The Songspear thought about it for a moment before answering. "It should not matter, but it does."

Valmont smiled; her answer seemed to please him. "The Snow Queen laid my chieftain low as an example to the rest of the clan. Some resisted, but most bent before her like a pine under the snow's weight. Of those who refused to do so, only myself and Frode lived to see the futility of our actions.".

"Kukardisch is a long way from Agmar's Watch," Aristoi commented.

"It is indeed. Under the cover of a moonless night, Frode and I pulled Hlruf from the stake where the Queen had left him tied, food for the crows." The boy bit his lip hard enough to draw blood, the pain stopping the half formed tears in his eyes. "Alone, we carried our chieftain's body across the tundra to the valley of graves. It was only then we realized the true breadth of her war upon the traditions of the wastes."

Hollis felt the collective gasp of indrawn breath around him.

"The barrows were laid bare like open wounds. The corpses of their precious contents mingled with those of the Bone Dogs who sought to protect their sworn charges. Among the charnel house that was the battlefield crept something that I at first assumed to be one of the Baenulf. It was not."

Valmont's hand disappeared into the folds of his fur-lined tunic. When it emerged, he held a dark metal nail on a thin leather thong. "On a whim, I had brought with me a fist full of iron nails from our battle with the Dread that Walks. Had it not been for that flight of fancy, I would have suffered the same fate as Frode." The boy's head dipped for a moment, as if he prayed for his lost comrade.

When he raised his eyes to regard Aristoi and the thief, a look as hard as the metal in his hand hung in his gaze. "When what remained of the Bone Dogs found me, the creature and I were wrapped in an embrace of blood and fur. Were it not for Sagaun, I would not have seen the sunrise." Valmont gestured to the cloaked figure across the fire from him. "She tended to my wounds and pulled me back from the brink of death."

From within the depths of her cloak, Sagaun said, "The Lady decreed that your thread still had a place in her tapestry." Even the flickering light of the fire could not pierce the shadows of her hood; it only revealed the gentle curve of her jaw, marred by a thick ribbon of scar tissue that disappeared into its depths. "That night, it was her will, not my own, that kept you from the eternal hunt."

"Since that night, neither I nor any of the Bone Dogs have been without a small portion of my salvation." In turn, each of the figures around the fire pulled forth a dark metal nail hanging from a leather thong. "Inspired by you, we forged spears made of pure iron. No amount of it offers protection from the beasts' foul gifts, however." Valmont studied the Songspear, an expectant look in his eyes. "You brought low the Dread that Walks. We ask that you bring your own crafts to bear upon its kin."

Aristoi nodded slowly. "I—" The rest of her words were drowned out. As if on cue, a low, mournful howl rose beyond the firelight. Just like in the library courtyard, its notes pulled at Hollis's heart. He drew a fortifying breath and wrapped himself in the soft cloak of serenity that was the "Understanding". The Bone Dogs had no such advantage.

Figures rose quickly, their furtive glances scanning the night for the source of the sound. The low keening rose again, seeming to hang on the winter breeze like the season's first snow. Crouched on the nearest barrow, silhouetted against the moon, was a broad, vaguely canine shape. It casually raised a disturbingly human forelimb and gestured towards the gathered Bone Dogs.

Chapter Three
An Unexpected Opposition

Seven figures crested the rise, broad-headed axes raised above their heads. Running past what Hollis could only assume was a gwyllgi based on the Songspear's story, the warriors charged towards where the Bone Dogs scrambled to overcome their terror. Pushing himself to his feet, the thief snatched his sheathed Wallin Fahr from where it lay on the frozen ground. Pulling the blade from its scabbard, he let the leather covering fall as he met their advance with bared Dwarven steel.

Behind him, he heard Sagaun speaking in calm, sure words that contrasted the chaos that surrounded the imminent melee. "Lady of the Tundra … Merciful Umma, grant your children the light of your wisdom on this, the darkest of nights." As if in response, the moonlight that had only extenuated the night's shadows threw the Bone Dog campsite into sharp contrast.

As the first interloper entered the aura of moonlight, he noticed that the man had a thick wooden shield strapped to his forearm. A half dozen paces ahead of his fellows, the warrior faced Hollis alone for a crucial few seconds. The thief lunged forward with two loping strides, dropping his shoulder as if he intended to crash into the solidity of the shield. When he saw the warrior contract his body, preparing to accept the collision, Hollis threw his body to the left.

His momentum drove him into a sloppy roll and past his surprised opponent.

Coming smoothly to his feet, the thief brought his sword around. The burnished blade struck the man in the thigh, just above the knee. Dwarven steel separated flesh and muscle with ease, pitching the warrior forward into the permafrost. Keeping his foe's comrades in his peripheral vision, Hollis drove the tip of his weapon into the prone warrior's back, between the shoulder blades. When he turned to face the remainder of the raiding party, the thief found himself flanked by Bone Dogs, having found their courage amid the still echoing howls that surrounded them. Ragged scraps of cloth hung from where they had stuffed them into their ears.

A quick look over his shoulder revealed that a trio of Bone Dog warriors stood protectively between Sagaun and the oncoming forces. The woman, having pulled a short bladed axe from within her cloak, stood protectively in front of a knot of children. Turning his attention back to the matter at hand, Hollis felt a smile come to his lips despite the desperate circumstances in which he found himself. After a month spent in Oizan navigating deception and politics associated with Asaege's rebellion, he almost relished the simplicity of the situation.

Again the gwyllgi's howl split the air. The thief saw everyone around him cringe at the sound, allies and opponents alike. As he parried a heavy overhead swing, Hollis looked past the melee; his eyes searched for the source of the undulating sound. Perched atop the same rise, the beast had thrown its head back. Approaching from the right were four figures, spears held before them. Aristoi's glaive-like weapon was not difficult to make out amid the collection of more conventional ones.

The thief heard Aristoi's voice cut through the cacophony of battle. He could not make out the words, but he could feel their slow plodding rhythm deep in his chest. The magic of her song made its presence known immediately. Although he could clearly hear the woman's song, every other sound around him became muted. It was subtle at first, the grunts of exertion and pain seemed to reach his ears through cotton wadding. Before he had time to wonder at the phenomenon, the only thing he could hear was Aristoi's song, clear as a church bell. The gwyllgi's howls, along with every other sound around him had faded to silence.

Hollis could tell that the mystical stillness had a profound effect on the warriors around him as well. Taking advantage of his opponent's distraction, the thief gripped the top of his shield and pulled the interloper off balance. As the warrior stumbled forward, Hollis drove a booted foot behind his knee and forced him to the ground. To his credit, the warrior rolled onto his back in an attempt to put his shield between himself and the thief's blade. He was a half a breath too late. Hollis drew his sword across the man's midsection, just below the ribs. All the interloper's fast thinking did was drive the Wallin Fahr's edge deeper into his gut.

On the hill, the gwyllgi had proven that, even deprived of its voice, it was still a formidable opponent. Where a moment ago, four stood against the beast, only two remained. Unmistakable with her broad bladed spear and thin braids, Aristoi stood beside the thin silhouette of what the thief assumed to be Valmont. Her song continued to ring in his ears and pound in his chest.

A momentary glance was all Hollis could afford. The half dozen Bone Dogs beside him had turned the tide against the interlopers, but he was far from safe. A massive Rangor charged through a pair of the thief's comrades of convenience, knocking them to the ground. An axe in each fist, the huge warrior swept his left arm down and sank one of them deeply in a fallen Dog's chest with a meaty *thwap*. The man lay still as the death that claimed him. Leaving his weapon embedded in the quickly cooling body beside him, the interloper pointed a beefy finger at Hollis as he shouted something in his harsh language.

"Alright, big man," Hollis said, his tone not betraying the understandable intimidation that settled across his heart as the man's true size became apparent. "If you wanted my attention, all you needed do was ask." Like every other sound around him, his voice faded into silence almost as quickly as it left his lips. Before the warrior's mass obscured the thief's view of his second victim, Hollis saw the woman beginning to stir. He felt a fleeting rush of relief before he was forced to dodge backwards out of the way of a powerful overhand chop.

Before Hollis could capitalize on his opponent's overextension, the warrior launched a wild backhand slash that would have easily separated his head from his body had he been an instant quicker. In the throes of the Understanding, the thief saw that what his foe lacked in skill, he more than made up for with viciousness. *It must be a Rangor thing*, he thought, *Ret and his brother, Ulrych, subscribed to the same theory*. After the combined years of bearing witness to both of them, Hollis knew how to turn it against the huge warrior.

Encouraged by his enemy's lack of offense, the Rangor launched himself forward with his axe leading the way. The thief lunged forward to meet him, only pivoting to the right at the last second. To his credit, his opponent rotated his body in mid leap in an effort to bring his weapon to bear. His enthusiasm was his undoing. Crouching as the warrior overshot him, Hollis brought his Wallin Fahr up diagonally across his foe's body. In turning towards the thief and lifting his arm to bring his axe around, all the interloper did was expose more of his midsection to Hollis's blade.

Although the blade bit deeply into leather and flesh, the monstrous man didn't fall. He brought his weapon down on the thief, the blood seeping from his mouth staining his teeth crimson. In a desperate attempt to avoid the thick axe blade, Hollis used his coiled legs to launch himself upward, meeting the blow halfway. The sturdy wooden shaft of the axe slammed into him with enough force to drive the breath from his lungs.

With his sword caught between himself and his opponent, Hollis had no choice but to release the weapon. Instead of scrambling away from the massive Rangor like any reasonable person, the thief interlaced the fingers of his left hand in the warrior's filthy furs and pulled him closer. Absorbing a teeth-rattling punch to his ribs, Hollis reached behind him for the broad-bladed dagger, sheathed scout-style on his belt. The knife was forged of the same Dwarven steel as his Uteli sword. As his opponent drove another fist into his side, the thief sank the dagger to the hilt in his armpit.

The Rangor opened his mouth to roar but all that emerged was a short, powerful cough. The change in Hollis's opponent was instantaneous as his punctured lung stole his breath. The next punch had almost no force behind it. As the brute leaned against him in an attempt to force more air into his ravaged chest, the thief released his grip on his side and wrapped it around the back of his neck. Pulling with all his might as he rose onto his toes, Hollis drove the crown of his skull into his opponent's face. To Hollis's surprise, it required another head butt to knock out the huge man. As he slid to the permafrost, the thief had an opportunity to see the interloper for what he truly was.

Although the Rangor had towered above Hollis, he could not have seen a score of summers. In the peace of unconsciousness, his bearded face took on an almost cherubic cast. Gone were the lines of fury that had etched themselves upon his brow; all that remained was the promise of youth. *What have I done?* the thief raged silently. Dropping his dagger to the frozen dirt, he crouched next to the fallen boy. Even with Aristoi's song still hanging in the air, Hollis heard the last, rattling cough of a child who would grow no older.

A white-hot anger filled his belly as the thief leapt to his feet. Around him, the Bone Dogs seemed to have won the day. Four of them stood surveying the battlefield, as dappled by blood as moonlight. Among them was the woman the giant had bull-rushed. She clearly favored her right leg but still stood with her comrades. The notes of the Songspear's spell faded into the night, allowing the other sounds around Hollis to return in a rush.

Denied an immediate target for his rage, the thief crouched down to pick up his fallen sword before making his way to where Aristoi and Valmont stood over a crumpled form. His comrade looked up as he approached. She raised an eyebrow questioningly when she saw his scowl. "Later," he mouthed, shifting his eyes to the corpse at their feet.

Hollis didn't know what he expected the gwyllgi's body to look like but the very slight, very human looking man lying there was not it. "Where is the beast?" he asked.

The Songspear nodded down at the dead man. "When a gwyllgi dies, it reverts to the form it possessed before being infected." Her eyes shifted to Valmont's face, half hidden in shadow. Aristoi reached out to place her hand on the boy's shoulder before saying, "His name was Gorm … he was one of theirs."

*****

Hollis could not get the giant of a boy's face out of his mind as he looked down at another young victim of the Snow Queen's ambition. Although he hoped with all his might that she and Mika were not one and the same, in his heart he knew the truth. As Silvermoon had been a father figure to the thief, the Mantrian warrior had often played the role of foster mother to him. At moments, their relationship had a tragically Greek quality, but Mika was there for Hollis when few others were.

Her reflection, Beatrice, had held Stephen when his parents died months apart. The thief could feel tears burning the backs of his eyes as clearly now as when they were shed decades previous. His tears that night were born of rage rather than grief. *If Mika is responsible for this*, he swore to himself, *I will make sure she pays for each and every death, whether by her hand or in her name.*

Hollis didn't realize the Songspear was at his side until she laid a gentle hand on his forearm. He tried to control the fire in his eyes, but some of it must have smoldered there. Aristoi's brows furrowed in concern. With a slight shake of his head, he quieted her questions before she asked them. It was a testament to their friendship that the Songspear let the matter drop. "Sagaun is said to possess the power to purge the spiritual corruption of the gwyllgi from those slain by the beast."

The thief nodded, still honestly only half listening.

Even so, he could not help but hear the disappointment in her voice. "Unfortunately, I am skeptical."

Shaking loose from his reverie, Hollis clutched his friend's wrist. "There is a world of difference between you and that thing."

Aristoi frowned. "I am not so sure, Northerner. Perhaps Gorm succumbed to the sickness of its touch more quickly, but from all accounts, the curse is like the creeping misfortune of flood waters. Its advancement is both sure and inevitable."

He shook his head slowly. "Those with the courage and patience to abide the haunting specter of its approach often outlast even the most certain catastrophe. I know from experience that you have both in abundance."

"I appreciate your faith, my friend, but the burden of it sits upon my shoulders like a millstone. It seeks to grind me beneath its incalculable weight."

The thief squeezed Aristoi's wrist. "It no longer sits on your shoulders alone. In sharing the load, we can both bear the burden of this thing."

The Songspear looked into his face, searching it as if she were seeing him for the first time. After the space of a pair of breaths, she found what she sought. With a sigh that spoke of both dread and relief, Aristoi breathed, "Thank you."

Shrugging off the seriousness of the moment, Hollis said, "You would do the same for me. Shit, you have done the same for me." Catching her eye, his expression turned deadly serious. "You are my friend, one of the few that remain to me. Your struggles are mine as well."

Before she could respond, both of their attentions were drawn to the circle of Bone Dogs around the fire. Three fur-wrapped bodies lay on the cold ground as still as the death that had claimed each of them. The firelight highlighted the stern faces of their comrades, reflecting from their tear dampened eyes. Stepping from their ranks, Sagaun's cloaked form approached the corpses. She knelt beside each in turn, bending down, as if to whisper in their ears.

After attending to the last body, the woman rose slowly and turned to those assembled. When she spoke, it was in the harsh northern language of the Rangor Wastes. Aristoi softly provided a whispered translation.

"Our ranks have been lessened this night, in quality as well

26

as numbers. Each of these warriors have paid the ultimate price. In doing so, they purchased their brothers and sisters an opportunity to continue our fight for our very way of life."

Sagaun swept her unseen gaze of those assembled. Hollis could feel her eyes on him despite the fact that they were hidden in the depths of her hood.

"The Lady tells us that, like the seasons, our lives ebb and flow. Each one blending into the next seamlessly in an endless dance."

She gestured towards the barrow that claimed the lives of all three Bone Dogs.

"But these brothers and sisters were not taken from us by the gentle touch of the Mother of Us All. They were snatched from our grasps by the taloned hand of her brother. From the confines of his cage of darkness and ash, the Master of Beasts caused their deaths through the predation of his foul abomination."

Sagaun turned back to her rapt audience, sweeping her finger past each of them.

"Make no mistake, Sharroth's shadow has fallen upon each and every one of us. Whether or not the Snow Queen's strings are pulled by him, she does his bidding nonetheless."

Hollis felt his jaw clench reflexively. *I wish it were that simple,* he thought bitterly. *My greatest fear is that all of this is Mika's doing alone.*

"However, we can not fight the darkness while still enveloped in its inky coils. We must step into the light. For it is only through exposing the gloom to the purity of the Siblings' sight can we drive it from our own."

Unaware of the conflict that waged within the thief, Aristoi continued to translate Sagaun's words. "Lady of Moonlight and Mother of Us All, look down upon the sacrifices of your faithful. Lay your hand upon the spirits of these fallen warriors and sweep away the filth of your brother's corruption. Guide your children into the Endless Tundra with your gentle touch."

For a moment, it seemed as if an opaque form interposed itself between the moon and those gathered beneath it. The crisp moonlight of the northern evening dissolved into a hazy half-illumination. The only objects in the Bone Dog camp not draped in the gauzy cloak were the three fur-wrapped bodies. Each of them was thrown into stark contrast against the night around them. The thief wondered at the fact that unnatural brilliance was so encompassing that it seemed to cast no shadow. As quickly as it surged, the light receded, returning the camp to its familiar state.

"The corruption has been purged." Hollis felt the Songspear's eyes on him as she whispered to him, an impressed tone obvious in her voice. Clearly sensing his discomfort, she asked, "What is it?"

The thief turned to face her, opening his mouth to make an excuse. The words froze on his tongue. As he looked beyond Aristoi, a shape stood out against the clear winter sky on a isolated rise. Even across the distance, Hollis could feel the creature's eyes on him, digging into his spirit and weighing it down with claws of lead. He nodded quickly in its direction but as the Songspear turned, the shape disappeared from sight, leaving only the haunting heaviness of its stare.

Chapter Four
An Uncomfortable Recollection

Despite the frigid temperatures of the tundra, Aristoi's sleeping body was soaked in sweat. Beneath the hood that protected her from the night air, her braids clung to her skull. Her muscles constricted in smooth, rippling waves under the thick blanket covering her tossing form. Each time a painful tide rushed across her body, a soft growl built in the back of her throat. The sound was equal parts agony and relief.

*****

Aristoi stood over the still form of her mother. Looming so large in life, the woman seemed so frail in death. The sudden illness that had swept through her household sickened them all, but it struck her mother hardest. She had watched as the woman who had been her example of strength throughout her childhood wasted away in a matter of days. In addition to being a ranking Songspear, her mother was also a talented herbalist. Neither her songs nor knowledge were potent enough to stem the tide of whatever swept through their family.

Clenched in Aristoi's hands was the ornately crafted wooden bowl containing the scraps of her mother's dinner. Among the remnants were the flattened black-and-brown husks of castor beans. It was only by chance that she had noticed the poisonous legumes in the dregs of the thick venison and vegetable stew all three of them had eaten that evening.

"How could this have happened?" As she had since she was a girl, Aristoi turned to her elder sister, Junwei, for aid and comfort.

Junwei snatched the bowl from her hands, squinting into its depths. "Are you certain they're castor beans?"

"What else can they be?"

"Something else ... anything else. Iya was beloved by everyone."

At the sound of the word Iya, the Kieli term for mother, tears welled up in Aristoi's eyes. "The proof is right there, sister. All three of us have felt the effects for a day and a half. Perhaps the poison was meant for one of us and Iya was an unintentional victim."

"Which of our neighbors would resort to such an action?" Setting the bowl down atop the mantle, Junwei took her sister's hand. "We will not solve this mystery ourselves, we must inform Ofin Taloi."

As the leader of the village council, Taloi wore the title Ofin only with the support of Aristoi's departed mother. He would mourn her loss as deeply as her family. She nodded slowly. "Taloi will know what to do."

*****

The rituals of passing left Aristoi physically and spiritually exhausted. As the daughters of the departed, she and Junwei had borne the responsibility of singing over their mother's funeral pyre until the last wisps of smoke had risen into the clear night. Her sister had nearly collapsed an hour into the ordeal. Concerned that Junwei may have been under the effects of the poison that had claimed their family's matriarch, Aristoi had insisted she return home to rest. Taking the entirety of the ritual duties upon her shoulders pushed her to her breaking point, but as she approached the humble home she now only shared with her sister, Aristoi felt that her sacrifice served as a fitting farewell to her beloved mother.

Light shined from the house's low windows, an odd thing considering Junwei should have been resting. Aristoi's stomach rose in her throat, fearing the worst. She wasn't sure she could bear the thought of losing both her mother and sister within the same week. Despite her exhaustion, she broke into a run and covered the thirty yards to the house. Throwing the door open, Aristoi rushed inside.

When she found Junwei sitting at their table, surrounded by Ofin Taloi and the rest of the Elder Council, Aristoi's first reaction was a rush of relief. Far from the pale, weakened state Junwei had

30

been in hours before, her sister seemed reinvigorated, even pleased.

Suddenly stricken by confusion, Aristoi blurted out, "What is going on? Junwei?"

Taloi turned to face her, barely contained rage etching lines into his face. "Aristoi. How could you?"

Her mind whirled, trying desperately to make sense of the Ofin's question. "How could I? How could I what?"

"That woman loved you above all others. It was to you whom she intended to pass her spear, her songs. Why murder her?"

Suddenly, combined with the satisfied look upon Junwei's face, his words made perfect sense. Taloi's suspicion of familial treachery was correct, his accusations were simply aimed at the wrong sister. Seeing herself as overlooked for too long, Junwei had taken matters into her own hands.

"Let me guess," Aristoi said, the combined weight of loss and betrayal threatening to crush her. "You found a cache of castor beans in my room?"

"Under your mattress," Junwei contributed helpfully.

"Of course you did. None of you thought to ask what I had to gain from the death of my mother?"

"The evidence speaks for itself. You will have an opportunity to dispute it during the trial." Taloi's words were hissed through pursed lips, his anger evident in every syllable. "Seize her."

Two of the council moved forward, but their advanced age gave Aristoi the advantage she needed to dash past them. Reluctantly pulling her furious glare from the smirking face of her treacherous sister, she focused instead on the spear leaning against the mantle. The ancestral weapon of her family, the songspear had been passed down from mother to daughter for generations untold. Aristoi would not see it pass into the hands of her mother's murderer.

Obviously guessing her sister's intent, Junwei rose quickly to intercept her. She was almost on top of Aristoi when she wrapped her fingers around the weapon's shaft. Aristoi swung her elbow wide as she turned to face her pursuers, catching her sister squarely in the face. Junwei slumped to the floor like a dropped sack of flour. The three council members cautiously approached, naked steel in their fists.

"I do not wish to do you harm. The murderer you seek lies there." Aristoi gestured to Junwei's unconscious form. "We have all been fooled by her duplicity."

Taloi's spittle coated lips pulled back in an angry sneer. "Put the weapon down, girl."

31

Studying the furious faces before her, Aristoi came to the sinking realization that any chance of a fair trial had passed before she entered the house. She wasn't a killer and had no intention of allowing those present to force her to become one. Aristoi feinted towards the approaching elders, causing them to instinctively flinch away from the perceived attack. She used the momentary distraction to charge towards the open window behind her.

As she fled her childhood home, she also left behind everything she had ever known. In that moment, she swore to herself that when she returned, she would do more than clear her name. She would claim her birthright as a member of the Songspear.

*****

Aristoi woke with a start, the memory-fueled dreams seeming as real as the permafrost beneath her. She brought a hand to her face, wincing at the slowly fading ache in her limbs. It served as both proof that she survived her sister's treachery and a reminder of the unrelenting course of events that betrayal had launched.

Rolling over carefully as cramping muscles slowly relaxed, her eyes fell upon Hollis's face. The hard lines of worry the thief wore while awake were smoothed in sleep. The soft snores emerging from his throat barely carried to her ears, but Aristoi focused on them as she settled back under her blanket. Their even and mild unpleasant tones gave her something to take her mind off the dreams that she feared waited for her behind closed eyelids. As the barking of a dog wards off unwanted visitors, so too Hollis's snores held off the nightmares, at least for a short time.

Chapter Five
An Inconvenient Occurance

Asaege leaned against the cold stone wall, allowing herself to slide down its rough surface to sit upon the filthy floor. A tapestry of exuberant voices and low moans of pain surrounded her as she closed her eyes against the sounds. Despite the advantage of surprise, the battle to take control of the Lord Mayor's prison had been brutal, with at least twenty of her own dead or wounded. The fact that more than twice the number of defenders found themselves in the same situation brought her no joy. In her mind, all of them were stains upon the souls of those who clung so tightly to their power that they willingly fed the kindling of their own people to the smoldering flames of rebellion.

Reflexively, she brought her hand up to pinch the bridge of her nose and recoiled at the clammy sensation of cooling blood upon her fingers. *Your own soul is not blemish free, Prophet,* she thought. *It is your words upon the lips of every revolutionary ... your cause in each heart.* Since the night in the courtyard of the Great Library, the theory of their movement had become all too real. What began as a demand for equality had gained a momentum all its own. Some nights, Asaege fought to keep her head above the tide that was her own rebellion.

For the scores of prisoners they had freed, the raid on the subterranean complex was nothing short of life changing. Had Asaege and her conspirators not intervened, the mixture of debtors and imprisoned rebels most likely would have not seen the sun again. Most would have lived in darkness until the day their bodies finally succumbed to the backbreaking labor and filthy conditions forced upon them by the Lord-Mayor's justice. The lucky few would have faced execution to serve as an example to their brethren who continued to struggle against the "way of things".

Anger flared in the woman's heart, burning away a measure of the guilt that had taken up residence there. Asaege opened her eyes, looking upon the carnage around her with a new perspective. A bitter thought stabbed at her thoughts like a jagged thorn amid the petals of a rose. *These men choose to serve the interests of the city leaders over those of their fellows. Their fates sit upon their shoulders, not mine.* Even as the vitriol oozed forth from the darkest depths of her mind, she felt her revulsion for the thoughts. *The only choice in this matter belongs to those who will never dirty their hands with its effects.* Although the prison guards served the Lord Mayor and his council of guild masters, the guards were as much victims of them as she and her people were.

A figure knelt beside the woman, placing their hand on her shoulder. "You are not hurt?" Toni asked in a soft voice. Asaege wasn't sure whether their concern was for her safety or for its effect on their own plans.

She shook her head. "No, just resting for a moment."

Toni glanced around the narrow corridor. "I fear that we only have the one. It is only a matter of time before the commotion draws interested parties." Bracing their hands on their knees, the neophyte guild-master levered themselves to their feet. "We should be long gone when that happens."

Asaege couldn't help but agree with their words. The path they used to enter the dungeons unseen necessitated that their group remain small and lightly armed. Although Rudelph had insisted that a contingent of his Binders accompany Toni and their thieves, Asaege had decided that speed and stealth was of more value than the martial skill that the sworn guardians of the Great Library offered. The commander hadn't been pleased but, for the time being at least, the Prophet still led the revolution.

Rising more slowly, Asaege tried to force from her mind the idea of the impending reinforcements that no doubt bore down upon them as she wallowed in her feelings. "Then long gone we shall be. It will be slower going than either of us would like, but I see no reason why we cannot escape via the same Underfoot paths that led us here."

Toni thought about it for a second before responding, "We do not have many other choices available to us." They pursed their lips and let out a sharp whistle. Each of the ten surviving thieves turned at the shrill sound. Toni held up a single finger and rotated their wrist, indicating that the time had come to take their leave. Despite losing two thirds of their number, all of them reacted without hesitation. Bending down to help the frailest prisoners to their feet, the members of Oizan's thieves guild herded their charges through a narrow culvert and into the rat's nest of tunnels that ran beneath the city.

*****

Even dressed in his armor and towering above the small Slazean man standing before him, Rudelph seemed to be at a disadvantage. Seran looked up at the Binder commander, a cocky half-smile pasted on his face. Rudelph seemed at the end of his legendary patience, evidenced by the blotches of crimson that colored his cheeks.

"— not how we are going to win the hearts and minds of the people."

Seran shrugged, causing the tight braids of bright purple hair that brushed his shoulders to bob. "I was unaware of the fact that I needed to concern myself with that." He breathed a light chuckle before continuing. "What is done is done, I suppose. I often find it better to ask forgiveness than permission." The wrinkles beside the aging thief's eyes became pronounced as his voice dropped to a growl. "Although, as far as I am concerned, I require neither from you."

Asaege watched Rudelph close his eyes in an effort to compose himself. "As you say, Master Seran." By the time his eyes opened, his tone had returned to the even cadence that she had come to expect from the Binder commander. His momentary pause allowed an intense silence to hang between the two men. "However ..." The word slithered from between Rudelph's lips like a serpent from its burrow. "If you would indulge my curiosity for but a moment," he continued. "With the hands turned against our not-insubstantial endeavor, would you not agree that making use of the chaos to pursue your personal vendetta seems unwise?"

Seran studied his fingernails, as if he would find some answer to the Binder's question written there. When his eyes shifted up from them, they settled on Asaege. Like the sun emerging from behind an autumn cloud, a smile blossomed on his face. "Perhaps that is a discussion for another time, my dear Rudelph. The triumphant heroes have returned." She saw the commander's shoulders tense beneath his stark white cloak but when the man turned, his expression bore no sign of his no doubt substantial frustration with the aging thief.

The Binder captain gestured toward the knot of filthy former-prisoners. "Although I celebrate your success, Prophet, my question is as relevant to you as it is to the guild master."

Asaege cringed at the title that had become as much a part of her identity as her own name in recent months.

"Co-master, if you please," corrected Toni. "No longer will the Brotherhood tie its fate to the will of any one individual."

Rudelph allowed a small smile to color his lips. "As you will, Master Toni." He turned back to Asaege. "Our fortunes are no brighter for the addition of mouths to our charge without an equal number of hands devoted to the cause."

Asaege felt her mouth turn down into a tight frown. "These mouths, as you term them, belong to the very same people our movement was begun to protect. I will not allow them to languish in the Lord-Mayor's prison for the crime of being born poor."

"While that is admirable—" the Binder began.

She cut him off, her words sharp as a knife's edge. "—if we forget the reason for our journey, there is nothing to prevent us from wandering from our intended path."

Rudelph raised his hands, palms outward in a soothing gesture that didn't quite have the effect he intended. Asaege felt the frustrations smoldering in her heart flicker into the slow burning embers of anger. "Please do not mistake my questions for apathy to these people's suffering. Although popular opinion remains on our side, it may quickly turn against us should our endeavor stretch on too long. If left to burn too long, the fires of revolution give way to a smoke that blurs the lines between the sides. All people know is that the life is being choked from themselves and their families."

The binder's words did nothing to soothe Asaege's frustration, but she couldn't deny their logic. Feeling contrary, she growled, "Then we will need to find a way to do both: force those arrayed against us to see the wisdom of our demands and keep those under our protection safe."

"That is indeed a tall order, Prophet."

Her teeth clenched as he used the title again. *As uncomfortable as it makes me,* she thought, *the Prophet demands a respect that Asaege simply does not.* "Tall or not, it is a necessity. The rebellion can not forget for whom it fights."

Mirroring his words to Toni a moment before, Rudelph said, "As you will."

Despite the affability of both word and tone, Asaege could see the cracks in his placid demeanor. *Who can blame him? The Binders are sworn to protect the Great Library and its contents, not the vulnerable masses of common folk that made up the majority of the revolution forces.* The soothing touch of compassion cooled the last coals of anger within her. Laying her hand on his muscular upper arm, Asaege said, "We will find our way, Captain Rudelph." She wanted to say more but any further platitudes felt like deception to her.

*****

As the newly freed prisoners shuffled into the courtyard, Asaege felt a firm hand on her shoulder. Seran's grip was both soft and undeniable, owing to decades spent in endeavors that demanded a light touch. "A moment?" Although, for all purposes, it was phrased as a question, she had no doubt that the elder thief hadn't intended it to be a request.

Allowing the buzzing tension that pulsed through her body to escape with an explosive sigh, she turned. "What is it, Seran?" There was no attempt to keep the weariness from her voice.

At his side, Seran held a vaguely conical object, wrapped in a blood-speckled, gold-embroidered cloak. "As you, no doubt, ascertained upon your arrival—" For some inexplicable reason, Seran's insistence on overly formal and often unnecessary vocabulary annoyed her to no end. It seemed as if he felt that he needed to prove himself more than the common thug many believed him to be. "—while you and my esteemed colleague were busy emptying the Lord Mayor's prison, I was not idle."

"I believe Rudelph termed it your personal vendetta."

He chuckled softly. "The captain can certainly be dramatic when he puts his mind to it." Any trace of a smile evaporated from his face like dew in the summer morning sun. "In this instance, he may not be too far from the truth. It was indeed a vendetta ..." Seran extended the swaddled object to her. "... just not mine."

So casually did the elder thief handle the bundle that its weight took Asaege by surprise. Combined with its distinctness of its shape, the gift's heft left no doubt as to its nature. She raised an eyebrow. "You brought me a sword?"

"I think you might have misplaced it during the unfortunate situation with Curate Reisling."

Asaege's heart leapt in her chest. In a bid to consolidate power,

37

the Plague Man had captured her while she and Hollis were within the Ivory Cathedral. During the struggle, her Uteli Tallis Fahr had been lost. It was a fine blade, razor sharp and exquisitely balanced. The quality of the weapon paled in comparison with the sentimental value it held. The sword had been a gift to her from Hollis. Originally given to him by a treasured friend, long since lost, the gesture still brought tears to Asaege's eyes.

Pulling the blood-dampened wool from the sheathed weapon with trembling hands, she whispered a heartfelt, "Thank you." In those two words, Asaege expressed more than she could have in the most impassioned soliloquy.

"The templar who carried it neither deserved it nor will he have need of it anymore."

Wrapping her hand around the sharkskin-wrapped hilt, Asaege pulled the sword from its sheath. The familiar weight felt good, natural. Her eyes darted to meet Seran's. "You returned to the Ivory Cathedral for this ... for me?"

A sly smile that spoke of half-truths graced his lips. "Among other things."

"Such as?" Asaege asked suspiciously.

Turning on his heel, Seran dismissed her question with a flick of his hand. "Content yourself with the return of your property, my dear. Some answers are not worth the price of their asking."

She opened her mouth to press him but declined to do so as the futility of continuing to address his retreating back occurred to her. As the elder thief passed through the door, a small shape separated itself from the shadows of the corridor and followed behind the man. The sight raised the hair on the back of Asaege's neck but she pushed the feeling from her mind. Returning the Talis Fahr to its sheath, Asaege wrapped her arms around the weapon and clutched it to her chest. A combination of her imagination and an intense longing for her beloved scoundrel brought to mind the familiar scent of the man himself within the soft aroma of oil and leather.

*****

The treasured weapon lay beside Asaege as she sat tailor-style on the simple straw pallet, a heavy tome balanced on her knees. Another gift from Hollis, the book of thaumaturgical formulae was far beyond her capabilities, but through necessity, Asaege expanded her understanding more each day. When Toni knocked lightly on the sagging door frame, she looked up from a particularly troubling passage with mild annoyance.

"I am sorry to disturb your study, Asaege." Toni never referred

38

to her as Prophet, something for which she was silently thankful.

Letting her irritation flow from her body with a slow exhale, Asaege carefully closed the book. Uttering a pair of words beneath her breath, she activated the protective spell laid upon the tome long ago. The tempo of the syllables echoed softly in her chest, marking them for the words of power they were. Content that the valuable secrets contained within the book were secure, Asaege pushed herself to her feet. "Do not be silly, Toni," she said. "There are much more pressing issues that should be attended to." She glanced back at the thick tome through squinted eyes. "Sometimes, I give into stubbornness longer than I should."

"It happens to the best of us." They tried to conceal the dire tone of their voice behind the quip but its ragged edges shown through.

"What is it?" she asked a touch too quickly.

"We have received word of a death at the Silver Courtesan."

The Courtesan's owner, Torae, was a friend of the cause. Part brothel, part social club, it was one of their best sources of intelligence within the unoccupied districts of Oizan. Even amidst the bloody revolution that raged in the streets, those that thought themselves above it all continued to live their lives, secure in the belief that eventually the rebels would "remember their place" and settle down. As foolish as they were, the patrons of the Silver Courtesan were a constant source of information for the revolution.

Wrapping her sword belt around her hips, Asaege cocked her head slightly. "I assume that the victim is someone of import?"

Toni snorted sharply. "In the minds of the council, yes. It was Meister Fremht."

She raised an eyebrow. "The Master of Commerce?"

"The same. His family has sat on the Ruling Council almost since the city's founding."

Asaege lowered her voice and tentatively asked, "Did we have anything to do with it?"

"No." The word was clipped, betraying their annoyance.

Asaege felt a rush of relief. By its nature, the rebellion had claimed lives on both side of the line, but the idea of assassination turned her stomach. "But the council is not likely to believe that."

They shook their head. "Torae did what she could to keep it quiet but Fremht dropped dead in the middle of the common room. The staff rushed him to a private chamber as quickly as they could but there is no doubt that people noticed."

Asaege's head spun, her thoughts a rush of possibilities, none of them good. Up to that point, the only causalities of the movement were professional soldiers and revolutionaries. Oizan's halls of power had remained untouched. The death of a council member would invite immediate and brutal reprisal. Amid the maelstrom of questions that raged in her mind, not a single solution made its presence known. The icy claws of doubt sank deep into her heart. *You are no leader,* Asaege thought, *a leader would know what to do.*

Toni must have seen the panic in her eyes because they stepped forward and laid a gentle hand on Asaege's forearm. "It is an unfortunate circumstance but not one that we can do anything about." Although their voice was low, its steady timbre offered a stability that she desperately needed. "We need to see the body for ourselves. If it was more than an inconvenient accident, we need to get in front of it." They pointed to the tome. "Is there anything in there that can help us figure out what happened to the old goat?"

Trying to quiet the cacophony of her thoughts, Asaege tried to remember the formulae in the book. Like the sun emerging from behind a spring raincloud, a gauze-like calm settled over her frenzied mind. She instantly recognized the presence of her reflection, Jillian.

Although separated by distance between their two worlds, the two fit together like a pair of lost puzzle pieces. Where Asaege struggled to retain the sheer volume of information found in the tome, Jillian remembered each word with perfect clarity. In times of need, Asaege had even found herself able to cast spells directly from her reflection's memory without the required memorization.

Clear as if the page lay open before her, Asaege saw the formula in her mind. *Saetae's Shrouded Speech* was a simple incantation that allowed communication with the spirits of the recently deceased. Her eyes tightly closed in an effort to block all other distractions, Asaege reviewed the spell. Nodding to herself, she allowed her eyes to flicker open again.

"I know of a way, but we must act quickly."

*****

Meister Fremht's face was contorted in an expression of agony, a sheen of half clotted blood staining his mouth and neatly trimmed beard. Asaege averted her eyes, waves of nausea crashing against the back of her throat. "What happened to him?" Although the question emerged as a raspy whisper, neither Toni nor Torae forced her to ask again.

"That is what I was hoping you could tell me." The proprietor of the Silver Courtesan spoke softly, placing a gentle hand on Asaege's shoulder. "He was taking his dinner in the common room with two guests—a pair of merchants that I had not seen before to-night. One of my girls was close, keeping the wine in both their wine glasses full and her ears open. Bethy said that Fremht faltered for a moment. His speech slurred for a moment before he was wracked with a hacking cough. Before anyone could do anything to help him, he began to bleed from the nose and mouth. He was dead by the time I arrived."

Toni crouched down, their nose wrinkling slightly as they studied the body laid out on the short silk divan. Reaching out, they dipped the tip of their pinky into the dead man's crimson mask. Cautiously, Toni brought the stained digit to their nose and took three short inhalations before frowning. After cleaning their finger on Meister Fremht's suede leggings, Toni rose slowly. "Grayshell causes exsanguination such as this, but the amounts required to act this quickly would leave the tell tale scent of rotten meat. The entire room would stink of it."

"I had thought of that," Torae began. "What about Plushweed?"

Toni shook their head. "Plushweed tastes like week old bile. There is no way that he could have unknowingly consumed it. Did you find any wounds on him?" Without waiting for an answer, the newly minted guild master grasped the body by the shoulder and rolled it onto its side.

"No," responded Torae, "the only person close enough to him before he started coughing was Bethy."

Toni raised an eyebrow, her unspoken question obvious.

"I trust my girls as I would trust myself. Besides, what would she gain from killing a member of the council?"

"What indeed?" Toni licked their lips nervously as they squint-ed at the unmarked silk blouse before them.

"If you have something to say, spit it out." Torae's tone was sharp as a knife.

Toni scratched absently at the tip of their nose with a blunted thumbnail. "I am not sure we can rule anything … or anyone out at this point." Their eyes refocused between breaths, becoming hard as steel. "It is best that your girl not take any unsupervised strolls until we figure this out."

Torae opened her mouth to object, but Toni cut her off.

"— if you can not handle it, I have people who can."

Through gritted teeth, Torae hissed, "Bethy is my responsibility. I will take care of it."

Fighting through her queasiness, Asaege stepped between them. "Perhaps I can shed some light on the situation." Before either could

41

respond, she gathered her skirt and knelt close to the body. Closing her eyes tightly against the sight before her, Asaege let slip her control of the turmoil that was her thoughts. Instantly, alien syllables surged forward, jockeying with each other to claw their way free from her mind. After holding the thaumaturgical formulae back for what seemed like hours, the lapse of discipline filled her with relief.

Knowing it for the trap that it was, Asaege clamped her mouth shut as the words formed on her tongue of their own volition. Focusing her will, she pulled the syllables of *Saetae's Shrouded Speech* to the forefront of her mind and forced the others back into their cage of willpower. Once Asaege was sure that all but the formula she sought were locked safely away, she exhaled softly. With her breath, came the words of power that made up the spell. As they hit her ear, they beat a counter rhythm to her heart. Each phrase pulled the air from her lungs, leaving her breathless as the last syllable escaped her lips like the air of a crypt too long sealed.

The sound of it hung in the air, echoing back upon itself in a cacophony of breathy notes. Ebbing and surging, the reverberation began to take shape into something understandable.

As ... ask ... ask of ... ask of me what you will.

Unsettled by the sudden clarity, Asaege was speechless for a moment.

The voice became more insistent. *I am weary ... ask what you will and then leave me to my rest.* Irritation colored the otherworldly voice.

"Are you Meister Fremht?" She felt foolish speaking to the empty air but feared what lay before her enough to keep her eyes pressed shut.

I am ... Ask what you will! Irritation quickly turned to anger.

"Who killed you?"

I do not know. As quickly as it flared, the voice's fury faded into a ponderous sadness.

"What do you remember?"

The roses of my garden ... in the spring, the air would dance on your tongue from their fragrance. An almost sleepy wistfulness hung in the air around Asaege. Under the scent of courtesan's perfume and the stink of drying blood, she could almost smell the aroma of blooming flowers.

Her mind drifted to afternoons spent with her sisters in the Garden District, wandering among the rainbow hued tide of meticulously cultivated blooms. Asaege could see in her mind's eye the azure summer sky, only broken by the most translucent wisps of clouds.

She could feel her older sister's hand in hers, the excitement of the day radiating from her skin. Choirs of unseen birds mingled their songs into a tapestry of melody. Amid their canticle, the spirit's voice became less and less distinct.

Like a cold burst of rain, realization struck Asaege. In the margins of the formula, Hollis's friend had written a warning. Spirits didn't want to help those who compelled their aid. Through threat or trickery, they will always seek to escape the influence of the spell. She saw the vivid memories for what they were: a distraction. Asaege clenched her teeth and forced herself to focus. "What do you remember about the night you died?" The tone of her voice was like a whip, more forceful than she would have liked.

As much as she instantly regretted it, the effect was immediate. Meister Fremht's spirit seemed cowed. In a meek voice, it responded, *I was meeting with a pair of grain merchants ... The uprising has made Oizan an undesirable place to sell their products ... The granaries are almost empty.*

"Did they kill you?"

No ... I felt suddenly light-headed ... as I lifted my hand to wipe the sweat from my brow ... my sight darkened ... I saw a strange place through my clouded vision.

"What did you see?" Asaege pressed.

Everything was washed out ... as if it were a blouse, too often laundered ... I saw a room I did not recognize ... everything was sharp angles and bare surfaces ... I saw ...

The spirit's words hung in the air, the weight of them settling on Asaege's heart like sodden wool. She could feel Meister Fremht's fear across the threshold of death that separated them. Firmly, she repeated. "What did you see?"

The spirit's panic flowed through Asaege as it stammered, *He is coming ... the rays of the sun glint in the mirrored edge of his knife ... No ... NO!*

Asaege felt a sharp pain in her chest. The piercing agony was only broken by the frigid bite of cold steel.

No! I do not want to die! Help me! Help me!

Although her mind understood that nothing she felt was real, the phantom assault continued. In rapid succession, her body exploded into blossoms of pain. With a fierce shove of her will, she forced the specter from her presence and let the spell fade.

As she slowly opened her eyes, the first thing Asaege saw was the look of abject terror forever stamped on Meister Fremht's crimson-masked face. Fighting her rising gorge, she turned from the corpse and pushed herself to her feet. As she turned, Asaege was greeted by the grim faces of Torae and Toni. Breathlessly, she said, "He was murdered, but not here."

"What does that mean?" Toni's voice was steady but tinged with bleak notes of concern.

The owner of the Silver Courtesan made no effort to conceal her own panic. "He died here. That will be more than enough for the city guard. I will be lucky if all they do is close me down."

Replying first to the guild master, Asaege said simply, "It means that we are out of our depth." She turned to Torae, grasping her wrist gently. "You should come with us. No doubt the guards' questions will go beyond Meister Fremht's death."

Pulling her arm free, she snapped, "Running will be as good as admitting guilt."

"Your guilt will be assumed whether you stay or go," Toni supplied, already turning for the door.

"Toni is correct, they will not wait for proof. You will find yourself in the Lord Mayor's prison before nightfall. I doubt that his inquisitor will stop at what happened here. Your only hope is to escape before they arrive."

"But what of my people? They count on me."

Asaege's heart ached for Torae. "If it helps, once it becomes clear you have fled, I doubt the guard will look much further."

"It does not."

Another emotion fought for dominance with Asaege's compassion: guilt. *Am I more worried about Torae's safety or what details can be pried from her about the revolution?* It broke her heart that she couldn't be sure of the answer.

Chapter Six

A New Adversary

Asaege split her attention between the hallway and the beautifully appointed bedroom. Although Torae gathered her things quickly, it didn't seem quick enough for Toni. The newly minted guild-master scowled impatiently at the woman as she stuffed clothing into a canvas sack. Once the proprietor of the Silver Courtesan finished packing, she whispered, "We can go now."

Toni let an exasperated hiss escape their lips, but made no further comment. They took the lead, moving past Asaege and into the hall. "Follow me, Asaege. Try to keep up, as we may need to move quickly." Any annoyance they felt towards Torae didn't carry over to Asaege. Their voice was as calm and steady as she had ever known it. Slipping into the corridor, she followed Toni with Torae on her heels.

By the time they reached the grand staircase leading down to the common room, the group could hear the commotion below. Toni held up a finger before crouching beside the ornate newel post. At first only the sandpaper-rough sound of raised voices reached Asaege's ears; their words muffled by distance and the pounding blood in them. Closing her eyes, she tried to calm her beating heart. In the back of her mind, she felt Jillian's comforting presence. A gauze-soft calmness settled upon her like winter's first tentative snowfall.

"—you will have your turn, whore! I was speaking to the boy." Asaege heard the meaty thwack of a shove followed by the sound of breaking furniture. "If I were you, son, I would answer Lady Markov's question before you join the harlot."

Asaege felt Torae surge forward against her back. Placing a restraining hand on the madam's arm, she whispered, "No."

"Where is the lady of the house, boy?" It was a woman's voice, full of velvet and sugar, but beneath its surface was the promise of wicked thorns. "Your fate is unimportant … to me."

Asaege heard the implied threat in that pause.

"As far as I am concerned, you could walk out the door, leave this life of degradation behind with a tidy sum in your pocket for your trouble. Would you like that?" The voice paused, waiting for an answer. When it didn't come, the woman continued, "Of course you would. Who would want to spend their life here?" She spat out the last word as if it were a bite of rotten fruit. "All you need to do is tell me where Mistress Torae is."

A small, mouse-like voice squeaked, "Truly, milady, I do not know."

"Remain on your knees, wretch!" The sound of metal against flesh followed the booming order.

Torae tried to push past Asaege, but again she was able to stop the woman. "Baern is just a boy," Torae's voice pleaded.

Shifting her eyes to Toni, Asaege saw the guild-master's face pulled into a scowl but still she shook her head tersely.

"Maybe you do, maybe you do not. I doubt you would tell me even if you knew where she was." The woman's voice took on a tone of boredom. "Claerius, I am through with him. Bring me one of the harlots … that one."

A baritone chuckle echoed through the common room. "Gladly, Lady Markov."

"No!" It was Baern's voice.

Asaege imagined the young boy throwing his tiny body against the armored form of the guard. The resulting sob of pain came close to breaking her heart.

Claerius grumbled, "None of them will talk, milady. Do you want me to set an example to loosen their tongues?"

"No," the woman responded. "Lirych, it is past time you earn your commission." In a voice that was both dark and joyful, the woman purred, "Break the girl."

"Enough," Torae hissed. This time when Asaege attempted to

halt her advance, the madam rolled her wrist in Asaege's hand and seized her forearm instead. With a firm twist, Torae forced Asaege to her knees and was on the stairs before she could react.

As the proprietor of the Silver Courtesan rushed past Toni, Asaege heard their wordless exhalation of irritation.

"If it is me that you seek, Markov. You need look no further. My people have nothing to do with this."

Toni looked back at Asaege, as if they debated their next action. Snorting sharply, the newly minted guild-master rose effortlessly and drew the thin Slazean sword at her side. "Follow me down." In a voice so cold it could have coated Asaege's ears in frost, Toni said, "Bar the door. None of them leaves the Courtesan."

*****

The guild-master rushed past Torae, using their momentum to carry them over the engraved oak banister. For a split second, they hung in the air, the embodiment of death come upon those below. Asaege lost sight of them as she dropped to the common room below. Torae didn't allow the dramatic display before her to interrupt her downward progress, although she took the more sane route the stairs offered. In a flourish of silk and velvet, the madam reached beneath her meticulously tailored dress. When it emerged, a jeweled stiletto was clutched in her fist.

The first clarion sound of steel on steel shocked Asaege into motion. *The door*, she chided herself as she rushed down the stairs behind Torae. It was only as she reached the bottom that it occurred to her to draw her own sword. What greeted her both shocked and amazed her.

Toni danced between two guardsman, their body in constant motion, their thin sword a blur of dark steel. Each time one of the soldiers swung their weapon, Toni's blade caressed it like a lovers' first kiss and angled it away from them. Before its wielder could recover, Toni drove the tip of their sword into shoulder or wrist. At their side, Toni held a long, thick bladed dagger. Any time a second guardsman took it into their mind to take advantage of Toni's distraction, the weapon in their left hand snapped up like a coiled snake, making them think better of it.

Torae stood between a guardsmen and a cluster of her "girls". Her eyes hard and her lips drawn back into a snarl, Asaege almost didn't recognize the soft spoken madam of an hour prior. At some point during her descent, Torae had ripped the bottom of her dress so it ended just above her knees. The torn fabric was wrapped around her left hand and wrist. Her stiletto held before her, she faced off against a clearly surprised soldier.

Moving past both battles, Asaege raced towards the door and set the thick bar across it, effectively locking the two groups in the Silver Courtesan. As she turned, she saw a hooded man leaning against one of the three marble columns in the foyer. His arms were crossed casually across his chest as if he were observing an impromptu street performance rather than a life and death combat. He made no move to interfere with either the ongoing melee or Asaege herself, but she gave him a wide berth.

Well out of danger stood an obviously well born woman, dressed in crimson and plum. She held a silk handkerchief to her face, although her eyes drank in the violence before her. To her left, the final guardsman stood. Although his sword was drawn, he remained stationed at her side.

"Lady Markov, I presume?" Having overcome her initial shock, Asaege felt only anger.

Markov exhaled sharply, a sound somewhere between a growl and a croak. "Claerius, deal with this ruffian. Please." The last word was added as an after thought and with an excess of scorn.

In the back of Asaege's mind, an itch formed. *That voice. That face. I should know them both.* Before she could pry the source of the familiarity loose, the broad city guardsman stepped forward, swinging his straight bladed Granatyrian sword back and forth tauntingly.

Although a few months ago, Asaege had only possessed the familiarity with violence that living in the Ash demanded, the revolution had forced her to learn quickly. She would likely never be the fighter that Toni was but Hollis and his mentor, Seran, had been adequate teachers. As ever, she was an apt pupil.

Putting her Talis Fahr between her and Claerius, Asaege angled her body to present less of a target. Her Uteli weapon surrendered the length advantage to his heavy broad sword, but its balance allowed her to strike as quick as a hiccup when an opening presented itself. Her opponent discovered that as he launched a clumsy overhand chop.

Asaege lifted her blade to meet his, angled slightly as she had been taught. The broad sword slid along its length, pulling its wielder off balance. Instincts driven into her by the smirking arrogance of Seran's lessons, Asaege snapped her weapon around and brought the Talis Fahr's razor sharp edge across the bare shoulder and bicep of the hulking soldier. Rolling her wrist, she launched her sword into a return slash, but Claerius interposed his sword between them as he leapt back.

"I think you will find me a little more trouble than a little boy."

Favoring his wounded arm, the guardsman sneered. "You took me by surprise is all, girl."

"Sure, I did." Wishing with all her might that she felt as confident as she hoped she sounded, Asaege leveled her weapon again, aiming its point at the center of her opponent's chest. In this way, she maximized the length of her weapon in a conflict where inches mattered.

Out of the corner of her eye, she saw one of the soldiers facing Toni fall to a knee. His leather cuirass was slick with blood from a hand full of deep punctures. His partner attempted to put his body between his wounded comrade and the guild-master's stinging blade. Unfortunately for the injured guardsman, all his well meaning friend did was obscure his vision. Toni's thin sword plunged into his throat like the two were connected by an invisible string. The soldier slumped to the ground with a tortured gurgle.

Behind them, Torae straddled a struggling guardsman as she drove her dagger repeatedly into his neck and face. The soldier fruitlessly attempted to ward off both the frenzied stabs and the flurry of kicks from the very people he threatened a moment ago.

The sound of a booted foot on the wooden floor snapped Asaege's attention back to her own predicament. Claerius pushed past her extended sword, leading with his own. Having no choice but to give ground, Asaege skipped backwards. In her panic, her feet became tangled. As she fell, Asaege felt the passage of the soldier's broad bladed sword above her head. Fighting the instinct to compact her body while in the air, she stretched out to help absorb the shock of her impact. In the process, she had to let her sword slip from her grasp.

Asaege still struck the floor with bone-jarring force but was able to scramble backwards on heels and hands as Claerius's sword carved a divot in the wood between her feet. Looking up into the leering face of her attacker, she felt fear squeeze her heart between its frigid talons. The sensation took her breath away. Just as he raised his weapon above his head, a soft cloak of tranquility settled across her chest as Jillian's thoughts surged to the fore. With them came the image of an open book. As clear in her memory as if it lay open before her, the thaumaturgical formula leapt off the page.

Reading the spell from her reflection's perfect recollection, Asaege felt the gathering of power into herself as if it were a deep inhalation of rich, balmy summer air. As fast as it was pulled into her body, the arcane words shaped and redirected it outward. An aura of hazy distortion around Claerius was the only warning that *Intrae's Instant Immolation* had taken hold of him.

Before the big man could bring his sword down again, a series of sizzling pops filled the air. Each was accompanied by a small burst of flame across his chest. The scent of burning flesh reached Asaege's nose as Claerius dropped his sword and began to pound himself furiously in an attempt to arrest the spreading blaze. His mouth slacked open for a split second before he let out a keening wail and dropped to the floor. Maintained by the power of the spell, his frantic rolling was only partially successful in smothering the flames.

Shocked into inaction, Asaege watched the aftermath of her efforts. The spell continued to gather power and channel it through her, even though she no longer spoke the words. Allowing sympathy to overpower her fear and anger, she turned her attention inward and tried to arrest the flow of energy. At first it was like trying to damn a river with a cobblestone, but Asaege turned all of her will to the task. In the back of her mind, she could feel Jillian lend her strength to the task as well. Slowly, the torrent ebbed into a stream and then ceased entirely.

Claerius's ragged gasps and twitching form told Asaege that the man still lived. His exposed skin was blackened, sections of it curled like ragged pieces of parchment to reveal blood-stained, ivory bone. Fighting back a retching cough, she averted her eyes and stumbled to her feet. At some point, the room had fallen into a tense silence.

Asaege recoiled when Toni laid their hand on her shoulder. "You had no choice," they whispered. Behind the guild-master lay the bodies of the two guardsmen foolish enough to cross blades with them. Beyond the carnage, Torae had gathered her employees behind her, their own assailant bloody and still on the floor.

The stillness was broken by Lady Markov's screeching voice. "Lirych! Do something."

The hooded figure at the door still leaned against the column in the foyer. "My commission was for interrogation and divination."

His voice was conversational, almost pleasant. It also had a familiar tone to it. Asaege herself had never heard it, but her reflection knew it almost as well as her own. That fact didn't do anything to prevent the shock both she and Jillian felt when Lirych reached up to pull back his hood and revealed Cyrill's face.

"Anything further will come with an additional cost." He looked around the room before adding, "Judging by the obvious proficiency of these three ladies, I will have to insist on half again my normal rate."

"Done," Markov snapped. "Just kill them all." She met Asaege's eyes, a satisfied smile blossoming on her lips. "I am not concerned with collateral damage, bring the whole building down if the mood strikes you."

Lirych drew a Mantrian longsword as he shrugged off his cloak. While not as physically imposing as the broader Granatyrian blades, the favored swords of their northern neighbor were more agile and tended to suit their more defensive style. "I am sure that will not be necessary."

Toni stepped passed Asaege, their own blade held casually at their side. "If you throw your lot in with these folks …" They indicated the four guardsman with a sweep of their sword. "… I am going to have to lay you beside them." Toni's voice was devoid of emotion, lending it the quality of razor-honed steel.

"I am afraid I am going to have to take my chances, my friend. A man has to make a living." The next words out of Lirych's mouth were lost on Toni, but Asaege recognized them for what they were: thaumaturgy. He didn't stumble over the phrases as she sometimes did. They rolled forth from his lips in an effortless stream, their power beating a staccato rhythm in Asaege's chest.

He stepped over the still twitching body of the victim of Asaege's last use of magic. She wasn't sure if the terror that crashed against her heart in pounding waves was natural or a product of Lirych's spell, but each undulating wave eroded the tranquil embrace of Jillian's presence. With her influence waning, so too would Asaege's ability to call upon formula she had not prepared earlier that evening.

"Run," she snapped.

Toni glanced over their shoulder, a questioning expression on their face. Behind their callous mask, Asaege could see the fear that also threatened to take the guild-master's nerve.

"Run," Asaege repeated. As she backed away from the advancing thaumaturge, she heard a door open behind her. Torae was pushing the last of her "girls" through the door and was holding it for Toni and Asaege.

The guild-master paused one moment longer and then gave into Asaege's advice, and their own instincts. The wide hallway beyond the common room was empty as Torae locked the door behind them. Toni opened their mouth to voice the obvious question but Asaege growled, "Later."

Content with that for the moment, the three raced down the

51

corridor, leaving the Silver Courtesan behind.

Chapter Seven

A Renewed Enmity

Jillian woke to a soft voice brushing against her semi-conscious mind. "… temperatures will continue to drop later in the week. By Saturday, we will be solidly in the single digits across the area." Her eyes flickered open as she attempted to wash from her memory the image of Meister Fremht's terror-stricken features. Despite the fact that she laid upon the pillow-stuffed futon that dominated the cluttered living room of her tiny apartment, the corpse's horrific, crimson mask was burned into her mind's eye.

She had fallen asleep on the futon the previous night. Since Hector had disappeared, and with him her supply of "Dreamtime Dank", she had transformed a small section of her apartment into a makeshift greenhouse to grow adder root herself. After almost three months, Jillian had still not mastered the dosage of the tea made from the green-and-purple plant. She had measured out what she thought was a moderate dosage of the foul tasting leaves before steeping them with a mild chamomile blend Marisol had given her. The half-full cup of cold tea still stood on the low coffee table between her and the inane morning news program on her second hand television.

"If you have elderly relatives or neighbors, please check in on them this weekend as well." Jillian focused on the way-too-perky reporter, bundled in a very camera-wise winter jacket. Her bottle-blonde locks brushed against the faux fur collar of the rose-red garment. In contrast to her dire warning, a warm smile was plastered on her face, revealing the bleached teeth behind her mauve lipstick. "With temperatures this low, bursting pipes are a real possibility. Please visit News Ten dot com for tips on preventing property damage during the winter season."

Behind the woman, a figure huddled against the corner of a nearby building. Wrapped in a tattered, over-sized olive-drab jacket and surrounded by black garbage bags, Jillian almost missed him. The incongruity of the reporter's sunny disposition against the despondency of the homeless man's circumstances ignited a sudden anger in Jillian. *Who is going to check in on him?* she thought bitterly. *Is there a tip for that on your website?*

In the back of her mind, she could feel Asaege's outrage add to her own. *These people are so invisible to society that they have become no more than part of the landscape.* In Taerh, her reflection fought a literal war against such casual neglect. In Jillian's own world, that war had already been lost. *Or has it?* she thought.

"Back to you, Ted." As the homeless man began to stir, the street scene cut quickly to a stern-faced man behind a wood grained desk.

"Thank you, Penny. Maybe it is a good week to settle in front of the fireplace with a cup of hot cocoa and a Christmas movie." His mouth turned up into a wry smile that was not reflected in the anchor's dead eyes. His chuckle was a dry and hollow sound, like dead leaves blown across a cobblestone walkway, A picture of a middle aged man dressed in a smart blue suit jacket appeared behind the anchor. "In other news, Freeholder Martin Fredericks was discovered early this morning in his home.

Jillian cringed. The Council of Elected Freeholders had been established after the American Revolution as the first governing body for the nascent county. As only free, land holding men were permitted to vote at that time, the title had been fairly accurate. More than two hundred and fifty years later, it had not changed with the times. The council existed in the ambiguous space between town and state government, and as such existed in tandem with the county courts to deal with business that fell between the two.

The Council of Elected Freeholders acted as both legislative and executive branches, the later conspicuous by its absence in county politics. They tended mostly to county infrastructure such as roads, bridges and education, but also could pass laws, approve budgets and spend funds, all without executive oversight. In his latest term, Martin Fredericks had championed a push to expand the council's power over the towns under its purview. As the freeholders' control expanded, that of their unofficial leader did so as well.

"Police say there were signs of forced entry and they believe that Mr. Fredericks may have surprised the intruder and paid for it with his life. Anyone with information about the events are urged to call the county sheriff tip line. Authorities are offering a thousand dollar reward for any tips leading to the prosecution of the perpetrator or perpetrators." A quick change in camera angle also zoomed in on the anchor's face. The altered perspective was unfortunate, as Jillian could clearly see the cracks in his exaggerated expression of sadness.

"Most recently, Freeholder Fredericks had been working with various community groups to regulate educational standards across the county. Whereas in the past, each town could set their own standards, the Council of Elected Freeholders passed a series of legislation aimed at consolidating them under one united set of guidelines. Several community groups rallied behind Fredericks, lending their support, both political and popular to his cause. Most notable among these organizations is the Coalition for Academic Responsibility and Excellence or CARE."

Jillian gritted her teeth at the name. In her opinion, the coalition's mission was the furthest thing from educational responsibility. After stacking the school boards of multiple towns in the county, they began dictating the academic procedures of the schools under their control, mostly through censorship and book banning. No vaguely controversial book seemed safe from their attentions: *Wrinkle in Time; James and the Giant Peach; Bridge to Terabithia; Are You There God? It's Me, Margaret.*

"After an unfortunate series of drug related incidents, leading to the deaths of two promising young men and her own husband falling into a persistent coma, CARE's current chairwoman, Veronica Moses, publicly decried subversive works easily found in school and public libraries as a major contributing factor. Citing authors such as Judy Blume and Shel Silverstein in addition to the role playing game Shadows and Sorcerers, or S&S for short, she initially launched a grass roots crusade against what she called 'the intellectual castration of the county's youth.'"

The newscaster's words cut through the angry buzz of Jillian's thoughts. *Moses. Where have I heard that name before?*

"Within the ranks of the Coalition for Academic Responsibility and Excellence, Mrs. Moses found a group of like-minded allies.

After running a very successful election for her own town's board of education, in which CARE affiliated candidates captured nine of the ten available seats, Mrs. Moses, herself, was elected chairwoman of the organization by a landslide."

Moses. A frigid ache echoed in Jillian's stomach as realization dawned on her. *Drug related deaths tied to a role-playing game? Stephen.* The name of Hollis's reflection came to her in a rush. When the thief activated the latest Well of Worlds on Taerh, he believed his twin in her world had perished, allowing the pair to become one. *Didn't he just say that her husband was in a coma?*

"Under Moses's administration, CARE threw their substantial support behind the late Freeholder Fredericks. In the three open board of education elections held, Mrs. Moses and CARE were successful in winning seventy percent of the seats they ran for. Before his death, there were serious rumors that Martin Fredericks had planned on endorsing Mrs. Moses in the upcoming Council of Elected Freeholders election."

Her eyes now glued to the television, Jillian felt herself torn between Stephen being alive and the fact that his not-so-widow was using his condition as a means to garner support for her crusade against education.

*****

The troublesome itch in Jillian's brain was still present when she climbed out of her car into the crisp, winter morning. Between her and the faded brick surface of Rolling Meadows Elementary School stretched a thin layer of ash colored snow, occasionally broken by a stray blade of grass. Despite the fact that students would not arrive for another thirty minutes, the building was a hub of frenzied activity. Taking a deep breath of the biting air to steady her nerves, Jillian shut the car door and walked towards what promised to be a long day.

"Hey, lady," a voice called to her.

Turning more suddenly than she intended, Jillian saw a salt-faded blue compact car pull beside her, its passenger side window already open. Leaning across the center console, she saw a friendly face. Marisol Diaz had been that to her and more since they both began at Rolling Meadows. United in a shared dissatisfaction with the status quo at the small elementary school, the two women bonded early.

"I'll resist the urge to shout 'dead man walking' after you, but please know that it's only with an abundance of self control."

"I can't sufficiently express my gratitude," Jillian responded in a low, droning voice.

Marisol shook a finger in her direction. "No, no, no. You can't sound so downtrodden already."

"Why's that exactly?"

Screwing her face into a only passingly serious face, her friend responded, "It's still early. There is so much more treading to be done."

Jillian rolled her eyes. "Thank you so much for reminding me." Despite herself and the seriousness of her thoughts, she laughed.

Marisol joined her before sitting upright again. "Give me a sec to get parked and we can walk in together."

She reluctantly nodded, thankful for the Latina's company. "Hurry up, though. I'm not sure I can sit through another of Peterson's 'if you're on time, you're late' lectures."

Her friend accelerated quickly, pulling into an empty parking spot at a truly terrifying speed. Hopping out of the car with an enthusiasm that Jillian envied, Marisol practically skipped across the grit covered asphalt towards her.

"What's wrong with his lectures? He obviously is just talking to hear his own voice. He never actually stops to make sure you're listening. I use them as an abbreviated free period."

Jillian always found her smile infectious; this morning was no exception.

Marisol knew her well enough to see the anxiety behind the grin, however. "What's wrong, Jill?"

Out of instinct, she shook her head, dismissing the question. Her friend placed a hand on her arm, seizing Jillian's eyes in her own. Despite her lack of any further words, Jillian felt the unrepeated question.

"I received some potentially upsetting news this morning."

"Is everything okay?"

Jillian shrugged. "I'm not sure. I mean, it could be really good but … I just don't know."

"Him?" She could hear the capital H in Marisol's voice. Since Jillian mentioned Stephen to her friend months ago, she had been like a bloodhound on a trail. Jillian refused to disclose his name, so Marisol took to referring to him simply as "Him".

Before she could stop herself, Jillian nodded. "It's complicated."

Marisol dismissed her objection with a wave of her hand. "It's been complicated. Complicated is the word people use when they're not sure what else to say. Plenty of people have made the long dis-

57

tance thing work."

"Not this distance." *But is he really all that far?* Shaking her head in a futile effort to dislodge the thought from her mind, Jillian continued. "Even if he were right in front of me, it's—"

"—complicated, I know," Marisol finished for her with a frustrated growl. "At some point, that just becomes another excuse to stop trying." Her tone was gentle but the words conveyed the seriousness of her message.

A flash of anger, hot and sudden, exploded in Jillian's chest. It caused her breath to catch at the back of her throat.

Squeezing her friend's arm, Marisol whispered, "I'm sorry. I shouldn't have said that."

As quickly as it blossomed, the rage dissipated. "That's okay, Mari. It's just been a rough morning."

"I just want to see you happy. As complicated as he is, there is no denying the sparkle in your eye when you talk about Him."

Jillian covered her face, feeling her cheek already coloring. "My eyes don't sparkle."

"I beg to differ, lady."

Peeking through her fingers, she saw Marisol's mischievous grin. In that moment, for just a second, Jillian let herself believe that everything could work out. And then she felt her phone buzz against her leg. Pulling it from her back pocket, the four words on the screen chilled her blood. *Hector's back in business.*

"I need to go," Jillian stammered, turning towards the parking lot.

Marisol's mouth hung open as she tried to form the question on her lips.

"Mari, just cover for me, please. I'll explain later, I promise." Without waiting for a response, Jillian ran to her car. She was pursued by a fear she thought long dead.

*****

The shop in question was a inconspicuous storefront in an equally unremarkable strip mall. A faded, unmaintained sign hung above the frosted glass windows. It read simply: *Florist and Holistic Medicine.* Not advertised on the understated sign was the store's less than stellar history. First opened by an outwardly kind old woman, the florist served as a means to grow and supply adder root to unsuspecting customers in a bid to lure their dreaming-selves into the world of Taerh. While there, it was the hope of the proprietor that she could sacrifice them to a mystical pool, granting herself the power of the Well of Worlds itself.

When Jillian had first heard the story, she had felt ridiculous simply listening to it. The fact that she had been visiting Taerh in her dreams at the time didn't make it feel any less absurd.

After the original owner had been killed in the pursuit of her nefarious goals, a more pragmatic squatter took possession of the space. Rather than selling an unexpected death, Hector sold marijuana from the back of the store while only nominally maintaining the florist's respectable front. It was only when it was almost too late that Jillian found that he, also, sought to take advantage of his customers using the adder root with which he laced his product.

Jillian sat in her car, staring at the abandoned storefront. It stood out like a darkened scar between All County Liquor and Kimmel's Best Bagels. She wasn't sure what she expected to find but a sense of foreboding kept her frozen in place, keys clutched in one hand and the other poised above the handle of her car door. While Jillian's squinting eyes tried to pierce the frosted surface of the store's windows, her memory wrestled with the image of her last interaction with Hector. More specifically, it had been with the man's reflection, the Plague Man.

Beneath the streets of Oizan and bolstered by the power of a possessed artifact, he had tried to kill Stephen's reflection, Hollis. Had it not been for Jillian's connection with her own double in Taerh, she had no doubt that Plague Man would have succeeded. The two women, separated by the distance between their two worlds, were able to cooperate in order to cast a thaumaturgical ritual to exorcise the ancient presence from the brooch and deprive Hector's reflection of its aid.

When he attempted to flee, Hollis rushed off in pursuit. Although she had not seen it with her own eyes, the thief swore that their final confrontation ended with Plague Man's broken body falling fifty feet to his death. If Cyrill's text was correct, Hector's perpetually slippery reflection had once again escaped his rightful fate. If Hector lived, so too did Plague Man.

It was that fact that kept Jillian borderline paralyzed in her car. Neither she nor her reflection were killers, or even particularly dangerous in a conventional sense. Her thoughts returned to Asaege's experience in the Courtesan. *Not like Toni or Seran ... or even Torae.* Bitterly, Jillian wished that she were more like any one of her reflection's allies. *What would Seran do?* she asked herself. When a flood of terrible things flooded her brain, she turned her attention to the more relatable motivations of Torae.

Pushing down the fear that had gripped her heart, she forced her hand to open the door and stepped out of the car. As soon as the frosty morning air carried the sour-sweet burning scent to her nostrils, Jillian knew something was wrong. As she searched for its source, her eyes instead seized upon motion behind the clouded windows of the florist. Although they concealed their identity, there could be no doubt that someone was inside. It was only once the shape moved passed the now clearly ajar front door and further into the depths of the shop that she saw the first flickering reflections of flames against the frosted glass.

Before she could think better of it, Jillian broke into a run. If whoever was inside had meant to leave through the front door, they would have done so before the fire cut off their escape. She remembered an exit from the shop's back room. It was definitely a less conspicuous egress for a potential arsonist. *What are you going to do when you get there?* Jillian asked herself. At a loss for an answer, she instead focused on not slipping on the ice-covered sidewalk as she turned the corner into the alley between the building and the diner next door.

Barely keeping her feet under her, Jillian reached the rear of the building as a broad-shouldered figure burst from the shop's back door. Dressed in a dirty, gray hoodie, the massive man's face was wrapped in a black and white checkered scarf. He turned to face her for a split second, as if considering rushing her before he spun and fled in the other direction. For an inadvisable second, Jillian contemplated giving chase, but quickly came to her senses.

As the door was swinging shut, she thought she heard a voice over the soft crackling inside. Not giving herself a chance to think better of it, Jillian ran to the door and caught it before it closed. Squinting against the furnace-like heat rushing past her, she tried to make out anything besides the dancing, orange tongues of flame that seemed everywhere. Through the half-consumed curtain that had divided the back room from the public facing front of the store, Jillian saw that the once ajar front door now stood fully open.

Hoping a good Samaritan had come to the same conclusion she did, Jillian called out. "Hello? I think someone is still in here!" The only response she heard was the snap-crackle-pop of the hungry flames. She tried to step further into the building but the heat within stole both her sight and her breath. Forced backwards again, Jillian scanned the fiery confines of the room once more. Lying amid burning piles of antique furniture was a single unmoving form.

Jillian took a step back as she felt her gorge rise in her throat. The door swung closed, mercifully cutting off her view of the body.

Chapter Eight
A Haunting Nightmare

Aristoi had struggled to remain awake, straining to keep her eyelids open for fear of what lay behind them. The closer she came to Agmar's Watch, the more intense her nightmares had become. The alien instincts calling to her from inside her own mind seemed encouraged by the presence of the gwyllgi and redoubled their attempts to coax her into surrender. To that point, the Song-spear's resolve had proven the stronger, but she feared there would come a time when that was no longer true.

Beside her, Hollis slept fitfully, rolling from side to side in search of peace. She feared that his discomfort wasn't merely physical. Just as her past rose to greet her, so did Hollis's. The thief would never admit it, but mere vengeance would not heal the wound he carried in his heart.

As she turned her attention to the evergreen boughs that surrounded them, a deeper shade of black against the night, Aristoi felt the twitches begin. At first they were just a tickle between her shoulder blades, but it quickly built into the sensation of white-hot needles stabbing into her flesh. She tried to focus on the pain, breath through it as a means to hold off the fatigue that wrapped around her like damp wool.

In the end, the sweeping ripples of pain blended into one another, only adding to her all-encompassing weariness. As her eyelids drifted closed, the ever-patient dreams were waiting for her.

*****

The beast waited until the night had cut its teeth before emerging from the cluster of clapboard structures. The Songspear silently wished that her roost afforded her a view of the hole it had crawled from. She took a deep breath, as if the intake of cold air could force the regret from her; nothing good could come from agonizing about a situation she could not change. It was only partially successful. Squinting into the darkness, she made out the massive creature below her.

Aristoi estimated that if she stood next to the beast, its powerful shoulders would easily reach her waist. Its dark mottled fur made what she could see of it blend seamlessly into the surrounding shadows; as it approached, it slipped in and out of the gloom as if they were one. The only part of the creature that she saw clearly were its baleful eyes, appearing rust-colored in the reflected moonlight. Those eyes narrowed to slits as the Songspear heard a deep wuffling on the wind. Despite the surrounding darkness, the beast turned its gaze to regard the Kieli woman in her perch.

Feeling her heart rise into her throat, Aristoi's grip tightened on the shaft of her spear. Instincts nestled deep inside of the woman warned against meeting the creature's piercing stare. Even a passing glance into the beast's sinister eyes caused a deep exhaustion to settle into the Kieli's bones. She tried to measure the distance between herself and the creature below her by eye, hoping her spear's superior reach would allow her to strike before it brought its own natural weapons to bear.

Having located an intruder in its domain, the beast growled in low, dangerous tones. Aristoi almost dropped her weapon when those tones formed themselves into words like wind through thatch. "You do not belong here. You do not smell of the tundra." They were two simple statements, but the snarling words turned Aristoi's blood as cold as the northern night. The creature reared up onto its hind legs, placing its front paws against the low building on top of which the woman crouched. On two legs, its head only lay an arm's reach below her; even a half-hearted jump would carry it onto the roof beside her.

Steeling herself, Aristoi drew her spear back and prepared to strike the first blow, not sure she would get a second one. From the corner of her eye, she watched the rust-colored orbs studying her for a moment before it withdrew from the building and settled onto its haunches. As the moon emerged from the swollen mass of clouds that crossed the sky, she saw the beast in all its glory. For the most part, it appeared as a large, muscular wolf. Each of its powerful legs ended in an appendage that was more hand than paw. Even as it studied her, its wicked claws dug furrows in the frozen dirt. A huffing laugh erupted from the creature as it pondered her from its seated position. "Tell me, outlander, what brings you so far afield."

Her knuckles white on the shaft of her weapon, Aristoi tried to keep her voice even and free of the shudder that ran through her entire being. "If I may be honest with you, my business is the last thing in my thoughts this evening." The woman's eyes focused on the lithe muscles beneath the beast's dark pelt, watching for any indication that it was preparing to leap. "I could ask you the same question. Agmar's Watch is the autumn domain of the Furred Serpents."

The creature's ears flattened against its skull as a wave of irritation rolled across its expressive muzzle. Deep within its chest, a rumbling thunder of a growl built. Aristoi rose to the balls of her feet in preparation for the beast's lunge. As quickly as it rose, the sound faded into silence. The creature's lips pulled back revealing its ivory colored teeth in a sinister smile. "That no longer seems to be the case." Its grumbling voice held an edge sharp enough to cut flesh. "The question remains: what concern is it of yours?"

"The Furred Serpents are crucial to acquiring something of great import to me," the Kieli answered.

"More important than your life?"

"I have traveled quite a distance and weathered a great deal of storms, both metaphorical and literal, in search of it."

"The question still remains."

Aristoi nodded slowly. "It is worth quite a bit to me."

Slowly, the beast rose to its feet, closing its eyes as it stretched lazily. As it did, the Songspear lunged forward to take advantage of the creature's momentary weakness. Its malignant eyes flashed open, seizing her in their unwavering glare, causing a sensation of exhaustion to sweep over her like a deluge. Aristoi couldn't pull her eyes away from the beast's, despite wanting to with every ounce of her being. As the encompassing weariness weaved its way into her bones, her steps faltered. No doubt, that was what saved the woman's life. As she stumbled to her knees, the edge of the roof broke contact with the beast's eyes.

As soon as she was free of the creature's influence, the exhaustion fled from the Songspear's body like water from a broken goblet. As the last vestiges of the sensation seeped from her, Aristoi brought to mind the same song she'd used with great effect upon the young Rangor the previous night. Its effects mirrored those of the beast's sinister gaze, but she figured that turnabout was fair-play. The creature landed lightly on the rooftop as the steady dirge completed its work.

Shaking its shaggy head, the beast crouched momentarily in place as it tried to make sense of the unexpected assault upon its own vitality. "You are full of surprises, outlander," it rumbled as it stalked towards her.

Lost in the depths of her song, Aristoi simply smirked as she gripped her spear in both hands and prepared for the beast's inevitable lunge. She didn't need to wait long. The creature drew its legs beneath itself and sprung forward despite the waves of exhaustion that clearly spread through its body. Sinking into a low crouch, the Songspear drove the spear into the beast as it came within reach.

Twisting in mid-air, the creature passed over the woman with only a deep slash creasing its flank rather than impaling itself on the weapon. It stumbled as it landed, visibly favoring its right side. Deep creases appeared in its head as its brow furrowed in confusion. Its eyes shifted quickly to the gash in its side as it continued to bleed. It growled, "Iron." It was clearly not a question. "Will your tricks never cease, woman?"

Shrugging, as her smirk blossomed into a broad smile, the song continued to fall from her lips. Pressing her advantage, Aristoi rose from her crouch, spear held low before her. Lips pulled back in a snarling sneer, the creature gave ground reluctantly. It moved closer to the edge of the roof as the Songspear extended another probing thrust. Although it was only a flesh wound, she saw the effects when combined with those of her song upon the beast. A short, sweeping slash forced it to the lip of the roof. Faced with a choice between the weapon and plunge, the creature chose the latter. Spiraling as it fell, the beast landed roughly on its feet; a violent exhalation–part pain and part frustration–exploded from the creature as it struck the ground. As the Songspear moved to the edge, the beast leapt again, but found the distance too great this time.

"You can only sing for so long. This wound is far from fatal. It will not stop me from feasting on your heart once your voice fails you."

Cold realization froze the Songspear's resolve as the words settled in her ears. Even though she sang in a strong and steady voice, she suddenly became aware of how each breath she drew rasped at the back of her throat. If her battle with the creature became a wait-

ing game, it wouldn't be one she could win. Trying to push the rising discomfort from her mind, she allowed her voice to settle back into a comfortable volume.

Retreating out of sight of the beast, Aristoi backtracked across the roof to the side opposite where it waited. Casting her spear to the frozen dirt, the woman sank to her knees before sliding over the edge and allowing her arms to take her weight. She hung there for a moment, waiting until there came a natural pause in the song that flowed from her lips. Between beats, she released her grip on the roof and allowed herself to drop the short distance to the ground. As her legs absorbed the shock of the landing, a soft grunt escaped from her. Praying that the unintended sound would not disturb the delicate balance of the ancient magic, Aristoi continued the song as she quickly scooped the discarded spear from the ground.

The soft crunch of claw breaking permafrost was the only warning she received before the dark shape leapt from the surrounding gloom. Although the Songspear continued to sing, it was obvious the spell had been broken. She allowed the notes of her song to fade into the night as she gave ground before the raging beast. Forcing the panic from her voice, Aristoi spoke, "Although the song is no more, the iron remains." Keeping the spear between her and the creature, she rotated to her left with smooth, sweeping steps.

"I will take my chances. I can smell your fear. The stink of it hangs on the wind like smoke." Although the gash on its flank still bled freely, it only caused the beast to slightly favor its right rear leg. Slinking low to the ground, it mirrored her movements as it bided its time for an opening in the woman's defense. "As your voice waned, so too will your strength, so do yourself a service. Look into my eyes and greet your death wrapped in a blanket of fatigue, rather than in the razor grip of terror."

Aristoi repeated its own words, "I will take my chances." She thrust her spear tentatively at the beast. She expected it to shy away from the weapon, but instead the creature deftly dodged to the side and advanced on the Kieli. Only the half-hearted nature of the attack allowed her to withdraw the spear and use it to defend against its rush. The dark wood shaft collided with the beast's skull, forcing its jaws sideways away from her thigh. She felt the creature's teeth snap shut inches from her leg.

She took two quick steps backwards to bring the iron head of the spear to bear. That split second allowed the beast to dance out of the weapon's range. As soon as it was free of its limits, the creature sank back into its stalking slither. Although the strike to its head was bone-jarring, it didn't seem to suffer any lasting effects. The two continued to circle, each probing the other's defenses, as if they were both waiting for the other to make a mistake. The longer the standoff lasted, the more real fatigue weighed on Aristoi's limbs. Fortunately for her, with time and exertion the creature's limp became more pronounced. Her steps quickened in an attempt to press her advantage. Each time she came within striking distance, the beast found enough of a reserve of strength to lunge forward, past the tip of her spear. Each time it lunged, she skipped back, bringing that same tip back in line with its broad chest.

Before she could strike, it would bound backwards out of range of the iron's bite. So, it went on for what seemed like hours, a dance more akin to waves on the shore than the life and death struggle that it really was. As her feet began to drag through the frozen soil, she noticed that the beast's jaws hung open, tongue lolling from between them. Marshaling her strength one final time, Aristoi lunged forward, her spear leading the way. Caught unaware, the beast's jump came a second too late. While it was able to prevent the iron tooth from being driven home, it still separated the fur and flesh of its shoulder. The wound left the underlying muscle open to the frigid night. The creature howled in pain; the notes of it hung in the air and floated there like the vestiges of a nightmare.

Something within that sound called to the Songspear's heart and she knew fear. As waves break upon the shore, so did the undulating tones break upon her resolve. With each note, more of her courage fled. Aristoi gripped the shaft of her spear to hide the tremors that threatened to pull the weapon from her hands. It was all she could do to continue to match steps with the creature before her. It cradled its left paw against its powerful chest. The awkwardness of its wound turned the beast's once fluid gait into a clumsy, stumbling step. The Songspear knew that with its wound, the advantage belonged to her, but every instinct within the woman screamed at her to flee.

The creature's muzzle pulled back onto a pain smile. "And now we come to the end of it, outlander." Aristoi's terror didn't subside with the beast's howls. "Your heart aches to run from me...as is the natural way of things. I am predator and you are prey."

The woman clenched her teeth to hide the trembling in her voice. "There is nothing natural about you, beast." She gathered her strength for one last lunge and found her reserves depleted.

Dark eyes studied her for a moment as the night fell into a tense silence. The creature broke the stillness with its deep voice. "And yet you will run." Throwing its head back, the beast's howl rolled forth like black blood from a gut-wound.

Aristoi fought the waves of panic for a split second before she became overwhelmed by it. She turned and fled, allowing terror to drive her steps. Aristoi, born and weaned among the great forests of Kiel, was lithe and swift of foot, but in the end, she was no match for the speed of the beast. Even loping on three legs, it was upon her as she cleared the last of the buildings and broke for the open tundra. An intense pain lanced through her thigh as she was viciously thrown to the ground. The dull thump of her head against the frozen ground sent her vision spinning. As everything around her grew dark, the only thing that remained pristine were the creature's glistening teeth.

*****

Aristoi's eyes snapped open, rolling away from the jaws of a beast that only existed in her memories. Only the popping of the low campfire broke the oppressive silence of the early tundra morning. Across the embers, Hollis studied her wordlessly. A tilt of his head asked, *Are you alright?* The Songspear nodded slightly, and then again with more authority. The thief went back to tending the coals, but she could still feel his eyes upon her.

Gathering her spear before slowly rising, Aristoi walked past her friend. She laid a gentle hand on his shoulder and squeezed softly. "I need to clear my head," she said. "I am going to take a walk."

"Do I need to tell you to be careful?"

She looked down at him, a smile brushing her lips. "No, Northerner, you do not."

"Be careful anyway."

The Songspear released his shoulder and moved to the edge of the copse of evergreens that served as their camp. In the distance, she could just make out the irregular shapes of low buildings. Within hours, she would again be standing on the site of the battle that changed her life forever.

Chapter Nine

A Reluctant Promise

The sour-sweet scent of charred flesh reached Hollis's nose before he saw the haphazard stack of bodies. Carelessly piled in the center of the ramshackle village, smoke still hung around them like a billowing halo. Agmar's Watch was only a village in the loosest sense of the word. It served as the seasonal home to at least three Rangor clans. The thief was unsure as to the identity of the one that should have been occupying it, but from the corpses that continued to crackle in the morning air, it had not served them well.

Behind him, Hollis heard Valmont's angry growl. Without turning, the thief asked, "Is this is how the Snow Queen seeks to unite the North? Slaughter any who do not follow her?"

Valmont stepped up beside him. "This is her way. Those that will not stand behind her must fall before her."

Hollis muttered to himself, "This is not the woman I knew." *But is that true?* he asked himself. His youthful memories warred with the all too real evidence before him. The Mika he had known always had a dangerous intensity about her, but he never would have believed her capable of this level of brutality. In a time when Hollis's world was blood and chaos, Silvermoon and Mika had become father and mother to him. They had offered a preferable counter point to Seran's "rules of the alley" and the thieves' guild's cut throat politics.

69

"What was that?" Valmont's voice cut through his reverie like a razor.

"Nothing." Hollis pushed his conflicting emotions from his mind and looked upon the scene with new eyes, ones granted to him by the Well of Worlds. While the mound of burned bodies naturally drew the eye, he had found that the key to understanding a thing was always in the details. Turning his back on the grotesque monument, the thief scanned the hard packed ground that served Agmar's Watch as a main street. The permafrost didn't lend itself to holding foot-prints, but that didn't mean that it was devoid of valuable informa-tion.

Untold pairs of boots had trod the path before him, their prints melting into one another until it was almost uniform, bordering on smooth. However, in places Hollis could see deep scratches in the otherwise unvarying surface. Dipping his finger into one of the larg-est, he could feel its ragged edge. The marks had been made recently, perhaps even that very morning.

As the thief was turning to call for Aristoi, the woman knelt be-side him. "You found something." Her voice was tight and restrained like a rope stretched to its breaking point.

"I am almost afraid to ask what made these gashes," he asked quietly, careful to keep his words between them alone.

Squinting at the dirt, the Songspear took her time to answer. When she did, it was not the response Hollis hoped for. "Do you see the angle and depth of the mark? Nothing natural made these."

"Are you certain?"

"They curl back on themselves, like this." She bent the fingers of her right hand into a claw and then folded them against her palm. "Do you know of any beast that is capable of that?"

"I assume that you do."

She nodded. "We tangled with one last night."

"Is there a possibility that—"

Anticipating his question, Aristoi cut him off. "— there is no way that Gorm was responsible for these."

"You are a constant source of sunshine, Southerner."

"I wish it were otherwise."

Hollis laid a hand on her shoulder, uncharacteristically at a loss for words. The Songspear's sad smile told him that she understood his silent consolation. "Forgive my limited knowledge on the subject, but I assume that this is not common behavior for the creature?" He gestured at the stacked corpses behind him with a thumb.

"It is unlikely that the gwyllgi is working alone. They are more

70

likely to eat their prey, preferring it raw."

Debating his next question, Hollis allowed a stillness to hang between them for a moment. Even amidst their dire circumstances, he felt the warm touch of appreciation for the comfort that had grown between himself and the Songspear.

"Before last night, how many of these beasts have you faced?"

Aristoi's answer was immediate, before emotion had an opportunity to creep into her voice. "Two. The first in this very spot six months before we met. The last within a day's travel of the village in which I grew up."

The thief raised an eyebrow in an unspoken question. *Coincidence?*

"I am not sure. When I faced down the gwyllgi here, it was a chance meeting, unlucky on both of our parts. The most recent was after I had finished my Long Walk and was returning to claim my position among the Songspear."

"Just after you and I parted ways?"

"Yes. I had just entered the forest my people call the Verdant Sea when I had an overpowering sense that something was hounding my trail, just out of sight." Aristoi frowned deeply. "The curious part was that where I would have expected fear to seize my heart, there was only anger. It was almost as if something deep inside of me resented being the hunted rather than the hunter."

"This inner voice seemed alien to you?"

The Songspear seized her bottom lip between her teeth and closed her eyes. Hollis had no doubt that moment was played again behind those eyelids. "It was like an animal had seized my soul between its teeth and shook it with all its might. The feeling was frightening and exhilarating in equal measures." As she opened her eyes, the thief saw reflected there the glimmer of guilt. "Part of me enjoyed it, relished in it. It was a part I did not recognize."

"The gwyllgi's influence?"

"I think so. I was almost relieved when the creature broke through the undergrowth. The corruption within me rejoiced at the opportunity to put an end to the challenger before me … the intruder that dared trespass on what was mine."

Beneath her guilt-laced words, Hollis could detect a subtle note of satisfaction. *Even now, the pollution clinging to her soul rears its feral head.* Words of consolation leapt to his tongue, but he allowed them to dissolve there. Aristoi didn't need empty platitudes.

"Whatever shard of the beast I faced here that night lay just beneath the surface, like a splinter. Surrounded by the pus of its malignancy, the insistent voice screamed for release."

"Release?"

The Songspear averted her eyes. "When it is at its strongest, I can feel my body changing … seeking to mirror the fell shape that haunts my soul."

"Like a werewolf?" In his panic, Hollis used the English word.

Even in the midst of her fevered tale, Aristoi paused and studied him.

The thief searched his knowledge of Trade Tongue for a replacement but none came to mind. *Lycanthrope? Loup-Garou?* Neither had direct translations in the common language of Taerh. He settled for, "A person that changes into a wolf."

She cocked her head. "Those are common in Stephen's world?"

He couldn't contain a small smile, despite the seriousness of their conversation. "Only in myth and legend."

"I wish the gwyllgi had stayed there as well." Aristoi's demeanor lightened slightly, allowing her to continue in a steadier voice. "The term werewolf seems apt. I have had the very same compulsion over the last few months but each time it rises in me, it seems stronger, more insistent." All levity evaporated from her face. "I fear it grows stronger by the day. I fear that one night I will be unable to resist its call."

Hollis wanted to comfort her, to tell her that could never happen, but he didn't want to lie to his friend. A dire sense of foreboding seized his own heart in its vise-like grip.

"Once that happens …" She paused, her eyes pleading. "… I am afraid it will be all that remains of me."

Reaching out, the thief seized Aristoi by the bicep, perhaps squeezing harder than he intended. "That is not going to happen. Now that I share this burden with you, it is carried by both of us. You are strong. Together we are stronger."

"Strength wanes, Northerner."

Hollis growled, his jaw tightening of its own accord. "Then we will find a cure. There are libraries full of tomes from across the Cradle and beyond. In one of them must lie the answer." Feeling his lips pull back from his teeth, he hissed through clenched teeth, "If all else fails, there are still two Heralds that draw breath. We will find a solution even if we have to pry it from the Risen at the point of a blade."

"I appreciate the gesture, Hollis, but—"

"—but nothing. You were there with me at the Well. You stood beside me when Plague Man took Asaege. Both of those you did without question, without hesitation."

"I assure you there were plenty of both—"

"—but stand with me you did. I refuse to not do the same." The thief looked past her, to the huddled pair of Valmont and Sagaun. "We can leave tonight. Let Mika have the North … to hell with grudges that should have long ago grown cold."

"No." Aristoi's voice had the iron weight of finality. "I believe you, Northerner. I am convinced you would turn your back on everything you hold dear for my sake." Hollis opened his mouth to interrupt her again, but she cut him off. "I am equally certain you would regret it with every breath you drew from this moment until your last. Deep inside, you would use the guilt of it to stoke the fire over which you torture yourself. You could not live with it, and neither could I."

"But Aristoi —"

The Songspear laid her fingers on the back of his neck, cradling his chin in her palm. "I am not saying no. Just not yet." She looked over her shoulder. "We are embroiled in something more than your personal issue with the Snow Queen, bigger than either one of us. Let us see it to its end. Then … if you still feel the same, we shall search for a solution."

Frustration and admiration warred within Hollis's heart. His mind wheeled, searching for a resolution that could address both concerns.

"Were the situations reversed, what would you have me do?"

Trapped by his own nobility, the thief reluctantly nodded. "As you will, my friend."

"I will ask one further thing of you, however." Aristoi's voice took on a tentative note. "If the corruption takes me, if I begin to change, you have to …" Even the Songspear's selflessness had its limits.

Hollis couldn't bring himself to look at her, but answered anyway. "I will do what I have to."

Still holding his head, she forced him to meet her eyes. "I will not become a monster. If the time comes, I may not have the ability … or the courage to prevent it. If my friendship means anything to you, Hollis …"

"If the time comes, I will free you of this burden … one way or another."

*****

By the time Valmont and Sagaun joined them, the pair had each recovered their composure. Although he tried to hide it, the way the young man looked at the wise woman left Hollis with little doubt of his feelings for her. The Rangor youth seemed to be the picture of a stoic warrior, except when it came to the furtive glances he spared for her when he thought she wasn't looking. He trailed just behind her, his spear held casually in his right hand and his eyes on the shape hidden beneath her fur cloak.

Once they closed within earshot, Aristoi gestured to the quickly cooling stack of flesh. "This is a message," she said, not hiding her contempt.

"This far north, it is clear for whom it was meant." Sagaun wrapped her fur-lined cloak tighter around her body. "The Snow Queen's forces can not hunt down the Bone Dogs, so they seek to use our people as a means to stay our hand."

"So, you believe this message is for you?" Aristoi's question was spoken softly but carried its own implications.

"I doubt she has given either of us much thought," Sagaun replied, bitterness dripping from her words. "It is doubtless a broader message for the Bone Dogs. As the last vestige of an ancient tradition, we present a threat she can not easily put to the sword."

"Are her fears founded?" Hollis pushed his desperate rationalizations aside in order to focus on the matter at hand.

"Absolutely. The clans of the north were once a proud people. Bolstered by the old ways and centuries of independence, we have no need of the so called betterment she offers." It was Valmont's voice. "It is just another form of enslavement."

The thief studied the boy with a fresh appreciation. Although lacking the sheer mass of either Ret or Ulrych, Valmont carried with him a fiery determination that would make either of Hollis's former companions proud to claim a shared Rangor heritage with him. "Do you not want to join the rest of the Cradle?" he asked.

Valmont frowned. "Join them in what? Imprisonment in their stone cages? Bowing before lesser men based on from whose loins they have sprung?" He closed his eyes for a moment and spread his arms, as if he sought to embrace the rapidly failing afternoon light. "We have all we need. All the silver and gold in their treasuries could not buy the freedom to walk the tundra beholden to none but my own counsel."

As much as he treasured his beloved Oizan, in that moment, Hollis couldn't argue the boy's point. When the burdens of civilization weighed too heavily on his own shoulders, didn't he find his feet upon the King's Road in search of something the city couldn't provide? *Perhaps savagery is society's way of venting its jealousy when confronted with a people who have no need of it.*

"Well put, Valmont." Aristoi smiled softly at the Rangor youth. "Although the clans may not choose to walk the Snow Queen's path, that road could provide respite from the pains of lean seasons."

"At what price?"

"It is just a thought." Hollis saw the Songspear catch Sagaun's eye. The wise woman nodded, seemingly understanding her train of thought. Aristoi suggested, "A leader with the true betterment of his people in mind could lead his people into the future on their terms."

Sagaun laid a hand on the boy's bicep. "A leader who understands that the old ways can change without forgetting them."

The thief saw a glint of pride spark to life in Valmont's eyes. Between breaths, he stood a little taller. *Good for him*, Hollis thought, *the best leaders are those who have no designs on the title.*

Before Valmont could respond, a shrill howl cut the still northern air. The sound raised the hair on the back of Hollis's neck. He felt the bony fingers of dread seeking purchase on his heart. With less effort than it would take another person to delay a breath, the thief pulled the cloak of tranquility granted him by the Well of Worlds around his shoulders. The insistent clawing became the feather-light caress of an autumn breeze.

Aristoi seemed similarly unaffected, as she scanned the twilight kissed tundra. Valmont and Sagaun were not so lucky. The pair stood their ground but their dancing eyes and tense postures told the thief that the full weight of the gwyllgi's song had settled upon them. "Stay here," Hollis called to them; he received a grateful look from each in return. Aristoi was already in motion, sprinting for the western edge of Agmar's Watch. The thief broke into a run, twenty yards behind her.

As he passed a clump of tightly clustered buildings, a hulking shape lurched out of the space between two of them. Throwing himself to the side, Hollis avoided the no doubt bone-shaking collision his ambusher had intended. Off balance, he tucked his shoulder and allowed his momentum to carry him to the ground. As he rolled to his feet, he saw a massive Rangor dressed in thick furs and boiled leather. Beyond him, a hand full of figures emerged from the claptrap buildings of the village, intent on Valmont and Sagaun.

The thief barely had time to draw his Uteli blade before his attacker was upon him, a pair of companions close on his heels. Out of the corner of his eye, he saw Aristoi disappear into the distance before turning his attention back to the more immediate concern before him.

75

Chapter Ten

A Bloody Sacrifice

O ut numbered three to one, Hollis dispensed with the wasted energy that dialogue would have required. Consciously forcing the tightness that had seized the space between his shoulder to relax, he held the Wallin Fahr before him, its tip angled toward the chest of the charging warrior. The guard position the Mantrians called *Lin Fuh* or Long Point had been drummed into him by Mika more than a decade ago. Its primary use was to establish and maintain distance from your opponent. It appeared that this particular foe wasn't going to cooperate. Trying to momentarily push from his mind the two youths a score of strides behind the lead opponent, the thief shuffled forward, meeting the warrior in mid charge.

Unable to arrest his momentum, the Rangor allowed Hollis inside his guard before realization colored his face. Crouching slightly, the thief allowed his opponent to impale himself on the razor sharp point of the Uteli blade. As soon as he felt the Dwarven steel sword pierce the space below the warrior's boiled leather breastplate, Hollis shifted his weight and pivoted his wrists, turning the weapon sideways. His opponent continued past him, opening his belly on the honed edge of the Wallin Fahr. Acting on instinct, the thief rotated his body, bringing the sword around to strike the already tumbling foe between his beefy shoulder and thick neck. When the Rangor struck the frozen ground, he lay still as the death that would quickly claim him.

Hollis hazarded a quick glance towards where Valmont and Sagaun stood surrounded by four hulking figures. A fifth lay moaning in the street, no doubt a victim of the youth's spear. Sagaun had drawn a bearded axe from within her cloak and swung it defensively, her back pressed against that of her companion.

The thief's immediate impression was that the remaining Rangor seemed to show a little too much respect for the pair's weapons. His experience with both Ret and his brother Ulrych had taught him that the northern warriors tended towards an abundance of confidence and brute force, with a decided lack of caution. Given their obvious numerical advantage, the group should have easily overwhelmed both of them.

His own desperate circumstances demanded that he turn his attention from that of his companions. Extending his sword into *Lin Fuh* once more, Hollis readily retreated before the Rangor pair's advance. His mind searched for a solution to the problem that the two battle-trained Northerners posed. Armed with round shields and broad bladed swords, they presented a more intimidating issue than had their overzealous comrade.

Forcing his racing thoughts to quiet through sheer force of will, the thief devoured the details of the scene through the filter of the Well's gift. One of the pair huddled behind the wooden barrier of his shield with a rigidity that spoke of an already shaken confidence. When next they advanced, Hollis continued to give ground but angled his retreat so as to put him closer to the nervous warrior. Again they surged forward, but this time rather than maintaining his distance, the thief met their advance.

Hollis stepped forward swinging his sword in a high horizontal cut, aimed at the less aggressive of the two. As he had intended, his enemy jerked his shield up to cover his face and thus blocking his view of the thief. The warrior's impeded perception hid Hollis's return swing from sight. The Dwarven steel blade cut deeply into the Rangor's thigh, just above the knee. Had his comrade not pressed an attack immediately, the sword's keen edge would have separated muscle from bone. The necessity to dodge backwards out of reach of the second warrior's own slash prevented Hollis from drawing his weapon completely across the leg, but it still left a vicious wound behind, grinning like a crimson maw.

The uninjured Northman exhibited more recklessness than his companion, showing Hollis more openings for counterattack, but the warrior's furious swings gave the the thief little opportunity to take advantage of them. Each time he was able to free his blade quickly enough from a parry, the Rangor's shield easily turned aside his blow. Whenever Dwarven steel met wood, it carved chunks off of the latter, but in the battle of yards that raged between them, those inches would be too little to affect the outcome.

Hollis could spare neither the attention nor time to glance over his shoulder to where Valmont and Sagaun engaged in their own life and death conflict, but the lack of sounds of a struggle didn't bode well. A wave of selfishness descended upon him. *If they both are dead, this is going to go from bad to profoundly tragic really quickly.*

The injured warrior hobbled up behind his unwounded comrade, his face tightened with resolve. As the thief beat back the latest attack, the freshly confident Rangor charged past his companion and collided full force into him. Hollis was able to twist his body, absorbing most of the impact, but the shield's sharpened boss dug painfully into his side. His leather vest held against the assault, but he felt something snap under the force.

A muffled cry attracted Hollis's attention, despite himself. His pair of companions still lived, but were ringed by an ever closing circle of fur-clad bodies. Valmont's spear lay only a few yards from the youth, an unmoving warrior laying beside it, but with an enemy interposed between them, the distance seemed insurmountable. A Rangor held Sagaun against his broad chest, one of his beefy hands obscuring half of her face. Other than their dire straits, neither looked the worse for wear.

Tearing his gaze from the fate of his companions, the thief focused on his own rapidly deteriorating situation. Once again the two warriors stood side by side, their shields presenting a unified front. He lunged forward suddenly. Hollis was relieved as that the injured youth recoiled from him with the healthy respect the deep leg wound had earned him. The feint invited a spirited counterattack by his comrade, but he still felt reassured.

A lopsided smile appeared on the uninjured warrior's face as he blurted out, "Queen want friends," in broken Trade Tongue. Side-stepping, he placed himself between the thief and the imperiled pair.

Hollis snorted at the absurdity of the words, regardless of his actual meaning. "I am sure there are better ways for her to find them."

The thief's clever quip was lost on the hulking young Rangor. "Queen want traitors alive."

I am not sure I like where this is heading, Hollis thought.

"She say nothing about you."

"Well, that sounds downright unfriendly."

Any further patter he had planned was cut short by a series of short, chopping overhead cuts. Hollis deflected each, redirecting their force away from him, but each still sent a bone-jarring shock up his arms. After the third, his shoulders began to ache. Moving in a slow, stumble-walk, the injured warrior pressed the thief from the side in an attempt to flank him.

Rotating his body, Hollis threw himself into the unwounded Rangor's shield, sending another thundering impact into his already painful shoulder. The Rangor shoved him hard, following up with another chopping blow. Pushing off with all of his might and using the warrior's added momentum, the thief launched himself at his wounded comrade.

Taken off guard, the injured warrior could only bring his own shield up between himself and the deadly missile that was Hollis. Repeating his earlier mistake, the Rangor exposed his legs. The thief planted a booted foot against the gaping wound in the man's thigh. He dropped to the ground, clutching his savaged leg. Hollis spun and quickly swung downward, but either luck or instinct allowed the screaming Northman to get his shield between himself and the Uteli weapon.

Before the thief could follow up, the second Rangor charged him. Faced with a choice between saving his own skin and finishing off his enemy, Hollis chose the former. Dancing backwards, he focused on keeping his feet underneath him; stumbling would have been a death sentence. Behind the massive warrior, the remaining three Rangor had subdued Valmont. They youth hung between the two of them while a third carried a bound and gagged Sagaun. One of them called out in their language. The youth pressing Hollis snapped back irritably.

Although he didn't speak more than a few words of the language, the thief understood the gist. *It will only take me a few more moments.*

"Don't bet on it," Hollis growled in English. Again the warrior launched himself at the thief. This time, Hollis didn't give ground. He bent his knees, sinking into a crouch. As the Rangor closed, the thief sprang forward, colliding with his shield. Suppressing a grunt when flesh and bone met wood, Hollis rotated his body to roll along the shield and let his opponent stumble past him. Before the warrior could arrest his momentum, the thief brought his Wallin Fahr down across his back. The dwarven honed edge of his sword peeled fur and leather like a ripe orange. Shifting his grip, Hollis drove his blade into the sweaty flesh beneath.

Expecting the man to fall to his knees, the thief pivoted to engage the wounded Rangor between him and his captured comrades. His expectations hadn't taken into consideration the dogged resilience of the northern clans. His sword was pulled from his grasp as the man he assumed mortally wounded spun on him. Hollis was barely able to draw his broad bladed dagger from the sheath at his back before he was wrapped up in a bone crushing bear hug.

With his arms trapped against his sides, the thief was unable to bring the dagger to bear. He struggled against the strength of the hulking Rangor to pull his weapon free. Pain exploded in Hollis's neck as the warrior's teeth sought his throat For the moment, the thin layer of leather and wool fended off the visceral assault, but he wasn't sure how long his luck would hold. Driving his skull into his attacker's cheek, Hollis felt bone break but neither the unrelenting pressure on his neck nor the vise around his chest lessened.

Just as his bones felt poised to snap beneath the iron bands that were the Northman's arms, the thief heard a wet, choking sound come from the warrior. The Rangor's grip slackened as great wracking convulsions seized his body. The pair fell to the ground, still intertwined. Lacking the ability to do anything other than gulp huge lung fulls of air, Hollis watched as blood poured from the hulking youth's nose and mouth.

The thief tried to roll away from the dying warrior but a massive hand seized the front of his vest. Preparing to drive his dagger into the man's chest, Hollis was struck by the abject terror in his blood shot eyes. Absent was any sign of the fury that had consumed the man a moment ago. These were the eyes of a frightened boy.

"Help me," he begged through blood soaked lips. "Please."

The weapon dropped from Hollis's suddenly inert fingers. The youth's desperate appeal was spoken in perfect English. Before the thief could process the events, the boy let out a rattling gasp and went limp. Stamped upon his crimson stained face was a mask of horror. Hollis's gaze was transfixed by the sight before him. Something in the back of his mind screamed at him to move. Surrendering to instincts honed long ago on the streets of Oizan, he rolled free of the quickly cooling body.

A sword cleaved the dirt on which Hollis had lain a second before. Above him stood the injured Rangor, an expression of hatred stamped on his scowling face. The thief clumsily climbed to his feet, searching franticly for a weapon. Having discarded his shield, the warrior held his broad sword above his head in two hands. The wild look in the youth's eyes told Hollis that something had broken deep inside him. Lurching forward in staccato half steps, the wounded man chopped at the thief with an intensity reserved for mad men.

As he retreated before the unreasoning assault, something impacted Hollis's calf. Looking down, he saw the hilt of his Uteli sword half buried under the dead Rangor. He crouched quickly and snatched it from the depths of the corpse, quickly celebrating his fortune that it came free without struggle. Placing the blade between himself and his crazed opponent, his Well-born senses provided him with a embarrassment of opportunities to end the melee. So intent was he on killing the thief that the warrior had completely abandoned any sense of defense.

"Run," Hollis hissed.

The youth kept coming, spittle flying from between clenched teeth.

"Run!"

The command's effect wasn't improved by repetition.

"Save yourself, you daft bastard."

Whatever had snapped within him, it was preventing the warrior from comprehending the thief's words.

"Alright," Hollis whispered, more to himself than his uncomprehending opponent. Tasting the bitter sting of guilt in the back of his throat, the thief met the youth's next stroke, deflecting it easily. Before the youth could raise his sword again, Hollis brought his blade around in a tight arc. The sword swept across the boy's throat in a horizontal slash. The warrior had half spun towards the thief before his body finally surrendered and slumped to the ground like a string-less puppet.

The thief sank down between the two youths, his sword slipping from his hand onto the blood-soaked permafrost. In the distance, the last surviving Rangor fled with their prizes. *Children, Mika,* Hollis thought, *not only are you killing children, but you are making me join you in the task.* A deep fatigue settled into his bones, radiating from his guilt-sick heart.

Hollis's eyes went to the face of the young Rangor who had begged for his life in English. A spark of recognition flared in his mind He knew the boy. *But from where?* He had only traveled north of Mantry a few times, and never this far into the wastes. The only Rangor he knew in more than passing terms were Ret and his brother, Ulrych. The boy had certainly not worn either of their faces.

Suddenly, it hit him like a sandbag to the gut; he was approaching it from the wrong direction. He had never seen the boy in Taerh, but Stephen had met him in his world. He'd been a friend of Robert's, a football player from a local high school. *What was his name?* Once he turned his attention to the problem, the answer came to him as smoothly as his childhood telephone number. *Erik Gunn.* The thief knew it was not his blows that had killed Erik's reflection; he must have met his fate in the other world.

A series of howls in the distance snapped him out of his introspection. Wearily, he climbed to his feet and reclaimed his sword and dagger. Looking in the direction Mika's people had taken Valmont and Sagaun, Hollis squinted ineffectually into the darkness. Turning on his heel, he jogged off into the night in search of Aristoi.

Chapter Eleven
A Savage Soul

The howls awakened something deep inside of Aristoi that filled her with excitement and embarrassment in equal measure. Once the keening sound reached her ears, it awakened something in her heart that went beyond words; it struck an instinctual cord in the very primal core of her soul. As the Songspear ran towards the source, she was perfectly aware that it boded ill for her and her companions, but her body was carried along, an unwilling passenger held aloft on the undulating notes of the call.

As she crested a small rise, a shape came into view. Its head thrown back in the fading light a vaguely canine silhouette stood out against the clear evening sky. Allowing its warbling song to fade into silence, the creature lowered its short muzzle and turned its attention to Aristoi. Its eyes were the baleful color of rust in the pale light of the tundra moon. Once that glare would have drained from her the will to do anything beyond surrender herself to its hunger. The only effect it had that night was to stoke the furnace of rage that bubbled beneath the surface of her resolve.

Risking a quick glance over her shoulder, the Songspear saw no sign of Hollis or her other companions. Uncertainty bloomed in her heart, only slightly tempering the rage smoldering there.

"Your friends will not be joining us." The beast's voice reminded Aristoi of gravel shaken in a glass jar. "I have made arrangements for them to be otherwise occupied."

The gwyllgi itself resembled a powerfully muscled, yet wiry wolf. Its coat was a mottled tapestry of ash and charcoal, lending it the appearance of being one with the night around it. Its massive head ended in a thick, blunt muzzle filled with wickedly sharp, but otherwise decidedly human looking teeth. Both of its corded forelimbs ended in a long, thick toed foot. A broad fifth appendage jutted out opposite the four claw tipped digits, making the beast's paw as prehensile as her own hand.

"You are an aberration," Aristoi growled, the depth of her voice unsettling her. "You profane this place with your very presence."

"Is that not the stream calling the river wet? We are the same, you and I, just at different places in our journey."

The Songspear hissed through clenched teeth. "We will never be alike, monster."

The gwyllgi let out a choking laugh, more cough than chuckle. "Even now, you muzzle the beast within yourself. You can stifle its growls, but you know the truth in your heart."

Aristoi felt a pang of self-doubt as the fears that plagued her for months were reflected in the beast's words. She fought a daily battle with foreign instincts that gnawed at the bonds that kept her baser urges in check. Hollis had promised to walk beside her until a cure was found, but deep down, the Songspear feared that the curse laid upon her soul had but one finale. It would end in nothing but blood.

The thought of dragging her friend into the abattoir with her frightened Aristoi more than succumbing to the feral presence within her. She had never met another like him. More than simple friendship, but devoid of romantic attraction, what they shared defied definition. His quietly unquestioning loyalty towards her ran counter to the Kieli warrior's decades of experience. Truly amazing to her, though, was the fact that her loyalty to him was just as absolute. Betrayed by her family and her tribe, the Songspear found true kinship in the most unlikely of places: a northern ruffian of questionable moral character.

She had to believe that bond was stronger than any curse on the face of Taerh.

Aristoi refocused her attention on the creature before her. "You know nothing of my heart, gwyllgi. You are not the first of your kind that has crossed my path. Behind me lies a trail of broken bodies attesting to the fact that, each time, they were found wanting."

The beast's mouth lolled open in a canine smile. "My poor

little Songspear," it purred mockingly, "you have never come across anything like me."

Aristoi's mind spun. *Songspear? It knows me.* Bringing her spear up before her, Aristoi closed the distance between herself and the arrogant creature. Leaping backward with a seemingly effortless motion, the gwyllgi easily landed outside of the weapon's range. It flexed its powerful claws, digging furrows in the frozen dirt beneath it. The creature pulled its lips back in a sneer, revealing razor sharp teeth the color of freshly fallen snow.

"Tooth and claw, gaze and howl … none of these things are the equal to iron and song." She drew out the final syllable, bending it into the first notes of an ancient dirge. Where the thaumaturges of the north relied on precisely worded formulae, concealing words of power within the mnemonics of the spell itself, the ranks of the Songspear harnessed the primal forces of the world around them through the phonics of those very same words. As the first notes of the song flowed from her lips, the tip of her spear was wreathed in a cloud of steam.

"Impressive." Low and dangerous, the beast's voice contained a measure of appreciation. "You think much of yourself and the traditions that sired you. What happens when both fail you?"

Maintaining the song left the Kieli unable to respond to the gwyllgi's challenge, but the time for talking had passed. The obscuring mist dissipated in an instant, the flames on the spear's tip burning them away as they sprung to life. Extending the burning brand towards the crouching creature, she slowly advanced.

Tightening its jaws, the beast forced a low, rolling sound from deep in its chest. Where the howl it has used to summon the Songspear was an axe, this baying was a scalpel. The gwyllgi sang its own song.

The force of it struck Aristoi like a great wind, even though not so much as a stray hair moved under its influence. Its effect upon the flames could not be denied. In a rush, they were snuffed out like a candle in a thunderstorm. Taking an unconscious step back, the Songspear's mind reeled with the horrifying revelation that the weapon upon which she most relied could be denied her.

The beast parroted her words back to her. "You are not the first of your kind that has crossed my path."

Tightening her grip on the spear, Aristoi ceased her retreat. "I shall be that last." With a sudden lunge, she charged forward. The iron tip of her spear unerringly dove towards the creature's heart. Surprised by the impetuous attack, the gwyllgi was forced to retreat to avoid the deadly kiss of the Songspear's weapon.

Pivoting, the Kieli allowed the spear to slide through her hands as she reached the apex of her thrust. Despite its hasty withdrawal, the extended spear sank a few inches in the beast's shaggy coat, and the flesh beneath. As it snapped reflexively at the offending object, letting out a short yelp of pain, she pulled the weapon from its reach. Swinging it in a short circle around her head, Aristoi sent the spear in a powerful horizontal slash. The gwyllgi snarled in frustration as it retreated again before the weapon's broad, single edged tip.

"You are a formidable warrior, Songspear. As much as I would enjoy testing my skills against yours, that is not why I arranged this meeting."

"Why should your intentions be of any concern to me, beast?"

"You are alone. Even in a tavern full of people, you remain an island among the masses."

Its words struck home, but Aristoi pushed her doubt away. "I am a Songspear, my brothers and sisters are beside me, in spirit if not physically. Behind them stand generations of my ancestors, back to before the Age of Legends."

"Brave words," the beast muttered. "It is a shame that they are naught but the assurances of a child against the threat of the dark." Its eyes fixed on the iron-tipped weapon, the gwyllgi approached cautiously. "If your fellows remain beside you, tell me why you are in this accursed place, so far from their support and company?"

Another knife of pain dug into the Kieli's heart. At the end of her Long Walk, her return was not all she'd hoped. Accused of an unforgivable crime for which she was not responsible, Aristoi had been forced to defend herself in combat. Although she still drew breath, her honor remained behind, broken in the ceremonial circle.

Sensing its advantage, the creature pressed further. "You throw all your hopes for belonging, for family into the Well's Child." An impossibly wry smirk appeared on the beast's blunt muzzle. "He will disappoint you as well. Whether by action or death, he too will cast you aside."

Its words were a step too far. Aristoi's connection to Hollis was undeniable. As was her friendship with Asaege and whatever it was that she shared with Seran. These people valued her for who and what she was. More than that, they cared for her. At least Hollis and Asaege did. Before leaving her kingdom behind, the Songspear had met with the Herald known only as the Branded. The protector of the Verdant Sea and the Kieli people within had assured Aristoi of her path.

The opinions of your village are not those of the Confederation, he had said. *Do not let their small minds poison your soul. I will speak to the Songspear elders on your behalf. You have great work ahead of you, I have seen it. Go forth into the world, secure in the knowledge that I labor on your behalf.* It had been a rare spot of sunlight in the otherwise dark shadow of her return. With the death of the Walker, the Branded was one of only two Heralds remaining. His support validated Aristoi's faith in her path.

"You know nothing of me or those close to my heart." The words were soft but carried with them the steel of strengthening resolve.

"The question is not what I know of them, but instead how well do you?" Slinking closer to Aristoi by almost imperceptible inches, the gwyllgi continued to taunt her. "I assume you have not shared with any of your so called 'brothers and sisters of the song' the conflict that wages within you."

As the beast drew within spear range, the Kieli lashed out swiftly and drove it back again.

"Of course you did not. At that point, you would become no better than me in their eyes, another monster to be put down."

"There are those I count among my friends who know what manner of heart beats within my chest."

"The boy-savage, Valmont? If he knew what you truly are, he would split your chest with iron before you could draw the breath to explain." The gwyllgi sank to its haunches. "Perhaps you mean the criminal, the self proclaimed Child of the Well. You are nothing more to him than a means to an end. His only loyalty lies in his own inflated sense of self worth."

It struck Aristoi how much the creature seemed to know about her. "In who, then, should I place my trust? You?"

Again, the beast responded with a coughing laugh. "Absolutely not. Trust in anything beyond the tip of your nose and the reach of your hand is an invitation to betrayal. What I offer is much more rational: a mutually beneficial alliance. I will make no promises of anything beyond what is in my best interest and will ask none from you."

"I will take my chances with my friends."

The gwyllgi drew back its lips in a bestial grin. "Maybe you place stock on the words of the Branded."

Aristoi felt as if a cold hand wrapped its clawed fingers around her windpipe.

"Go forth into the world, secure in the knowledge that I labor

89

on your behalf."

She lunged forward, swinging her spear side to side. "Keep his words out of your mouth, aberration!"

Dodging backwards, the beast stayed out of range of the deadly weapon. "I fear that his words are all that remains. As much as he wanted to maintain his oath, the Herald will be unable to do so."

"No." The Songspear backed her denial with the fervent hope that the gwyllgi's words were untrue.

"Your dilemma weighed heavily on his mind. That was not to his benefit when he and I finally met. The Branded was as formidable as tales tell. However, in the end, I was able to snatch victory from the jaws of defeat. If you will excuse the pun."

"You lie." Even as she spoke, Aristoi knew the creature spoke the truth.

"Many of my own family fell before his mighty spear and puissant magic, but in the end, he was devoured mind, body and soul."

An excruciating wave of spasms ripped across her shoulders, as if something deep inside her own body was trying to claw its way out. Through pain-clenched teeth, she repeated, "No."

"Even now, you hear the call of your kind. Surrender, Aristoi of Kiel. Give in to the inevitable echoes inside of you."

The tearing pain shot down her back into her hips. Muscles and ligaments contorted under her skin, straining to force her bones into inhuman shapes. Incapable of words, Aristoi bit back a moan of agony.

"You have died in this place before. Yet you continue to walk in the land of the living. There is a price for that blessing."

"Curse." The word was all the Songspear could manage through the razored ripples of pain.

"Blessing or curse, it is all a matter of perspective." The beast cautiously approached Aristoi; she could do nothing to stop him. "The harder you fight, the more your body will suffer. You might as well stem the tide with a paper fan. Let the change overtake you. In but a moment, you will feel the shackles of your humanity slip from your wrists. It is freedom. It is bliss."

Falling to her knees, the woman closed her eyes against the crimson mist of agony that engulfed her. There she found a moment of solace. Her mother's kindly face hovered just out of reach. Although her lips didn't stir, Aristoi could hear her mother's voice.

You still possess what matters most: pride, tradition and honor. None may take those; they may only be sacrificed by you.

They were the same words spoken to her by her long departed

mother when her soul straddled the chasm between life and death. Those same words rang true on this night. The curse could not take her, the gwyllgi had told her as much. She needed to surrender to it, lay her very humanity upon the alter of its influence.

The beast was close enough that Aristoi could feel its foul breath on her skin. She opened her eyes and pushed the pain aside by sheer force of will. Wrapping her hand around the shaft of her spear with a grip that she feared would splinter the weapon or the fingers themselves, the Songspear slowly climbed to her feet. Her heart still pounded in her ears, a physical manifestation of the fury that seized every fiber of her being. She had a target for that anger now, one outside herself.

Aristoi stabbed at the beast, a wordless scream flowing forth from her lips. In that primal cry was every ounce of terror and rage that had built up in the months toiling under the yoke of the gwyllgi's curse. The iron tip of the weapon creased its side, but it was able to leap away before she could solidly connect. It had taken most of her tenacity to make the attack; she could not seem to follow it up.

Before the echo of her shout had fallen into silence, the creature stalked toward her again. "There is much fight in you, little Song-spear. Perhaps once that is beaten out of you, surrender will seem a more attractive option."

She lifted her spear, but had spent most of her strength fighting the curse. She was unsure how much she had left.

Just as Aristoi's desperate scream faded into nothingness, another sound replaced it on the evening wind. A chorus of low howls wove a tapestry in the air. Whereas the baying that had brought her here had evoked a jealous fury, the call that hung in the night spoke of fellowship. It was a bolstering cry rather than one of challenge. In the midst of memories of loss, it reminded the Songspear of those that stood beside her, even when she struggled alone. Perhaps she could find the strength to rise again after all.

The call seemed to have the opposite effect on the beast before her. Wincing at the undulating notes as if they were physical blows, the gwyllgi halted its advance. "You are not ready, girl." Its head swayed side to side, searching the darkness furiously. "Not yet." Pivoting like water over cobblestone, the creature disappeared into the night.

The howls faded into the distance as Aristoi collapsed to the frozen ground. *This was your most difficult test yet, Songspear*, she thought, *for the moment, you have proven the stronger.* The crunch of permafrost heralded an approaching figure. She rose to meet the new challenge. An explosion of relief threatened to steal what strength she retained when Hollis emerged from the darkness, Dwarven steel blade glinting in the moonlight.

Chapter Twelve
An Uncomfortable Coinscidence

Jillian looked around the featureless cinder block room for what seemed like the hundredth time. Painted a grayish-blue, the room seemed more sad for it. She momentarily considered sitting in one of the unpadded plastic chairs tucked beneath the scratched surface of the wooden table, but dismissed it immediately. Although her feet had begun to ache in the hour since the police had asked her to wait "just a few minutes," she chose the devil she knew over the chiropractic nightmare the chairs promised.

Turning on her heel, she paced towards the massive mirror that dominated the wall opposite the room's only door. She had seen enough television to know that beyond its reflective surface, no doubt someone studied her every move. *You give yourself way too much credit*, she chided herself. *Most likely, the cops are too busy finding the arsonist to question you.*

Jillian chuckled softly. She had graduated high school with half the officers she had seen as she entered the station. If their decade-ago selves were any indication, her brief look at the fleeing figure would be the last anyone saw of him. She was so deep in her cynical reverie that the door's sudden opening caused her to jump in surprise.

An older man in wrinkled khakis and a navy polo stood in the door, obscuring the hallway beyond with his massive frame. Although Jillian had never met him, his visage still burned brightly in Asaege's memories. The detective's own reflection was none other than the vicious guardsman, Claerius.

"Ms. Allen, I'm sorry to keep you waiting." As the door clicked closed ominously behind him, he said, "My name is Detective Russell Blaine. If you would have a seat, we can try to get you out of here as soon as possible."

Pulling one of the plastic and chrome monstrosities from beneath the table, Jillian winced as she settled into its torturous confines. She began to fidget immediately as the chair's hard surface dug into her tail bone. *With these things, they don't need to beat confessions out of suspects. I'm ready to admit to just about anything just to stand up again.*

Blaine studied her with something approaching satisfaction, his hands steepled before him on the table. "So, Ms. Allen, why don't you tell me what you thought you saw?"

Thought I saw? A powerful temptation rose in her to reach across the intervening distance and smack the smug smile off of the detective's face. She was only partially convinced that the feeling came from her reflection.

"I can tell you what I witnessed. Will that work?" Jillian spoke slowly, focusing with all of her might to fix her face. Even so, she was sure that Blaine read the disdain written there.

"Whatever you remember ... ma'am." He added the last word with a sneer.

Not a great place to start. "I stopped for a bagel on my way to work—"

"—and where is that?"

" Rolling Meadows Elementary."

He wrote something down in a small spiral bound notebook. "Continue," he prompted. The smug smile had returned.

"I stopped for a bagel and noticed the front door of the florist was ajar. Seeing as the shop has been closed for a few months, I went over to take a look."

"Why would you do that?"

Jillian bit her lip to arrest the scowl she felt forming. "Curiosity?" She paused, waiting for Blaine to respond. He simply jotted again in his notebook. "As I approached, I smelled smoke. Through the half open door, I saw that the shop was on fire. I thought—"

He interrupted her again. "—what possessed you to go around back rather than calling 911?"

Taking a short breath to compose herself, she continued. "I thought I heard someone inside. As the flames had made the front door impassable, I hoped that I could help them out through the back."

"That was—"

She cut him off in turn, "—brave?"

"I was going to say stupid. What made you think the door was unlocked?"

Jillian shrugged. "It was better than doing nothing. If I hadn't, detective, you wouldn't have any description of the arsonist, would you?"

Blaine flipped through his notes. "A large figure dressed in a gray hoodie?"

"It's more than you had before I walked in."

"Mmm hmm." Looking up from his notebook, the detective took a deep breath. "Tell me, Ms. Allen, had you been to Marcheur's Florist and Holistic Medicine before today?"

"Perhaps. I don't remember." Jillian hoped her expression didn't betray the lie. "I get my bagels at Kimmel's. As I said, it's on my way to work."

"Are you aware that the owner died six months ago?"

She shook her head.

"What would you say if I told you that since then, we've suspected it was being used as a front to sell drugs?"

"I guess someone did your job for you."

Blaine's cheeks reddened with anger. "We've had it under surveillance for the last month. Every person who even looked sideways at the place was captured on video." In his tone was an obvious threat.

"And?" A cool relief washed over her. That afternoon was the first time Jillian had returned to the florist since Plague Man's death in late September.

"If I'm going to see you on that video, it's better for you to tell me now."

"I thought you were looking for an arsonist," she asked sweetly. Beneath her saccharine tone was a core of steel. "Are you accusing me of something, Detective Blaine?"

"Should I be?"

"Not that I'm aware of." In the back of Jillian's mind, she could feel the soft fingers of Asaege's presence lending her strength.

The two of them sat in silence for an uncomfortable moment. She broke the stillness of the bleak room. "Did you need anything else from me?"

"Not unless you want to share something you haven't told me." The detective's voice held the expectant tone of a fishing expedition.

Jillian eyed him warily. "Nope, that's pretty much it."

"Then I guess you are free to go." As she rose, Blaine added, "If anything else comes up, I'll be sure to contact you."

The woman opened her mouth to respond but thought better of it. She hurried past him and out the door. As soon as she stepped into the hallway, she noticed the mood in the police station had changed since she had gone into the interrogation room.

There was a palpable frenetic energy hanging in the air of the squad room. Uniformed officers moved among the small cluster of desks as if they searched for something they were destined to never find. Jillian quickly scanned the faces before her. It didn't take her long to find the one she searched for.

If someone had given Jillian a hundred tries, she never would have guessed Billy Parr would have chosen law enforcement as a career. The man before her only marginally resembled the unrepentant bully she had graduated with. His once full head of curly hair had dwindled to a muted horseshoe that haunted the edge of his scalp. Even at his most malicious, his eyes had held a twinkle that granted him a rugged charm despite his actions. At some point in the intervening years, that luster had become the dull stare of dispassion.

Truth be told, Jillian felt sorry for her former classmate. Whether through self reflection or circumstances, it seemed that his youthful cruelty had taken its toll on him. His attention focused on the laptop between them, Officer Parr didn't notice her until she was beside his desk. "Heya, Billy."

His head snapped up, an apathetic frown pasted on his face. The sneer dissolved into a sad smile when he recognized Jillian. "Jillie! It's been a minute."

She chuckled. "Long enough that I go by Jillian now."

For a second, the carefree boy she had known possessed the unhappy man before her. "I know the feeling." He tapped the half-buried nameplate on the desk. *Off. William Parr.* "No one has called me Billy in years." The transformation was fleeting. Between one breath and another, Billy became William again. His melancholy eyes scanned the room behind her. "You're not in trouble are you?"

Jillian had to think about it for a moment before shaking her head slowly. "I don't think so. I got a quick look at the man who set fire to the florist down on Winter Ave."

"Allegedly," William said helpfully. A pale smile colored his lips as he said, "Sorry. It's a force of habit."

She returned the gesture with a warmer grin. "No worries. I suppose it's a danger of the job."

A frown reclaimed his face as he indicated the room she had just departed with a bob of his head. "Did Blaine question you?"

Jillian didn't have to ask how her high school friend felt about the detective, his distaste for the man seemed to radiate from him like the heat of a summer fever. "Yes. He's obviously not in the running for Civil Servant of the Year, is he?"

William leaned in, lowering his voice to a conspiratorial whisper. "Be careful with him, Jillie—" She nodded towards his own nameplate. "—an", he added quickly. "Blaine likes to close cases, even if they're not the one he's working on."

She raised an eyebrow, the detective's questions suddenly making more sense.

"You didn't hear it from me." His voice held a pleading tone that she would have thought him incapable of a decade before.

Jillian pressed the tips of her thumb and forefinger together and made a zipping motion across her mouth. Gesturing to the hive of nervous energy that was the squad room around them, she asked, "Is that what all this is about? The fire?"

William shook his head quickly, opening his mouth to respond. His jaw hung slack for a moment as he visibly debated saying more.

"Who am I going to tell, Billy?"

An impulsive sparkle bloomed in his eye. "I guess it can't hurt. Erik Gunn died this morning." He sighed softly.

Jillian wished desperately that the name meant something to her. Her confusion must have shown on her face.

"Erik Gunn …" When recognition didn't register on her face, William elaborated. "Three time All State linebacker for the Pope Innocent Pumas …"

She shook her head.

"He was looking at a full ride to any top 25 college team he wants."

"Football?"

William chuckled. "Yes, football. He finished this season with just over forty sacks and three hundred total tackles."

"I assume that's good?"

He just studied her beneath furrowed eyebrows.

"He passed away today?"

"Yes." It seemed that William wanted to say more, but instead allowed an awkward silence to hang between them.

"That's terrible. An accident? Natural causes?"

William's mouth pulled into a tight frown. "It's not clear yet." Again, his face betrayed the fact that there was more to the story.

In a soft voice, she asked, "Murder?"

His eyes shot to a small glass enclosed office in the corner of the room.

Turning to follow his gaze, Jillian saw the words *Bruno Stewart, Captain* stenciled on the door in broad gray letters. "I need you to answer one question for me, William."

His attention returned to her. After studying her for a second, William responded. "Why do I think that this is going be something that will get me in trouble?"

"I'm going to take that as tacit agreement." Before he could reply, Jillian continued. "Were you involved with the Martin Fredericks case?"

William's eyes grew huge in an expression that struck a balance between shock and fear. "That's an open investigation, Jillian. I can't comment on it."

Focusing her attention on his face as she spoke, Jillian whispered, "How similar was the causes of death between Erik and the Freeholder?"

He stammered a few times before closing his eyes. "It's still ongoing. I could lose my job if I talk about it." The flesh at the back of her neck crawled with a nervous chill that she couldn't quite explain. Jillian didn't need anything more than the way he clenched his bottom lip between his teeth to tell her that there was more than a passing connection between the two deaths.

*****

"Was that Billy Parr?" Having left her car in the strip mall parking lot, being unable to reach Marisol, Jillian had no choice but to call Cyrill to pick her up at the police station.

"Who would have thought he would become a cop?" Sitting beside her friend in his car, she did her best to put from her mind Asaege's experience with his reflection, Lirych.

"In middle school, he pushed me into my gym locker after third period." There was an edge to his voice that wouldn't let the image fade. "I was trapped in there so long, I missed lunch."

She laid her hand on his shoulder. "Billy was a nasty little shit back then. Now he just seems …" Still grappling with sitting so close to the reflection of Lady Markov's "hired gun", Jillian searched for the words to describe her interaction with the bully that made so many of their lives miserable a decade before.

"Different?" Without waiting for her response, Cyrill continued. "The torment he inflicted on kids that only wanted to get through the day is unforgivable. He doesn't get to pretend that those things didn't happen."

"I was going to say sad."

"Good," he snapped. "As far as I'm concerned, sad is the least that he deserves. Do you remember what he used to call me?"

Although they had known each other since childhood, Jillian and Cyrill hadn't really become friends until college. Still, she remembered the nickname that the middle school bullies had come up with for him. *Semen the Greek.* Lucky for him, Cyrill had found his place within the fickle society of high school, leaving behind a lot of the artifacts of his younger years, including the unfortunate moniker. Others were not so lucky.

Jillian frowned. "For a lot of people, Billy was the center of the universe of misery that was their school years. I am in no way making excuses for him but—"

"—there is no but. I didn't even get the worst of it. Do you remember Richard Stein?"

Jillian winced. He had gone by Richie, but Billy and his friends had decided early on to call him Dick Stain. Cruel as school aged children tend to be, the name stuck. It followed Richie through middle school and into high school. He was a nice kid; the way he recoiled from the hallway chants broke her heart as much in that moment as it had years prior.

"I heard he tried to kill himself a few years back. His neighbor found him in time, but his brain was without oxygen long enough that he's been in a coma ever since."

She momentarily forgot about Cyrill's reflection. She covered her mouth, gasping into her hand. "Oh my god. Suicide? Poor Richie."

"He's been in Church Hill since then ... or so I heard."

Jillian remembered reading about Church Hill Long Term Care Center. In the 1960s it had been had been Calvary Hills Memorial Hospital. Although small, it was the only hospital in the county. In 1986, Belmante Medical Systems built a state of the art trauma center less than a mile from Calvary Hills.

Soon after CHMH was forced to declare bankruptcy and close its doors. Belmante bought the building out of foreclosure for pennies on the dollar and within a year, Church Hill Long Term Care Center, a Belmante subsidiary, opened for business. Its main selling point being cut-rate residential and rehabilitation services,

Church Hill became a popular destination for patients whose families weren't fond of them and those who couldn't afford better.

The tragedy that began on an elementary school playground had ended in the dreary medical-green halls of a budget nursing home. "Poor Richie."

Neither of them seemed to know what to say, so the car fell into a tense silence. The only sound to break the stillness was the dull drone of the road beneath their tires. Within the soulless hum, Jillian replayed Asaege's memories of the Silver Courtesan in her mind. Her nose stung with the scent of burned flesh and fresh blood as if she were still in the common room beside her reflection. More than the recollection of the violence of that day, she was shaken by the image of Lirych's indifferent expression as it occurred around him, the face that he shared with the man sitting beside her.

"I guess Hector's out of business again." Cyrill's gallows humor struck her differently given the events of the past day. "Was he there when the place went up?"

Cyrill is not Lirych, Jillian told herself. Although, in the strictest of senses, the statement was true, it still rang false in her head. *If they are tied as Asaege and I are, there must be a small part of that jaded thaumaturge-for-hire in my friend.*

Distracted by the doubt that filled her heart, she stumbled over her words. "Um … I saw something that could have been a body in the flames."

"Really?" There was real sadness in Cyrill's voice. "That's …"

His words floundered as he was overcome by emotion for a moment. She turned to study his profile as he drove. Her friend's breaths came in short, controlled bursts as he fought the tears that clearly hung in his eyes. It was not the hard, apathetic bearing carried by his counterpart in Taerh. His knuckles were white on the steering wheel, an indication of the pain he fought within himself.

"That's terrible. Hector could be a jerk but no one deserves that … to die like that." A single tear traced its way down his cheek. It hung on the edge of his jaw for a split second before falling to his denim clad thigh. Reaching up retroactively, Cyrill wiped away any trace of its passing. "Did the police have any ideas who it may have been?"

"I'm not convinced they are looking, at least not in any real way. The fire department got the blaze under control fast enough that the only store affected was Hector's. From what I gathered from my short interview with the detective, he never actually had any right to be there. It seems he just moved in when the last owner died.

Detective Blaine seemed more interested in the shop's off-the-books business rather than who may have set the fire."

"But Hector died!" Cyrill's voice cracked as he raised it. Softening his words, he asked, "What are they going to do about that?"

"He had more questions about whether or not I'd ever visited Hector for pot than who was responsible for what happened today."

He took a deep breath, holding it for a second before exhaling in a long, slow breath. The gesture reminded Jillian of her own technique for communing with Asaege in times of stress. "What do you think he knows?" The question was devoid of the quiver Cyrill's voice had held a moment before.

Pushing down the acid bite of dread at the back of her throat, Jillian kept her tone even. "He said that they have had the florist under surveillance for the last month." After saying it out loud, an obvious question occurred to her. *If they had been watching the shop, they should have a record of the arsonist.* She felt a twinge of annoyance at having not picked up on it earlier. *Either Blaine was lying or they really don't care about who set the fire, just to whom Hector was selling.*

"A month? I was just there last night." Whether due to shock or other, more devious reasons, Cyrill said it as a statement of fact, free of any real alarm.

"Did you buy any Dreamtime Dank from him?" Jillian wasn't sure how much of the worry in her tone came from her concern for her friend and how much stemmed from a fear that through the adder root laced pot, his reflection had a grasp upon him.

"I did. I figured we could split an eighth."

Her mind spun, searching for an excuse to not go back to his place. "Sounds good," she said, trying to keep the trepidation from her voice. "But not tonight. I have a ton of papers to grade and a make up lesson plan to get done before tomorrow."

Cyrill seemed unfazed. "Sure. I'll catch up with you tomorrow."

As they approached the entrance to the strip mall, he still had neither slowed down nor put on his turn signal.

"Cyrill," she prompted. "This is me up here."

Her friend regarded her from the corner of his eye. "Of course." He flipped his directional and applied the brake, both with a little more zeal than was strictly necessary. Jillian was forced to grab the safety bar above her to prevent herself from pitching forward. As he stopped behind her car, Cyrill turned to face her.

"Thanks for the ride," Jillian said, reaching for the door handle.

He placed a hand on her arm. "One more thing, Jill."

She looked down at it like it was a snake but kept her tone even. "Yes, Cyrill?"

"Be careful. You still don't know who was behind the fire and who may want to keep it quiet."

"Thanks," she muttered, pulling free from his grip and stepping from the car. As she wrapped her coat more tightly around her body, Jillian wasn't convinced that the chill that bit into her bones came entirely from the frigid night air.

Chapter Thirteen
A Whispered Reassurance

As Asaege pulled herself through the trap door, she felt the muscles between her shoulders relax. There was no doubt that access to the passages beneath the city provided by Raethe, King of the Underfoot, was one of the things that made the revolution possible. The act of traversing them, however, made her skin crawl. Ash-born, Asaege was comfortable with the claustrophobic confines that made up the slums of the city of her birth, but even in the tightest alley, a thin ribbon of sky remained above her.

In the bowels of Oizan, there was a darkness so pure that it became something more than a simple lack of light. It pulled from those who walked in it the very will to put one foot in front of the other. Lanterns were a pale succor against the smothering void that struggled against their radiance. Or at least that's how it seemed to Asaege.

Behind her emerged Torae and those of her employees that had nowhere else to go. The Silver Courtesan had been a constant in Oizan society for decades before Torae assumed ownership of the brothel. Within the span of an hour, it had become another causality of the Prophet-led rebellion. It wasn't its owner whose glare Asaege avoided, however.

"Now is not the time, Toni."

The guild-master stood with their arms folded across their chest. "I disagree."

Turning her back on them, Asaege addressed the unemployed madam instead. "Get your people settled." Unable to meet her eyes, she simply promised, "We will fix this, Torae."

Desperation warred with anger on Torae's face. Instead of pressing the issue, she wrapped her arms around the shoulders of the nearest girl and guided her towards the hallway beyond.

"You cannot promise that," Toni growled.

When Asaege turned to face them, she found their mouth drawn into an angry scowl. "Add it to the stack of crimes laid at the feet of the Prophet."

"You could have put an end to Markov tonight ... Markov and her hired thaumaturge."

"Perhaps," Asaege snapped. "But would that have lifted the suspicion from the Silver Courtesan and its staff? When Markov did not return, do you believe the council would decide it was just an unfortunate coincidence?

"Markov would have been dead, thus making our lives easier."

"That is the key, is it not? Our lives?" She gestured towards the huddled group rushing from the room. "What about their lives? We started this with a higher purpose in mind."

"Your higher purpose is getting my brothers and sisters killed."

The cold bite of disappointment danced with burning notes of anger. "My purpose. Was it not our purpose, Toni? All of ours?"

Their countenance softened. "Of course. I just do not want to be responsible for putting the final nail in the coffin of the Brotherhood of the Night."

"You do not bear that burden alone." Asaege hadn't noticed Seran's entrance, but the elder thief leaned against the door frame, his hands steepled against his lips. Partially obscured behind him was a slim figure. She assumed it to be the boy Seran had brought back with him from the Ivory Cathedral.

Toni rolled their eyes. "So my absentee colleague returns from Olm-knows-where, hollow assurances sharing space with venom-soaked platitudes upon his tongue."

Their words were greeted with an arrogant smile. "Not all contributions to the movement are made on the edge of a blade, Toni."

The conflict between the two of them had grown more heated in the months since the death of Guild Master Dhole in the tunnels beneath the city. Asaege was privy to only the most public of their disagreements, but it had become clear that, whatever the spirit of brotherhood within the guild, it could not serve two masters.

"Tell me, Seran, which of your personal grudges contributed to the revolution while we were—"

"— babysitting a whore?"

His interruption only served to anger them further. "Torae is an ally, one who has proven her value to us at every turn."

Asaege added, "She is also a friend. There is no need to call her that."

He raised an eyebrow. "Is it not true? At the core of their profession, does not the most respected courtesan sell an intimate portion of themselves to those who are willing to pay for it?"

Of all of those thrown together in the revolution, she had the most difficulty getting an accurate impression of Seran. He often spoke velvet words in a rose-scented tone, but the underlying meaning always seemed designed to elicit the worst in his audience. Almost in the same breath, he selflessly risked his life for those around him before twisting those same people to his own purposes.

"Although the currency may differ, which among us is free of that particular sin?"

Seran's smile broadened. "Eloquently put, my dear. At any rate, I did not intrude upon your no doubt engaging discussion to trade clever barbs. While you were ..." He paused dramatically. "... tending to the most hospitable of our allies, I was looking into a troublesome detail of my own."

Toni licked their lips as they turned up into a devious smile. "Do you mean that something keeps Seran, master of all he surveys, up at night?"

"Of course not, my dear comrade. I sleep the slumber of the innocent, reserved only for saints and children. It occurs to me, however, that the Templars have been unexpectedly quiet for the last week or so."

"Is that why you invaded the Ivory Cathedral? Killed their soldiers and kidnapped your new ward?" Toni indicated the slight boy still hiding in the elder thief's shadow.

"Among other reasons. Even after last night's events, the warriors of Olm remain shuttered in their chalky sanctuary. Their uncharacteristic behavior vexed me."

Asaege blinked hard. "You wanted them to retaliate against us?"

"Want has very little to do with it. I expected them to at least make a token reprisal, but nothing."

Toni chuckled. "That is a good thing."

"Is it? There are a great deal of truly frightening things in the world. Each one of them is less so once you understand it. I could not fathom why the Olmites would abandon their allies to our machinations. I found that unsettling." He paused, expecting them to inquire further, his silence practically demanding it.

Asaege humored him. "What did you find?"

"How kind of you to ask. With the Hand of Light dead, the Olmites of Oizan and its surrounding countryside had fallen under the auspice of the templar commander. It was he who made the compact with the council of guilds; it was he who ordered the forces of the church into the streets. As happens with all good things, ill fortune must also come to an end."

Toni raised an eyebrow. "A new Hand?"

Asaege shook her head. "The Hand of Light is bestowed upon a worthy successor by the Father of Justice himself. They are not appointed by any collection of mortals."

"I am never disappointed by the breadth of your knowledge, esteemed Prophet."

She cringed but allowed him to continue.

"The church itself is a massive endeavor, unwieldy for even Olm's chosen. The Hand appoints three representatives to aid in administrating to the three pillars of the Olmite faith: acquisition of knowledge, eradication of heresy, and waging of war. Called the Triad, each is considered absolute in matters of their purview, outside of the Hand themselves."

Asaege felt the air leave her body. "One of the Triad is coming here?"

"I am afraid so. Grand Inquisitor Remahl of the Falling Water arrived in the city two nights ago."

Toni sighed heavily. "An inquisitor does bode well for us."

Seran shook his head. "Not just an inquisitor, *the* inquisitor. They call her the Crimson Sister."

A passing guild-member spun on the trio, his face ashen. "The Crimson Sister? It is said that she dyes her robes with the blood of heretics. If she stands against us, our cause is lost."

Seran's scowl was enough to convince the apprentice to keep walking. "Whether or not she actually poses a threat, her reputation itself is a concern." His eyes bore into the back of the fleeing boy. "It does not take an abundance of imagination to envision why."

*****

"The Crimson Sister? No shit?" Speaking in English, Hollis's voice was a whisper. Asaege wasn't sure if the sensation of it against

106

the tender flesh of her cheek was wishful thinking or a side effect of the trinket she held before her lips. Unimaginatively called a whisper stone, the charmed, small vaguely orb-shaped object allowed the possessor of it to communicate with someone holding its mate. Seran had given the pair to Hollis before the thief had left for the northern wastes. When pressed about their source, Seran had been evasive to say the least.

"Try not to sound so impressed," Asaege responded in the same language. When they had agreed to use it in lieu of Trade Tongue via the device, it had seemed an overabundance of caution to her. Jillian's experiences on Earth, combined with her own in Taerh had made her believe that their safeguard may not have gone far enough.

"Okay, but under any other circumstances, it'd be fairly impressive."

"I'm worried about what it means for the rebellion. You and I know that Plague Man killed the Hand but I'm not sure even all of our own people believe it."

"You've dealt with everything that's come up so far. I'm sure you'll find a way around this as well."

The calm sound of confidence in his voice lit a smoldering heat in Asaege's chest. His unwavering faith in not only her, but her ability to deal with anything put in front of her reminded Asaege of why she fell in love with the thief in the first place. She desperately yearned to say, "It'd be easier if you were beside me," but wanted to put neither that pressure nor guilt on him. Asaege settled for, "Thank you, my love."

"You've got this, Magpie."

"I feel like I'm juggling a dozen balls. I just get one in the air as two more fall towards my hands." Outside that room, Asaege worked hard at keeping up the facade of the Prophet. If her people lost faith in her, their shared endeavor would fail as well. During her hushed conversations with the thief, however, she could let down the barriers and reveal the roles that were more comfortable: teacher and idealist, lover and friend. With him, she didn't need to be anything other than what she truly was. He loved her without conditions or limitations.

"Just because you can do all things, doesn't mean you should have to. Although the Prophet leads it, the revolution belongs to more than just one person. Toni and Seran, Rudelph and Torae, each of them is capable of dealing with some of the things that threaten to get away from you."

"I know I can be a bit—"

"Bossy?"

107

Asaege let out an only slightly annoyed snort. "I was going to say can be a bit of a control enthusiast."

Hollis laughed. It was a comforting sound, like a warm wind over a sandy beach. "That too," he agreed.

"In the last week or so, I've noticed some unsettling changes in the people around me."

His tone became serious. "Like what?"

"Small things like Toni pulling back, putting the needs of the guild before the rebellion and Torae expressing worry about her people. Both are understandable. but I worry about cracks beginning to form in what was once a united front."

"You know as well as I do that holding together such a band of disparate factions, each with their own motivations, is a herculean task. If anyone is capable of herding them together, it is you, Asaege."

"I'm touched that you think so highly of me."

"Without a doubt, you are the most capable person I know. The one place where you falter is in seeing your own worth."

"Hollis," she began.

Before she could argue further, he continued. "My dearest wish is that you could see yourself through my eyes."

Asaege was speechless for a moment. Silence replaced the breathy whispers in the dim room that served her as both quarters and office. Rather than awkwardness, the stillness between them was filled with a gentle longing.

Lost in the moment, she blurted out, "I wish you were here with me." Regretting it immediately, Asaege tried to explain herself. "What I meant was—"

"— I know what you meant, Magpie. It's not weakness to want something for yourself. Although I am leagues away, my heart always beats beside yours. Aristoi and I will finish our business and be home as soon as we are able." There was a tension in his voice, but the thief did his best to hide it. As much as she wanted to press, Asaege allowed him to believe he had succeeded.

"I will be waiting for you when you return."

"You are my home, my dear. Without you, Oizan is just another place to rest my head." Another sweet quiet hung between them. This time, it was Hollis who broke it. "Has Seran been behaving himself?"

"Your beloved mentor has been present less and less, often returning after things have begun to fall apart. He claims to have been attending to personal business but refuses to divulge any but the most

108

general details."

"That's Seran's way. He basically raised me and I still could count the things I know about him on two hands, with fingers to spare. Besides the randomness of his presence, has he given you any other reason to distrust him?"

"He's been ... nice."

"Nice? That's not a word I would've ever used to describe Seran."

"He brought your Talis Fahr to me, the one I lost when I was captured. He claims to have taken it off the body of a templar."

"It's yours now, Magpie—"

"—when he returned from the Ivory Cathedral, he had a boy in tow."

"A boy? Even in my childhood, my mentor was never the paternal sort. If Seran rescued him, he has ulterior motives."

"I came to a similar conclusion about his recent benevolence."

"Keep an eye on him, Asaege. While Seran is a powerful ally, in the end, his only loyalty is to himself."

A light knock at the chamber door reminded the woman of her surroundings. "Asaege," a voice on the other side called, "a city patrol has cornered some of our people near the docks. They have Lirych with them."

Aware that the stone wouldn't transmit any sound above a whisper, she tried to keep her fear from her voice. "I've got to go, Hollis."

"Don't be a stranger." He tried to keep his voice casual, but Asaege heard his reluctance.

"Come home to me soon, Scoundrel."

"There is nothing in heaven or earth that could keep me away, Magpie."

Chapter Fourteen
A Convenient Deception

"There is nothing in heaven or earth that could keep me away, Magpie." As the connection was broken, Hollis tucked the stone into the pouch at his waist, caressing its smooth surface with his fingertips before letting it drop into the leather depths.

Aristoi's voice broke him out of his thoughts. "Everything alright in Oizan?"

He exhaled slowly before answering. "Not by a long shot. Asaege keeps it from me, but there is more at play than the Crimson Sister and revolutionary interpersonal issues."

"No doubt, she does not want you to worry."

The thief squinted in her direction. "I would never do that."

"I assume you told her that the two of us harry the trail of a half dozen Rangor in pursuit of captured companions, hounded at every step by a bloodthirsty beast of claw and shadow?"

"Of course not, she—"

"—Then save your objections, Northerner."

"There are some days when you are positively infuriating, do you know that?"

"You may have mentioned it on occasion." The Songspear prodded the low-burning fire between them with the tip of her spear. "She will be fine, Hollis. She has a good head on her shoulders, which is more than I can say for either of us."

The thief rubbed his hands together and extended his palms towards the flames. "A more inconvenient truth, I have not heard." His heart was still heavy with worry, but his companion's shared confidence in Asaege's abilities relieved a measure of its weight. Before he could lose himself beneath what remained, a low, keening howl rose in the distance. Hollis reached for his sword.

Aristoi shook her head. "The creature will not make another attempt tonight."

"What makes you so sure?"

"I am not certain if it was your timely arrival or the howling that was heard right before, but the gwyllgi was clearly spooked by one of them."

"Do not get me wrong, I am glad that I found you in one piece, but there is nary a mark on you, my friend."

The Songspear frowned. "That was the strange thing. All he wanted to do was talk."

Hollis noticed that she had gone from referring to the gwyllgi as "it", a creature to be slain, to a more personal pronoun. "Talk?"

"Yes. He seemed to know all about my run in with the beast that infected me."

There it was again. "He? Are you so sure that it is male?"

"I was not sure before speaking with him. I am still not convinced, but there is something so familiar about the way he spoke." Aristoi scratched at the back of her head in an exaggerated gesture. "It is like an itch at the back of my brain, just out of reach."

"What did he want?"

"He believes that we are the same, he and I. The frightening thing is I am not certain he is mistaken."

"We have been over this. There are leagues between you and that monstrosity."

"He kept encouraging me to give into the bestial voice that has sunk its claws into my soul. Each time it rises in me, I can feel my body twist under its direction. Could losing myself be as simple as giving in?"

"I hope we never need to find out." Concentrating on keeping his tone even, Hollis felt a sinking feeling in his gut. *What am I going to do if I have to follow through on my promise to put her out of her misery?* The thief honestly couldn't answer the question, even to himself. "When you went home, was there no one there who could shed some light on the problem? Are the Songspears not the keepers of lore back to the Time of Legends?"

Aristoi studied the ground before her, avoiding his eyes. "It is not quite that simple. Although, as a group, my brothers and sisters have access to a staggering amount of knowledge, they are never in the same place. That means the lore is never all in the same place. Given time, perhaps I could find the right collection of Songspears to assemble the pieces of what has befallen me."

"Then, that is what we must do—"

"—but I cannot do that."

"Why?"

"It would require confiding in my people about the conflict that rages within me. The gwyllgi, known in Kiel as *Bulch Dalk* or Black Dog, are hunted by the leaders of my order."

"Yet you had never heard of them before being attacked?"

Through gritted teeth, the Songspear growled, "They kept it from the people."

From his vantage point across the campfire, Hollis saw the furs in which his companion had wrapped herself ripple in the flickering light. The thief wanted to attribute it to a trick of shadow and an overactive imagination, but he couldn't quite dismiss the feeling of dread that had taken residence between his shoulder blades.

"The council had decided that knowing that the *Bulch Dalk* were more than just stories to keep children in bed would cause the general public unnecessary distress."

"Fantastic. It is always better to be eaten by a fable than pre-pared for a monster." Sarcasm dripped heavily from Hollis's words.

"Those were my feelings on the matter as well. Besides your-self, the only person to whom I have told my story is the Branded himself."

"The Herald? And he could not just …" Hollis waved his hand in a vaguely arcane looking gesture. "… mojo it away?"

"That would have been convenient, but no. The curse is older than our magic; it is almost as old as the Heralds themselves. The solution will no doubt be a hard fought one."

"Based on the fact that we sit here tonight, I assume the Brand-ed does not share the council's fervor."

"No. He offered to work on my behalf to search for a cure, but only on the condition that I remain far away from the Verdant Sea until he called me home. Despite his oath as a Herald, the Branded's first priority has always been the Kieli people. I guess, even in his eyes, I represent too much of a threat to them."

"So that is good, right? Solving the mystery has to be magni-tudes easier with the aid of a Herald."

"If the gwyllgi is to be believed, that aid may never come. He claimed to have slain the Branded shortly after I spoke to him."

"Do you believe him?"

Aristoi shrugged, but the heaviness in the gesture told Hollis all he needed to know.

"Then we do it ourselves."

"If the beast can best the Branded, what chance do we have against it?"

"Do not forget, we slew the Walker less than a year ago. She was no Songspear, but both of us can attest to the puissance of her magic."

His words didn't seem to lift her spirits. "You killed her through trickery."

For a moment, the same self doubt that plagued Stephen all of his life stabbed at the center of him. *Maybe she is right. Perhaps we have gotten ourselves in over our heads one time too many.* Images of Silvermoon and Rhyzzo mixed with those of Alan and George in Hollis's mind. *So many people have paid the price for my survival.*

A voice screamed at him from deep within the thief's own psyche. He was so accustomed to their integration that, at first, he didn't recognize it. *We left that bullshit behind at the Well.* It was Stephen in his purest form, free of their merged consciousness for a moment. *For too long, I ... we believed the words of those who sought to pull us down to their level. They never beat us. Each time, we defeated ourselves. Every battle has its casualties, but every one of our lost comrades died so we could continue to fight.*

"Aristoi." Hollis's voice had the snap of a cracked whip. When she looked up, he locked eyes with her. "Dead is dead. It matters not what tools were used, the deed was done." His and Stephen's identity melded together once again. "Anyone who does not believe the pair of us to be very dangerous people will quickly learn that lesson, to their detriment."

Chapter Fifteen
A Distressing Reunion

Trying to push her doubts about Cyrill from her mind as she drove, Jillian turned her attention to that morning's revelation, one that, in the turmoil of the day, she had overlooked. *Stephen is alive ... at least if his not-quite-widow was telling the truth.* A burning sensation built deep in her chest as she thought of the less-than-esteemed Mrs. Moses. The faceless CARE chairwoman had impacted her life from the shadows for too long.

Her crusade against "inappropriate educational practices" had begun with banning books in both school and public libraries, but in the last month, the CARE dominated school board had begun "suggesting" changes to lesson plans that didn't meet their approval. Jillian couldn't think of one of her co-workers whose curriculum wasn't affected. From restricted topics to whole sections being stricken from previously approved textbooks, everyone had been forced to scramble to reassemble already established lesson plans.

While Mrs. Moses's effect on her professional life was profound, Jillian wasn't sure it was the source of white-hot animosity that threatened to rise into her throat. Hollis hadn't been overly verbose about Stephen's life prior to the Well of Worlds, but the little he did say about the wife he left behind was far from complimentary. Knowing Hollis's heart through her own reflection's recollections,

Jillian felt confident that she had a pretty good read on Stephen's as well.

His soul would have been wasted with a woman like that, she thought bitterly. Recognizing the feeling as equal parts resentment and jealousy, Jillian decided she didn't care. *It may be petty, but she didn't deserve him. She still doesn't.*

*****

The hyper dog downstairs started barking almost as soon as Jillian had put her key in the door, but she didn't mind the sound as much since the territorial little beast had warned her of Hector's presence months ago. "Bark on, you furry little dust mop," she muttered as she locked the deadbolt. The dog seemed to gladly oblige her as she climbed the single flight of stairs to her one bedroom apartment, its yapping increasing in both volume and pitch.

The room that served her as both living and dining areas was just as she left it that morning. Since Plague Man's reflection had broken in, Jillian found herself more observant when it came to things out of place, or at least out of place for her. Pillows lay stacked haphazardly on the battered futon that served her as a couch and books on various subjects were stacked on every conceivable flat surface. Some may have enjoyed the clean lines of a sterile living space, but she preferred the warm embrace of controlled clutter.

Flopping down on the cushion-laden surface, Jillian pulled her laptop from the coffee table. As she flipped it open, the screen leapt to life. In her browser window was an article on growing rattlesnake weed, singularly unhelpful when it came to keeping her dwindling supply of adder root alive. Closing it with an exasperated huff, she opened a new tab. *Might as well start from the beginning*, she thought.

Jillian's fingers stabbed at the keyboard, typing: *Stephen Moses* into the search bar. Nothing on the first page of results was related to Hollis's reflection. After a few unsuccessful tries at refining her search, Jillian was able to find a small article that had run in the local newspaper.

June 15. Gerry Hahn, Staff Reporter.
Local Man, Stephen Moses, was found unresponsive in his home last night. The county sheriff's department released a statement this morning detailing Moses's potential involvement in the deaths of two local young men. Alan Lightner and Michael Ryan, both seniors at Pope Innocent XIII Regional High School, passed away a week ago from suspected drug overdoses. Although both investigations are

116

*still ongoing, Sheriff Wilson Moore indicated that they believe that
the cases are related.*

*A Pope Innocent alumnus himself, Moses had been a student
of Jeffery Lightner, Alan's father a decade ago. The senior Lightner,
his brother and a family friend, also passed away under mysterious
circumstances. Sheriff Moore has not ruled out these older cases
being related as well.*

*Mr. Moses was discovered by his wife of seven years, Veroni-
ca. When sheriff's officers arrived, an empty plastic bag was found
clutched in his hand. Traces of an unknown substance were found
inside the bag, although the sheriff's office has not released any
further details.*

Jillian's stomach clenched as her eyes ran over the words. She
knew the unearned guilt that Hollis carried regarding the deaths of
his friends. The knowledge that he was being held responsible by
both law enforcement and the press would drive that self-wielded
dagger even further into his heart.

Clicking the left pointing arrow harder than she had intended,
Jillian navigated back to the search page. After scanning a handful of
summarized results, all asserting the same salacious assumptions, she
found a link to a much more recent article. The title stood out to her
by virtue of its clearly pandering title:

*Local Community Leader Takes a Stand for the Children
November 5. Gerry Hahn, Assistant Editor*
*CARE chairwoman and social advocate, Veronica Moses, could
have been broken by the two-fold tragedy that struck within the confines of her own home less than five months ago. Accused of narcotic
distribution and involuntary manslaughter, her husband of seven
years attempted to take his own life by overdosing on an unidentified
cocktail of his own product. Ultimately unsuccessful, Mr. Moses has
been in a coma ever since.*

Jillian felt her jaw tighten as she felt her blood turn to magma
in her veins. Thick and hot, her rage burned the back of her throat as
she read the blatant lies written about the man she had come to care
for as deeply as did her reflection.

*Rather than wallow in the betrayal of the person closest to her
heart, Mrs. Moses chose to take it as an opportunity to better her
community and, in doing so, prevent those around her from expe-*

117

riencing the pain she knew so well. Her first order of business was shedding light on the true nature of "role-playing games," specifically Shadows & Sorcerers, the game played by her husband until the day of his suicide attempt.

Known as S&S by its supporters, Shadows & Sorcerers encourages players to assume the identities of fictional characters with the nebulous goal of achieving fame and riches. The game involves neither board nor time limit, leading to a sensation akin to addiction in those who participate in its serpentine mental labyrinth of youthful grooming. Shadows & Sorcerers played a part in not only Mr. Moses's self-inflicted overdose but the five deaths he was suspected of being involved in.

Mrs. Moses's grass-roots movement, Save Our Youth or SOY, gained statewide acclaim when they amassed 8,000 signatures to remove books sold by S&S publisher, Griffin Publishing, from public libraries across the county. In addition, SOY-led demonstrations indirectly led to the closing of two local comic book stores who refused to cease selling the objectionable material.

Mrs. Moses herself credits SOY's campaign against Griffin Publishing for attracting the attention of the Coalition for Academic Responsibility and Excellence. In the three months since SOY and CARE combined their efforts, the parents' rights organizations have seized practically every school board election into which they threw their hats. "When chairperson elections came up on November first," said three term CARE treasurer, Millie Roestock, "voting for Veronica was a no-brainer."

Despite the agony and embarrassment he has brought her, Mrs. Moses still visits her comatose husband at the Church Hill Long Term Care Center on a daily basis. She is an inspiration to anyone who has ever been dealt an unfavorable hand. Burdened with tragedy and betrayal, Veronica Moses responds with loyalty and selflessness.

Her hands were shaking as she finished reading the article. Below it was a full color photograph of Veronica Moses beside the bed of a thin figure, almost lost among a nest of blankets, wires and tubes. Jillian felt the heart within her chest break as she recognized the unconscious man. Always larger than life in Taerh, Hollis—or rather Stephen—looked so fragile in the image. It was bad enough that the reflection of the effervescent thief languished in such a state, but for that shrew of a woman to exploit it for her own gain was appalling.

118

Jillian's rage cooled in an instant as a frigid wash of dread swept through her body. The face hovering above Stephen's motionless form, the soulless gaze staring back at her from her laptop screen was none other than that of Lady Markov.

*****

Jillian hadn't shaken the feeling of disquiet by the time she pulled into the parking lot of Church Hill Long Term Care Center. Lady Markov's tight, smug smile had been haunting her thoughts since her reflection had encountered the Oizan council member. Although she hadn't raised a finger during the events in the Silver Courtesan, there was no doubt in Jillian's mind that Markov bore the majority of the responsibility for what occurred.

She had convinced herself Lady Markov remained in Taerh, a literal world away. The realization that her reflection not only existed but was so intricately intertwined with the man of which she was so fond shook Jillian to her core. Far from the petty, feckless woman Hollis had described, Veronica Moses's eyes held the same arrogant cruelty as Asaege had seen in Lady Markov's. Besides her isolated experience with Hector, the risks posed by her nocturnal excursions to Taerh had always stayed behind when she woke. Those days were obviously behind her.

Shutting off the car's engine, Jillian took a moment to compose herself before emerging into the crisp winter evening. No doubt, the building's parking lot had been maintained, but since being obtained by Belmante Medical Systems, it clearly had fallen into disrepair. Less than half of the hulking overhead lights functioned well enough to spill their luminescence onto the cracked asphalt. The isolated pools of pale light somehow made the shadows between them appear even more threatening.

The facade of the building itself was a mixture of cracked brick and worn stonework, evoking the image of an abandoned manor house, stranded in the midst of a cursed, British moor. Above her loomed a checkerboard of softly lit and pitch black windows, giving the impression that the entire building was a jagged toothed jack-o-lantern, biding its time until it devoured any who dare cross its threshold.

As she approached the column-flanked entrance, Jillian took note that it seemed the only part of the exterior in good repair. Large floor-to-ceiling windows revealed the lobby's polished white granite floors and spectacularly intricate Persian rugs. Scattered amidst the grandeur of the airy reception area were clusters of overstuffed Queen Anne wingback chairs. Each collection surrounded a low oak

119

table.

The cloying scent of lavender and vanilla assaulted Jillian as soon as she stepped through the door, but her sinuses stung from the acerbic undertone that hung in the air. The combination of deodorizers and scented candles almost masked the aroma of antiseptic and urine originating from further within the facility. Like the richly appointed lobby, the fragrance was a carefully cultivated facade that couldn't quite conceal the threadbare condition of Church Hill.

A uniformed young man leaned against a massive oak desk chatting with the receptionist, half-hidden by its bulk. The clearly bored woman's half-lidded gaze followed Jillian's progress across the floor. Oblivious to both the disinterest of his companion and Jillian's presence, he continued to babble as she approached.

"—then I said, 'You don't pay me enough to clean that up.' Old people are so gross."

The woman beside him responded with a non-committal, "Mmhmm." Her head visibly bobbed as she obviously studied Jillian from head to toe. Pursing her lips as if the air was suddenly bitter on her tongue, the receptionist murmured, "Can I help you?"

Only through sheer force of will was Jillian able keep her expression placid. "I would like to visit a friend. Richard Stein."

"One moment," she replied. Although she began typing on the keyboard in front of her, it took the young woman a long second to drag her eyes from Jillian. "Are you family?"

Biting back an exasperated sigh, she said, "I'm a friend," emphasizing each word.

The receptionist seemed to either not notice or not care. "He's in the medical assistance ward. Room M26—"

"—and where's that?"

A wan smile formed on her face. "Only family is allowed in that ward, ma'am." The last word dripped from her lips like rotten honey.

Jillian opened her mouth to argue, but the receptionist cut her off.

"—Unless …" The receptionist's eyes shifted to stare meaningfully at the small purse that hung from her shoulder. "I wouldn't want to come between two old friends. What about you, Henry?"

The security guard beside her chuckled lightly. "I'd hate to do that, but I'm supposed to make sure that people follow the rules." An arrogant smirk tugged at the corners of his mouth. "If I'm on break, perhaps an early dinner, I can't exactly stop you."

"Let me guess," Jillian said, "you're not the brown bag type?"

He shook his head. "I'm not much for PB&J. I was hoping to grab something from Mickey D's." He turned to the receptionist. "How about you, Taylor? Are you hungry?"

"I could go for a six piece nuggets and fries."

The security guard's smile broadened. "The thing is, though, I'm strapped for cash until pay day."

Jillian rolled her eyes, reaching for her purse. "Well, I can't have two responsible kids such as yourselves going hungry." Pulling a twenty dollar bill from inside, she held it out to him. When he reached for the money, she folded her fingers in towards her palm, pulling it out of his grasp. "For this, I expect there's going to be a line at the drive thru ... maybe you wait for them to fix the ice cream machine."

"This time of night? A Mickey D's run is always good for forty-five minutes."

She extended the bill again. "Bon appetit."

Snatching it from her fingers, Henry replied, "Gracias," before spinning on his heel and walking away.

Every instinct in her teacher's heart screamed at Jillian to point out to the boy the differences between Spanish and French. Instead, she turned to Taylor. "Isn't Veronica Moses's husband here, too?" The words might as well have been sand on her tongue.

"The drug dealer?"

Swallowing hard to bite back her anger, Jillian nodded.

"He's in M42. It's a fancy private room ... completely wasted on him."

Not trusting herself to speak, she nodded again.

"Mrs. Moses comes every day to visit him. If it was me, I would have dumped him so fast he would have gotten whiplash."

Faced with the the choice of slapping the taste out of Taylor's mouth and walking away, Jillian chose the latter.

*****

Richie's chest rose and fell rhythmically as he lay under a dingy, threadbare blanket. His face had a certain serenity, but his hollow cheeks and gray pallor made him almost unrecognizable. On the bedside table lay the pair of perpetually repaired glasses that he had worn since junior year. Beside them was a battered copy of J. R. R. Tolkien's *The Fellowship of the Ring*. The spine of the book had been lovingly repaired with clear tape after Billy Parr had torn it in half.

A yellowed curtain separated the room in half. Jillian assumed that Richie's roommate lay on the other side of it, but she hadn't pulled it aside to confirm her suspicion. For a moment, the awkward stillness in the room was only broken by the ragged sound of Richie's breathing. Seating herself carefully in the unforgiving wooden chair at his bedside, she gently took his hand.

"Hey, Richie ... it's Jillian," she started, unsure of herself. "I would have come sooner, but I just heard about your ... um ... accident."

Accident? she thought, *nice, why don't you just say suicide?*

"Well ... anyway, I'm sorry we lost touch after school." A wave of guilt crashed against her heart. "I should have made more of an effort. Maybe if you'd had someone to talk to, things wouldn't have gotten so bad."

Unsure of what else to say, Jillian allowed the room to fall into silence once more. She held his cold, limp hand between both of hers, hoping with all her might that their warmth brought her friend some comfort, however small. Watching his impassive face, she let her mind wander to her evening's true purpose. Would Stephen's hand feel as lifeless? Would she find herself at the same loss for words at his bedside?

Feeling suddenly ashamed, Jillian forced herself to be present in that moment. So many people had given up on Richie or simply overlooked him entirely, he deserved her full attention. "I'm so sorry this happened to you. You deserved ..." A liquid burning began behind her eyes as tears formed and began to roll down her cheeks. She squeezed his hand gently. "... you still deserve so much better."

In the stillness of the medical assistance ward, the echos of footsteps interrupted her tearful soliloquy. Laying Richie's hand down with as much care as she could, Jillian leapt to her feet. Peeking around the door frame, she saw the hallway was empty, but the telltale sounds of approaching people grew louder. Sprinting from the room, she was able to turn the corner before anyone appeared from the other direction.

Leaning heavily against the pale green painted surface of the cinder block wall, Jillian tried to quiet her breathing enough to hear what was happening in the hallway beyond her hiding place. The footfalls grew louder, matching pace with the pounding of her heart. She was preparing herself to duck into one of the half dozen open doors before her when they stopped just short of where she hid.

"Hello, Richie." It was a voice she recognized, but only because she had so recently heard it. It was Officer William Parr. Jillian heard the chair she had just vacated creak beneath Billy's weight. "So, when we last left our brave hobbits, they had entered the Barrow-Downs while fleeing the black riders." His voice was soft and soothing, a stark contrast to his interactions with Richie years before. "I think they may be in for some more trouble. Let's find out how much."

A smile crept onto Jillian's face. *Perhaps a leopard can change its spots after all. Apparently, I'm not the only one struggling with guilt over the last few years.* Turning to make her way down the hall towards room M42, she almost collided with a figure that had been standing behind her. Jillian had been so focused on the voices from Richie's room that she hadn't heard him approach.

Dressed in a simple black sports coat over the same color shirt and slacks, there was no mistaking the face that stared back at her. Although there was a white clerical collar at his throat, Jillian couldn't shake the nagging feeling of dread that gnawed at her guts as she stood in arms reach of Seran's reflection.

"Are you lost, miss?" he asked in a soft, almost gentle voice. "I still get turned around myself sometimes."

At a loss for words for the moment, Jillian just shrugged. Of all of the people Jillian had come to know through Asaege's eyes, with the possible exception of Plague Man, Hollis's mentor evoked the most dread in her. The thief's oldest friend, Seran was only nominally an ally as far as she was concerned.

"Perhaps I can be of some assistance."

Somehow the man standing before her seemed different, however. His eyes held a warmth that were lacking in those of his reflection. "Thank …" Jillian began, choking on her words as her mouth became suddenly dry with fear. Swallowing hard, she continued. "Thank you. I'm here visiting a friend."

"In the medical assistance ward?"

"Yes, he's just down the hall."

"Please accept my best wishes for both you and your friend. Sadly, the ward tends to be a longer term solution than I would like to see."

There was a compassion in his demeanor that Jillian thought Seran incapable of. "Thank you. We're trying to keep our hopes up." Turning to look behind her in an obvious searching gesture, she forced a smile to her face. "Like you said, I just needed to get my bearings. I'm sure I can find his room now."

For a second, a spark of recognition flashed in his dark eyes. A wry smirk teased the corners of his lips as he offered his hand. "My name is Reverend Albacete. I serve as the in-house chaplain for Church Hill."

She took his hand hesitantly, memories of his reflection still stirring the paranoia in her mind. "It's nice to meet you, Reverend."

"Please call me Mateo, if you like. One of my theology professors often said, 'Anyone who stands on ceremony is always on uncertain footing.' I'm not sure I understood his meaning at the time, but over the years I have come to appreciate it more and more."

"Thank you, Mateo, but I really should be getting to my friend's room. Visiting hours are almost over."

"I'm afraid that ship has sailed. They have been over for at least ten minutes, Miss ..." He paused, obviously expecting her to provide her name. When she didn't speak up, he said, "It occurs to me I never asked your name." His half-lidded eyes studied her in an all too familiar manner.

She debated lying to him but there was something in his stare that made her feel that it would be a fruitless gesture, only serving to make her seem more suspicious. "Jillian," she supplied.

"If it brings comfort to your friend, I see no harm in ignoring the posted visiting hours this once, Miss Jillian."

She felt her body relax, releasing the tension that had built up in her neck and shoulders like an overflowing levy.

"I'd advise you not tarry too long, however. The nurses may not share my forbearance."

Obviously, he and Seran share some qualities in common. He and his reflection seemed to hold a mutual fondness for five-dollar words. "Thank you again, Mateo."

"It was my pleasure, Miss Jillian."

She flinched as he reached into his jacket. Jillian's second-hand experience with Seran honed her paranoia to a fine edge. When his hand emerged with a business card rather than the expected weapon, Jillian chuckled at her clear overreaction.

"This is my office number as well as my cell." Curling it back towards his palm, Mateo flicked his fingers and flipped the card in one effortless motion. "My email is on the back. It's my role to comfort patients and loved ones alike." He held it out to her, a gentle smile gracing his face.

She took it and said, "Thanks again, Reverend."

Bobbing his head in a gesture of humble acknowledgment, he said, "Have yourself a nice evening." As he walked away, Jillian noticed that his hard soled shoes only seemed to echo in the empty hallway until he turned the corner.

*****

Thankfully, she was able to find room M42 without further

incident. The sorrow that seized Jillian's heart when she saw Stephen's condition in a photograph was a whisper compared to the cacophony of emotions that swept through her as she witnessed it in person. Hollis's reflection lay still as death beneath a colorfully patterned quilt; the various shades of green in the log cabin style pattern accentuated the pale skin of his hands as they lay across its surface. Asaege was unused to seeing the face she associated with his reflection freshly shaven. A trimmed horseshoe of hair graced the bald pate she associated with Hollis as well. She struggled with the overwhelming desire to rush across the room to him, to take those hands in her own.

Instead, she stood just inside the doorway, fists clenched at her sides. She had been wishing for a variation of that moment, dreaming of it for so long, but when it arrived, it wasn't at all what she imagined. The more she reflected, the less sure Jillian was of where her own feelings ended and where Asaege's began. *Could my infatuation with Stephen be nothing more than an echo of her love for Hollis?* The thought rang false as soon as it crossed her mind. As she stood just out of arms reach of Stephen, she felt a heat rise in her cheeks that had less to do with her reflection's passion than her own admiration for the man himself.

As she took a faltering step forward, the room swam before her eyes. Transposed over the heartbreaking scene of Stephen's room were flashes of a torch-lit tunnel. Reaching for the door frame, she closed her eyes and braced herself against its cold metal stability. A sensation of vertigo threatened to overcome her as the image before her continued moving despite the fact that she stood stock-still.

The inexplicable odors of mold and filth mingled with those of cleansers and bodily fluids expected in a hospital. A phantom chill clung to her bones despite the layers that had held the night's frigid bite at bay earlier. Against the backdrop of her clenched eyelids, the faraway scene continued to unfold. She could make out a half dozen figures ahead of her, their forms made hazy by the flickering torchlight. The tunnel through which she moved somehow looked familiar, although she had never personally laid eyes on it.

Exhaling slowly, Jillian tried to force her pounding in her chest to subside through will alone. She was only marginally successful. The staccato beating of her heart in her ears eased slightly; it was enough for her to partially gather her wits. Since she had begun reflecting, her connection to Asaege had increased. Jillian was often able to call upon her memories and emotions, but never before had she experienced Taerh while still awake.

Taking a measured breath, she put from her mind the nauseating cocktail of stenches from both worlds that seemed to cling to the back of her throat. Her own fear mixed with that of her reflection, each building on the other. Exhaling again, Jillian pictured those negative emotions flowing from her body along with her breath. Forcing her eyes open, she tightened her grip on the door frame as she felt her knees weaken beneath her. The duplicity of the conflicting images before her caused her stomach to lurch.

Come on, Jillian, she chided herself, *you can do this*. Focusing on the scene that was more real—at least to her—she willed that of Asaege's journey through the Underfoot to fade. It began as only a slight feathering at the edges, but quickly her vision of Taerh fell in on itself like a collapsing balloon. Jillian still felt her reflection's presence in the back of her mind, stronger than ever before, but her perception belonged to her alone once more.

The room looked just as it had before her episode; Stephen remained unconscious and still beneath the fashionable quilt. Somehow, everything seemed to have taken on a darker aspect. The stillness of the ward suddenly seemed oppressive, as if something waited just out of sight to prey upon the unwary. Even the sight of Stephen in the bed was affected.

Where he appeared at peace previously, now Jillian could not help but see the entire scene as carefully staged. The room itself was bare of anything extraneous. Missing were any cards or well wishes. Only a vase of fresh cut flowers stood on the table beside the bed, the water held within crystal clear. Absent as well was any sign of occupation. Any cables or wires attached to the machines that flanked Stephen were meticulously lain across his body or tied out of sight.

This contrasted starkly with the state of Richie's room, where everything appeared to be set up in a way to make access as convenient as possible for his caregivers. It seemed to Jillian that the room and its sole occupant were primarily meant to be a photo opportunity and Stephen's care was of secondary concern. *Another sin that can be laid at the feet of the esteemed Veronica Moses.*

She took a cautious step forward and was again besieged by the personality of her reflection. Prepared for it, Jillian furrowed her brow and focused on her own perceptions. The acrid smell of bleach and urine. The sandpaper dry air against her skin. The infuriatingly staged image before her. Although she was more aware of the other world than she had ever been while awake, Jillian remained rooted in her own.

Another few steps brought her to Stephen's bedside. Looking

down at the face she knew so well, yet had never seen with her own eyes, she felt a yearning that belonged to her alone. Through Asaege, Jillian had come to know Hollis. Through the thief, she had come to care for a man she had never met.

Chapter Sixteen
An Unwelcome Gaze

The man sat in the dim confines of the room across from Stephen's, still as a guilty thought. Perpetually empty, the space afforded him a convenient vantage point from which to observe any after-hours visitors. When he saw the woman skulking through the hallway, he was able to backtrack quickly enough to reach the shadowed safety of his refuge before she reached the bedside of his charge.

He had debated intervening when he first saw her, but decided against it. His employer might disagree with his choice, as was her right; however, he felt it was the most prudent course of action. There was no telling who the woman was or, more importantly, who knew of her nocturnal destination, at least not yet. There would be time to discover those things and more. If she posed a threat to their plans, he would eliminate her as he had Freeholder Fredericks.

When she tentatively reached down to take Stephen's hand, the man almost regretted his inaction. His employer would want to know someone had been to see Mr. Moses. It would no doubt be an uncomfortable conversation, but there would be no avoiding that. Once he had not intervened to prevent her entry, it had become prudent to allow the situation to play out.

The man's hopes that Stephen's unauthorized visitor would

tarry long enough for the night shift nurse to catch her mid-dalliance were dashed as the appointed time came and went without anyone checking on him. The shadowed observer made a mental note to bring it up with his employer. He was sure that they would ensure such a lapse never happened again.

He settled back in the chair, sinking further into the shadows, as the woman crept to the door. After verifying that she wasn't being observed, she exited the room and hurried down the hallway. *If she only knew,* the man thought to himself as she disappeared from sight.

Chapter Seventeen
A Scalding Reception

The clamor of steel-on-steel assaulted Asaege's ears as soon as she emerged into the close air of the small warehouse. After the confines of the tunnels, she had hoped to have a moment to revel in her freedom from them before being thrown into the conflict that raged in the streets of the Dock Quarter. Alas, it was not to be.

Judging by the volume and direction of din, the life and death struggle lay mere yards from where Asaege and her small group stood. That small distance and the building's thin walls were all that separated them from the tide they intended to turn.

"The damn fools have led them back here," Toni cursed. "After tonight, this whole section of tunnels will be useless to us."

While Asaege agreed with their assessment, she also sympathized with the rebels' terror-born desire to escape at any cost. With the fighting close at hand, she felt the need to jump into the fray; that urgency cooled somewhat when she felt the powerful syllables of thaumaturgical magic resonate in her bones. Unheard but still recognized, the words of power reminded Asaege of her hesitation in the Silver Courtesan. *None of these people can afford me to freeze up again*, she chided herself, *myself least of all*.

During Asaege's brief moment of introspection, all eyes had expectantly turned to her. The weight of those gazes compounded the already-hefty guilt she carried for the hours since fleeing the brothel. Although not as intense as in the Underfoot, she felt Jillian's presence at the fringes of her thoughts. Her reflection's conviction strengthened her own.

"If this place is lost to us, then let us collect its full worth from those who would take it from us." Asaege hoped that when said out loud, her words were as inspiring as they had been in her mind. More than that, though, she hoped that no one had heard the quiver in her voice as she spoke them.

Toni led the charge, throwing open the wooden door leading to the alley beyond. Once that fragile barrier was removed, the sounds of combat seemed to be right beside Asaege. Four guild thieves followed their leader, short chopping swords already drawn. As she moved to join them, the arcane words to match the pounding against her chest became audible.

Pulling up short, Asaege strained to identify the formulae that hung in the air. Based on the soft vowels and almost song like tempo, she narrowed the spell's general category to either enchantment or conjuration. By their natures, both thaumaturgical fields of study shared many qualities in common. Unfortunately, her revelation came too late to affect its intended outcome.

A wash of superheated air slammed into her like a blast furnace. For a tense second all the sounds of battle fell into silence. Only the soft crackling of flames reached Asaege's ears. As suddenly as the stillness had fallen, it was split by cries of agony. Taking a small step into the doorway, her stomach twisted in fear and revulsion at the sight that greeted her.

Flanked on either side by two story warehouses, the tight passage was clogged with a thick, almost sweet-smelling smoke. Vague silhouettes moved within the billowing confines of the swirling cloud, occasionally thrown into stark contrast by the tongues of fire that licked at their bodies. The only thing Asaege could make out with any clarity, flitting amidst the panicked figures like a toddler on holiday, was a waist high creature of animated flame. Lirych had conjured a fire elemental to do his bidding.

By their very nature, elementals were beings of pure chaos. Fickle and stubborn, they were either incapable or uninterested in communication with any but their own kind. The closest a thaumaturge could achieve to control of one was aiming it in the general direction of their enemy and setting it loose. This was precisely what Lirych had done. Rebel and guardsman alike fled from the creature's scorching tendrils. Amid the screams and pleas for aid, Asaege swore the sizzling and snapping almost sounded like laughter.

She released a marginal amount of her control over the formulae pressing against her thoughts. Immediately, a barrage of esoteric phrases rushed forward, each one straining to blot out the others in their mad rush to be set free from their intellectual prison. Asaege had studied the spells earlier, committing each word to memory for use at a later time. For one of them, that time had come.

Closing her eyes against the fury pressing against her mind, she isolated the words of the formula she sought. *Sarcune's Spectral Shield* summoned before her a patch of glowing yet still-translucent energy. The barrier would absorb any physical force thrown against it, no matter its source. Stepping into the alley, Asaege prayed that would include the immolating caress of the creature before her. The description of the formula in her inherited spell book was unsettlingly vague on that point.

On the pages following those detailing *Sarcune's Spectral Shield*, there had been a more appropriate, but much more complicated spell. She cursed herself for not examining *Duraethur's Dimensional Bulwark* more carefully. Created specifically to deal with entities not native to Taerh, the more advanced formula would have made combating the fire elemental much easier.

Reigning in the remainder of the unspoken spells, she continued into the roiling bank of smoke and ash. She passed a body so badly burned that she was unsure if they had started the day as ally or enemy. Memories of Claerius's charred face leapt into her mind. Forcing them from her thoughts, Asaege approached the blazing center of the billowing cloud.

The elemental's rippling form flowed across the ground, undulating tentacles of flame lashing out at her hungrily. Asaege winced as the first flaming limb contacted the ghostly surface of her spell. Her shield held against its assault, but its pale blue glow flashed an angry red in response to the fiery touch. Although *Sarcune's Spectral Shield* deflected the flames themselves, it did nothing to diminish the skin searing heat that they produced. Asaege was forced to close her eyes against the wash of blistering air that swept across her skin like a desert wind.

Even if the protective energy could prevent the elemental from setting her ablaze, the heat its flailing attacks brought with them would eventually fry her with no less certainty. However, Asaege noticed with rising concern that with each whip-crack strike of its blazing tentacles, the glow of her shield dimmed. The spell was meant to forestall physical attacks, not the elemental's primal barrage.

133

The creature surged forward in an angry burst, thrashing wildly against the barrier in an effort to shatter it and reach Asaege. Each blow exploded against the rapidly weakening shield, buffeting her with a super-heated blast of air. In the midst of the assault, Asaege found inspiration.

After losing control of *Intrae's Instant Immolation* in the Silver Courtesan, she had no wish to commit the formula to memory so soon. In its place, she had gone in the opposite direction and chosen *Gaxby's Forceful Gale*. Trying to put from her mind the savage assault quickly barraging her defenses, Asaege relaxed her control once more and allowed the incantation to surge forward.

As the words fell from her lips, she caged the other spells trying to force their way free in the prison of her will. Even before she uttered the formula's final syllable, a cool breeze began to caress her skin. For the moment, the stinging pain on her face abated. The gentle current quickly built, doubling itself in the space of breath.

The elemental's barrage slowed, although it wasn't for the creature's lack of effort. It continued to launch strike after strike in Asaege's direction, but the building wind dissipated each blazing tendril before it could reach the mystical barrier between them. The elemental surged forward angrily in an effort to overwhelm the shield with its mass. She saw that, as it approached, the fire that made up its body began to dance in the building wind.

Narrowing her eyes, Asaege focused her attention on the creature. Like a candle placed too close to a draft, its flames began to flicker. Mustering her concentration, she gathered the erratic currents around her into one concerted zephyr. In the blink of an eye, the elemental was extinguished, banished to its fiery home. Asaege used the last vestiges of the spell to clear the smoke from the tight confines of the alley. Like a curtain being pulled back, her efforts revealed the smiling face of Lirych.

*****

"Hello, again," Lirych cooed. "As hard as it will be for you to believe, it truly is nice to see you again." His voice was sweet to the point of being cloying. "I do so wish that it had been under different circumstances."

"Why is that?"

"My employers feel that the revolution has been going on too long."

"Is that so?" Asaege hoped to keep the mercenary thaumaturge talking long enough to bring to mind one of the last two spells that strained at her self control. Choosing between *Flynn's Float-*

ing Trance and *Murdael's Murder Flies* wasn't a difficult one. The former was the most rudimentary spell of levitation while the latter was a particularly nasty conjuration formula. Precisely as it sounded, *Murdael's Murder Flies* summoned a swarm of thumb-sized, flesh-eating insects, a nightmare brought to life.

"The fact that the passage of ships into and out of the city has been affected represents a rather substantial embarrassment to them. As such, the revolutionary forces' control of the docks must be broken."

"So you thought releasing a fire elemental in the middle of the Dock Quarter was the best way to accomplish that?" Allowing her eyes to grow unfocused, Asaege brought the words of the formula into the forefront of her mind.

"It seemed the most expedient given my understanding of the situation at the time. I am afraid that my contract in this matter is very specific: no rebel is to be left alive." Lirych shrugged helplessly. "I have a feeling that you and your friends are meant to be a lesson to your fellows. There is little that can be done about it."

Even if she wanted to respond to him, Asaege would have been unable. The arcane phrases in her thoughts launched forth from her mouth as if they had a mind of their own. As soon as the first syllable was spoken, a low drone began to rise from all around her. Asaege tried to put from her mind the thoughts of the destruction which the insects she summoned were truly capable. *At least my spell is focused at a single target, unlike his scorched field tactics.* She wasn't sure that her rationalizations would absolve her of the guilt afterward, but Lirych had made his intentions crystal clear.

The mercenary thaumaturge's saccharine smile dissolved like a hand full of sugar in the rain as he recognized the incantation. Without further comment, Lirych let words of power fall from his lips. Although she knew the timbre and cadence as conjuration, the organization of his formula somehow seemed wrong. It wasn't until she felt the power drawn in by her own spell disappearing as quickly as it gathered that she realized his purpose.

He must have realized that no matter what formulae he had at his disposal, anything he could cast would be woefully too late. Even if he could complete an incantation before the murderous insects reached him, there were only a few that could stop them from devouring his flesh. Lirych had instead elected to use the raw force of one of the spells committed to his memory to counter-weave her casting of *Murdael's Murder Flies*.

Asaege remembered reading about the process but, like most

of the massive book given to her by Hollis, it was more complex than she felt comfortable attempting. Obviously, Lirych had no such doubts as to his ability. The power around her continued to slip from her grasp like water through cheesecloth. As she let the incantation fall into silence, she felt the arcane syllables fade from her memory like a prematurely ended dream. Drawing the Uteli short sword at her waist, Asaege closed the distance between them before he realized she had stopped chanting.

Looking up in shock at the sound of her footsteps, only Lirych's instincts saved him from being disemboweled, but the razor-sharp blade still slashed through his silk shirt and opened a deep gash across his stomach. Pressing her advantage, Asaege brought the Talis Fahr down in a backhanded cut that caused her opponent to continue to scramble backwards. In the mad rush to avoid her sword, all Lirych could do was fumble for his own weapon. Her furious assault left him no opportunity to call upon any thaumaturgical formulae that remained in his mind.

Once he was able to free his Mantrian long sword from its scabbard, Lirych tried to bring it to bear, but Asaege refused to him the space to do so. Each step of distance he surrendered, she gladly accepted in order to stay within the perfect range for her own weapon while denying him full usage of his own. In the back of her mind, she could hear Seran's taunting voice. *Fighting is more than thrusts and parries, little girl. Frustration has killed more people than any technique known to man.* Despite the fact that each time they sparred, Asaege held the advantage of her longer weapon, she could never quite wipe the smirk off of the infuriating man's face. It was her hope that she could evoke in Lirych a measure of the vexation she felt in those moments.

"Help me, you fools!" His voice quivered with effort of keeping Asaege's blade from his flesh. A flash of fear crept up her spine, envisioning a group of guardsmen at her back. She hazarded a glance over her shoulder and immediately realized her mistake. Toni and her people held off a large detachment of soldiers at the mouth of the alley. None of the men who had weathered the elemental's attack seemed interested in coming to Lirych's aid, no matter which side they had owed allegiance to before he set it loose in their midst.

However, Asaege's lapse in concentration provided her opponent with the respite he sorely needed. She cursed to herself as he was finally able to put enough distance between them to extend his straight-bladed sword into a proper guard. She lunged towards him, but he easily beat back her assault. Unhurriedly, Lirych's lips began

136

to move. The words barely brushed Asaege's ears but she could feel their power, nonetheless. Each word struck her heart, eroding the confidence she had built in the previous moments. He spoke deliberately, each syllable measured, allowing him to continue to defend himself while gathering his spell.

Asaege reached into the back of her mind, praying that she would find more than a simple levitation formula there. What she found brought a gradual smile to her lips. Having made use of adder root before drifting off in her world, Jillian was waking in Taerh. Her reflection's presence lifted Asaege's spirits, giving her a sudden burst of courage. "Alright, Lirych," she said more to herself than the man before her. "Let us dance." Rapid fire bursts of images flashed before her mind's eye. Laid before her was the entirety of her prized spell book.

Immediately, she decided on one of the incantations written on the recalled pages, more for the speed with which it could be cast. *Podrae's Forceful Push* was a very simple formula, taught to most apprentices as a skill-building exercise. Unimaginatively named, it functioned just as one would expect from its title. Its only purpose was to generate a substantial, if not particularly deadly, surge of force. If unexpected, however, it could easily knock a full-grown adult from their feet … or disrupt the necessarily consistent rhythm of a thaumaturgical incantation.

Thrown off balance, Lirych was forced to windmill his arms to maintain his balance. Asaege felt the power he had been gathering evaporate into the ether as his concentration turned to the more pressing matter of keeping himself upright. Quickly turning the page in her mind, she searched the alley for an object to use with her next spell. Lying on the cobblestones was a wooden gear, part of a broken tackle.

Closing her eyes for a split second, Asaege spoke the words on the page in her memory. The natural evolution of the formula that had staggered Lirych, *Balm's Forceful Barrage* imparted the same momentum to a small object. She snapped her lids open in time to see the piece of debris strike the mercenary thaumaturge in the chest. Queasiness and satisfaction warred within Asaege at the muted cracking of his ribs. In the end, satisfaction won.

The images of the casualties of Lirych's reckless summoning sprung to her mind, friend and foe alike. Asaege felt Jillian's revulsion and anger as intensely as her own. Without conscious thought, her memory turned to a page she knew all too well, the one that held *Intrae's Instant Immolation*. The sensation of performing thauma-

137

turgy was invigorating, bordering on addictive. The more spells she cast, the more it felt like falling into a rushing river. The power held within the formulae carried her along so that all that mattered was the act of commanding it.

Asaege glared at Lirych. The man held his sword before him one-handed. His other arm was wrapped protectively over his broken ribs, his breathing coming in short, tentative gasps. Gritting her teeth, she dismissed both the memory and her thoughts of vengeance from her mind. *He is beaten,* she thought. *He can barely breathe, much less cast.* He didn't deserve her mercy, but she wasn't doing it for him. *When magic becomes the end rather than the means, the motivation for its use, then I prove to be no better than he is.*

"Asaege!" Toni's call broke her out of her self-reflection. Stepping backwards, Asaege kept Lirych in her peripheral vision as she turned to see the guild-master rushing towards her. On their heels was only half the number of rebels that had emerged from the Underfoot minutes ago. "We need to go," they hissed. "Now."

A squad of templars, armored and fresh, stood in the mouth of the alley. "The Olmites choose now to make a stand?" She felt the weariness in her own voice.

Interlacing their fingers in her blouse, Toni pulled Asaege after them. "It seems the Crimson Sister has made her decision."

Chapter Eighteen
A Tested Bond

Jillian came to her senses slowly, the comforting gray and mauve confines of her own bedroom not assuaging the conflict that raged within her. Asaege's second experience with Cyrill's reflection had been more disturbing than her first, but together they had proven equal to the task. She tried to put the intense craving that casting so much magic in such a short time had awakened in her from her mind. More frightening than the longing that still clung to her heart, even a world away, was the apathy it induced in her to the circumstances of those around her.

Throwing off the heavy down comforter and rolling to her feet, Jillian felt the brief head rush that came with rising too quickly. For once, she reveled in the soda-pop carbonation disorientation; it offset the vestiges of that unsympathetic longing. Forced to close her eyes against the sensation, she took a few deep breaths to push through it. When it had cleared, all that remained of the craving was its memory.

Jillian walked rapidly down the narrow hallway leading to the living area of her small apartment. Its tight confines reminded Jillian a little too much of the claustrophobic depths of the Underfoot. The room at the end of the short corridor was just as she'd left it the previous evening after returning from Church Hill, her purse and laptop bag casually thrown beside the coat on her futon-couch.

Jillian snatched the remote from the low coffee table and turned on the television. After the vicarious adventures seen through Asaege's eyes, its pillow-strewn surface looked inviting. She forced herself to walk past it and into the small galley kitchen.

The sound of the morning news was an indistinct drone in the background, but Jillian preferred it to the soundtrack of her internal monologue that silence encouraged. Even through its influence, the loudest of her thoughts broke through.

What does it mean that Stephen is still alive? Is his wife keeping him in that wretched place as nothing more than a prop in her public relations campaign? The timing of Veronica's rise to power on earth and Lady Markov's own sudden influence among the Council of Guilds in Oizan just seems too coincidental. Similarly, I can't believe that Seran's reflection popping up at Church Hill was just an unfortunate accident.

The unanswered questions stemming from Jillian's visit to the long-term care center compounded her already oppressive anxiety over the changes she perceived in Cyrill. Her friend and his reflection seemed to be such polar opposites. *But are they really?* she thought. Despite knowing him since they were children, Jillian and he had only had grown close in college. Before that, Cyrill had always struck her as too much a fan of himself.

Amid the ever changing tides of teenage popularity, Cyrill had been a disturbingly constant fixture among the in-crowd, no matter the composition of the rest of the group. Popular throughout high school, it was only after he lost the support system he had built there that they had become friends. *What kind of man would he have grown into had that bastion not been denied him during that pivotal time? Am I seeing his true nature or is Lirych a more accurate representation of his character?*

An acrid burning stench interrupted the downward spiral of Jillian's thoughts. Looking down, she saw the blackened wreckage of her breakfast. Jerking the pan from the flame, she turned the burner off with a flick of her wrist. Dropping it to the stove-top with more force than intended, she stalked from the kitchen. As she turned to face the television, Jillian was greeted by the face of Veronica Moses.

"... such a tremendous loss. I'm certainly no stranger to tragedy but the loss of Martin Fredericks has struck me, has struck us all, particularly hard." Mrs. Moses averted her eyes for a long second before seizing the camera in her hard gaze, a single tear standing out against the pristine backdrop of her pale cheek. The gesture seemed too smooth, too practiced. "Our thoughts and prayers are with his family in this difficult time. I understand how important those can be at such a heartbreaking moment." The tear picked up speed, rolling down her face. "As you know, I lost my husband to a drug overdose several months ago. The support of those around me meant so much. As we bid farewell to Freeholder Fredericks tonight, I hope that the great people of this county do not let his legacy die with him."

Jillian's stomach turned as she realized the woman's intent.

"Martin and I had lunch a few days before his death. He had been an incredible support in my campaign to take back the pillars of our educational system. In a short time, we in the Coalition for Academic Responsibility and Excellence have managed to gain traction on many school and library boards. The final gift we intended to give to the youth of the county, both present and future is true legislative change to ensure both their safety and welfare." Veronica reached up and dramatically brushed away the tear. "Freeholder Fredericks expressed to me how important that is to the well-being of our children." She looked away again, her voice trembling slightly. "That's why I can't let my dear friend's dream go unfulfilled." Snapping her eyes up, Mrs. Moses's voice hardened. "I am officially announcing my acceptance of his seat on the Board of Elected Freeholders."

Jillian sat down on the couch, her legs suddenly weak. *Days after his death, the woman is snatching Fredericks's seat before it's even cold.*

Her words more satisfied than somber, Veronica concluded, "You can rest now, dear friend. Those of us that loved you will carry on in your name."

*****

Jillian returned to school to find the substitute had ignored her filed lesson plans. Her morning passed in an uneasy blur of irritation and anxiety. As she watched her students walk towards the cafeteria, she only felt a measure of it lift from her spirit. Remediating the classroom setbacks, however annoying, had served as an ample distraction from the less immediate but equally pressing matters that held her mind in their grasps like a vise.

Questions about Lady Markov and her earthly reflection still weighed on Jillian's thoughts. The more she contemplated them, the less comfortable she felt dismissing them as coincidence. On the few occasions Hollis had mentioned Stephen's wife, he had always given Asaege the impression that she was more idle parasite than politically savvy crusader.

From what Jillian could gather about Markov from her own reflection's limited knowledge of the woman, she was the daughter of

141

a well known, if not particularly powerful, merchant family. Known among the servant-class of the Ash as petty and vindictive, there was little to differentiate her from others of her station. Inheriting her father's seat on the council after his death, Asaege remembered little else of note about Lady Markov until a short time ago.

Like an itch she couldn't quite scratch, the ghost of an idea remained just out of reach. Closing her eyes, Jillian focused on what she knew. *The two women floated on the tide of mediocrity until they both seemed to develop a desire for more about six months ago.* Like a ray of sun emerging through a gash in the clouds, the light of re-alization illuminated her perception of the situation. *Six months ago ... the same time Hollis activated the Well of Worlds, the same time Stephen fell into a coma.*

Jillian remembered the first time she experienced reflection as more than inexplicably detailed dreams. Hollis had been beside Asaege in her small second story room. Both she and her reflection had assumed it had been his experience with the phenomenon that had reduced the distance between them. What if his instruction had been only part of it? What if, by virtue of his presence, the thief had weakened the barrier between Earth and Taerh? Suddenly, the increased intensity of the bond shared with Asaege at Stephen's bed-side made perfect sense.

Through his experience in the Well of Worlds, Hollis and his reflection didn't merely share a soul, they were effectively the same one. From what he and Aristoi had told her, when the mystical well consolidated the consciousness of one of its "children," the earth-bound member of the pair died, pruned like the dormant stem of a rose bush, to maintain the health of that which remains. *What would happen if, whether through interference or fortune, that elimination couldn't occur?*

"I was concerned when I didn't hear from you this morning." She was so lost in her thoughts that Marisol's voice caused her to jump. "I'm not sure if seeing you daydreaming in the doorway of your classroom is any less distressing."

Jillian spun on her friend, Marisol's levity providing a momen-tary balm for the dizzying complications making her mind spin. "It's been a morning."

"So I've gathered. Mrs. Shelton took your class yesterday. No one can tell her how to teach a class. After all, she has—"

"—thirty-five years in the classroom," Jillian joined in. Both she and Marisol had their fair share of experiences with the substitute teacher. Despite the weight of her thoughts, Jillian couldn't help but

142

laugh with her friend.

"You'll get past it," Marisol counseled. "Even Sheltie can't do that much damage in one day."

Still chuckling, Jillian said, "You wouldn't think so, but this morning felt a lot like a rigged game of whack-a-mole."

"Did you get 'em all?"

"I think so." Jillian took a deep breath, exhaling slowly. "I needed that. How's your day going?"

"In their minds, my kids are already on winter break. It's been like riding a bucking bronco all day."

With everything going on, the upcoming holidays had slipped Jillian's mind. With her parents in southern California for the winter, she was most likely spending them alone anyway.

It was a credit to Marisol that she noticed the change in her friend's demeanor. "I'm not sure what you're doing, but the family would love for you to join us for Christmas dinner." Before Jillian could argue, she added, "My mother's making her turkey."

Jillian felt her mouth begin to water. "I do love your mom's turkey. Can I let you know?"

"Of course." Frowning, Marisol tilted her head. "It's not the holidays that have you down, is it?"

Before she could think better of it, Jillian said, "It's not."

"Would you care to share?"

As close to her as a sister, she always felt comfortable talking to Marisol. Their conversations always shed enough light onto a problem that it never felt quite as daunting afterward. Since her first reflection, Jillian had avoided the subject with her friend for fear of the woman's reaction. That fear warred with the guilt of keeping such an important aspect of her life from the woman that had often been her only confidant. Just the prospect of sharing her secret with someone outside of Taerh felt like a weight lifting from Jillian's chest.

"You know what? I think I very well might."

"Fantastic." Marisol watched her expectantly.

"Not here. What are you doing after work?"

"Coming over to your place so you can tell me all about it." There wasn't a trace of a question in her words.

"How about five o'clock?"

"I'll grab Chinese on the way. Won-ton soup and Singapore noodles?"

"You know me too well." Jillian wondered if her friend would ever look at her the same way again.

*****

143

Jillian had almost changed her mind by the time the doorbell rang. Marisol was her closest friend; the woman's respect meant more to her than the minor catharsis unburdening herself could offer. A cold sheen of sweat formed on Jillian's brow as her mind furiously searched for an alternate path of discussion. Her secret had been so built up by her unwillingness to discuss it earlier, Jillian was not sure Marisol would easily let the matter drop.

Forcing a smile to her face, Jillian opened the door. Marisol stood on the wide concrete steps leading to her apartment two bulging plastic bags clutched in her hands. "Dinner!" she announced in a much-too-chipper voice.

"Finally." Jillian tried to match her tone but failed, even to her own ears. "I'm starving."

Marisol laughed and stepped past her into the tight alcove. "I couldn't decide between shrimp toast and dumplings." Smiling guiltily, she added, "So I got them both."

Jillian locked the door behind her before following her friend up the stairs. By the time she reached the top, Marisol had begun unpacking the bags onto the recently cleared table. Looking around the apartment, Jillian felt a tinge of pride at how quickly she had been able to declutter its common areas. It had been at the expense of the small bedroom at the end of the hall, but no matter how honest she chose to be, she had no intention of letting that particular secret slip.

"Let me grab us some plates," Jillian announced as she walked into the kitchen. "Can I grab you something to drink? I have water …" She opened the refrigerator and was suddenly reminded of how long it had been since she went shopping. "… or water. Sorry."

"Water is fine," Marisol called, her voice muted by the dumpling already in her mouth.

"Two waters coming up." Jillian clutched both glasses between the fingers of one hand while she carried the stacked plates in the other. Her friend had already opened one of the white paper boxes and dug in with the wooden chopsticks provided with their order. "Did I need to bother with plates?"

The expression of a child caught with their hand in the cookie jar plain on her face, Marisol simply shrugged. "Only if you want to be fancy."

*****

With their bellies full of Chinese food, Jillian and Marisol sat on the more reasonably cushioned futon-couch. Under most circumstances, Jillian would have felt at complete ease beside her closest friend. On that night, however, a tense silence hung between

144

them. Marisol waited patiently as Jillian rolled the best way to begin around in her mind.

"So, you wanted to know what has been bothering me …"

Marisol nodded, a sudden look of apprehension taking over her features. "Yes. It's not something I did, is it?"

Jillian squinted, taken out of her game plan by her friend's question. "You? Of course not, Mari. Why would you think that?"

She shrugged. "You've been a little distant the last few months. You invited me over to talk about it. I assumed it was a permutation of 'the talk.'"

With the anticipatory stress that had been building all afternoon, Marisol's understandable assumption caused Jillian to laugh nervously. "I'm sorry if I gave you that impression. You are so very dear to me. This has everything to do with me … well not precisely everything … but …" She searched for a way to get back on track.

Marisol rested her hand on Jillian's arm. "Take a deep breath and start from the beginning."

Jillian closed her eyes and sighed. Laying her hand over Marisol's, she squeezed it lightly. "The beginning. I wish it was that easy." Meeting her friend's gaze, she said, "Mari, you have to promise me one thing. I'm going to tell you some crazy things, things that I didn't completely believe myself at first. You have to listen with an open mind and let me finish."

"Of course," Marisol quickly replied.

If only she realized what she's promising, Jillian thought. "Do you remember the man I mentioned a few months back?"

"Yes, the gentle, dangerous scoundrel. Did something happen? Did he hurt you?"

"Yes. No. Let me get this out, please. I'm not sure I can get though it more than once."

Marisol's eyes were filled with questions, but she denied them a voice.

"His name is Hollis. It is also Stephen."

Marisol opened her mouth, but was able to restrain her curiosity enough to remain silent.

"It didn't actually begin with him, but it might as well have." Standing, Jillian walked to the collection of pots that took up most of the floor space closest to the apartment's large windows. Picking one up, she brought it back to where Marisol sat expectantly. Handing her the pot, Jillian sat down on the futon again. "That is adder root. It's thought to be a distant relative of rattlesnake root but the effects of the two plants could not be more different. While its cousin claims to be able to cure everything from asthma to snake bites, adder root has a very specific use."

She mustered the courage to continue. *Now for the hard part.* "When consumed, it induces a deep slumber during which you see things, experience things not of this world."

Unable to contain herself any longer, Marisol said, "It's a drug? A hallucinogen like LSD?"

Jillian shook her head. "I wish it were that simple. There is another world parallel to our own, separated not by distance but instead by some sort of barrier. While asleep, adder root allows a dreamer's consciousness to slip through that barrier and into the mind of a version of themselves on the other side."

"Like an evil twin?"

"Not always. You and your reflection share either the best or worst parts of each other."

"Reflection?"

"It's the term Hollis uses. Your duplicate is known as your reflection, thus the act of traveling to Taerh is called reflecting."

"And Stephen is?"

"Hollis's reflection ... or Hollis is Stephen's. In the end it all amounts to the same thing." Jillian felt a pleading tone invading her voice. "I know it sounds insane, like the rambling of an addict or crazy person. I didn't believe it at first either. I've seen things Mari, both here and in that world, that have no other explanation. Do you remember that Sherlock Holmes quote?"

Still reeling, Marisol raised a questioning eyebrow.

"When you have eliminated the impossible, whatever remains, however improbable, must be the truth."

"This is pretty improbable."

"But, as it turns out, not quite impossible."

"If you say so."

The look of disbelief in Marisol's eyes came close to breaking Jillian's heart. *Have I irrevocably shattered the closest friendship I've had in years?* "Do you trust me?"

"You have to understand how unbelievable this all is."

"Do you trust me?" Jillian repeated.

As much as it stung, her friend contemplated the answer to her question. Biting her bottom lip, Marisol slowly nodded. "I would trust you with my life, Jillie ..." She let her words trail off.

"But?"

Another silence hung in the air for what seemed to Jillian to be forever. Finally Marisol broke it. "But nothing, Jillian. I trust you,

146

full stop."

"I want to show you."

Hesitation warred with curiosity on Marisol's face. "How does it work? I don't like needles and the last time I smoked, I got bronchitis."

Jillian chuckled. "I originally discovered adder root when Cyrill gave me some pot laced with it. Thanks to Hollis, I learned how to make tea from it. With my dealer gone, that's become the only way to reflect."

"He is gone as in ..." Trepidation dripped from Marisol's voice.

Jillian reached for the tin containing her latest batch of dried adder root. "One thing at a time. I'll only give you a little to start ..."

Chapter Nineteen
A Sickening Display

The atmosphere that greeted Asaege as she emerged from the Underfoot was markedly different than when they returned from the Silver Courtesan. The survivors of the Dock Quarter wore weary smiles, despite the half-dozen victims of Lirych's arrogance who still lay among the scorched cobblestones of the alley in which they died. Even Toni's normally steady demeanor had skewed towards celebratory, when they shared a brief one armed embrace with one of their apprentices.

Accepting Toni's offered hand, Asaege allowed them to help her to her feet. "Not too shabby."

"Thanks?" Asaege's confusion was evident in her questioning tone. While she celebrated their escape, its cost weighed at her heart.

"Markov's hired thaumaturge will think twice before locking horns with you."

Before she realized what was happening, Asaege was surrounded by a vague cloud of grinning faces. The cacophony of praise around her blended together until it sounded more like the panicked squawking of barn fowl than congratulations. Hands patted and squeezed her from every direction, filling Asaege with a burning desire to flee their presence. Occasionally snippets of order stood out amid the clamor.

"... make them give us our due ..."

"... Asaege showed them what true power is ..."

"... only a matter of time before the council flees like the dogs they are ..."

"... snuffed the flame beast out like a candle ..."

If only they knew how thin my margins of success had been from the moment we stepped into that alley. Asaege shuddered at the thought of what could have been ... if she had been a breath slower with her formulae, if Jillian had not reflected at that very moment.

Brushing off the clinging grasps around her, Asaege pushed her way through the crowd and rushed from the room. In her wake, she left shocked faces and murmurs of confusion. As she reached the calm bastion of the hallway, she heard a soft voice behind her.

"Thaumaturgy requires more than good intentions and pretty words. No doubt, Asaege needs some time to compose herself after such a resounding victory."

Turning quickly, she saw Seran's slim silhouette leaning against the door frame. Although she had walked right by him, Asaege hadn't noticed the elder thief. Beside him was the ever-present shadow of the boy he'd rescued from the Ivory Cathedral. Past him, a few stragglers that had meant to follow her into the hall seemed to have thought better of the idea.

"Thank you," she said, her voice flat with exhaustion.

He spread his hands apart and bowed his head slightly. "It was my pleasure, but it also was not for you."

Asaege raised an eyebrow.

"The people in there need a win. In their desperation to find one, they will make diamonds out of pig shit if need be."

"And when their fervor fades, they will find their hands covered in manure."

Seran shrugged. "That may very well be the case, but there is nothing to be gained in pointing that out now."

"People died, Seran, people that I am responsible for."

"Had you not intervened, how many more would have joined them? You count the losses. Perhaps that makes you a good leader." He indicated the celebrating figures behind him with a tilt of his head. "Those people only know that you came for them. They saw you risk your life to bring them home. Magic is something they will never understand, only fear. It has been a tool of the rich, used to keep them in their place for so long that when one of their own is able to match their practitioners spell for spell, it gives them hope."

"I did not exactly—"

Seran cut her off. "—in their minds you did. In this case, reality matters less than their perception of it."

Asaege looked past him, this time with new eyes. The mill stone of revolution grinds down everyone involved with it, but in the room before her, she didn't see broken men and women, just seeking to survive another day. For the time being at least, they were invigorated, their sparking eyes seeking the change that had been promised them for so long. She couldn't bear to take that away from them.

As if he sensed her change of heart, Seran walked towards her. "Perhaps you would like to see the other side of the coin?"

"What do you mean?"

"Their perception of today's event is not the only one that is skewed. You dealt a stinging blow to the council today. With the Academy Arcane in revolution-controlled territory and the majority of Oizan's thaumaturges more interested in their studies than who holds power in the city, the guilds were forced to look for an outside solution to your unique skills."

"Lirych."

"Correct. From what I hear, he sells his skills to the highest bidder. Right now, I am not sure Markov and her friends feel they got their money's worth. A few minutes before you returned, I received word of the Council of Guilds' intention to hold a public meeting to address our little movement."

"A few minutes? How?"

Seran smirked softly. "I have my ways." He patted the pouch that hung at his waist. "I have picked up a trick or two over the years. All you need to know is that it will be held on the steps of the council building at three hours after noon."

Asaege debated whether to trust the smiling man. *Is the potential information worth the risk that I am serving Seran's purposes and not my own?* In the end, she decided that it didn't matter as long as, for the moment, their objectives aligned.

"If you hurry, you may be able to bathe and change clothes first." The elder thief chuckled as he walked past her. "Smelling like that, no one will need to recognize your face to tell you do not belong."

*****

Taking Seran's advice, Asaege decided on a simple green dress after cleaning herself up. Saved from traveling though the Underfoot in her clean garment by a convenient thieves' guild pass-through, she had arrived in Guild Square with plenty of time to spare. The massive brick building that dominated the small piazza was the center

151

of Oizan's government. Lively on the slowest of days, Guild Square was absolutely packed as Asaege eyed the crowd.

Groups of craftsmen clustered together, speaking among themselves. Standing apart, flanked by house guards dressed in colorful livery, were the city's chosen sons and daughters. Blessed by birth, representatives of the Nine Families were the closest thing Oizan had to nobility. Although some dabbled in the day-to-day affairs of the city, most of the residents of the exclusive High District spent their time enjoying the wealth and power their position afforded them. No doubt, however, they all took an acute interest in the day's proceedings. Only a twenty-foot wall and the Library Gate separated their gilded oasis from the rebel-controlled University District.

Conspicuous by their absence were the retinues of servants that normally accompanied each noble. Missing as well were the craftsman's ever-present cadre of apprentices. As far as those outside the revolution were concerned, its greatest sin was depriving them of the labor they had come to rely upon, and forcing guild member and noble alike to dirty their own hands. Asaege wasn't ashamed of the satisfied smile on her face.

The cold drizzle that fell from the sky gave her a reason to enter the square cowled. Her attempts to hide her identity would have had the opposite effect had the sun held sway that day. Asaege wasn't overly concerned about being recognized, the fact that she and the Prophet were one and the same was only known to a select few within the ranks of the rebel leadership. Her secret was as safe as could be expected. *Then why do I feel so unsettled every time someone looks in my direction?* Her inner circle consisted of Seran, Rudelph, Toni and a single young apprentice. All of them should have been trusted confidants and stalwart allies, as their fates had become intertwined. *Yet, each has their own agenda, their own objectives for the revolution.*

Exhaling sharply, Asaege tried to put the suspicious voice of her internal monologue from her mind. Worrying about a phantom dagger in the hand of a friend could very well lead to her missing a very real one in the grasp of an enemy. Glancing around with a renewed vigilance, she saw that most eyes were directed to the council building's massive oak doors. The disparate conversations around her quieted as they opened.

A dozen richly dressed men and women appeared on the dais ten feet above the crowd. Asaege recognized Lady Markov immediately. Her uninterested gaze swept over the throng before her as if they were so much cattle in a pen. Markov's eyes passed over

Asaege's hooded form with neither pause nor recognition. Turning casually, she spoke to a bearded youth to her right as if the gathered crowd wasn't there. His gaze hung upon her as if hers was the only voice worth hearing.

A few hushed discussions started around Asaege, but her gaze remained on the council members above her. *If only I could read lips as Hollis does*, she thought. The image of the thief caused a warm, yet hollow sensation to form in her gut. They had only just begun exploring their feelings for each other when he left Oizan for the Rangor Wastes. She had meant every word she'd said when counseling him to finish his business with Mika and the Well, but she missed him dearly.

Lady Markov nodded quickly to the youth beside her and stepped forward. "Good day, gentle folk." What her voice lacked in conviction, it made up for in volume. Despite her distance from the speaker, Asaege had no difficulty hearing her words. "I see many familiar faces this afternoon. To the Nine Families, especially that of our dearly departed Meister Fremht, I offer the council's sincerest condolences. The filthy rebels will pay for his death —" A roar rose around Asaege. "—with interest!" Again, the crowd reacted, many throwing up their hands. She felt her heart begin to beat faster, almost as if it unconsciously reacted to Markov's words.

Feeling suddenly vulnerable, she pulled her cloak tighter around her body. In the back of her mind, Asaege felt Jillian's presence. It acted as a barrier between her and the venomous rhetoric that came from the dais above. Among the clamor, angry words crashed into clarity.

"—deserve to be broken on the wheel!"

"Hang the traitors!"

"—burned at the stake like the heretics they are!"

"Death is too good for them!"

Each struck Asaege like a cast stone. Hazarding a glance, she found herself surrounded by spittle-flecked lips and toothy sneers. Those closest to her began to turn their eyes her way, having drawn attention to herself by not spewing venom as they had.

Ironically, she was saved by Lady Markov herself. "All in due time, my friends. All in good time!"

The razor-filled eyes around her turned to the speaker once more. Asaege retreated further into the crowd, before they looked her way again.

"Meister Fremht's loss has struck every one of us hard, each in their own way. Larger than the personal tragedy, more painful than loss of his keen intellect, is the gaping wound his death has left in the council. If those ungrateful dirt-people thought to break us, break the city of Oizan itself, it is of utmost importance to show them how very wrong they are!"

Again, a cheer rose around Asaege. This time, she felt it best to join in, although it turned her stomach.

"The night before his death, the meister and I had a terribly frank discussion. At the time, I felt that it was both fatalistic and unnecessary. I did not believe the traitors would resort to the cowardly act of murder. It is a testament to the brilliance of our lost colleague that he not only believed them capable of it but planned for their deplorable actions."

A low grumble filled the plaza, an almost palatable aura of hate hung over the gathering.

"Although I can not hope to live up to his example —"

On the edge of the crowd, where the representatives of the Nine Families stood, other emotions were etched on the faces found there: surprise, disbelief and anger. It seemed that they, like Asaege, anticipated Lady Markov's next words.

"—our beloved Meister Fremht asked that I take his seat on the Ruling Council of Oizan."

An acclamation of support rocked the square as the crowd displayed their approval. The nobles on the periphery were silent and stone-faced.

"Of course, I understand that under normal circumstances, the Meister of Commerce is appointed by the Nine Families from among their own. During this time of upheaval, after so recently losing one of their own, it was Meister Fremht's belief that it would be best that his replacement be chosen from outside their ranks." Lady Markov extended her hand, palm upward. In times gone by, the same gesture was used by kings and queens when demanding fealty from the barons under them. "Lords and ladies, would you see the final request of our esteemed meister denied by the rebellion that tears at the very foundation of our way of life?"

As one the crowd turned their gaze on the nobles and their retinues. There was hunger in their eyes, raw and brutal. Faced with the unveiled fury of the mob, those representing the Nine Families had little choice. Each of them nodded their ascent, extending their own hands towards Lady Markov, palm down in acceptance. Again the throng surged, turning their attention back to their new Meister of Commerce. The nobles apparently didn't care to hear the remainder of her speech. One by one the representatives and their entourages turned and left the plaza.

With them gone, Asaege remained on the periphery of the crowd. Markov began again, her venomous rhetoric continuing to spur the crowd into an increasingly maddening fervor. Thankfully, her hateful words were quickly swallowed by their cries. Also on the edge of the throng, a figure wrapped in a blood-red cloak stood out by virtue of their still and silent consideration of the proceedings. Curious, Asaege approached the lone observer. Their hooded head turned to regard her, revealing a face unknown to her, yet very familiar to her reflection: Marisol Diaz.

*****

The woman before her misinterpreted Asaege's surprise tightened features. "Peace, friend," she counseled. "I wish to observe and nothing more." Asaege recognized the voice from Jillian's memories. It belonged to her reflection's friend Marisol. Although she's never met the woman on this side, Asaege felt a measure of the comfort her reflection found in Marisol's presence. The woman extended her open left hand from the depths of her cloak. Before it closed around her again, Asaege saw that her right wrapped around the hilt of a curved Oenigh knife. Prized on the streets of the desert city-state, it seemed as out of place here as the woman herself.

"I mean you no harm," Asaege said as she held out her own empty hands before her. "I saw in you a kindred spirit."

The woman tilted her head, a gentle smile on her lips. "Interesting observation. I am curious how you came to it."

"You seem to be a faction unto yourself. When the Families' representatives departed, you remained, but keep your distance from the …" Asaege searched for a diplomatic term for the gathering before them.

"… mob?" the woman supplied.

"If the description fits, I suppose."

Looking over Asaege's shoulder and past her, the woman said, "Perhaps I do not stand alone after all." She offered her left hand to Asaege, palm downward.

The gesture was too close to Lady Markov's of moments before. As Asaege accepted it, she rotated the grasp into a more conventional handshake. "So it seems." Feeling uncertain, she debated introducing herself. *It is bad form to begin a friendship with a lie,* she mused.

The woman saved her the trouble. "You may call me Remahl."

Without meaning to, Asaege's grip tightened around her hand. "Remahl of the Falling Water?" She stood within arm's reach of the

155

Grand Inquisitor of the Church of Olm. As a member of the Triad, no one commanded more respect among the Olmites short of the Hand of Light themselves. Only hours ago, it was the Crimson Sister's troops that had forced Asaege and her rebels to abandon the Dock Quarter to the council forces.

She saw the woman's shoulder slump slightly in disappointment. "Some days, I wish that name had remained free of the weight time has placed upon it."

Mentally reaching back into her memory, Asaege quickly took stock of the single formula that fought for freedom there. While quite useful in many circumstances, *Flynn's Floating Trance* wouldn't serve her particularly well against the Crimson Sister. The dagger strapped to her leg would need to suffice should their interaction turn sour. "I would have thought the Grand Inquisitor would travel with a detachment of templars. Yet you stand alone." Releasing Remahl's hand, she took a small step backwards giving her room to draw her weapon.

Remahl's eyebrows furrowed, surprised either by Asaege's line of questioning or her lack of deference. "Over the years, I have found that seeing the truth is easier when free of distractions."

Although Asaege's heart pounded in her chest, she refused to cower in the presence of the Olmite. Letting her fingertips brush the material of her dress, she felt the reassuring shape of the weapon beneath. "And what do you see here, Sister?"

Shifting her gaze to the crowd once more, Remahl said, "I see a maestra conducting frustration and anger as if they were an orchestra. It is as terrifying as a symphony is beautiful." Meeting Asaege's eyes once more, she asked, "Would I be wrong to assume that you do not have an ear for her brand of music either?"

"Lady Markov plays for herself alone. I imagine she is unconcerned with my opinion."

Remahl's tongue flicked out to wet her lips. "But I have a suspicion that she should be. You are quite a remarkable woman, ..." She searched for Asaege's name before the realization that it had never been provided dawned in her eyes. "... quite remarkable indeed."

Asaege watched as the Crimson Sister wavered a bit, seemingly unsteady on her feet. "Are you well, Remahl?" In spite of the danger the woman posed to both the revolution and her personally, she found herself genuinely concerned.

Remahl's right hand snaked out from the depths of her cloak to wipe a bead of sweat from her forehead despite the chill that hung in the air. "I am quite alright. My travels may be catching up to me is all."

When her hand strayed from the knife at her waist, Asaege knew in her heart it was the moment to strike. It was also her heart that stayed her hand. *I will not murder this woman on naught but the words of others. To this point, she has treated me fairly and with respect.* As the Crimson Sister pulled her hand back into her cloak, Asaege thought, *I just hope I do not come to regret that decision.*

At some point, the cold drizzle had evolved into a bone-chilling sleet. "Perhaps you should retire to less hostile surroundings."

Her distraction evident by her unfocused eyes, Remahl nodded in agreement. "Perhaps you are correct." Sweeping her gaze over the crowd one final time, her mouth twisted into a distasteful frown. "Although, I am not sure the weather is the most objectionable part of this evening."

"On that, we agree, Remahl of the Falling Water." Asaege's use of her name rather than the more nefarious sobriquet by which she was known displaced the woman's scowl.

"I have a feeling we will meet again, my friend." Remahl turned on her heel and began to walk away, calling over her shoulder, "Then, perhaps you will share with me your name."

Chapter Twenty

An Unforeseen Complication

Jillian's eyes darted between her watch and the tranquil lines of her friend's sleeping face with consternation. *Did I give her too much? What if she reflected into a dangerous situation?* Her fingers went to Marisol's wrist, feeling for a pulse. The tempo she felt there was steady and regular. When Marisol's eyes flickered open, she had to suppress a yelp of joy.

"Do I have something on my face?" Marisol asked, rubbing sleepily at her cheek.

Jillian's tension released itself through a nervous laugh. "Not at all."

"Do you know how creepy it is to wake up to someone staring at you?"

Her mind filled with images of Hollis's face, looking at her expectantly as her reflected consciousness awakened within Asaege. Despite the admittedly off-putting sensation of the memory, it brought a smile to her face, nonetheless. "Yes, I believe I may have a sense of it."

Marisol slowly pushed herself to a seated position, her movements deliberate, as if she moved through honey. In the months she had been reflecting, Jillian had never awakened so groggy. She reached out to steady her friend as Marisol wavered.

"Are you alright?" While her first question was the more pressing, Jillian's follow-up one was the one that burned in her mind. "What did you see?"

Laying her hand on Jillian's forearm, Marisol gave her a gentle smile. "I'll be fine. I'm just trying to make sense of everything."

"So you did see something?" Although Jillian had faith in her own experiences, having someone other than Hector corroborate them still put her mind at ease. She felt that if Marisol shared her experiences in Taerh as well, the last question of whether or not they were a flight of her imagination was answered.

Marisol closed her eyes and exhaled sharply. "There's no doubt I saw something. I'm just not sure what."

"Tell me," Jillian said, a touch too eagerly.

As they opened again, Jillian could see the tears hanging in her friend's eyes. "At first it was a maelstrom of thoughts not quite my own, yet still familiar. The harder I fought to get my bearings, the more turbulent the confusion became."

Jillian covered her mouth guiltily. "I should have warned you. The process can be quite disorienting if you and your reflection are not acquainted."

Rolling her eyes, Marisol murmured, "Now you tell me."

"I'm sorry. It's been so long since Asaege and I reached our ..." Jillian searched for the proper term. She settled for, "Understanding."

"As I struggled, it seemed as if I were a passenger in my own body. Only it didn't belong to me alone."

"Your reflection," Jillian provided.

"Despite not being in control, I experienced everything she did. I felt the chill of the air. I heard every word exchanged between my reflection ..." Her lips wrapped around the word as if it were an only half understood language. "Between my reflection and yours."

Excitement and an inexplicable dread swirled in Jillian's chest. "You met Asaege?"

"Yes, we did." Marisol placed a hard emphasis on "we." "Remahl isn't sure what to make of her, but she is quite certain Asaege is more than she appears."

"Remahl? As in Remahl of the Falling Water? The Crimson Sister?" Jillian didn't wait for Marisol's nod of confirmation. "That's not good ... not good at all." *My two closest friends on Earth are arrayed against us in Taerh.*

When she tried to pull her hand from Marisol's arm, her friend placed her hand atop Jillian's. "It's not a terrible thing. The buffeting tides of confusion didn't prevent me from getting a sense of the woman herself."

Jillian felt her eyes widen. "She's the Grand Inquisitor. They don't call her the Crimson Sister because she favors the color."

"I felt her heart, Jillie. No matter what the rumors say. Remahl is a gentle soul that seeks to not only serve the church to which she has sworn herself but the people who depend on it." Squeezing Jillian's hand firmly, Marisol's voice became soft but insistent. "Did you ask that I trust you?"

"Yes."

"Did I do so with no hesitation?"

Again, Jillian responded, "Yes."

"I'm now asking the same of you."

Jillian opened her mouth to argue but found her words tasted bitter on her tongue. *At our centers, Asaege and I are alike. The same can be said of Hollis and Stephen. On the surface, Asaege's scoundrel is a killer and a thief. Had I known him exclusively through rumors and hearsay, would I have placed my trust in his heart?*

"Of course, Mari. My faith in you is absolute." Jillian wasn't sure if she spoke what was in her heart or if by speaking the words, she fortified them there, but her trepidation evaporated like dew before the summer sun.

A silence hung in the air between them. Far from being uncomfortable, the stillness said more of the women's bond than any conversation ever could.

It was Marisol that spoke first. "Even in their short interaction, Remahl developed a fondness for Asaege." She frowned so deeply, the lines at the corners of her mouth appeared carved in stone. "The same can't be said for Veronica Moses's reflection."

"Lady Markov." Jillian felt her lips turn down as well.

"Even Remahl recognizes how dangerous she is. Please be careful around her." Marisol's brows furrowed as if she weighed something. Her tone more question than statement, she said, "Tell Asaege the same? Does it work like that?"

Jillian chuckled. "Sort of ... and not at all. Once you and your reflection find an accord, you —" Her explanation was cut short by an explosion of battering fists on the door. She leapt to her feet and both women's eyes went to the staircase leading to the apartment's only entrance.

Before either could speak, a fresh wave of pounding commenced. It was accompanied by a voice, raised in fear. "Jillian! It's Cyrill! Let me in!"

Jillian was frozen momentarily. She's known Cyrill since elementary school and the panic in his voice nearly broke her heart. She had also had first-hand experience with his reflection, Lirych. The thaumaturge-for-hire had tried to burn her to death, along with a dozen other people. On the other end of Lirych's leash was the devious Lady Markov, aka Veronica Moses. Could she put it past either of them to attack her in her own home?

"Please, Jillian!" he begged. "He's coming!"

"What are you doing?" Marisol asked. Jillian had not shared with her friend the identity of Cyrill's reflection.

Stopping only to grab a pair of pruning shears from the table, Jillian raced down the stairs to the door.

Cyrill stood on the concrete stoop, his face ashen and slick with a mixture of tears and sweat. He let his fist, raised to pound on the door, fall to his side with an exhaustion that seemed more emotional than physical. "Thank god," he said in a breathy exhalation. Glancing towards the shadows of the half-lit parking lot, Cyrill whispered, "We have to get inside. He was right behind me."

Sympathy not quite overcoming her suspicion, Jillian remained planted in the doorway. "Who, Cyrill? Who was right behind you?" Looking past him, she saw no movement among the darkened shapes of the cars.

"I don't know. I was driving home from Lobster Johnnie's and a car came up behind me." Again he hazarded a peek over his shoulder. "Can we please talk about this inside?"

Jillian heard Marisol at the top of the stairs and relented. Taking a small step backwards, she cleared the way for Cyrill to enter.

He rushed by her, taking the stairs two at a time as he repeated, "Thank you. Thank you," over and over.

Squinting into the winter night once more, Jillian thought she saw something dart between two cars in the distance. The possibility that it could be her imagination didn't stop her from quickly closing the door and locking the deadbolt with a flick of her wrist. A last look through the peephole before climbing the stairs herself revealed nothing out of the ordinary.

*****

If Cyrill's fear was an act, it was a good one. In order to keep his hands from shaking, he clenched them into fists so tightly that his knuckles were white. Marisol sat beside him, a comforting arm over his quivering shoulders. "— don't know where he came from. I looked in the rear-view mirror and he was just there."

"Calm down," Jillian began, channeling her reflection's recently learned calmness under pressure. "You're safe here." She wasn't

162

sure of how true her words were, but she did her best to maintain a confident tone. "Start from the beginning."

He lifted his glazed eyes from his lap, the pleading look in them indicated he desperately wanted to believe her. "I went to Johnnie's for an early dinner before heading home. As I walked out the door, there were a half dozen people hanging around outside. I didn't think much of it; smokers gotta smoke." The ghost of a smile crossed his lips, but it was a tight, transient gesture. "It wasn't until I was half-way to my car that I heard someone behind me. The parking lot was packed, so I had to park in front of the old bookstore ... you know that national chain that went bankrupt a few years back."

Jillian nodded, not wanting to disrupt the flow of his story now that it had gained momentum.

"I guess whoever owns the building doesn't want to waste money on lights for a property that's not providing rent. Or maybe over the years, they didn't keep up with the maintenance. Either way, it's always pitch black over there. When I turned around, all I could see was his silhouette."

Cyrill unclenched his hands, revealing the deep, crimson indentations his fingernails had pressed into his palms. Jillian sat on the coffee table in front of the couch, sinking to his eye level.

"You couldn't make out anything about him?"

He shook his head. "Not other than the fact that he was huge and walking towards me like I was the only thing in the parking lot. I tried to defuse the situation. I said something stupid like, 'It's a bitch about the lights, huh?' As soon as I stopped, he lunged at me. If he'd been a few feet closer, he would have grabbed me before I could run."

"So you ran?" Marisol's voice was gentle, as always, but Jillian could hear the tension hidden within.

"Fuck yeah, I ran. I didn't stop until I got to my car. The last I saw of him was his big ass disappearing in my mirror ... until I was on Route 92. As I passed the old one-room schoolhouse, a pair of headlights came up on me fast. Before I knew it, he'd slammed into me. The wheel jumped in my hands and I was spinning towards the building. I was able to get the car under control before I hit it, but I took out thirty feet of fence first."

"Are you alright?" Jillian's question came from genuine concern for her friend.

"I tweaked my neck a little but other than that, I'm fine." He closed his eyes for a second, regathering his thoughts before continuing. "When I looked out the side window, the big bastard was out

163

of his car and running towards me. I threw it in reverse, taking half of the chain link with me and tore out of there like the devil himself was behind me … which I'm not completely sure wasn't true."

"At the door, you said he was right behind you."

"He turned into the complex just as I was pulling into your parking lot."

Marisol spoke up. "Are you certain it was him? Could it have been someone else coming home? A lot of folks live in these apartments."

Cyrill's eyes were wild, the whites of them standing out against his olive complexion like stars on a cloudless night. His fists were once again clenched against his stomach. "Yes … no … I don't know." The adrenaline that had kept him one step ahead of his attacker now seemed to be clouding his thoughts.

"Just breathe, Cyrill," Marisol counseled. She fixed Jillian in a reproachful glare. "You can take as long as you need. We're all friends here. Let's just get to the bottom of this and then we all can figure out where to go from there."

Cyrill visibly calmed. Marisol had that effect on people. His first breath was raspy, a staccato intake of air. By the third, his breathing became smooth and steady. Slowly his hands relaxed as he let them slump onto his lap.

After a reassuring nod from Marisol, Jillian spoke as gently as she could. "Now, are you sure the man followed you from the accident scene?"

He shook his head. "I'm not certain. He was out of his car and twenty yards from it when I drove off."

"Alright, then." Jillian kept her voice soft and reassuring. "For the time being, let's assume that he was unable to follow you here. As a historical building, the schoolhouse has lights to deter vandalism. Did you get a better look at either the man himself or his vehicle when he was approaching your car?"

Cyrill's brows furrowed. "He was wearing a black knit cap. Between it and the shadows caused by the headlights of the passing cars, I couldn't make out his face."

"You said he was huge. Was he muscular or fat?"

He looked up, panic creeping into his voice again. "I'm not sure. I —"

As gently as she could, Jillian cut him off before he worked himself up again. "—That's okay. What about his vehicle. Was it a sedan?"

He shook his head.

"A truck?"

"No." The word had the quiver of indecision.

"A SUV?" Marisol suggested.

"Not quite. It was smaller."

"Like a crossover?" Jillian asked.

He nodded. "I think so. It was dark and the headlights were in my eyes."

"It's more than we had a few moments ago." Jillian picked up the cell phone beside her. "I'm going to call the police. You don't have anything in your car that will cause you problems, right?"

Cyrill chuckled softly. For the first time that night, a trace of a real smile could be seen on his face. "No, I finished the last of the Dreamtime Dank last night."

Marisol raised an eyebrow, but Jillian ignored the gesture. "Good. They're most likely going to at least look at your car, and we don't need to give them any reason to doubt your story." The memory of the last time they'd come to her apartment stood out in her mind. Hector had broken in to retrieve the journals she'd stolen, and their timely arrival had forced him to flee without them. Although the officers' dismissive attitude left Jillian feeling patronized, they had most likely saved her life. "After the last time they were here, we're working from a deficit as it is."

Marisol laid a hand on Jillian's shoulder, her eyes soft with concern. "The last time?"

"It's a long story. Someone came looking for something that belonged to neither of us. At any rate, they're going to love talking to me again."

*****

As Jillian locked the door after seeing the police out, she paused for a moment at the base of the stairs. Above her in the apartment, she heard the drone of indecipherable conversation between Cyrill and Marisol. Much like Jillian's earlier experience with them, the officers told him to not get his hopes up. Between Cyrill's non-specific description of both the attacker and his vehicle, the chance of actually finding him was extremely low. Even if they did, without concrete proof, the situation would be seen as the attacker's word against Cyrill's. No prosecutor worth his law school tuition would take it to trial.

Turning to climb the stairs, Jillian thought about where that left the three of them. She had known Cyrill for most of her life and they had been friends for more than a decade. In that time, she had borne witness to his occasional bouts of casual arrogance and their effects on the people around him. Jillian herself had been tempted to hit him more times than she liked to admit over the years. If he was feeling full of himself, there was a better than average chance this evening was a case of a stranger's anger turned road rage. It just seemed too much of a coincidence.

First Martin Fredericks was killed in his home, then Hector's shop was burned down around him. If the death of the high school football player that Billy had told her about was involved as well, the attack on Cyrill would make four assaults resulting in three deaths over as many days … in a county that only saw twice that many in a year. *The question is, what do they all have in common?* The question still hung heavy in Jillian's thoughts as she pulled a kitchen chair over to the futon where her friends sat.

Cyrill looked up at her, his twitchy gaze demonstrating how much of his panic remained, even after speaking to the police. "Do you think they're right?"

"About not finding the guy who ran you off the road? As much as I hate to say it, if anything, I think they were being optimistic." Jillian laid her hand gently on his shoulder. "It'll be okay, Cyrill." Although she felt obligated to try to soothe his fears, she wasn't sure she did him any favors by doing so.

"I know. I'll probably never see him again." His voice's desperate tone sinking the frigid knife of guilt further into Jillian's heart.

She debated the wisdom of pressing the already frazzled man further. *It's like ripping off a band-aid*, she thought. *It's better everything come at once.*

"Can I ask you something?"

"Of course." Cyrill tried to muster cheerful voice, but it sounded forced.

"While you were smoking 'Dreamtime,' did you notice anything … well … unusual?"

He studied Jillian for a moment. She was unsure if she saw confusion or hesitation in his face. "Unusual? You're gonna have to be a little more specific."

No turning back now. "Did it give you strange, yet very vivid dreams?" She felt Marisol's eyes upon her and tried to keep her focus on Cyrill's face. In that moment, she would have given just about anything for Hollis's "Understanding."

His thoughts were inscrutable behind the tight expression born out of the strain of the night. "Of course. Hector warned me about that possibly … hell, he all but touted it as a bonus."

"Tell me about the dreams." The words fell from Jillian's lips

166

before she could temper her eagerness. Cyrill recoiled from her naked interest. Out of the corner of her eye, she also saw Marisol's brows furrow as she started connecting the dots.

Withering beneath the unintended intensity of her gaze, Cyrill stammered, "Um ... okay."

Consciously softening both her eyes and her voice, Jillian prompted, "Were they always of the same place?"

A ghost of suspicion crept into his features. "Same place? Yes. They were always set in a fantasy world ... like Shadows and Sorcerers type shit."

"Were you always the same person?"

Cyrill's eyes narrowed, his uncertainty growing. "I was always me, but not." He lifted his right hand, wrapping it around his left fist as he brought them to his lips. "It was only a dream, right? The combination of the weed and an overactive imagination?" He sounded as if he were trying to convince himself of that fact, rather than her.

"I don't know. You tell me." Jillian watched the stricken man's face for any indication of Lirych's unfettered arrogance. All she saw was fear and uncertainty.

"It has to be." Far from a definitive tone, his statement was that of a child seeking validation of the fact that there was nothing to be afraid of in the dark.

Yes, Virgina, Jillian thought sardonically, *there are monsters under your bed.* As gently as she could, she asked, "Can you tell me about this person that wasn't you?" She felt Marisol's hand on her shoulder, but refused to look at her friend.

"He was everything I've always wanted to be, but at the same time, all the worst things in life."

Jillian waited patiently, allowing Cyrill to expand without additional prompting from her that might have shut him down completely.

"Lirych is confident." The name struck Jillian's heart like a knife. "He always has the answer, whether it's to an argument or a fight. He's secure in his place in the world. I've not felt that way since graduating high school. It was nice to feel that way again, if only for a little while."

Cyrill's teen-aged popularity had made him insufferable for the four years they had spent in high school. College, however, had been a rude awakening for him. It wasn't until he experienced that bit of reality that they had been able to form a real friendship. The idea that, absent that ordeal, Cyrill and Lirych would have been one in personality as well as body, chilled Jillian to her core.

"But there is a coldness about him, a detachment from the world around him. It is almost as if he sees it and those around him as nothing more than tools to serve whatever purpose he has at the moment. Those that can't benefit him are either immaterial or playthings for his amusement. I'm not like that, I don't want—" As he spoke, the tempo of his words increased to a frenetic pace, as if he were running from something he could never quite escape.

Marisol squeezed Jillian's shoulder hard. Laying her hand on top of Marisol's, Jillian interrupted him. "—You're not, Cyrill."

Gratitude flashed from his damp eyes. "I wasn't always my best self, Jillian. I know that but …" Cyrill searched for words that would not emerge from his panic-cluttered brain.

"But nothing. You are a good person." Before she could change her mind, Jillian lied to her friend. "It was only a dream. Like you said, it was the unfortunate combination of pot and imagination."

The words felt as if they burned the back of her throat, but their effect on Cyrill was immediate. He settled back on the futon, closing his eyes. His hands relaxed once more, resting on the cushions on either side of him.

"Let's both agree to avoid Dreamtime Dank in the future."

"Good idea," he agreed.

"Why don't you both spend the night here and I'm sure things will look brighter in the morning light."

Chapter Twenty-One
An Earnest Plea

A ristoi lay huddled near the low burning fire, its fading heat and the furs wrapped around her body fending off the lion's share of the bitter cold of the Rangor night. Deep in slumber, her brow furrowed as visions of the past haunted her dreams.

*****

The wordless melody brushed Aristoi's consciousness. Gentle at first, the sound was insistent in its steady, comforting rhythm. As it rose and fell in an undulating cadence, the song caressed the Songspear's ears with a velveteen touch that she remembered from her childhood. The melody became more urgent as it filled Aristoi's ears and flowed through her being. As the tide carried the small fishing boats from which her tiny village derived their existence, so too did the song lift her heart. It carried her along with it as the trepidation she felt melted away; all that existed were the warm, almost siren-like notes.

Wrapped in that sheltering bastion, the Songspear's eyes slowly flickered open. Her head lay pillowed on the moss-covered root of an ancient kapok tree, the dappled sunlight filtered through its blade shaped leaflets. The tree, called the Wooden Giant among her people, towered above the surrounding vegetation, its parasol shaped crown sheltering the trees beneath it. Vaguely, Aristoi recalled the biting cold of the northern wastes, but here among the silent sentinels of her childhood home, it was relegated to a distant memory. The melody that filled her dream continued to roll across her perceptions.

Lazily sweeping her eyes across the forest floor, she quickly discovered its origin. A figure was standing a handful of yards away from her supine form. The setting sun behind the figure cast its features into shadow, but as the Songspear's head began to clear, the voice was unmistakable.

"Iya?" Aristoi spoke the word for mother softly in her native tongue, her questioning tone having more to do with disbelief than doubt. Tears came to her eyes as the memories of laying her mother to rest flooded her senses. A funeral pyre had been made from a stand of red gum trees planted on the day of her mother's birth. She could still smell the aromatic smoke as it wrapped around her, doing nothing to numb the razor-sharp claws of grief that raked her heart with every breath. She tasted the salty tears that rolled down her cheeks, although they had nothing to do with the thick smoke.

The figure didn't approach the prone warrior; she simply continued to sing as she beckoned her with a thin hand. Climbing to her feet, Aristoi squinted into the luminous aura that the sun cast about the woman before her. Memory filled in the details lost within the blinding corona; her mind told her that the mother lost almost a year ago could not possibly stand before her; her heart wanted to believe that she did so desperately that it pained the Songspear. Out of habit, Aristoi's eyes scanned the forest floor for her spear, finally locating it in the figure's grasp.

She questioned again, "Iya?" Again, the figure gestured for her to come closer. As Aristoi took a step forward, her feet felt unreasonably heavy. The second step came more easily, but still the sensation of great weight remained. With the resistance came a hot rush of anger. The emotion swept through Aristoi as the circumstances of her mother's death came unbidden to her mind.

The fury was like a physical weight, tethering Aristoi to the ground. As it burned in her heart, so too did its burden settle on her limbs. So preoccupied was the Songspear with her inner turmoil that she didn't notice that the figure before her had ceased singing and simply watched her, arms akimbo. Aristoi tried to take another step, but her foot felt like it weighed as much as a draft horse. The figure spoke in a soft, sympathetic whisper, "You cannot cross into the realm of the ancestors while you carry that anger.

"Iya ... I cannot lose you again."

"Then lay down your burden and come to me, sweet child."

Aristoi's mother took a step forward out of the glare of the perpetually setting sun. The Songspear made out the woman's plump cheeks and well-earned laugh lines. Her heart felt as if it would burst in joy as she laid eyes upon her beloved parent. The delight momentarily freed Aristoi from the ponderous anger; as she rushed into her mother's arms, she felt as if her steps were as light as air.

The woman enveloped Aristoi in her embrace, feeling to her as real as the earth beneath her boots. Here in her mother's arms, the Songspear felt at peace for the first time since the woman's death ... since she was taken from her. With that thought, the unreasoning fury returned tenfold. The strength of the emotion was so intense that her mother released Aristoi as if burned.

Her mother repeated, "Lay down your burden."

Clenching her teeth against the bitter taste of rage, Aristoi growled, "Junwei murdered you."

Her mother nodded sadly. "Yes, she did, child. She will need to answer for it when she steps before the Twins on the night of her death. Yet you are the one who carries it."

The Songspear began, "But she took you from me."

"And yet it is you who keep us apart. Lay down your anger and we may walk together among the trees of the Everlasting Forest." Her mother's eyes misted in sadness. "But alas, that is not to be." Aristoi's mother extended the spear to her. "Junwei has indeed taken a great deal from you, but you still possess what matters most: pride, tradition and honor. None may take those; they may only be sacrificed by you."

Aristoi glanced at the spear, but did not reach for it, as if by doing so she could extend this moment forever. "I would sacrifice all that and more to bring your daughter... my sister to justice."

"You seek vengeance, not justice."

"Is there a difference?"

The woman smiled sadly and said, "That you would ask the question indicates that you would not comprehend the answer." She seized her daughter's eyes, Aristoi couldn't break her intense gaze. "You are a Songspear, my daughter. More than strength of arm ... more than magic of melody and word, our power comes from tradition ... lessons remembered do not need to be learned again. Our power comes from pride ... if you have nothing to fight for, you have nothing to fight with. Our power comes from honor...what is worth fighting for when you are not yourself worthy?"

Aristoi's mother closed her eyes slowly, allowing her daughter to break her gaze. Aristoi looked away, suddenly ashamed, "I am

171

sorry, Iya."

The spear was pressed into her hand. "Your sister disregarded the wisdom of the ancestors. That is why you are my heir and she is not."

"Junwei is the elder sister," Aristoi began.

"The council honored that above my wishes?"

The Songspear's mouth drew into a tight frown. "Junwei painted a picture that gave them little choice." Her mother's eyes drifted down to the weapon that stood between them. Aristoi continued, "I could not allow her to keep the honor of our family, although she surely has taken mine."

"She has done no such thing, child. However, I see now that more than your anger holds you from the Everlasting Forest."
Sadness clouded her mother's face as she released the haft of the spear. "You have other paths to walk." As the weight of the weapon settled into Aristoi's hand, the forest around the pair was blanketed in a rising fog. The mist brought with it a knife-like chill that sliced into the Songspear's flesh. As suddenly as it rose, the fog withdrew, revealing the harsh tundra of the Rangor Wastes. "What has put you on this path in particular, my daughter?" Aristoi's mother's voice was a mixture of concern and genuine curiosity.

"I cannot prove my innocence without the spear... I cannot prove my worth to carry it without completing my training."

"This is your Tikha La ... your 'Long Walk?' What lost lore could you hope to find in this place?"

Aristoi's face warmed into a smile. "Veltim Vilt ... the Well of Worlds." Her mother raised an eyebrow, a glint of pride in her deep brown eyes. "I have studied the etchings in the Mountain of Fire as well as the wells found in Slaze and Utel. They all pointed me north."

"Impressive." Her soft smile turned downward. "Yet you stand here between the world of the living and that of the ancestors."

"A creature stands between me and the Well. The tribesman agreed to allow my access but first ..."

"... you have to remove this beast for them," her mother finished her thought.

Aristoi nodded. "I have to slay the beast."

Her mother pulled her shawl closer around her shoulders and sat tailor-style on the permafrost. She gestured for her daughter to do the same, "Tell me of the creature."

Aristoi did as she was bid. "But Iya, what would you—"

Her mother frowned. "Lessons remembered ..."

172

It was the Songspear's turn to complete her mother's thought, "Do not need to be learned again."

"Tradition is as much a weapon as it is a shield. Tell me of the creature."

"In shape and size, it is very much like the wolves that stalk the forests of home. Its paws end in long toes as capable of grasping as your hand or mine. Each of these are tipped with a vicious claw." Aristoi's mother listened, still as a stone. "Despite its wolfish muzzle, it is capable of speech ... as a matter of fact I have held less refined conversations with a good deal of our own kind." A shudder ran through the Songspear. "The worst part is its eyes. The color of dried blood, there exists behind them a calculating maliciousness that puts to shame any foe I have faced. To lock eyes with it is to feel your very strength drawn into the dark void that is the beast's wickedness."

Her mother spoke softly, but her voice rang out clearly, "When it howls, does it seize your heart as if death itself whispered in your ear?"

Aristoi nodded. "My resolve broke like a wave upon the rocks."

Her mother folded her hands on her lap. "Allow me to tell you a story, my daughter." Already agitated by the recollections of her encounter with the beast, Aristoi did her best to remain still. From experience she knew she had little choice. "In the Age of Legends ... just after Olm banished the elves from his sight by the might of his hammer and the Fair Folk retreated to their stony halls, humans were just taking their first steps into the light of the day. With them, they brought the gifts bestowed by the Sibling Gods, Olm and Umma. They also carried inside of them a gift from their brother, Sharroth. Known as the Father of Lies and Lord of Beasts."

Despite herself, Aristoi felt herself pulled into the story, just as she had when she was a child. Her curiosity overcame her impulsiveness.

"This gift is the greatest of all those granted us by the gods. It is the gift of free will."

"Is not any gift from the Father of Lies a trap?"

Her mother shook her head, "Many would have you believe such. It, like anything else, is a tool, an inert thing. In and of itself, it is neither good nor evil. It only becomes such based on the intent of those who use it. Free will allows us to choose our path through life. That path may take one through sun-dappled fields or shadow draped swamps, according to the wishes of the traveler."

"As long as you only choose your own path, that is fine. Often others are pulled into the mire beside those who choose the path of darkness."

"There can be no heroes without choice. There can be no villains." Her mother waited the space of three breaths for Aristoi to speak and then continued, "Among the first of our kind, there were a handful who seized upon this divinely granted freedom to, as you put it, drag their fellows into the mire. The greatest of these was a northerner called Gwyllgi."

Aristoi frowned deeply. "A Rangor?"

Again, her mother shook her head. "Remember, my child, that the Age of Legends was before the kingdoms you know were even a thought. All we know is that Gwyllgi was not of the south ... Not Kieli."

"Convenient," was all Aristoi muttered.

"Quite. Gwyllgi capitalized upon the trust and gentle nature of his fellows to steal from those around him, killing those who wouldn't quietly surrender what was theirs. When his existence came to the attention of the Mouhn, the law bringers of the First King, they fell upon him in an effort to make an example for those who sought to emulate the man. Sharroth, having developed a fondness for Gwyllgi, granted him a measure of his own shadow."

Aristoi leaned forward, hanging on every word that fell from her mother's mouth.

"The man's cunning and malice the god left intact, adding to it a sliver of the darkness that ran through his own veins. Sharroth placed the pull of the goblin moon in his eyes and the call of the night in his throat. When the Mouhn met Gwyllgi's gaze, they felt the exhaustion of a score of midnights; when they heard his howl, they felt the fear all men have when lost in the darkness. As the Master of Beasts, Sharroth twisted the man as the god himself had been twisted, leaving the beast you faced this night."

"It was a legendary beast I fought?"

"No, Aristoi, simply one of his children." Aristoi's mother rested her hand on her arm. In Aristoi's childhood, her mother had used such a gesture to counsel patience. "Taken by surprise, the Heralds were forced to surrender the field of battle. Emboldened by his success, Gwyllgi began to cut a swath of chaos and pain across the face of the Cradle, always driving unerringly towards his master's ultimate prize, the Ivory City. It was on the outskirts of Aerh that Gwyllgi and the Mouhn battled a second time. Before the church of Olm himself, the creature tore into the chosen of the First King. Sharroth was not the only god present that day, however. The Father of Justice, Olm, stood beside the bringers of his laws. Despite

Olm's favor, two of the Mouhn fell beneath Gwyllgi's claws. The last of their number, a woman whose name has been lost, even to the ancestors, impaled the beast upon the iron gate that surrounded the holy place."

"You mentioned children."

A sad smile flickered across her mother's lips. "That I did. In his march north, Gwyllgi left behind himself a trail of broken and bloody corpses. Those who fell beneath tooth and claw but didn't cross into the Everlasting Forest did so by seizing upon the darkness that lay within themselves. They nurtured it as one does a fledgling flame on a winter's night. This darkness staved off the call of death, but in its place left the dark inheritance of their killer." The sadness of her smile crept into her eyes as she watched her daughter.

"Your eyes are saying something that you are not. What is it?"

Her mother did not answer her question, but simply nodded before continuing, "Since that time they have been known by many names: black dog, churchyard beast, ajadu. They most commonly carry the moniker of their progenitor: gwyllgi." Aristoi watched her mother with hooded eyes, but didn't repeat her question. "They can be slain, as their forefather was, by iron. This, too, he passed to those he cursed."

"How do you slay something that can strike to the heart of you with its very voice?"

Her mother's eyes glinted with moisture, but tears did not fall though Aristoi expected them to. "Lay down your anger, Aristoi. Walk with me and leave the beast to others."

The Songspear saw her mother shift her position upon the grass. She was clearly hiding something. "How do I defeat the creature?"

"There is a song. It is an ancient melody without word or lyric. It demands a heavy price, but if sung properly, it will be the only sound heard. Its magic will abide no competition." She squeezed Aristoi's arm in a vise grip, "The dawn comes, and the day does not belong to the dead." Behind her, the sun had finally begun to move, disappearing behind the horizon with startling speed. "Lay down your burden. Walk with me."

Aristoi allowed the temptation to pull at her heart for a moment and then her resolve hardened within her. "Do you have the time to teach me the song?"

"Leave the creature to others."

"Others do not have the song."

Her mother's shoulders sagged, as if under a great weight.

175

"Just enough time remains."
   "Teach me the song."

*****

Aristoi's eyes fluttered open slowly. Compared to the night-mares that had recently plagued her, the recollection of her mother's last gift lifted the Songspear's spirits. In the place between worlds, between darkness and dawn, she was able to learn one final lesson from her beloved Iya. What came before or after couldn't take the sweetness of that moment away from her.

As she pushed herself into a seated position, Aristoi saw the thief moving in the dusk's approaching darkness. Just as she had prepared to face the horror of the gwyllgi that night months before, he faced his own poisonous dilemma. Just as she had, he chose vengeance over peace.

Chapter Twenty-Two
A Crushing Defeat

The night was mature by the time Hollis and Aristoi reached the outskirts of the camp. The Songspear's skill with tracking rivaled even that of his former mentor, Silvermoon. Well after dark, the pair was able to continue their pursuit, thanks to her magic. With only a soft, wordless hum from the back of Aristoi's throat, the ground before them had been cast into a pale, almost ghost-like contrast.

As they lay upon the frozen dirt, its icy fingers digging their way into muscle and bone, the two figures were no more than deeper patches of night. A collection of elk-hide tents spread out before them; it wasn't the temporary site they had expected. Instead, they looked upon a semi-permanent encampment made up of two dozen smaller structures surrounding a large pavilion. Eight evenly spaced bonfires ringed the camp, leaving few options to approach unnoticed.

Leaning close enough to his companion that Hollis could feel the heat of her skin, he whispered, "Why am I thinking we have misjudged this situation?"

She rotated her head to place her own lips near his ear. "Perhaps because we have. The ambush among the burial mounds, the trap in Agmar's Watch, the gwyllgi's sudden appearance, all of them were related. Each of them drew us closer and closer to this place, this point in time. At every juncture, we thought ourselves the hunters. In truth, we have been the hunted since we entered the domain of the Bone Dogs."

Replaying the events of the last few days in his mind, Hollis didn't need the "Understanding" to see the Songspear's point. Since the first attack on the Bone Dog camp, the pair had been lured away from the safety of the clan's numbers and then led on a merry chase that ended with them isolated on the outskirts of an enemy encampment. He had no doubt as to the author of their troubles. He had seen her execute countless similar plans, on a much smaller scale.

When faced with unfavorable odds, Mika had a knack for drawing overconfident opponents into circumstances that benefited her alone. Knowing full well who it was he chased, Hollis had still allowed himself to be led along her intended path like a hound following his nose. Preoccupied by his selfish need for vengeance, sprinkled with a healthy dose of arrogance, the thief executed his former comrade's plan as if he were in on it.

"We put ourselves precisely where they want us to be." Hollis's tone conveyed the apology that his words didn't.

Aristoi laid her head lightly against his. The gesture spoke of both shared responsibility and forgiveness. "They may well find themselves regretting that desire. We are, after all, very dangerous people."

Pushing aside his guilt, Hollis growled, "Hell yes, we are."

Turning his attention back to the encampment before them, the thief studied it with the benefit of his Well-born gifts. Although the bonfires burned around the perimeter of the camp, he didn't see any shapes moving among them. The only movement between where the pair lay and the first ring of tents were the flickering shadows cast by the flames. *Any guards must be posted beyond them,* he thought. *Any intruders would need to pass through the light, revealing themselves to anyone scanning the perimeter.* If they could just get past the watch fires, a few dozen yards of darkness separated the pair from the shadows of the tents.

Hollis whispered, "Can you do anything about the—"

"—Fires?" Aristoi finished his thought. "I can shift the wind for a moment, darkening a path for no longer than a score of breaths. If I hold the song any longer, the wind may become too strong to escape notice."

"Do you think you can make it to the tents in twenty breaths?"

He felt her sneer in the darkness. "It is not my ability that concerns me, I am not the one ironically described as slender."

178

Resting his hand on his ample belly, Hollis said, "Don't let the jealous words of the malnourished fool you, I can move when I need to."

"I just thought with all the honey cakes you ate during your recovery —"

"—Brother Traemont told me to keep my strength up."

"I am not sure that was what he intended."

"Then he should have been more expansive in his explanation."

"Interesting choice of words."

The thief didn't need to see his comrade's face to know her expression. "You worry about your song, let me worry about my fat ass making it between here and there."

"It's not your ass that concerns me." She patted her own stomach in the darkness.

Hollis slowly rose into a crouch. "I bet you say that to all the boys."

*****

The shadows cast by the tents settled around his shoulders like a well-worn cloak, the thief scanned the camp beyond them. Small cooking fires of various sizes were scattered before him, but none was large enough to substantially cut into the darkness filling the distance between him and the large pavilion at the center of the camp. In the dim light, he could just make out Aristoi's silhouette beside him. True to her prediction, the Songspear had reached the tents a few strides ahead of him. *But it was close*, he thought bitterly.

Rangor warriors gathered in groups of threes and fours around each fire, sharing mead and stories. The thief couldn't make out their words, but the accompanying raucous laughter filled the night air like the peals of church bells. After verifying that the attention of the Rangor in sight was turned inward, Hollis tapped the Songspear's shoulder as he rose to his feet. Quiet as a whisper, the pair raced across the distance between them and the massive elk-hide tent. Any sound of their passage was easily drowned out by the zealous mirth of the gathered warriors.

Dropping into a crouch as he reached the pavilion, the thief pressed his ear against its rough surface. He was forced to cover the other with a hand to blot out the noise of the camp. The same laughter that covered their movement had worn out its welcome. Over the muffled guffaws, Hollis could make out a handful of baritone, stern voices. He was unsure if he could have understood the muffled words, even if he spoke any of the Rangor dialects, but the meaty slap that followed made their intent unmistakable.

179

The thief pulled his broad bladed knife from its horizontal sheath at his back. Aristoi laid a light hand on his forearm. She couldn't have helped hearing the blow from within the tent. She tapped her temple and then gestured to the camp around them. *Think about it*, the gesture said.

Hollis nodded, pointing to the tent and then his eye. *I am only going to take a look.* The Songspear removed her hand and turned her attention back to the scattered clusters of warriors. Carefully cutting a slit in the elk hide near the ground, the thief lay against the frozen ground to peer through it and into the tent beyond.

The pavilion was vaguely circular with a ten yard diameter. Tied to the center pole were two bloodied figures, surrounded by three fur-clad Rangor. One of them crouched near the prisoners, their back turned to Hollis's vantage point. Again, the deep voice rumbled, its words again obscured by distance and the language barrier. One of the bound figures shook their head adamantly, their blood-soaked hair swaying in the dim light. The thief recognized Sagaun's swollen features hanging between those sodden curtains.

With a frustrated exclamation, a massive Rangor burst through the tent flap. Easily a head taller than any of his gathered clansmen, Hollis would have recognized the man by his size alone. The tent's flickering torchlight made that leap of logic unnecessary. Although his chestnut brown beard had developed streaks of gray in the decade since the thief had last seen him, he could never mistake the craggy face beneath for anyone but Ret.

In the days when Hollis and his companions were known as the Band of Six, Ret had served as both older brother and partner in crime to him. Often brash and impulsive, the massive Rangor warrior had taken the thief under his wing at a time when Hollis thought himself incapable of being anything but the killer Seran had trained him to be. His stubborn, often violent, demeanor hid a brutally honest yet fiercely loyal heart.

They had not parted on the best of terms; the inexplicable loss of two-thirds of their friends certainly hadn't been ideal circumstances. While Hollis chose to escape his pain by climbing into a bottle, Ret set off for the northern wastes in search of answers. *I should have gone with him.* No doubt Ret's hunt had led him to Mika, and after ten years, there was little doubt in the thief's mind whose word the big man would believe. Hollis had spent most of the journey north preparing himself for a confrontation with Mika. The thought of also crossing swords with Ret as well just about broke his heart.

Pulling away from the tear in the tent, the thief looked to Aristoi's featureless shape in the dark. "We have a problem."

Raised voices from inside covered the pair's words. "What do you think you are doing?" It was Ret's booming baritone. "Violence on the battlefield brings honor. Beating bound prisoners brings nothing but shame to yourself and your ancestors!"

"Only one?" she whispered in response.

"Another one," Hollis corrected. "Ret is here as well."

"That certainly does complicate things." He had shared with the Songspear the history leading up to their first meeting early in their friendship. She knew the esteem he had for the Rangor and exactly how much he regretted how they had left things. "His presence cannot be a coincidence."

The thief couldn't argue the point. "If he is here, I feel Mika cannot be far behind."

The silence was broken by an only barely restrained cry of pain.

"We have a choice to make." The tone of Aristoi's whispered words said there wasn't really any choice at all.

"I only see one." As much as Hollis had loved Ret in his younger years, he wouldn't allow Sagaun or Valmont to suffer for the sin of wanting to be free. "There are four warriors, including Ret. Their attention is focused on our companions tied to the center pole."

"No doubt they have posted guards at the pavilion's entrance, so those odds are likely to double within seconds of breeching the tent."

Hollis tapped the elk-hide before him. "If there is no advantage to taking out the guards beforehand, I am of the mind to make our own door right here."

The Songspear stretched out a hand to test the tent's surface. "That could work. If we combine our efforts, we should be able to cut it open before anyone inside notices."

"Can you make sure no one hears their cries for aid?"

"I have something in mind, but there are two issues."

The thief didn't ask the obvious question, trusting his companion to provide any complications.

"First, you will be between my song and its intended target. You will be caught in it as well."

"That's a small price to pay to keep bad odds from getting worse."

"More importantly, it will take a moment to take full effect. For that time, you will be alone in there with four northern warriors."

"I will have to endure." Hollis found himself grateful for the darkness that lay between them. He didn't trust that he could keep

181

the trepidation at the prospect of what lay before him from his face. He drew his Dwarven steel sword and set its point against the side of the tent just above the level of his head. "On three?"

Aristoi extended her spear, laying its tip besides his. "One."

The thief gathered himself, allowing the Well-given serenity to pull the cold fingers of fear from his heart. "Two."

"Three," they hissed in unison. Both weapons bit deeply into the elk hide, tearing it at opposite angles. The side of the tent buckled as a triangular section fell inward.

Hollis felt more than heard the soft melody of Aristoi's song as the sounds of celebration around him faded into silence. It was a credit to Ret's still-sharp reflexes that his were the first eyes turned in the direction of the makeshift door. Putting from his mind the certainty that within moments, he would need to cross swords with the closest thing he had to a brother, Hollis surged forward. As the nearest warrior began to turn, the thief swept the razor-sharp edge of his Uteli blade across the back of his knee. The Rangor collapsed into a heap at Hollis's feet. Before the man hit the ground, the thief's return stroke opened his throat.

Before either of his companions could draw their weapons, Hollis was past them and free of their reach. He saw Ret's lips moving, but Aristoi's song swallowed the sound before it emerged. In the midst of his Well-born calm, the thief's profound sadness at the inevitability of fighting his friend seemed distant, almost like the memory of a tooth ache. Ret's shock at seeing Hollis seemed to stay his hand for a split second, allowing his warriors to charge forward first. *Ret's a problem for "thirty seconds from now Hollis"*, he thought. *"Right damned now Hollis" has more pressing concerns.*

Although both the Rangor were truly massive, out weighing the thief by at least fifty pounds, he was shocked by their speed. He was forced to dance backwards out of the range of their short, bearded axes. However, they didn't have the monopoly on unexpected quickness. Both Aristoi and Asaege were fond of reminding him that he could benefit from a diet richer in vegetables and poorer in honey cakes, but even with the extra weight Hollis carried, he was extraordinarily agile.

Feinting right, the thief switched directions so swiftly that he was able to lunge past the slower of his two remaining opponents, scoring a shallow but solid hit across her naked bicep. She transferred her axe to her left hand so smoothly that he was unable to follow up the strike, but the damage, no matter how minimal, had been done. Skipping back a few steps, Hollis watched for another opening as he bought time for the Songspear to join him. He felt a wash of relief as the Kieli stepped through the tear in the pavilion's wall.

The comforting warmth turned to ice in his veins as Ret moved forward to block her path. *Perhaps he is as unwilling to fight me as I am him.* The thief was unable to find any true relief in the thought, as it left Aristoi to deal with the northern warrior. Although momentary, Hollis's lapse in concentration allowed the two Rangor to close on him. Trained for battle from the time they could walk, it was rare to live long enough to regret losing focus for a moment while fighting a member of the barbarian clans.

Forced to place his trust in the Songspear's skills, Hollis turned his full attention to the pair before him. Holding his Wallin Fahr before him, its point at eye height, he sought to maintain what distance his distraction hadn't surrendered. Thankfully, his Uteli blade more than made up for the natural reach advantage granted by the Rangors' height. Between that and the agile nature of the sword compared to the short, chopping axes wielded by the warriors, Hollis felt comfortable that he could hold them at bay long enough for one of them to make a mistake.

That opportunity presented itself more quickly than he could have anticipated. Possessed by more frustration than sense, the uninjured Rangor leapt forward in an attempt to overbear the thief. He waited until the overzealous warrior had fully committed before deftly sidestepped, turning the charge into a clumsy stumble as the man tried to keep his balance. Hollis brought his weapon down across the back of the Rangor's neck, separating flesh and muscle to reveal the gristly smile of vertebrae beneath. The Dwarven steel blade bit deeply into the warrior's spine; he dropped to the ground like a string-less puppet.

Shifting his eyes to the side for a split second, Hollis saw that Aristoi and Ret continued to circle each other warily. There was a time when the big man was a less patient fighter, led more by his heart than his head. *Apparently, the years have been teacher to us all.*

The final warrior gave Hollis the respect earned by the deaths of her two comrades. Her eyes were narrowed as she watched him; in those eyes, he saw a trace of justifiable fear. Had the Songspear's spell not robbed him of his voice, the thief would have given her the option of surrender. She still presented a very real threat to him, but with her wounded arm, time was Hollis's real enemy. Although he trusted in the effectiveness of Aristoi's song, their presence wouldn't go unnoticed forever. If they could end things quickly, there still was a chance they could rescue their comrades and slip from the camp unseen. Each moment it dragged on, that chance became slimmer.

End things quickly, he thought. *That would mean putting Ret down hard enough that he cannot get up to stop us.* Having firsthand experience with Ret's capacity to absorb damage, Hollis wasn't sure sufficient force to accomplish that task wouldn't kill the Rangor. *Am I prepared to take it that far?* One look at Sagaun's bruised and blood-stained face solidified his resolve.

When the thief lunged at the Rangor woman's already injured arm, she understandably recoiled, turning her body to pull it out of reach of his blade. In doing so, the axe in her uninjured hand rotated as well, leaving her entire left side momentarily unguarded. *If things had been different ...* Hollis didn't bother finishing the thought. Dwarven steel sliced through leather and flesh alike. The Rangor looked down in shock as her stomach and legs were instantly stained crimson. She took a faltering step toward the thief before pitching forward, no doubt a victim of shock.

Moving past the unconscious warrior, Hollis rushed to where Aristoi and Ret fought. Having moved past the initial "feeling out" period, both of them were locked in a life-and-death struggle. Aristoi indisputably held the reach advantage, but unable to strike at her, Ret focused his hammering blows on the shaft of her spear when it tarried too close to him for too long. The length of the prized weapon of her mother, and her mother before her was scored by jagged gouges. Ret seemingly paid for defiling the sacred weapon; his leather breeches and bare chest were coated in a thin sheen of blood and sweat.

As the thief approached the pair, mustering the determination to attack his former friend, the flap covering the pavilion's entrance was pulled back. Standing in the opening, flanked by a half dozen Rangor warriors was a lithe shape, naked steel clenched in her right fist. Even if she hadn't held Silvermoon's sword, Hollis couldn't have mistaken Mika for any other person on the face of Taerh.

At Mika's raised hand, Ret cautiously retreated to where she stood. Its usefulness at its end, Aristoi let her song fade into silence. In a rush, the sounds of the night returned like flood waters after a sudden thunderstorm.

"Please, Hollis, join us." Mika's voice held a casualness that enraged the thief. "If you wanted a reunion, all you needed to do is ask." She gestured at the three bodies littering the pavilion's floor. "None of this was necessary."

Hollis stepped up beside Aristoi, laying a hand on her shoulder. "You know damn well I am not here for a reunion, Mika."

"I had assumed as much, but an old lady can hope." Unlike Ret, the years didn't appear to have had such a profound effect on the woman before him. No trace of gray marred her deep brown mane of hair and her flashing green eyes still held the clarity of youth. The only compromise to the passing years were the fine lines etched into the corners of her eyes, but somehow they made Mika seem more appealing than Hollis's memories of her.

The thief forced the ghostly influence of childhood infatuation from his mind. "That hope can be laid in a grave next to the men you betrayed. I am here to take everything from you ... just like you took everything from me."

Mika tapped Ret's shoulder with a closed fist, looking meaningfully at the Rangor warrior. "Not everything." The massive man's features were unreadable as he studied the thief.

"Ret and I will have our own reunion once I am through extracting my blood price from you." Hollis was shocked by the coldness in his own voice. Until she walked through the flap, the motivation for his travels north were purely supposition. Now that it had suddenly become so very real, the thief hadn't found himself as conflicted as he would have thought.

"Blood price? Bold words. Ret, do you remember the scrawny youth that came to us, more passion than sense?"

Ret's shaggy head bobbed. "He is no longer that boy, Mika."

"That he is not, my friend." Turning her attention back to Hollis, she asked, "Tell me, boy-no-longer, for what do you think I owe you blood price?"

"Your betrayal cost two good men their lives; it cost me much, much more."

"I never laid a finger on Marcus." Hollis saw Ret's eye twitch at the mention of the thaumaturge's name.

"You might as well have plunged a knife into his chest. You traded the lives of the people I loved for what? Glory? Power? What did the Well deliver to you that was worth the sacrifice of everything you should have held dear?"

"Held dear? It seems you were the only one of us that never saw the world for what it was. Silvermoon would have done the same to me given half a chance."

"No!" Hollis's voice became hard as bared steel. Aristoi's hand on his wrist was the only thing that prevented him from launching himself at Mika. "He would have done no such thing," he said through clenched teeth. "Even after Haedren was dead, you let his toxic words poison your heart. Silvermoon loved you like a sister. He

185

would have gladly laid down his life for any of us, especially you."

Mika squinted, studying the thief for a quick second before responding. "And so he did."

Hollis pulled free from the Songspear's grasp, bringing his Wallin Fahr up as he crossed the distance between himself and his former friend. Before any of her escorts could move, Mika met him halfway. Silvermoon's stolen blade met Hollis's gifted one. *Damned, but she is as fast as she ever was ... maybe faster.* As she slipped sideways in an attempt to flank him, the thief mirrored her motion, keeping his blade pointed at her sternum. Hollis wasn't sure it was shock or respect he saw in Mika's eyes, but she disengaged with a small half-step backwards.

"Careful, boy-no-longer, do not allow your heart to goad you into a fight the rest of you cannot hope to win. While we may disagree on my motivation, there can be little doubt as to the results of my visit to the Well of Worlds. If you insist on crossing blades with me, I will be forced to show you what it means to be a Child of the Well."

Forcing a self-assured smirk to his lips that he didn't quite feel, Hollis said, "I may have some idea what that is like."

She allowed the tip of her sword to drop slightly. "What are you saying?"

"The site of your betrayal was not the only Well." He gestured to the gathered warriors. "These people may need to take your word for what it means to be a Child, but you can save your lies. I know the truth of it."

Mika's eyes grew distant for a second, as if she were processing the situation and debating her next move. Before Hollis could take advantage of her distraction, a smile blossomed on her face. "This is wonderful news."

"How do you figure that?"

"I know you believe I have wronged you, Hollis, but put aside your anger. Not since the Age of Legends have there been two Children of the Well in the same place."

"I plan to rectify that in short order."

Mika gave him a doubtful look, continuing as if he hadn't spoken. "Do you not understand? We represent something truly special, doubly so together."

"You are right, we are special, but the Wells were not meant to promote any one person's fortunes. They were meant to help all people, to help all of Taerh."

"I am helping these people. For uncounted generations, they

186

have been forced to scratch out a living up here in the north, no better than animals. I give them purpose; I give them a better life for their sons and daughters."

"If I truly thought you believed that, we would have something to talk about. You serve only yourself, as you have always done. Much like Silvermoon, Marcus and the rest of us, these people's interests correspond to your own, however briefly. When they cease to do so, they, too will be cast aside."

He saw anger creep into Mika's face. "I understand," she growled.

"I do not think you do."

"It is your wish to be the only Child. You want the power for yourself."

"What about your knowledge of either myself or Stephen would lead you to the conclusion that we desire solitude?"

Mika's sneer spoke volumes. "Do not speak of that place, nor of the small people that populate it."

"Your seizure of the Well's power did not give you mastery over it. You doomed those closest to you in order to fuel it, but in your refusal to accept the Well's true purpose, you have set the two sides of your nature against themselves. I did not realize it at the time, but Samantha made the same mistake, and look at what it cost her."

A condescending smile covered Mika's face. "If you held sway over the Well's full potency, you would have struck me down before I could have drawn a blade. The fact that I still live proves that neither of us has a perfect understanding of the Well's purpose. Perhaps together we can pry its secrets from the universe itself."

Hollis shook his head slowly. "No, Mika. Although we both have been blessed by the Well of Worlds, we are no more alike than a candle and a forest fire. I seek to use the gifts I have been given to light the way for those around me. All you desire is to consume everything within reach to feed your unquenchable hunger."

"You are making a mistake. I did not allow Silvermoon to come between me and my destiny, what makes you think you can take this opportunity from me?" The tip of Mika's blade snapped up with the swiftness of a serpent's strike.

"Because I'm the only one who can." Hollis pulled a cloak of serenity around him once more as he embraced the "Understanding" for what he hoped wasn't the last time.

The tip of Mika's sword flashed in the flickering torchlight as it darted towards the thief's face. Giving ground, he parried the blow, letting his blade ride along hers. He allowed his sense of touch as much as his eyes to guide his riposte. Taking a small step to the side, Hollis lunged forward. With a deft twist of her wrists, his opponent turned the thrust aside and disengaged as easily as a normal person would tie their shoe.

Hollis turned the "Understanding" on her, probing for weaknesses that he could exploit and found ... nothing. For the first time since being granted the Well's gifts, they failed him. The gathered Rangor warriors surrendered their secrets like open books to him. *A bored fidgeting here, a barely restrained zealous charge there.* Even Ret's suppressed conflict was plain on his face. Mika, however, was as empty as a patch of midnight. Through the cultivated cloak of calm that hung around the thief's heart, he felt the pangs of fear.

It stood to reason that as each person was unique, the gifts bestowed upon them by the Well would be tailored to each of its children. Growing up in the Ash, born to tragedy and weaned on often unpredictable acts of violence, Hollis's survival often depended on judging his father's mood before he could take it out on the boy. The Well of Worlds simply magnified that talent, granting him the knack for knowing how things worked, even people.

Mika, on the other hand, had been born into the Mantrian warrior caste. When the child had reached out for a toy, she had been given a weapon instead. It stood to reason that when she sacrificed Silvermoon to the Well's glowing waters, it enhanced her already formidable martial aptitude. When Hollis studied her, it wasn't that the "Understanding" had betrayed him in his time of need, when it came to swordplay, the warrior woman simply had no weaknesses to expose.

Before his new found realization could completely settle upon his mind, Mika leapt forward, swinging her sword in a tight horizontal arc. Hollis matched her lunge, meeting her stolen blade with his own. As steel met steel, both of them rotated their weapons so they slid past each other. As Hollis pivoted on his lead foot, turning to face her, Mika's sword was there to check his charge. Although it was only a half-hearted thrust, if he hadn't reversed his movement, it would have impaled him through the chest.

Turning his backwards hop into a sidestep, the thief brought his Wallin Fahr down in an overhead chop. Again, Mika's blade was there. Rather than halting the sword, she allowed its momentum to add to the strength of her own blow. Hollis barely was able to recover from his swing to get his weapon between them. *Fighting her is like slashing at a wave*, he thought. *Every time I think I have the upper hand, she just flows around me.*

Mika's stolen Uteli blade slid along Hollis's, its tip biting deeply into his shoulder. Skipping backwards once more, her follow-up swing missed the thief by the slimmest of margins. Mika's small, almost casual steps ate up the distance between them like a starving man as she pressed Hollis into a purely defensive posture. It was all he could do to escape her unyielding assault.

The thief's breathing came in great bellows like gasps. The sweat of his exertion stung his eyes and mixed freely with the blood from the dozens of nicks and cuts that covered his arms and torso. Each one bore silent testimony to a missed parry or ill-timed retreat. To all appearances, his opponent might as well have been in the midst of an evening stroll rather than the life and death struggle in which they found themselves.

Each time he saw an opening, Hollis pounced, only to find Mika's blade there to close it and make him pay dearly for the attempt. After what seemed an eternity, he had lost count of the minor wounds that covered his body. With each, a bit of his cloak of serenity was torn from him. Soon Hollis realized two things. The first was, even with the "Understanding", he was no match for his former friend. The second and more distressing revelation was that Mika was toying with him.

Mika didn't make him suffer under the burden of that knowledge long. She launched a vicious flurry, batting Hollis's blade aside before striking him soundly behind the ear with the pommel of her sword. As the tent's interior darkened before his eyes, the thief saw the group of Rangor warriors close around Aristoi. The last thing he heard was Mika's voice, without even the hint of exertion. He assumed she spoke in Trade Tongue for his benefit. "Be gentle with the Kieli. Any who deny the Hungered his prize will serve as his next meal."

189

Chapter Twenty-Three
A Necessary Alliance

"You didn't need to come with me." Jillian studied Marisol from the corner of her eye as she drove.

"I know," her friend replied, watching the road ahead of them. An uncharacteristic look of concern was plain on her face. "With everything that's happened in the last twenty-four hours, I didn't feel comfortable letting you go alone."

"Is that the only reason?"

"Truth?"

"Truth."

"No. None of this makes any sense. If I had to sit home alone, I would have been climbing the walls. My mother is already suspicious."

"What's she suspicious about?"

"She doesn't know and that makes it so much worse. CIA interrogators have nothing on Puerto Rican mothers, except they don't need water boards and black hoods to get the truth. Abril Diaz works in guilt and meaningful looks like sculptors work in marble."

"So you would rather come to a wake?"

"Than face my mother with a secret in my heart? Every day of the week."

Jillian laughed softly. "I do love your mom."

"So do I, but if you stay at my house for a few more days, hospitality comes to an end and you're fair game as well."

Marisol shared a home and mortgage with her parents, an unfortunate price of the occupation that she and Jillian had chosen. Although they were literally responsible for the future, their paychecks never seemed to reflect it.

"I wanted to thank you for letting me stay with you. After that thing with Cyrill —"

"—You know our guest room is only ever a phone call away. Besides, last night has me shaken up as well." An unasked question hung in the suddenly awkward silence of the car.

"What's on your mind?" Jillian asked softly, the ever-increasing weight of her guilt feeling like a sodden wool sweater across her shoulders. Not for the first time since the previous evening, she found herself regretting pulling her friend into her troubles.

"Do I have to choose just one?"

"Why don't we start with the first and see where we go from there?"

"All of this is insane."

"Granted," Jillian agreed. "That doesn't make it any less true, however."

"How long has this been going on?"

"I first reflected in late September ... so three months."

"And in three months, you couldn't find an opportune time to let me in on the secret?"

"Would you have believed me?"

Marisol bit her bottom lip, her lack of reply was a response all its own.

"That sounds a lot like a solid no."

"Do you blame me?"

"Not at all. That's the thing. I've been having a hard enough time deciding if I were crazy or not. I'm not sure I could have convinced anyone else of that fact."

"What made you change your mind?"

"About my sanity or confiding in you?"

"Either? Both?"

"I suppose the answer is the same regardless." Jillian focused on the road before her, so she didn't have to witness her friend's expression, even out of the corner of her eye. "Things on both sides have suddenly become all too real. At first, everything happened in Taerh, in my dreams. It was easy to dismiss it as an active dream life."

"What happened?"

"Hector broke into my apartment looking for a pair of journals belonging to Stephen's friend."

"Your drug dealer?"

"The same."

"How did you get the journals?"

"I stole them—"

"Jillian!"

"—but Hector got them from someone who in turn stole them from Stephen, so they really weren't his to begin with. Stephen's friend, Jeff, documented his own jaunts to the other side, including the events that precipitated his death."

"Death?"

Jillian nodded. "He wasn't the only one. Around the same time of Jeff's passing, three more people died under curious circumstances. One murder, one suicide and an unexplained brain embolism."

"But things just started getting real a few months ago?"

"Until I read the journals, I had no idea about any of this. The first sign I had that Taerh was bleeding over into our world was when Hector tried to take the journals back."

"You could have told me then."

"Things moved very quickly. By the next day, we thought everything was over. Hector's reflection was thought killed, taking my earthbound problem with him."

Marisol's sudden intake of breath seemed deafening in the confines of the car. "Jillian," she gasped, "we're talking about someone's life."

Jillian found herself shocked at her own casual dismissal of Plague Man's death. "I must sound like such a terrible person, but …" Her words trailed off as she heard herself rationalizing something that would have been anathema to her less than a year before.

To her credit, Marisol didn't drive home the point she knew she'd already won. "But what?" she asked softly.

"Plague Man … Hector's reflection was … is one of the most evil people I've ever known. Through Asaege's eyes, I saw the depths to which he was willing to sink in the name of power and revenge." Even in the warmth of her heated car, Jillian shivered with the thought of the masked villain.

"You didn't kill him. Did you?"

Jillian tried to ignore the indignation that arose in her chest. "No, he fell off a cliff. When Hector disappeared, I assumed the worst. The best? I assumed that both he and his reflection were dead."

"Yet that wasn't real enough to loop me in?"

"For good or ill, it was over. With Hector gone, I had lost access to his adder root spiked weed, so my dream-travels to Taerh also came to an end. No matter how I felt about it, I had to move on."

"Except?"

Jillian felt a small, guilty smile creep onto her face. "Except I didn't want to."

"What did you do," Marisol asked in a vaguely scolding tone.

"The journals were quite clear about the fact that adder root was the key to reflecting. Between Google and online retail, it was actually pretty easy to start growing it. I'm still working on getting the dosage right but within a month of Hector's disappearance, I was reflecting regularly again."

"I'm going to try to ignore the fact that you let me reflect using a plant of which you were unsure of the dosage."

"People are dying again, Mari. Freeholder Fredericks. Erik Gunn." When Marisol wrinkled her nose in confusion, Jillian expanded. "A promising high school athlete. Hector's shop was burned to the ground, most likely with him in it. Now, last night someone tried to kill Cyrill."

"You told him it was most likely a coincidence."

"I lied. He was barely holding it together." It was only half the reason for Jillian's withholding of her suspicions, but it sounded more sane than "Cyrill may be a sociopathic thaumaturge in Taerh," at least for now.

"Do you seriously think they're all related?"

"I'm not sure, but I also can't afford to be taken by surprise if they are." Not for the first time since involving Marisol, Jillian heard the craziness of her own words. She was saved from continuing her train of thought by their arrival at the funeral home.

"Is that why you're crashing the wake of a local politician?"

"I'm sorry, Mari. You must think I'm delusional. You don't have to—"

She caught Jillian's face between her palms. "Stop. You're my friend, probably the best I've ever had." Releasing Jillian's head, Marisol gestured to the full parking lot. "All of this is just ... well, it's simply insane."

"I know—"

"—but it's an insanity that I witnessed with my own eyes. I can't say I know what's going on, but whatever it is, it's important to you. I trust you, Jillian. If you're going to see how deep this hole

194

goes, I'll hold the flashlight."

Relief flowed through Jillian's body, relaxing muscles unconsciously tensed like ice melting in the sun. "Thank you, Marisol."

"That's what friends are for, right?"

*****

Jillian didn't know what she expected, but the funeral home was packed. People stood shoulder to shoulder in the foyer, slowly filing past a stern faced man in a dark blue suit. Checking each person's name against the list before him, he directed people either into the gallery to his right or the state room to his left where the dark oak surface of the closed coffin could be seen.

"I don't suppose we're on the list," Marisol said trying to keep her balance among the shoving throngs of hopeful onlookers.

Jillian felt a pang of disappointment. "I thought it seemed too easy." Her words were as much for herself as her friend.

"Do you have a plan?"

"I'm working on it."

As they got to the front of the line, Jillian put on her best do-me-a-favor smile. "We responded a little late and may not be on your list."

With a bored tone, the man droned, "Everyone's on my list, or they're in the gallery."

A voice emerged from the crowd behind the suited clipboard-jockey. "It's okay, Graham, they're with us." Following it through the throng came a familiar uniformed face.

"Officer Parr, this is most inappropriate."

Billy smiled lopsidedly. "You asked for off duty volunteers, didn't you?"

Graham frowned deeply. "We assumed they would be in uniform."

"You know what they say about people who assume things, right?"

Shaking his head slowly, Graham's eyes had already moved on to the next people in line. "Make sure they stay quiet and out of the way." Without waiting for Billy's reply, he waved Jillian and Marisol through and addressed the mourners behind them. "Names, please."

Jillian ignored Graham's scowl as the pair walked by. She mouthed, "Thank you," to Billy as they approached him. The time-dulled memories of his bullying ways seemed to soften when combined with the more recent image of him reading to Richie at his bedside.

"It won't be a big deal ... unless it becomes one," he said

195

scanning the crowd. "We have plenty of plain clothes officers here, including your old friend, Blaine."

The thought of the detective and his reflection, Claerius, sent shivers up Jillian's spine.

"Rumor has it that Mrs. Moses requested him specifically."

Turning to Marisol, Jillian explained. "Detective Blaine questioned me after the fire at the Florist."

"I take it the two of you didn't become fast friends?"

"Let's just say I won't be holding my breath for a Christmas card."

"That's putting it mildly," Billy added. "He must have seen us talking, because after you left, Blaine plopped himself down on the edge of my desk for a chat."

"What did he want?"

"You. More specifically, anything I could remember about you from high school."

"What did you tell him?" Jillian heard the desperation in her own voice.

"Nothing, I don't scare easily. It's one of few advantages of a misspent youth." Through the bravado that he put forth, she heard a note of regret in the man's voice.

In this instance, I think fear may be the right choice, she thought bitterly.

Marisol cleared her throat, looking meaningfully at Billy.

"Oh, I'm sorry. Marisol, this is William Parr. We were friends in high school."

Billy extended his hand. As Marisol took it, he said, "Jillian is too kind. I would have gotten in less trouble had she and I been friends in school. The truth is, I'm not sure I would've wanted to be my friend back then."

"Billy ..." Jillian struggled to find words of consolation but couldn't find any that wouldn't be outright lies.

He shook his head. "I know what I was like, Jillie. As much as we all would like to change the past, it's beyond our ability. I hope that the person I am now, in some way, makes up for the stupid kid I was."

Hesitant to mention the fact that she had overheard his interaction with Richie, Jillian settled for, "I think you're doing a pretty good job, William."

At her use of his full name, the man stood a little straighter.

Marisol smiled softly as she said, "At any rate, it's a pleasure to meet you, Officer Parr."

"Ditto, Marisol." He turned back to Jillian. "Speaking of unexpected meetings, may I ask what the two of you are doing here?"

Quickly, Jillian responded, "What makes you think we're not friends of the family?"

"Not on the list."

"Campaign donors?"

"If Fredericks had a voter base, you'd be the farthest thing from it." Before Jillian could feign indignation, he added, "That's not a bad thing. By all accounts, his political role models were Machiavelli and Boss Tweed."

"That's a pretty bad combination," Marisol commented.

"Yes," Billy said. "Yes, it was. Which makes me wonder why the vice president of our high school's chapter of the ACLU would be paying her respects."

Seeing as he put himself at risk by vouching for them, Jillian figured Billy deserved some measure of honesty. "We're less interested in the deceased than we are in our fellow mourners."

He tilted his head and frowned. "I don't understand."

As luck would have it, right at that moment, Veronica Moses stepped through the door. Flanked by a small retinue, she bypassed the line and approached Graham. His voice, an octave higher than it had been when speaking to Jillian, greeted her.

"Mrs. Moses! This way please. We have a seat reserved for you in the front row." Snapping his fingers, Graham gestured for one of his associates to take his place as he walked towards the state room.

Billy didn't fail to notice Jillian's intense focus on the new arrival. "Never mind. I think it's becoming clearer now."

Among the group of people that accompanied Veronica was a college-aged young man. Even from Jillian's vantage point, it was clear that his eyes never left the woman's black clad figure. He looked vaguely familiar to Jillian, but she couldn't place where she'd seen him before. The empty, hungry expression he wore on his face wasn't one of an assistant or relative. Veronica stopped momentarily to extend her gloved hand. He snatched it immediately as a drowning man would a bit of floating flotsam.

"Who's the kid?" Jillian couldn't hide the curiosity in her voice. Phantom wisps of Asaege's memories tickled her brain.

Billy smirked slightly. "That's Robert Maris. He was a friend of her husband before his overdose."

Her lips turned down into a tight frown, but he seemed to not notice.

"If Mrs. Moses captures the young vote, he'll be the reason

why. He played football in school and continues to be active in county college. After her husband's … um … incident—" Perhaps he had noticed after all. "—Maris spread her message among his peers, taking a public stand against drugs and other influences that led to his friend's downfall." Billy made quotes in the air with his fingers as he said the word "friend."

"You doubt his sincerity?" Marisol caught Billy's attention, giving Jillian a chance to compose herself.

"Oh, he's passionate alright, but I'm not sure it has anything to do with the issues." As the group disappeared into the crowded state room, Veronica laid her free hand over the one clasped in her other. "It doesn't take a sharp eye to see that she's got him wrapped around her finger."

Like the surge from a broken dam, realization crashed upon Jillian. She had seen Maris at Lady Markov's rally. The bearded young man beside her on the steps must have been his reflection. First Detective Blaine and now the lovesick boy, Mrs. Moses's connection to Taerh became increasingly obvious the more Jillian learned about the woman.

*****

Although the polished wooden casket was surrounded by enough flowers to choke a hundred bee hives, it was far from the center of attention. After a dramatic show of consolation with the widow, she had moved to the rear of the room to hold court. At some point, Detective Blaine had joined her entourage. He stood behind her, his squinting eyes sweeping the crowd as Moses entertained her admirers. Robert remained close as she chatted quietly with a collection of politicians and civic leaders, his gaze never leaving her for long.

Now that she was finally faced with her nemesis in two worlds, Jillian was at a loss as to her next step. Her heartbeat felt like it was in her throat as her smoldering dislike of the woman quickly burst into the flames of hatred. Before her stood the woman who not only sought to set education in the county back seventy years but also used Stephen's unconscious body to do it, as if he were nothing more than a puppet dangling from her fingers. Meanwhile, no telling how much chaos her reflection was responsible for on the streets of Taerh as she whipped her supporters into a borderline murderous frenzy. If she didn't already have blood on her hands, they soon would be covered in it.

"I have to talk to her," Jillian announced, unsure who her words were meant for.

"Mrs. Moses?" Billy asked. "Why?"

Jillian just shook her head, her eyes projecting daggers into the woman's meticulously dressed body.

"Are we going to have a problem?" His voice gave the impression that he may have been regretting his choice to get the pair past Graham.

"There's not going to be a problem," Marisol assured him. She leaned close to her friend. "Is there, Jillian?"

"I just need to speak with her alone for a moment." Reluctantly pulling her eyes from Veronica, Jillian turned them to Marisol and Billy. "But I can't do it with Blaine or her boy-toy there. I have a suspicion they won't give me the chance."

"You're probably right," Billy agreed. "I can distract Blaine for a few minutes, but I'm not sure what I can do about Maris."

"You may not have to." Marisol softly smiled. "If Mrs. Moses's young admirer is looking for an audience for her rhetoric, I think I can hold his attention long enough for you to have your conversation. Draw the detective away, William, and I'll take care of the rest." She turned to Jillian, "You owe me ... big."

*****

True to Marisol's prediction, Veronica's young admirer left her side when the young woman gestured to him. A moment later, Billy stepped up behind Blaine, whispering in his ear. Jillian made her move as he and the detective stepped away.

As she pushed through the circle of people, Jillian said, "May I have a quick word, Ms.—"

Veronica interrupted her without letting her finish. "That is Mrs. Moses." Contempt clung to her words like curdled milk.

Consciously reigning in the anger that made her feel as if she vibrated within her skin, Jillian repeated, "May I have a quick word?"

Sighing heavily to indicate her annoyance, Veronica turned to face her. "I am far too busy—" When she laid eyes on Jillian, a visible tremor ran through her body. For the first time since her grand entrance, the nascent politician looked unsure of herself. On the other hand, Jillian found the comforting calm of Asaege's presence settle over her.

"It will only take a few moments."

Nodding shallowly a few times, Veronica gestured towards an open room away from the crowd. As Jillian led the way, an unpleasant chill arose along her spine, as if the woman behind her were searching for a place to plant a knife. As she heard the door close,

199

Jillian turned to face Lady Markov's reflection. Any advantage she had gained with her unexpected appearance had passed.

"Do I know you?" Veronica's question was sharp, a honed steel edge dripping with suspicion.

"We have met in passing, although it has recently come to my attention that we have a shared acquaintance in common."

Veronica wrinkled her nose and sniffed sharply as if she smelled something offensive. "I highly doubt that, Miss …" She paused, obviously waiting for Jillian to provide her name.

She didn't oblige the woman. "I was no less surprised to find that someone whose opinion I respect would associate with the likes of you." Veronica's mouth turned up into a vicious snarl, a cutting retort obviously on her tongue. Jillian didn't give her the chance. "But everyone makes mistakes."

"How dare you!"

Honed by Seran's training, Asaege's reflexes took over. Jillian stepped close enough to the woman to smell her overpriced perfume. "Bluster all you like. You know that all you ever were to him was a mistake." Hissed through clenched teeth, the menace of words not entirely her own surprised even Jillian.

Veronica took a half step back, seeming to compose herself as she did so. "Him?" Her scowl morphed into a self-satisfied smile. "You're a friend of my husband." The emphasis she placed on the final word felt like a dagger in Jillian's heart. "It's curious, isn't it?"

As much as she shared Jillian's anger, Asaege's consciousness did its best to temper it. "What?"

"The fact that the only worth he ever possessed came after he …" She paused for a split second, her eyes burning into Jillian's. "… overdosed."

"Is adder root a controlled substance now?

Veronica shrugged her shoulders, dismissing her question.

"I don't know what you're doing with him, what part you force him to play in your sick game, but it's going to stop."

Veronica raised an eyebrow. "Is it?"

Jillian's jaw clenched so tight, her ears began to ache.

"Keep in mind, bitch, we're not in some thinly gilded whorehouse. All I need to do is scream and you'll be in cuffs before the echo fades."

Thinly gilded whorehouse. She's talking about the Courtesan. Jillian's thoughts raced. Veronica was not only Lady Markov's reflection, she remembered what occurred in Taerh. She was an active participant.

"I fear that if Detective Blaine took you to jail tonight, a pretty girl like you may not last the night." Pursing her lips in a feigned expression of concern, Veronica murmured, "It's just a feeling that I have."

Did she just threaten to have me killed? A cold wave of realization washed over Jillian. *Is she responsible for the death of the man she is here to mourn?*

"He should be grateful. After making a mess of his opportunity in your friend's establishment, your appearance here offers him the chance to put it right."

Jillian held up her hands, open palms outward. "We're just talking. The detective won't do a damned thing, because he has no cause to."

Veronica patronizingly purred, "That's a good girl." She stood up a little taller, regaining a measure of the arrogance Jillian had witnessed earlier. "Now that we have established our respective positions in the world, I'll expect no further trouble from you, no matter where we meet again."

Jillian opened her mouth, ill advised words perched on her tongue. They were interrupted by the door bursting open. On the other side was a red faced Blaine, Billy close on his heels. Over the detective's shoulder, he mouthed, "Sorry."

"Ms. Allen," he snarled. Veronica's smug grin widened at the sound of his voice. "What are you doing here?"

Jillian seized her with a hard stare. "I was just leaving, Detective." On her way to the door, she passed close to Veronica. "I'll be seeing you around."

*****

"I'll just be a minute," Jillian called to Marisol as she walked down the short hall to her bedroom. After the funeral, she had thought to pack a few things for her short stay at her friend's house. The realization that Veronica might be actively working with Detective Blaine on Earth, just as her reflection worked with his in Taerh, opened a flood gate of worries in her. In her bedside table, Jillian had a small plastic accordion folder containing her important papers. They included her birth certificate, social security card as well as a handful of other documents that could be used against her by a determined party.

Alongside them in the drawer, Jillian had stowed the few journals she'd been able to take from the florist while Hector wasn't paying attention. Those very same books had resulted in his breaking into her apartment a few days later in search of them. As much damage as the contents of the plastic folder could do to her on Earth, the journals could represent just as large of a threat to Asaege in Taerh. If Blaine came to visit while she was away, Jillian couldn't afford him to find any of them.

As she reached for the light switch, Jillian felt the pang of an uneasy feeling. It caused her to fumble for it in an unsteady rush. When the rarely used overhead light threw the room into stark illumination, it also revealed the source of that apprehension. Sitting on her bed, the tattered fabric of his hood draped over his head, was Hector. The shadow it cast only partially hid the angry red burn that dominated the left half of his face. His eyes tightened in a pained grimace as he drew a raspy breath to speak.

"Close the door. We need to talk."

Part Two:

Shadows of the Moment

"The instruments of darkness tell us truths,
Win us with honest trifles, to betray us
In deepest consequence."

-William Shakespeare

Chapter Twenty-Four
A Cherished Refuge

Jillian took a step backward into the hall. "You can't be here," she whispered but even she wasn't completely sure if she meant his presence in her apartment or among the living at all.

"Believe me, Jillian," Hector said slowly, every hoarse word emerging from his throat radiating pain across his face, "you weren't my first choice of sanctuary."

"The police think you're dead."

"I'd prefer to keep it that way, at least for the foreseeable future." His voice crackled like boots walking across a patch of dry leaves. "The son of a bitch that tried to burn me alive is still out there, and I don't plan on giving him a chance to finish what he started."

Jillian stepped into the room and closed the door behind her. "Did you get a good look at him?"

Hector shook his head. "Big guy in a dark hoodie. He already had something wrapped around his face when I turned around. He hit me across the temple with some sort of club and dragged me into the back. After that, I was more concerned with surviving the fire than figuring out who set it."

"I saw a body in the flames, but there was no way to get to you."

Hector raised an eyebrow. "After everything Plague Man put you through, after everything I did, you still considered saving my life?"

"You say that like there could be another choice."

"I guess not for you."

"All I saw was someone in need. Merit never entered into it."

Hector tilted his head, digesting her sentiment. "I was able to crawl into the walk-in cooler and get the door closed." Even the short statement robbed him of his breath. He had to pause for a moment before continuing. "The former owner had a trap door installed in there leading to the basement." Another pause. "I was able to climb halfway down the ladder before falling the rest of the way."

"No one found you down there?"

"When I woke up, everything was quiet. Something must have fallen across the door, blocking it from above. With all the damage, the firefighters must have missed it." Hector's words came in bursts, broken by raspy gasps for air.

"Did you go to the hospital? It sounds like all that smoke did a number on you."

He dismissed her question with a backhanded wave. "I'm in much better shape than that big bastard had intended. Hospitals report to the police … there's no need to put up a sign pointing out that I'm still alive."

Without meaning to, Hector had corroborated the fear that had haunted Jillian since her run in with Veronica Moses. "Do you think the police are involved?"

"The cops have been watching the shop for the last month like I was giving away free donuts. Maybe they figured if they couldn't get something to stick, no one would miss another drug dealer."

Jillian remembered Blaine's words from the night of the fire. *We've had it under surveillance for the last month. Every person who even looked sideways at the place was captured on video.* Veronica had all but said that Blaine worked for her. If the florist shop was burned down at her request, she also had a record of everyone Hector sold to as well. The question was: how were the woman and Hector connected? Was it, like Stephen's comatose body, another public relations tool in her search for political office?

"You're not the only one that's been attacked." She searched his face for signs of surprise and found them written all over it. His eyes widened quickly and then squinted as he contemplated the ramifications of her revelation. "Why you?"

"Who else?"

Jillian repeated, "Why you?"

Lifting the fingers of his left hand to lightly brush the cracked, red skin of his cheek, Hector's lips turned up in an expression that was half smile, half grimace. "Listen, Jillian, there's more going on here than either of us is aware of. No doubt, you've already come to the same conclusion that I have."

"Which is?"

"What we don't know will certainly kill us." He closed his eyes for a second. In his excitement, his words had outstripped his limited lung capacity. When he began again, his voice was softer. "We'll never be anything close to friends; too much has passed between us for that."

"To say the least."

"However, the unfortunate truth is that we're in this together. Both of us have our own pieces to this puzzle. Each of us is likely to take those pieces to our grave unless we can somehow make sense out of the entire thing."

"You can't be suggesting we work together. Not after what you, what Plague Man did."

"I admit it's not an ideal situation, but it's better than the alternative."

"How can I trust you?"

"You can't."

At least he's honest, Jillian thought.

"But if you've figured out anything about me since we've met, you know I'm mostly concerned with my own well-being."

"That's been very clear from the start, yes."

"Whoever is behind this has already tried to kill me once. As long as they're out there, I need your help. You can't trust me, but you can rely on the fact that as long as you're valuable, you also have nothing to fear from me."

Why am I even considering this? "If we're going to do this, we need ground rules."

"Obviously. What did you have in mind?"

Jillian held up a finger. "First, no more dropping in unannounced. This is my home, and I never want to see you here again."

He nodded. "Done."

She added a second finger to the first. "Second, you tell me everything. If I even suspect you're holding back, I go to the police and let them know you're still alive."

"As long as you're as forthcoming with me, I can live with that … literally."

207

Jillian put up a third finger. "Lastly, this is between you and me. Plague Man is to know nothing about it. That means for the duration of our investigation, no adder root, no Dreamtime Dank, nothing."

Hector hesitated, agonizing over her last condition.

"Or you could take your chances with the folks that tried to burn you alive."

"Fine," Hector snapped, his already husky voice cracking. "You realize that no Plague Man means none of his unique skill set, correct?"

"I'm willing to make that sacrifice."

He murmured, "I'm glad one of us is."

"What was that?"

"Nothing. If we're not going to meet here, then where?"

"Stone Path Mall food court. There are a few tables tucked behind Casa Pizza. It'll provide some privacy while still being a public place. I don't suppose you have a cell phone."

"Not anymore. It was on the counter when the back door was kicked in."

"Pick us up two burners and we'll meet up tomorrow night at six pm." Jillian looked over her shoulder at the closed door before turning back to Hector. "Now, hand me the folder and journals out of the top drawer of my night stand."

He opened the drawer and gave her the accordion folder, but clutched the leather bound books for a moment. "I haven't forgotten where you got these."

She held out her hand. "I didn't figure you would."

Reluctantly, Hector extended the books towards her. As she took them, he rasped, "Someday, I'm going to want those back."

"I'm sure you will." Jillian turned to the door. "My friend and I are going to leave. I assume if you broke in, you can lock up after yourself on the way out."

*****

Jillian drove in silence for five minutes before Marisol broke it. "This isn't going to work if we're going to keep secrets, Jillie."

She dismissed her initial instinct to feign ignorance as to what her friend meant. "I know, Mari. I'm so used to going it alone on this side that I've grown accustomed to using secrecy to protect those I love."

Marisol exhaled slowly, the sound of her breath mingling with the drone of the road beneath their tires. "That's no longer the case. I'll be honest with you, all of this is a lot—"

"—I'm so sorry—"

"—Let me finish. It's a lot, but I imagine it weighed so much more when you carried it alone. I'd be lying if I said that I'm glad all of this is happening, but I could never regret sharing this burden with you."

"Thank you."

"However, I can't help you carry it if you only share the parts you feel I can handle." Jillian could feel her eyes on her in the dark interior of the car. "Or what I can figure out for myself."

"Hector was waiting for me in the bedroom when I turned on the light."

"Hector? I thought he was dead."

"Until that moment, so did I. He was able to crawl into the basement and avoid the worst of the fire."

"Did he see who set the fire?"

"He didn't get any better of a look than I did."

"Are you sure he wasn't involved? From what you've told me, Hector and his reflection aren't the most trustworthy men." Marisol said "reflection" as if the word rolled around on her tongue under its own power.

"He's pretty badly burned and can barely speak from the smoke. Neither of them strikes me as the type to put themselves through that sort of punishment just to sell a story."

"What did he want?"

"Hector's understandably angry and is looking to find whoever tried to burn him alive. He realizes going it alone will only result in much the same result, if not worse, a second time around."

"If he is reaching out to you—"

"—he has to be desperate," Jillian finished.

"Not quite the words I would have chosen. To the point though, I suppose."

"Both he and Plague Man give new meaning to the word unpredictable, but when it comes to them both, there is one thing you can count on. They always act in their best interest. Hector's injured and frightened, with neither friends nor resources to rely on." Although the logic was sound, Jillian hoped that her words seemed more confident than they did in her own thoughts.

"So he turned to the only person he knows has knowledge of both worlds?"

"He thinks he is taking advantage of my desire to prove the difference between us."

"Isn't he?"

"Yes … and no. He knows that I can't let him be murdered, but in his arrogance, he fails to see that the situation goes beyond him. As much as he thinks he's using me, I'm benefiting just as much."

"We," Marisol corrected.

"Mari—" Jillian started to argue, but her friend cut her off.

"Either we're in this together or we're not. As much as you're tempted to go back on that choice, it was made the minute you opened my eyes to the other world." Marisol's comfort with the concept seemed to grow with every mention of it.

"I can't ask you to take that kind of risk."

"You're not asking ... and neither am I."

Fear for her friend mixed with profound relief in Jillian's heart. She wouldn't have to face the coming days alone. "Thank you," was all that she could muster before her voice began to crack.

"I've said it before, Jillie ... that's what friends are for. Now, tell me everything he said."

*****

As Marisol opened the front door, Jillian could hear the low drone of the television in the family room beyond. The house Marisol shared with her parents was filled with the savory scent of dinner, no doubt kept warm for their arrival. Despite the trials of the day, Jillian's mouth watered at the prospect of Abril Diaz's home-cooked meal.

"Mami," Marisol called, lovingly using the familiar term in Spanish for her mother. "We're home." It always warmed Jillian's heart to witness the casual, close relationship she had with her family. Her own upbringing was more formal, and although she never doubted her parent's affection, it tended to be a little more reserved.

Abril emerged from the brightly lit kitchen, wiping her hands on the towel laid across her left shoulder. With a smile warmer than the aromas that filled the house, she cooed, "Mari ... Jillian, are you hungry?" Jillian loved the way Abril pronounced her name, softening the J and making it sound like the feeling of morning sun on your face.

The grumbling of her stomach was the only response Abril needed to hear from her.

"Come, come," she prompted, "I made you both a plate." A platter was more like it. Each of the eggshell-colored dishes was piled high with shredded turkey, black beans and an aromatic yellow rice.

"Thank you so much, Mrs. Diaz," Jillian began.

Abril scowled softly at her, a gentle scolding obvious on her face.

"Mami," Jillian corrected.

She nodded, her warm smile returning. "By the time you girls get cleaned up, the cake should be out of the oven."

Initially hidden by the enticing scent of dinner, the sweet smell of dessert hung in the air just beneath it. "Cake? You didn't have to."

"Don't be silly." Abril herded the pair towards the large washroom off the kitchen with casual flicks of her fingers, as one would uncooperative geese. "Your dinner is getting cold."

True to her promise, by the time they had washed up, a white sponge cake sat cooling on the counter. When Marisol reached out to tear off a small chunk, Abril playfully swatted her hand. "Dinner first."

As she was sitting down, Jillian recognized a familiar voice from the other room.

"—it took this to finally drive home the true state of not only our educational and library systems, but our county as a whole." It was that of Veronica Moses. "Critics will say that announcing my intent to fill Martin Frederick's seat is premature, even disrespectful, so close to his death. Even if it is just days, those people want to see the status quo continue for just a little bit longer. To them I say: drugs, corruption and immorality have been allowed to flourish in our community for far too long. If they cared for the health of the people of the county, they wouldn't want things to continue as they are for another hour, much less the weeks or perhaps months they deem an appropriate period of mourning."

Jillian's appetite evaporated as the woman's voice dug its way into her gut, causing her stomach to churn with nausea. Although playing upon a different set of fears, her words too closely mirrored those of her reflection to be coincidental.

"I'm sure you all are as tired of politicians filling their pockets while the very fabric of our community is devoured by the rot to which they turn a blind eye. Last year, Freeholder Fredericks began a crusade to replace a lot of the corrupt collaborators in both town and county government. However, his work is far from done. I, for one, will not let his dream for our county to become a victim of the very depravity that tragically took his life."

Jillian wondered how it was that no one seemed to see through the veil of fear-mongering and poisonous rhetoric Veronica spun. By the sound of the sporadic and enthusiastic applause that punctuated her speech, however, the crowd seemed to not only be fooled, but were active participants in their own deception.

"It's time the people standing against us realize that the will of

211

the people is stronger than their immoral hold on our community. Reach out to your representatives. Tell them to fill our fallen Free- holder's seat, and to put someone in it that represents the county you want, not the one you are forced to accept. Don't let them hide behind excuses and rules. Let their decision dictate what sort of men and women they truly are. Any that are worth your support will make the right choice."

Just as Markov did with the representatives of the Nine Fam- ilies in the square, Veronica sought to weave a trap for those with the power to appoint her to the Council of Freeholders. Rather than hemp and knot, she used cables of flesh and opinion. Pushing her plate away, Jillian found herself confident that the results would be much the same.

Chapter Twenty-Five
An Unpleasant Surprise

Asaege sat atop a stack of boxes, one leg folded under the other. Across her thighs her spell book lay open and forgotten. A flurry of activity buzzed around her as Binders and guild thieves organized the crates and barrels that cluttered the large, open room. After the events in the Dock Quarter, Toni had felt it wise to relocate the rebellion's base of operations. The chosen building had served as an inn when the Common Quarter had been less common. Situated against the thick wall that separated the Elm District from the Merchant's Quarter, it wouldn't have been Asaege's first choice, but secrecy served as better armor to the revolutionaries than stone ever could.

For the most part, Asaege had forced the clamor around her into the background as she lost herself in her thoughts. With the eidetic aid of her reflection's consciousness, she reviewed the events of the previous evening in her mind. Jillian's recollections of the parallels between Lady Markov's words and those of her twin on Earth contributed to Asaege's general uneasiness. The only bright spot in the otherwise dim outlook of Jillian's situation in her world was her friend's validation of Asaege's first impression of Remahl. *If the Crimson Sister is indeed the fair and rational person she appears to be, perhaps the revolution can be concluded without the deaths of everyone involved.*

"Do you have a moment?"

Rudelph's sudden appearance beside her caused Asaege to jump. The thick tome fell to the dirt floor with the loud slap of leather and parchment. "In Olm's Name, you nearly scared the life from me."

"My apologies, Asaege. Perhaps next time I shall have to announce my approach with the fanfare of trumpets." The sarcasm in his voice was sharp but good natured. He repeated his request. "Do you have a moment?"

"Of course, Rudelph." Hopping down from her perch, Asaege collected the fallen book. She muttered the locking phrase before tucking it beneath her arm. "Lead the way."

The Binder commander crisply turned on his heel and walked to the curving staircase leading to the second floor. When they reached the top, Rudelph scanned the line of sagging doors that lined the hallway. Seemingly choosing one at random, he held it open for Asaege to enter first.

Anything of value in the small room had been stolen long ago, leaving only a splintered bed frame and a pile of moldering blankets to indicate its use in days past. One of the room's shutters hung on its last rusty hinge, half-open and ready to tumble to the street below. Behind her, Asaege heard his heavy footsteps enter the room and the door close behind him.

"I have concerns." His tone was casual, but beneath it was a grit that Asaege had come to know as worry in the man.

"You are not alone. Is there anything in particular that is vexing you, Rudelph?"

"You were present for Lady Markov's little town meeting yesterday. Did anything strike you as odd?"

"Other than the riot she seemed intent on stirring up?"

"The guilds, Toni's people aside, cannot seem to agree amongst themselves whether the sun rises in the east or the west, but everyone present seemed to unite under the banner of a virtually unknown minor noble? Given the contentious past of the council of guilds, it seems a little too neat, too absolute."

Having been in the center of the mob, Asaege had been more concerned with her own safety than the lack of opposition within it. Given the perspective of time, Markov's control of the crowd did seem astonishing. It had only been through Jillian's influence that Asaege herself hadn't gotten swept away.

"And you want to know if she had some sort of thaumaturgical aid?"

"It would provide an explanation."

"I was in the midst of the crowd, but did not sense any magic being cast." Asaege thought for a moment. "However, if she possessed some sort of enchanted item, I would be unable to detect its use ... unless I was specifically looking for it."

"Which I assume you were not."

"In the moment, I was only concerned with not being torn to pieces by her supporters."

"I am not ashamed to admit that mobs frighten me." Again, Rudelph's conversational tone hid the uneasiness in his voice. "Soldiers, guardsman, even petty thugs I understand. A mob is something completely different. While a pseudo-military unit has some sort of central authority, a commander or leader, a mob is an unthinking being unto itself. It seeks chaos and destruction no matter the cost to its individual members."

"I do not get the sense Markov has much more concern for their welfare."

"If we could only convince her supporters of that fact, we could make some headway towards putting an end to the bloodshed."

Asaege frowned deeply. "You were not there. You did not see the fire in their eyes. They would follow her anywhere; how can reason compete with that?"

"Meanwhile, our numbers continue to grow, just not in any way that helps us. While freed prisoners and rescued courtesans certainly represent propaganda victories, they are also hungry mouths that do not add to our combat effective ranks."

"It is not their fault they are not soldiers, Rudelph."

"I never said it was. As long as they are under our protection, the Binders will treat their lives as our own. However, their presence does put all of us in a difficult situation."

Asaege remained silent, waiting for him to continue.

"Each base of operations must be chosen with them in mind. A portion of our forces must always be left behind to protect them."

"It was our rebellion that put them in this position in the first place."

"True, but it does not change the fact that caring for them takes away from the revolution we are supposed to be fighting. It is a little like climbing a hill with a rock tied to your back."

"I am sure none of them would appreciate the comparison."

"That does not make it any less true."

"Is that why you called me up here?"

215

Rudelph nodded.

"What would you suggest?"

"To continue to mount an effective resistance, we require a force that can move quickly and adjust even quicker. We cannot do that tied to those who cannot fight for themselves."

"So cut them loose?"

"Not at all. I propose that we split our numbers. The main force could remain in a semi-permanent headquarters with those we have freed but have nowhere else to go. Meanwhile, a few, smaller collection of cells can operate more independently, relocating more frequently between less heavily defended accommodations."

"Have you discussed this with the others?"

"Toni took a small team out an hour ago to scout some appropriate locations."

"Seran?"

"I saw no need to seek his counsel."

"What about mine?"

Rudelph refused to meet her eyes. "Toni and I felt alacrity was more important than consensus."

"Well, is that not convenient?" Any further discussion was interrupted by a loud crash, followed by the sound of shouts and clashing steel.

"Later," Rudelph snapped as he threw the door open and ran into the hall.

Asaege drew her Talis Fahr and followed him.

As they came down the stairs, Rudelph and Asaege walked into a maelstrom of violence. The revolutionary forces clashed with cloaked soldiers of the city guard in what was once the inn's common room. More guardsmen poured through a hole that marred the building's wall. Asaege could see the cobblestone streets of the Merchant's Quarter through the deep passage. As Rudelph launched himself into the fray, she searched for the source of the gaping entrance.

Asaege heard Lirych's next spell before she saw him. The harsh syllables marked his incantation as one of conjuration. Her first instinct was to attempt to counter weave his spell, as Lirych had done to her at the docks. Uncertainty froze the words in her throat, as even the warm influence of Jillian's presence cooled at the thought of attempting something so difficult. *Think*, Asaege scolded herself. *Any more delay and whatever he is summoning will appear, and then you will have to deal with both of them.*

She took a split second to smile as an idea struck like summer lightning. Closing her eyes quickly, Asaege brought to mind her book of formulae with Jillian's aid. There on the page before her mind's eye was the spell she sought. *Tallow's Warding Ban* was a simple spell, half the length of any of the other dimensional abjuration formulae collected in Marcus's book. Quick and dirty, its effects only lasted for the space of dozen breaths, but Asaege only needed half of that to foil Lirych's summoning.

As the last word left her lips, the air in the room suddenly seemed to double in weight. Asaege felt a bellow of anguish deep in her chest as the dimensional corridor opened by Lirych's spell collapsed under the room's sudden mystical pressure. From the depths of the tunnel, she heard the mercenary thaumaturge's curse. Before he could recover his wits, Asaege closed her eyes again, mentally flipping pages furiously.

She resisted the temptation to open them as the sounds of combat grew so close she imagined being able to reach out and touch the combatants around her. Finding the spell she sought, Asaege's eyelids snapped open to see a pair of Binders between her and the handful of guardsmen intent on putting an end to her casting. Past the reassuring solidity of their white cloaked backs, she could see the soldiers' hard set features twisted into hateful scowls.

Putting them from her mind, Asaege let the words of the formula flow from her memory to her lips in an exhilarating rush. The room immediately cooled, raising gooseflesh on her exposed arms as the spell took effect. The temperature drop was not so severe as to cause more than minimum discomfort, but the chilling of the air was an unintended side effect of the formula.

White-gray wisps of vapor began forming as the cool air conjured by the spell mixed with the warmer air near the floor. In the space of a few heartbeats, the mouth of the tunnel was obscured by a bank of billowing fog. *That should prevent him from casting unless he emerges from his hiding place*, she thought. *Let us now see if we can make his sanctuary less welcoming.* Asaege seamlessly moved on to the next stanza of the formula held in her mind's eye. Its effects became apparent as soon as the words spilled forth from her lips. Sparks of violet began to pop and flash within the swirling clouds of vapor. Subtle and sporadic at first, their frequency and magnitude grew as she forced the last words from her throat.

The scent of ozone and burned flesh heralded the first desperate cry of pain. A broad silhouette was thrown into stark contrast, momentarily revealing the figure's companions retreating further back into the depths of the tunnel in an attempt to escape the effect of *Killian's Killing Fog*. As another discharge of lightning flashed,

Asaege saw a shape standing alone within the fog bank. The arcing electricity sparked against some sort of unseen barrier and raced to the ground like a nest of amethyst vipers.

The sight of Lirych stepping from the depths of the billowing cloud, violet tongues of lightning arcing around him, was enough to cause enemy and ally alike to give him wide berth. Asaege saw his questing gaze seize upon her from across the room, the last vestiges of crackling electricity casting his grinning face into a macabre mask. With a sure voice, Lirych began to chant the words of another spell. She recognized it as an enchantment by its soft, almost airy tones.

While Marcus's book contained a fair amount of Enchantment formulae, it had been obvious to Asaege on her initial read through his disinterest in that particular branch of thaumaturgy by his complete lack of notes. Although they were separated by a decade and her mentor's death, she took his lead and also neglected her study of it as well. In that moment, Asaege wished she hadn't. Beyond identifying Lirych's spell as enchantment, she was at a loss as to its intended effect.

Her momentary ignorance forced her to turn to other methods of counteracting her opponent's formula. Asaege shuffled through her reflection bolstered memory of her treasured spell book. She quickly found the page she searched for. *Laerot's Lightning Strike* required a substantial gathering of clouds, but the effect of *Killian's Killing Fog* satisfied that need nicely. As she recited the words before her mind's eye, Asaege extended her will to the bank of already charged fog behind him.

A rapid series of flashes pulsed through the swirling mass of vapor, each one adding to the building rumble of thunder within. The growl behind Lirych reached a crescendo at the same time he shouted the last word of his spell. The room seemed to fall into silence for a split second as the air itself held its breath. Shielding her eyes against the assault she knew followed, Asaege saved herself from the blinding flash that filled the room right before the fleeting stillness was broken by a massive crash. Based on the shared chorus of shock and discomfort, she may have been the only one.

Turning her attention to where Lirych stood, she saw the man on his knees. The last vestiges of his mystical shield fell to pieces against the backdrop of arcing fingers of electricity. Asaege was denied the satisfaction of gloating as the effect of his spell became immediately apparent. The two Binders, who moments ago had been her protectors, blearily turned on her. The enchantment Lirych

218

had laid upon them didn't do anything to protect their eyes from the blinding flash that had filled the room seconds before; that fact alone had been Asaege's salvation.

Backing quickly up the stairs, she drew the Uteli sword at her waist. The pair swung their heavy, straight-bladed swords cautiously before them, cutting the air where a moment before Asaege's body had been. Risking a furtive glance past her allies-turned-attackers, she saw that the room's occupants were quickly regaining their senses. Unfortunately for Lirych, the revolutionary forces felt the same pressing need to remove him from the conflict as the guards had shown towards Asaege.

One look was all she could afford. As their vision obviously began to clear, the Binders' advance pressed her further up the stairs. Due in no small part to Seran's tutelage, Asaege's skill with a blade had improved by leaps and bounds in the months since the events beneath the Ivory Cathedral. Even so, faced with two professional soldiers, armed with Granatyrian long swords and broad heater shields, she had low expectations for her survival if she stood her ground.

Pivoting quickly, Asaege sprinted up the remaining stairs. Taking two at a time, she heard the pair storming up the steps behind her, but she didn't hazard a backwards glance. One of the elder thief's lessons stood out in her mind. *Never fight on anyone's terms except your own*, he had said. On the wide staircase or in the hallway, the Binders held the advantage; they could press forward together, easily overwhelming her. Asaege fastened her eyes on the open door before her. In their haste, she and Rudelph had neglected to close it behind them.

In that doorway, she could force them to press her one at a time. The cold realization that she would still be facing a soldier with decades of experience chilled Asaege's heart, but an advantage was an advantage. As she entered the room, she slammed the door behind her with all of her might. The solid sound of the lead Binder impacting with the thick oak door brought satisfaction, but no real joy.

Throwing it open once more, Asaege found that the soldier filled the door frame. Momentarily stunned by the unexpected collision, he didn't react to her sudden reappearance. She felt her gorge rise in her throat as she lashed out with her sword. Her thrust pierced his leather vest at the seam, sinking into his side, just below the ribs. As the city guard's attack was unexpected, the Binder had not donned a chain mail hauberk beneath it. Asaege appreciated the man's misfortune, although she couldn't bring herself to celebrate it.

As she withdrew her sword, Asaege hesitated for a heartbeat

before thrusting it into him again. That delay allowed the soldier to stumble backwards and out of range. His companion, combat-trained and battle-tested, surged forward to replace him. Asaege's blow found the frustrating solidity of the Binder's shield.

Unable to gather her wits enough to draw upon either the spells pressing against the back of her mind or those just out of reach in Jillian's memories, Asaege was forced to depend on her swordsmanship alone. Even if their skills had been equal, the Binder's shield would have tipped the odds in his favor. Instead, it just made his advantage almost overwhelming.

Behind his glassy, unblinking eyes, Asaege saw the soldier's consciousness straining against the chains Lirych's spell had placed upon it. While his body followed the mercenary thaumaturge's commands, the distraught expression on his face betrayed the Binder's struggle.

"You do not have to do this," Asaege begged. "Fight it. Fight him." The only visible effect of her words was the appearance of a single tear of frustration that traced a path down the soldier's grime-coated cheek.

He brought his sword down in an overhead chop. She met the blow halfway, redirecting its momentum into the wooden door frame. When the Binder pulled his weapon free, a large chunk of wood emerged with it, falling to the floor with a clatter. Asaege swung her own blade in a short horizontal motion, but the shield absorbed its impact once again. Only the tight confines of the doorway prevented the soldier from pressing his advantage. By staying inside the ideal range of her shorter weapon but too close for his own to be swung effectively, she was able to hold him off, but only barely.

When she felt the pounding words of power in her chest, Asaege almost gave up hope. She knew she couldn't hold off the Binder's attacks while addressing any formulae Lirych would bring to bear. A small voice in the back of her mind, no doubt Jillian's, told her that all was not as she feared. While she felt the reverberations of spell casting, the words themselves never reached her ears. Lirych wasn't near enough for them to be audible; the spell wasn't directed at her.

The sharp scent of charred wood was Asaege's only warning before the hallway burst into flames behind the soldier. A furnace blast struck her in the chest and burned her eyes, forcing her back a few steps. Turning her body against the unrelenting waves of heat, she strained to see the Binder's next attack through her tear-clouded vision. All Asaege could make out beyond the door was a rippling

220

curtain of fire. Eyes closed against the inferno, Asaege forced her way forward, feeling for the door. Gripping it with stinging fingers, she slammed it shut. The relief from the heat was instantaneous, the close air around her feeling like a cool autumn breeze by comparison.

As she raced towards the room's only window, Asaege heard the door begin to crackle under the hungry embrace of the flames on the other side of it. She perched on the sill and studied the alley below. A group of rebels poured from the building, stained with blood and soot. Rudelph stood at the head of a small group of Binders arrayed before the exit, his helmet conspicuous by its absence. Revolutionaries passed through their ranks, but no guardsmen emerged.

If Lirych's spell did not kill them all, they must have fled back through the tunnel, Asaege thought. *Lirych will need to be dealt with sooner rather than later. That is if his own people do not deal with him first.* Asaege felt her simmering anger with the mercenary thaumaturge mingle with Jillian's memories of his reflection. Putting aside her conflicting emotions for the moment, she released her hold over the formulae pushing against it at the back of her mind. She let the words of *Flynn's Floating Trance* surge forward while reigning in the others.

The spell rolled from her lips as she stepped from the ledge and into the empty air above the alley. She wobbled for a second as she found her balance. Once she felt secure, Asaege exhaled slowly, allowing herself to sink slowly to the street below. As her feet touched the ground, she wheeled on Rudelph. "This raid was not a stroke of luck on their part."

"I am inclined to agree with you."

"The spell Lirych used to burrow through that wall is fairly limited. He prepared it specifically for this purpose."

"Which means he had advance warning of the fact that it would be required. There was not time for rumor of our location to spread. That leaves one possibility."

"We were betrayed." Asaege looked around at the faces of the people who had placed their lives into the hands of the revolution's leadership. "Did you notice anyone missing right before the attack?"

Rudelph thought for a moment before responding. "You and I were upstairs right before the wall came down." He turned to the Binder to his left. "Gaelt?"

The soldier shook his head slowly. "I can think of no one conspicuously missing beforehand."

Rudelph sighed softly. "Neither the guards nor Lirych showed any care once they entered, leading me to believe that their informant was not present."

Asaege's lips pulled back into a sneer. "I want to know who was not here when the guards attacked. Starting with who left with Toni today."

Chapter Twenty-Six

An Overdue Conversation

Hollis woke in darkness, slowly lifting a hand to his throbbing temple. His fingers gently probed a painful knot just above his right ear as he tried to remember how it came to be there. Through the mists of what was no doubt at least a minor concussion, memories of the previous evening returned in a flood. Despite the stabbing pain that shot through his skull, the thief tried to roll to his feet. As he rose into a crouch, he felt the cold caress of steel against his bare scalp.

Reaching above his head, Hollis wrapped his hand around the bars of the cage that held him. Pale moonlight filtered through roughly stitched elk-hide was the only illumination available to him. He could barely make out the details of his makeshift prison, even with his extraordinary night vision, honed over decades in the shadow-draped alleys of Oizan.

The cage itself measured two yards long by one yard wide. It was high enough for him to crouch comfortably but not rise any further. Next to him in the tent's dim interior was a second cage, although that one seemed empty for the moment. Hollis's thoughts went immediately to Aristoi. His last memory before waking was Mika ordering his comrade's capture. Her absence didn't bode well for her fate. He tried to put his concern for his friend from his mind

223

as he studied the dim confines of the tent itself.

It seemed to contain nothing besides the two cages, lashed to the tent's center pole with thick, coarse rope. When he followed it, he found the securing knots tied well out of reach of his searching fingers. Although distance was hard to judge in the darkness, Hollis estimated that at least three yards lay between his cage and the tent's roughly secured flap.

Convinced that his environment was devoid of anything useful to his escape, the thief turned his attention inward. They had taken his boots before throwing him in the cage, and with them the picks he kept within their linings and the pair of razors he'd hidden in their soles. His cloak was also missing, denying him the thin wire he had woven into its collar. *I should expect no less from Mika,* he thought. *As much as I deny it, there are few people alive that know more of my tricks than she.*

As his thoughts turned to his former comrade, they darkened. There was a time when the thief had felt more than friendship for her. During a period of his life when he was unsure of who he was meant to be—thief or hero, killer or protector—Mika had represented everything he thought he wanted. She wore her confidence like armor and wielded her mind as effectively as the blade at her side, often times more so.

In the eyes of a young man who'd always been a cog in the machine of another, she'd been nothing short of everything his heart desired. What his youthful eyes failed to see was that she had only been able to become the person he saw by putting herself above everything and everyone around her. He wasn't alone in learning that particular lesson too late. *It had cost Silvermoon his life, and may still cost me my own.*

The white-hot rage that had burned in his gut since his discovery of the circumstances of Silvermoon's death flared again. His overconfidence had led him to believe that finding vengeance would be as simple as putting his mind to it. That fire in his belly suddenly turned cold with the memory of how he matched his Well-given gifts against Mika's and found himself hopelessly wanting.

The skeletal fingers of despair clawed at him. Even if he could free himself from the cage that imprisoned his body, the knowledge of his defeat would still shackle his heart. *If I am able to free myself, my only hope of survival lies in escape.* That would mean leaving his comrades to their fates. Valmont. Sagaun. Aristoi. Could he ever look at himself in the mirror again if he traded his life for theirs? *For years, I have tortured myself over my inability to help those I have lost. I have told myself, 'if only I had been there for them, I could have made a difference.'* The sharp teeth of fear seized him by the throat. Not since his childhood had Hollis felt so powerless, so overmatched.

Dread and self-pity warred with the stubborn idealism that had served him as the iron core of his life, even in the worst of times. As different as they were, the thief's two surrogate fathers, Seran and Silvermoon, had drilled into him the same lesson. It was presented very differently by each man, but they both had taught him to never give up the fight until the fight is done. Although Hollis had lost the first battle, the fight was far from over.

*****

The thief was sitting quietly when the tent flap opened. He'd lost count of how many times he had reviewed the events of the previous evening, but couldn't help but feel that he'd missed something important. The shuffling of booted feet on the tent's dirt floor offered a welcome respite from what had become a frustratingly circular exercise.

Hollis slowly opened his eyes and turned them towards the hulking silhouette that filled the opening. "About time," he called, "I was beginning to think no one would be by to take my breakfast order. I dearly hope you have more to offer than bread and cheese."

"Why is everything always a joke to you, boy?" It had been more than a decade since the thief had heard that booming voice, but he could not mistake it for any other.

"Ah … Ret, I was wondering when you were going to make an appearance. I've been told it is a defense mechanism." Although the words were in Trade Tongue, the concept was clearly beyond the big man's understanding.

The Rangor frowned at him, a demand for explanation clear in his features.

"That would have killed in Jersey." When Ret's scowl deepened, the thief dismissed him with a wave of his hand. "It is not important. What brings you to my little piece of the world?"

"I came to ask the same thing of you."

Hollis's voice became serious, taking on sharpness of steel. "You may have fooled a lot of folks with your dumb northerner routine over the years, Ret, but I never believed it. You understand very clearly why I am here. The reason for your presence, on the other hand, is less so. When we parted ways, you were headed home."

"So I have." Ret stepped forward, his movements more tentative than the thief would have expected. "When I left you in Oizan, I hoped you would find worthy companions once I was gone. You find yourself in dangerous company, my friend."

"Speaking of which, I need you to know something."

The Rangor leaned forward. "What would that be?"

"There was a southern woman with me before Mika's and my … discussion. Friendship or not, If I find that you or your clansmen have harmed her in any way, you and I are going to have a problem."

"Ever the loyal comrade. The woman was subdued with minimal damage. Her fate is in her own hands now."

"What is that supposed to mean?"

"Yours was not the only unexpected reunion this evening. She has business with the Hungered."

"The Hungered? I find that the arrogance inherent in referring to oneself as 'The-Anything' is a good judge of poor character. There was a time when you would have agreed with me."

"Who is to say that I do not now?"

"The fact that I am in this cage and my friend remains in the grasp of someone calling themselves The Hungered speaks loudly."

Hollis saw a flash of shame in the big man's face before he averted his gaze. "Did you even ask her what happened to Silvermoon and Marcus? Did you care?"

Ret's eyes narrowed and his lips pulled back to reveal his teeth. "How dare you? I had been risking my life beside the forester since before you had your first man's growth of beard. He was like a brother to me."

"And yet you curl up at night before the fire at the feet of the woman who murdered him."

"I have only your word for that. Mika tells a very different story."

Hollis raised an eyebrow. "By all means, regale me her version." He tapped his fingers against the steel bars of his cage. "It appears I have little left to me but time."

Ret winced at the dull clang. "I wanted to return to Oizan, to bring you into the fold, but—"

"—She would not allow it," Hollis interrupted. "Did you ever wonder why that was, Ret? If her part in Silvermoon's death was so blameless, why would she feel the need to keep me in the dark about it? For that matter, why would she seek to keep her survival a secret?"

"She wanted you to live your life unencumbered by the tragedy."

More to himself than the man before him, Hollis said, "Too

226

many people have used that excuse over the last year. It does not make any more sense tonight than it has any other time I have heard it." He turned his attention back to Ret. "Does that sound like me? In the time we have known each other, when have you ever known me to let something go? Not at Maggie's farm. Not with Haedren in the stables of the Virgin Mermaid. Not when you lay dying outside of Kaelstrom, a pair of arrows in your gut." The thief felt guilty mentioning the night he refused to abandon the wounded Rangor in Mantry, but it illustrated his point. "Not now."

"I—"

"—Wanted to believe her," Hollis interrupted again. "I understand that. Silvermoon could have found the strong sword arm he saw in you anywhere. The night I met him, there were plenty of journeyman thieves more skillful than I to choose from. He found in you the same thing he found in me: need. You can call it a need to be valued or a need for family, but whatever you call it, every member of the Band of Six was missing something that the group provided. With Silvermoon gone, you hoped that Mika would be able to give you what he no longer could. There is no shame in that."

The thief longed to reach out and lay a comforting hand on his friend's arm. For all his bluster, Ret had a heart the size of the Rangor Wastes itself. He hid it well, but the warrior loved as passionately as he fought. Mika had taken advantage of that. *That is yet another sin for which she must pay.*

"She was defending herself," Ret stated. Beneath his rough, confident tone, the thief heard a quiver of doubt.

Hollis sat back against the uncomfortable surface of the bars behind him. "Tell me then. Tell me a version of the story where Alexei Silvermoon sought to betray a member of his family."

"Haedren's words ... those of Theamon's spirit within him enchanted both the forester and his brother. The sound of his voice turned their hearts from a pure path to one of selfish desires."

"The sound of his voice? Silvermoon and Marcus were tempted by his voice alone?"

"Yes. The power of Theamon's words turned our friends."

The thief sat forward. "It was not Theamon's spirit that corrupted our dear friend, Haedren, in the first place. We were mistaken. It was something much older, much more evil."

Uncertainty flashed in Ret's eyes for a moment. "How could you know that?"

"I have spoken with that which is only known as the Shadow. Not four months ago, my companions and I purged it from

227

the brooch that housed its malign consciousness. It had been using people for longer than anyone knows, Theamon and Haedren were simply its latest victims."

"So Silvermoon fell under its sway then."

Hollis shook his head. "I am afraid not. The brooch that contained the Shadow was more prison than tool. Only those in direct contact with it were open to the corrupting influence held within. Did Mika mention Silvermoon touching the brooch?"

Ret averted his gaze, but didn't address the question. "As Haedren lay dying, the brothers turned on her. They sought to use her soul to gain the power of the Well itself."

"She told you that, did she? Marcus and Silvermoon attacked her before Haedren had breathed his last?"

"Yes."

"I happen to know that after Haedren was slain, all three left the chamber to lick their wounds. The battle was costly on both sides. It was only after Mika and Silvermoon returned that the Well was used. I have it on the authority of someone whom I trust completely."

"That is not true." Hollis could hear the desperation in the Rangor's voice. "She was forced to defend herself, to shed blood in the holy place. The Well itself honored her valor by gifting its vigor to her."

"That is not how the Well works, Ret. In order to use the Well of Worlds, one must—"

"That is enough." From the tent's entrance, Mika's voice cut through the night. "Ret, the scouts are returning. I need you to meet with them. We are so close to stamping out the Bone Dogs' resistance; our next move must be the right one."

The woman's presence bolstered Ret's weakening resolve. "Of course, Mika." The Rangor avoided Hollis's gaze as he turned and walked into the night.

"So nice to see you again, Mika," the thief cooed. "It would be a shame if he were to learn the truth."

She glared hard at the caged man, her eyes wrinkled with either rage or concern. It was hard to tell in the dim light. "Truth is more clay than rock, Hollis. Those who survive often mold it to their needs."

The thief had watched as the inroads he thought he was making with Ret seal themselves tight with the warrior's faith in Mika. A small smirk crept onto his face. *Even the tightest seals leave cracks in the repaired surface.*

Chapter Twenty-Seven
An Ethical Disagreement

Aristoi had regained consciousness moments before, but she kept her eyes closed and focused on remaining still. The ground beneath her body was covered in thick rugs that had a faint musty scent covered by too much perfume. They held the chill of the ground at bay but the dampness of the cloth seemed to soak into the southerner's bones. The bonds of leather around her wrists and ankles dug into her flesh unmercifully. Deep within her, something raged at the thought of being restrained.

The bestial aspect awakened by her first experience with a gwyllgi demanded release. It whispered promises to her in a voice only her heart could hear. *You could be free in the space of a thought. All that is needed is for you to stop fighting me. Accept what you are, who we are.* Twisting her wrists savagely, the Songspear drowned the voice in the depths of the pain. Beneath the muted sounds of Rangor voices, she could hear the steady, raspy breath of whatever shared the tent with her.

"Open your eyes, Songspear," a voice growled. "There is little purpose in your ruse. I could hear your heartbeat quicken the moment you awoke."

Aristoi slowly did as she was bid, levering herself into a sitting position. The single lantern hanging from the center pole cast the tent into a flickering dance of shadow and light. Laying on its side, rust colored eyes studying her, was the large gwyllgi she had fought outside of Agmar's Watch. Propped against the tent's wall was her spear, well out of Aristoi's reach, even if she hadn't been tied at wrist and ankle.

"I regret the barbarians' rough treatment of you, doubly so the necessity that you remain bound for the moment. You and I did not part on the best of terms. I was not anxious to repeat our last encounter." His thick tail swatted the ground beside him with a dull thump. "It is my honest hope that we can have a more productive discussion this evening."

"I am not sure what sway you hold over the Rangor, beast, but I can assure you it does not extend to me."

Rolling to its feet, the gwyllgi stretched slowly. "Sway? The only emotion I engender in these savages is fear." As it slowly approached Aristoi, the creature's expressive muzzle broke into a mockery of a smile. "I made the same offer to the Snow Queen that I extended to you. She was simply wise enough to accept."

"I am at a loss to figure out who got the worse end of that deal."

Ignoring the dig, the gwyllgi answered in an earnest voice. "Oh, without a doubt, she did. In exchange for my knowledge of the spirits of the north, she provided … well, you. Once you and I reach an accord, we shall leave the Snow Queen to her barbarian civil war and return south."

"What makes you so sure we will, as you say, 'reach an accord'?"

"A little bit of faith, but mostly experience with human nature."

"But you and I are no longer human, you said as much yourself."

"Those were my words, that is true. However, despite the evidence to the contrary, you still cling to your humanity. Even if it is false, your belief in it still leaves you vulnerable."

"I would rather die in the dream of humanity than live forever in whatever truth you preach."

"We shall see, Songspear. We shall see. Two Children of the Well cannot coexist, one must subsume the other. After this evening's performance, there is little doubt in my mind who will emerge victorious when your friend faces the Snow Queen again.

Aristoi's heart sank. She hated to admit it, but the gwyllgi spoke the truth. Hollis had been outclassed by his former comrade. It was clear to the Songspear that Mika had been playing with the thief, he never truly had a chance of besting her in combat.

230

"Of course, that assumes that she does not just have him killed out of hand." For a second, the gwyllgi's eyes grew distant. "A siblings' quarrel will shake the pillars of creation." The beast sat back on its haunches and studied the Songspear for a moment. "I am not sure about you, but I have no intention of being around when that happens."

Something about the words struck a chord in Aristoi. "A siblings' quarrel. Where have I heard that before?" Her voice was free of anything but interest.

The gwyllgi chuffed in approval. "Very nice, Songspear. It is part of a larger quote: The falling of the final night will be heralded by the wolf lying down with the child. In the darkness, a siblings' quarrel will shake the pillars of creation. When the final voice of Taerh's past is shouted into silence by its future, two dawns will shine as one."

Aristoi finished, "When these three signs come to pass, the walls shall crumble and the chaos contained finally released." A knot formed in her stomach. "You are talking about the Night of Two Dawns? The End of Times?"

"In one interpretation, yes. I choose to believe it speaks of a new age. Just as the Age of Myth came to a close, as did the Age of Legends that followed, the sun must set upon our own. Have you ever asked yourself what would come after? What the face of Taerh would look like as it opened its eyes on a new era?"

"The changing of the ages has always been borne upon tides of blood. They never pass in peace."

The creature huffed dismissively. "Why should we care? The gwyllgi were born in the Age of Legends. When time ground our contemporaries into the dirt, we endured. The great dragons fell into deep slumbers, leaving only wingless wyrms in their place. The Griffin kings retreated to their aeries high atop mist-covered mountains, there they hide from a world they only barely recognize but fear all the same. We thrive in the hearts of the people of Taerh, haunting their dreams and hunting their flesh. What have we to fear of chaos and upheaval?"

"Stop speaking like we are the same."

"You and I are more alike than you can imagine."

"Just because we had the misfortune to suffer a similar fate does not mean we have anything else in common. Even lying here among my enemies, I remain myself. Bound hand and foot, my heart remains unchained. Can you say the same, abomination?"

"I am free to do whatever I please."

"You are free to do whatever the corruption of your soul pleases, you mean," Aristoi corrected.

"In time, Songspear, you will find the difference is negligible."

"Not to me. I am stronger than the darkness seeking my soul. If you were wise, you would end our rivalry now. I assure you when the advantage is mine, I will not return the favor."

Aristoi heard the beast's jaws shut with an angry gnashing of teeth. "You will not goad me into ending your life," it hissed.

"Is that what I seek?"

"It is clear you seek release from what you see as torment. That could not be further from the truth. The instincts awakening within you are the first signs of your true self. Embrace them and you need never suffer again."

"I am not sure that is necessarily true. Plenty of gwyllgi have suffered on the tip of my spear. Their instincts seemed a poor balm for the bite of cold iron."

In a rush, the beast charged Aristoi, the lantern's light blotted out by its mottled black body. The gwyllgi was close enough that she could feel its hot, stinking breath on her face. In a harsh whisper, it promised, "Your fortitude is not endless, little southerner. You will run beside me. This may end no other way."

The Songspear's only response was to drive her forehead into the creature's muzzle. A snarling whimper arose in its chest as she felt bone crack beneath the blow. The gwyllgi shredded the rugs beneath its claws as it backpedaled, blood dripping from its nostrils.

"Guards," it called through already swelling lips. "Get her out of my sight."

As two Rangor youth dragged her from the tent, Aristoi heard the creature call to her. "After the Snow Queen puts your friend in the ground, we shall speak again. Perhaps you will feel differently when you have no one left to mourn who you were."

Chapter Twenty-Eight
An Unfortunate Victim

Jillian stood in front of her class, the stylus in her hand perched over the smart board. Mid-sentence, she had lost her train of thought. Her lesson on the Lenni Lenape evaporated in favor of a rush of anxious thoughts. *Was the fire some sort of elaborate trap by Hector? What is Veronica doing to Stephen? What is Cyrill's true personality: Lirych or the friend she had come to know? What if involving Marisol gets her hurt? What if it gets her killed?*

The morning had passed in a blur. Her students were young, but they had to have noticed her distraction. To their credit, none of them had tried to take advantage of it. Before Jillian could find her place, a hand shot up from the back row. It belonged to Thomas Krieger. His behavior and study skills had been a concern in the beginning of the year, but with some extra attention, the boy seemed to be finding his way. He still sometimes had issues staying in his seat during longer lessons but for the most part, his focus has improved.

"Yes, Thomas?"

"What is the third sister?" He looked up at her with the rapt attention of true interest. Something in that look struck Jillian as familiar. "Corn and beans are the first two. What is the third?" Thomas had of course expressed curiosity before, but the expression hit her differently. It was like she had seen it somewhere else, under different circumstances.

Jillian felt herself being pulled out of the moment and into her own thoughts again. She consciously pushed the building confusion from her mind. "Squash, Thomas. The three sisters are corn, beans and squash. The corn grows tall, giving the beans something to climb on. The large leaves of the squash shade the roots of both plants from the heat of the summer sun. It is an example of how three seemingly very different things have a better chance of survival when they work together."

Turning back to the board, Jillian could feel her decision to trust Hector weighing on her. *When it comes to him, survival and betrayal go hand in hand, but I think my choices are growing thinner by the day.* He would be loyal to her only as long as it benefited him. That was something she could count on. It wasn't much, but it was something.

"The wisdom of the three sisters applies to more than just farming. It also can be used in our daily lives." Jillian knew that the approved lesson plan only included the literal significance of the planting method, but felt that expanding on it couldn't hurt, especially given how applicable it felt at that moment. "Here in school, as well as at home, we all need to see not only the differences in each other but how those differences make us stronger as a community. Can anyone tell me a difference that could be something positive?"

A half dozen hands shot into the air.

"Betsy?"

A girl in the middle row sat up a little taller as she said, "What other languages we speak? My grandmother was from Italy and has taught me a little Italian."

"Very good. Anyone else? Brian?"

"What our parents do for work? My father is a plumber, so we never have to call one!"

"That's a good one." She noticed that Thomas had his hand up again. Twice in one class period, it had to have been a record. "Thomas?"

"Money?" Jillian's heart ached for him. She had only met his mother a few times but each time, she had seemed in a rush, never wanting to discuss her son or his progress. She was fond of saying that her son's education was the school's problem, not her own. Always wrinkled and disheveled, Jillian had always found Mrs. Krieger too twitchy for comfort. "My mom always says that not having a lot makes us grateful for what we have."

The soft tones of laughter began to rise, but Jillian silenced them with a stern sweep of her eyes. "I think that might be the most important lesson of all. Learning to be grateful is a hard lesson but one worth remembering." Before she could continue, the muted sound of a bell rang in the hallway. "That's the lunch bell. Please line up in the hallway and once Mrs. Schmidt's class is ready, we'll all head to the lunchroom."

As she was gathering her things, Jillian noticed Thomas watching her tentatively from the back of the room. She smiled at him in a way she hoped was reassuring. With half the day gone, she had no expectation that the afternoon would pass any easier.

*****

As the bell rang marking the end of classes for the day, a conflicted feeling settled upon Jillian. Having never quite quieted the anxious voices in her head, she was relieved to have made it through the day. In having done so, however, she could no longer delay thinking about her meeting with Hector that evening. Jillian was no more sure about how far she trusted the man than she had been that morning.

With as much enthusiasm as she could muster, Jillian called out to the departing children. "Have a great night, guys! Remember that tonight's homework is on the board, in case you need to copy it down." All of them filed from the room giving neither the board nor what was written on it a second glance. She sighed softly, not able to muster the energy to fight that particular battle.

Turning to her desk, Jillian began packing her laptop bag with a yellow folder containing assignments that needed grading and her lesson book. She thought fondly of a time where grading papers was the only thing keeping her awake at night. As she zipped the bag, Jillian looked out her classroom window at the chaotic throng of children rushing to climb aboard the blocky school buses filling the parking lot. Her eye was caught by an inconsistency, something that didn't belong.

Thomas Krieger stood on the sidewalk, a calmness in the storm of children around him. He was perched on his tippy-toes, straining to see over the heads of his classmates. When his balance gave out, he sank down to his flat feet, his shoulders sagging in disappointment. Although Mrs. Krieger rarely came to the school for conferences, she normally picked up her son at the end of the day.

Hanging her bag over her shoulder, Jillian shut off the classroom's lights and closed the door behind her. A few minutes and more polite platitudes to co-workers than she liked later, she stepped out into the chill afternoon air. Most of the buses had departed with their enthusiastic cargo, but Thomas still stood on the sidewalk, furiously scanning the quickly emptying parking lot.

"Thomas," Jillian said as she approached, "is your mother running late?"

He turned slowly, his jaw tight and eyes glistening in the late afternoon sun. Jillian wasn't sure if the emotions that clouded his expression were sadness or anger. In truth, it was most likely a combination of both. "I guess so, Miss Allen." The downtrodden acceptance in his voice pulled at her heart.

When he started to walk away, Jillian put a hand on his shoulder. "Where are you going?"

In a soft, resigned voice, the boy said, "I'm gonna walk home. It's not far."

Jillian knew for a fact that it was a few miles on more than one busy road. "I can't let you do that, Thomas." She thought she saw gratitude in the boy's face. "Why don't we wait for your mother inside? I'm sure she'll be along any minute."

Thomas thought about it for a second and then slowly nodded. "Okay."

Jillian didn't have Hollis's gift of understanding, but the hollow ache in the pit of her stomach told her that the delay wasn't a simple matter of traffic.

*****

Thomas was quietly working on his homework when the police arrived. Jillian saw the uniformed officers enter over the boy's shoulder. One of them was Billy Parr. She didn't recognize the other.

"Stay here, Thomas," she said as she rose and met the pair halfway.

Billy refused to look her in the eye. "Hey, Jillian. This is Officer Valentine."

Jillian nodded politely but never took her eyes off of Billy. "What's happened?"

"Is that Thomas Krieger behind you?"

"It is, but you're not getting anywhere near him until you tell me what's going on."

"There's been a ..." Billy paused for a second, measuring his next words. "... an accident."

Jillian lowered her voice to a whisper. "Mrs. Krieger?"

"I'm afraid so, ma'am," Officer Valentine provided. "She's been killed."

Her eyes bored into Billy's. "An accident or something else?"

"It's an ongoing investigation, ma'am." Valentine provided the

236

standard response. "I'm afraid that's all we can say at this time."

Billy didn't have to speak for Jillian to read everything she needed to know in his face. She silently mouthed, "Just like the others?"

He almost imperceptibly nodded, still studying his shoes.

Turning to Billy's partner, Jillian said, "I assume you brought someone from social services."

"Yes, ma'am. They are just outside."

She looked over her shoulder at Thomas's small form, huddled over his notebook. She wanted to allow him to remain that way for ever, ignorant to how his life was about to change. "You should probably go get them."

*****

True to her word, there was a small alcove tucked behind Casa Pizza. It was only big enough for a few cafe tables, but Jillian figured it would suffice as a meeting place. Hector was waiting for her when she arrived. He sat slouched over the back of a chair, leaning forward over his lit, and very much prohibited, cigarette.

"About time," he growled as she came around the corner. As he looked up, Jillian could see the bright red evidence of his experience in the fire. If he was lucky, the minor burns on his face and hands wouldn't scar.

"I was delayed. If you had a cell phone, I could have let you know."

Taking a deep drag from the cigarette in his hand, he reached into his long, olive drab jacket with the other. Jillian didn't realize that she had flinched until she saw the patronizing smile on Hector's face. "It's just a phone, princess." He slid it across the small table to her. "I picked up a burner this afternoon. Put your number in it."

Jillian picked up the phone, unlocking it with a flick of her thumb. Without taking her eyes off of it, she said, "There better not be anything in that beyond surgeon general approved cancer."

"I am nothing if not a man of my word."

She brought up the burner's settings menu and transcribed its number into her phone before adding her own to Hector's empty contact list. She slid it back to him. "I'd say not to take my dubious-ness personally, but I'd prefer to keep up my part of our agreement of honesty."

"Ouch." He swept the phone off the table with a smooth motion of his hand. It disappeared into the jacket faster than Jillian's eyes could follow.

A man of your word, my ass.

"What kept you?"

"Not that it's any of your business, but I was held up at work."

"As far as I'm concerned, everything is my business when it comes to this situation. I'm surprised you don't feel the same." He took another drag, allowing the smoke to ooze from between his uneven teeth like honey from a broken hive.

"I am very familiar with the level of honesty you are capable of. The definition of insanity is taking the same action over and over, expecting different results for your efforts."

"And for all your faults, princess, you're not insane."

Ignoring the nickname he'd apparently devised for her, Jillian leaned forward. "Are we here to try to get to the bottom of all this, or are you just in need of a captive audience?"

"Fair enough." Hector's eyes became hard. "What kept you?"

"There was another murder."

He raised an eyebrow. If he'd meant the gesture to distract her from noticing panic tighten his body like a plucked guitar string, he failed. Jillian could hear the tension in his quickened voice. "And you didn't think to tell me?"

"I would have gotten around to it. I'm not sure it's related."

Lifting it to his lips with a trembling hand, Hector took a deep pull from his cigarette. "You don't get to make that decision."

"Apparently, I do … you know … as the only one of us that can actually show their face in public."

"You're enjoying this too much."

Jillian smiled grimly. "I think I'm enjoying it just the right amount."

Hector exhaled forcefully, appearing for a second like a kettle left too long on the stove. He obviously thought better of whatever outburst he'd planned. Instead, his voice became soft and reasonable. For some reason that scared Jillian more than if he'd raised it. "Tell me about the murder."

What's the use of a detente if I'm not going to take advantage of his counsel? Jillian felt she had antagonized Hector enough for one day. It was less than he deserved, but any further distraction from the matter at hand served no purpose.

"It was a local woman, Lillian Krieger."

His eyes lit up with recognition. "Lilly Kay?"

"You know her?"

"She is … was a good customer. She left a lot to be desired as a mother, always bringing that kid of hers around and all, but I could always count on her to pay in cash."

238

Jillian's mind went to Thomas's contribution that morning. *My mom always says that not having a lot makes us grateful for what we have.* Suddenly, her sadness for the boy increased exponentially as her sympathy for his mother decreased in equal measure. "Did she buy Dreamtime from you?"

"Among other, less natural merchandise. Oxy was her product of choice."

Mrs. Krieger and Cyrill were both Hector's customers. That can't be a fluke. "Did you also sell to a football player? Erik … something." She searched for the name.

Hector provided it with a smile. "Erik Gunn. Good Ol' Shotgun Ricky was in twice a week like clockwork once the season was over."

"I think I see a commonality forming."

He leaned in, his voice a harsh whisper. "Me?"

"With the exception of Freeholder Fredericks, four people have been targeted. Two of them are dead: Gunn and Krieger. Two survived, just barely."

"Who else got away?"

Jillian wasn't sure if it was her complicated feelings about her friend and his reflection that led to her quick disclosure, but the name rolled off her lips before she could reconsider. "Cyrill."

"Nice." Hector strangely looked impressed. "I didn't think he had it in him."

"Fredericks didn't happen to be a customer as well, did he?"

"Martin Fredericks? Getting high would mean taking that stick out of his ass, and I'm convinced he'd have to get that thing surgically removed."

"So no?"

"No."

Jillian frowned. "That would've made things too easy, too neat. It would've been nice though."

"Maybe he's not involved? The esteemed freeholder bought it the night before the fire. The next day, XXL Hoodie torched the shop, with me in it. When did the kid die?"

As he spoke, Jillian touched her thumb to her forefinger and then the middle one, as she mentally tried to put events in order. "The same night you were attacked. Cyrill was run off the road two nights ago." Ring finger. "And Lillian Krieger was killed sometime today." Pinky.

"How do you know?" For just a moment, Hector lost the frightening aspect of his reflection. Jillian saw an earnestness in his eyes that couldn't be faked.

"She dropped her son off for school before eight."

"The cops have been watching me. Could it be them?"

Jillian remembered the conspiratorial glances between Veronica and Detective Blaine during the Frederick's wake. "Perhaps, but the only people we know to have been attacked were 'special' customers." She made quotes in the air with her fingers as she said special. "Have you ever actually sold flowers or was the shop completely a front?"

Hector narrowed his eyes, looking insulted for a second. "Of course I sold flowers. You can't run a florist without them." A note of pride crept into his voice. "I was actually getting pretty good at it … flower arranging, that is. Do you know that in Japan, the samurai would arrange flowers in their down time?"

She let a smile creep onto her face. *Under different circumstances, in a different world, perhaps things could have gone another way for Hector.* Like a blast of super-heated air from an open oven, Jillian's memories of Plague Man, Hector's reflection in a different world. *I can't forget who and what he is,* she scolded herself.

Jillian cleared her throat to shake the tremor from her voice. "Let's focus. If they were just going after anyone who went into your shop, there would be other casualties that had nothing to do with your side business."

His brow furrowed in thought as he took a drag from his almost-forgotten cigarette. Half of its length had turned to ash in his fingers while they had been talking. He flicked it with his thumb sending a blizzard of gray-white detritus to the floor. His head snapped up as an idea occurred to him. "My book."

"Your what?"

"My log book. I assumed it went up with the shop."

"You kept a log of your illegal drug transactions?" Jillian hissed in a low whisper.

"Everything was coded. I kept it just in case?"

"In case what? You wanted to send out a newsletter?"

An expression between annoyance and embarrassment crossed Hector's face. "In case anyone turned me in, I would have leverage."

"Well Archimedes, someone decided to beat you to death with your own lever."

Chapter Twenty-Nine
An Unheeded Lesson

Hollis's eyes opened slowly as a bound figure was carried into the tent. Even in the dappled moonlight filtering in through the entrance, he could make out the Songspear's braids thrashing as she fought against the hands of the Rangor holding her between them. Even tied wrist and ankle, she was putting up a respectable struggle. The thief didn't speak any of the Rangor dialects, but got a general sense of her words from her tone and their furious body language. *Curse them out, Aristoi*, he thought as they cast her onto the frozen dirt of the floor.

Rising to a crouch, Hollis scrambled forward and pressed his face against the bars of the cage. One of the massive warriors raised his foot to kick the prone woman. "Turn around and walk away." His voice was a sword's edge in the still night air, hard and dangerous. "As of yet, you have done nothing unforgivable. If that blow lands, you best grow accustomed to looking over your shoulder for the rest of your short life. The one time you forget, I will be there to sink a knife into your back."

The Rangor's foot paused long enough for Aristoi to scramble backwards out of its path. He turned on the caged thief, the sneer on his face revealed in a beam of moonlight. "Brave words ... from caged man." The warrior's trade tongue was broken and halting, but

241

he was able to get his point across.

"Think about it for a second." Hollis tapped the steel bars with his thumbnail. "I sit here stripped of weapons and tools, yet Mika insists I remained caged." He watched as both of the Rangor digested his words. "Perhaps she knows something you do not."

"You are southerner … soft and weak."

A slow smile came to the thief's face. From beside him, a barely perceptible hum began to build. "Perhaps. Why don't you open the cage and find out?" He was unsure of the intent of Aristoi's song, but meant to give her ample opportunity to finish it. Gripping the bars in both hands, Hollis shook them in an attempt to keep both men's attention on him. "The keys are next to the tent flap. If you want to test me, they are but a few steps away."

Just as the warrior turned to fetch them, his comrade growled something in the northern language they shared. Like a bear just awakening from its winter's sleep, he rumbled, "I … think not." Tearing a piece of the filthy tunic extending below his chain shirt, he approached the Songspear.

"So much for Rangor pride," Hollis taunted, his heart pounding in his ears.

The warrior drove his boot into Aristoi's gut, eliciting a grunt from the bound woman and bringing her song to an end. He forced the cloth into her mouth and knotted it behind her head. Turning from the Songspear, he tapped a thick finger against his temple. "Ret say … you clever. You stay … in cage, clever man." A booming laugh emerged from his throat as he walked from the tent. The sound echoed in Hollis's memory long after the voice fell into silence.

*****

After being marched through the brightness of the northern morning, the dim interior of Mika's tent seemed like a different world. Hollis had closed his eyes prior to being pushed through the entrance, but the stark contrast still cost him a moment of disorientation. As he tried to regain his bearings, he was shoved from behind again, driving him to his knees. With his hands tied behind his back, the thief could only tuck his shoulder in an effort to cushion his fall. The impact against the frozen dirt still sent a wave of pain into his neck and spine.

"Ake, Hollis is our guest. Kindly treat him with a little more care." Mika's conversational tone hurt the thief's pride more than the fall ever could.

Resisting the urge to leap to his feet, Hollis lay on the ground for a moment. Emboldened by the apparent effects of his unprovoked attack, Ake stood over the prone thief. Curling his legs in towards his belly in a gesture of pain, Hollis brought his feet in line with the warrior's knee.

"Hollis," Mika warned.

Ake looked down at him, his face paling as it dawned on him what Hollis had planned. Stumbling back quickly, the Rangor nearly tripped over his own feet and joined the thief in the dirt.

Mika stood from her fur-covered campaign chair. She dismissed the warrior with a backward wave of her hand. "That will be all, Ake." From a safe distance, the Snow Queen looked down at Hollis. "You have developed a temper over the last decade, boy."

"An eye for an eye, is that not what you taught me?"

"He pushed you. You were preparing to cripple him. Where is the equality in that?"

Hollis shrugged. "He and I had a conversation last night. I thought he could stand an illustration of my point."

"Do you believe he understands now?"

The image of the warrior's brutal kick to Aristoi's gut still fresh in his memory, the thief growled, "I think sometime soon he may require a refresher."

Mika chuckled softly. "I owe you an apology, Hollis."

"I am not sure that a simple mea culpa is going to make up for your murder of my friends." As there was no direct translation, he used the original Latin expression. The words' effect on his former friend was immediate and impossible for her to hide.

Wincing as if she had been physically struck, her lips pulled back in a sneer. Through clenched teeth, she hissed, "Not for that." To her credit, she recovered quickly, but Hollis filed the reaction away for future consideration. When she spoke again, her voice had returned to a more affable tone. "I underestimated you, judged you on the boy you were and not the man you have become."

"Did you have your goons drag me all the way across camp so you could apologize for making assumptions? Do you know what they say about people who assume, correct?" He watched her carefully as he used the English word for assume, rather than the Trade Tongue equivalent. The pained expression that crossed her face was subtle but obvious to his eyes. *Interesting.*

"Not exactly. I hoped that after some time to contemplate, you would reconsider my offer."

Hollis did a double-take. "You put me in a cage, hoping that when I came out, I would feel more sympathetic towards your plans for domination?"

243

"When you put it like that, it sounds insane."

"That is because it is."

"While I would rather work with you, I will not have you working against me."

"That sounds vaguely like a threat."

"It is not so vague."

Hollis tried to maintain a stoic expression, but felt his thoughts bleed through to his face. *Judging by the ease with which she beat me in our first encounter, it seems like a threat Mika is more than capable of accomplishing.*

She crouched down beside him, steering clear of his unbound legs. "I do not want to fight you, Hollis."

"To what do I owe this change of heart? You certainly had no such qualms last night."

"Last night, you gave me no choice. I should have known you would not respond to threats of force. You have always been thick-headed when it came to your own safety."

I do not like the sound of this. "I learned from the best. You do remember the man you murdered, right?"

A bitter smile crossed Mika's face. "Of course. The two of you were cut from the same cloth. You fed off each other."

"Do you mean made each other better?"

"No," she said plainly. "That is not what I meant at all." Rising slowly to her feet, the Snow Queen walked back to her campaign chair and sank into its depths. "For what it is worth, I asked him to leave you behind on more than one occasion."

Her admission struck Hollis more severely than any sword blow.

"I begged him to give you some money and send you on your way. Free from the influence of the thieves' guild, you would have made a fine farmer. You could have settled down with a wide-eyed farm-girl and had a herd of pie-faced children. That life would have made you happy."

"Are you claiming that anyone else's happiness was ever your primary concern?"

"Whether it was or not, one truth remains. If Silvermoon had set you free, we sure as hell would not be having this conversation."

Anger rose in the thief. "The reason we are in this situation lies purely with your choice to betray your friends for power. Everything else is smoke and mirrors, lies you tell yourself so you can sleep at night."

"I have had no trouble sleeping recently, my dear boy." Reaching into the collar of her tunic, Mika pulled out a familiar stone hung on a leather cord. She held his missing whisper stone in her fist. "When the concerns of the day weight too heavily on my mind, I let the hushed pleas of your lady-love soothe me into slumber."

Rolling to his feet with no plan beyond the handful of seconds directly before him, Hollis charged the seated woman. "You have no right!"

With an agility that made her scramble out of his path seem effortless, Mika rose and allowed the thief to collide with the bone and fur chair. As both man and furniture crashed to the floor, she chided, "Now, Hollis, let us not have a repeat of last night. As uncomfortable as change is for me, I am trying to adopt a less bloodthirsty method of conflict resolution."

Hollis lay amid the splintered wreckage of the chair, his bound wrists trapped beneath his body. He seized his former friend with a hard gaze. "She is beyond your reach."

Mika nodded slowly. "Indeed, she is. Her heart, on the other hand ..." Twirling the thin leather around her finger, her voice took on an icy edge. "It is clear from her words that she cares deeply for you. What would become of her if I responded to her breathy pleas with the news that you lay bleeding your last upon the snow? Do you think dear, sweet Asaege's pain would be any less than if I plunged steel into her?"

Conflict filled the thief's thoughts. She was easily more than a match for him when his hands were not bound behind his back. In his current state, he stood next to no chance. Mika tended toward straight-ahead thinking; his only hope lay in working the corners. That would take more consideration than was available to him at that moment.

Fortunately for Hollis, his old friend misinterpreted his silence. "Take some time to grow accustomed to the idea. We shall speak again soon."

The feeling that came over him wasn't quite relief, but it was better than nothing.

"Ret," Mika called. When the bearded Rangor stuck his head past the flap, she said, "Take Hollis back to his tent. As long as he behaves himself, I see no reason for him to return to the cage."

*****

Ret and Hollis walked in silence for a few moments, each lost in their own thoughts. As they approached the tent in which the thief had been confined all night, he stopped. The massive Rangor took a pair of long strides before he realized that his former comrade was

245

not beside him.

"Hollis," he began, "please do not make this more difficult than it needs to be." There was a weariness in his voice that the thief hadn't heard before.

"You were listening." It was not a question.

He didn't respond, which was a response in itself.

"I never knew extortion was the northern way."

"You know it is not." Ret's voice was harsh, but his words seemed designed to convince himself as well as the thief.

"She leads you, does she not? When Mika, Snow Queen of the Rangor people speaks, she speaks for the north. Am I wrong?"

He gripped Hollis by the upper arms, lifting him easily from the ground. The thief didn't resist.

"Do not seek to confuse matters, Hollis."

In as gentle of a voice as he could muster, Hollis said, "If you are confused, my friend, it is not my doing. No matter how tightly you shut your eyes, at some point you will have to open them again. If you are beginning to doubt the tapestry Mika has woven for you, it is because you have seen it fraying at the edges."

"Mika is my friend." Ret opened his huge hands and let the thief drop from his grip.

Hollis landing lightly on his feet. "Silvermoon was a friend to us both. Neither my words nor hers should have more weight than your conscience." He continued on alone, leaving Ret to the internal conflict that raged within him. Before he stepped under the tent's flap, he said over his shoulder, "When given the opportunity, the man I knew always seemed to find his way to the right decision. The question is: what kind of man are you now?"

Chapter Thirty

An Unconventional Investigation

"Are you certain it is still working?" Asaege's voice was a tense whisper as she extended the whisper stone to Seran by its leather cord.

The elder thief raised an eyebrow that spoke volumes. *You choose now to bring this up?*

On first glance the two story daub-and-timber building they stood beside seemed no different from its neighbors in the tight alley. Its defining characteristic was not the structure itself, but rather who dwelled within. Dael had recently joined the ranks of the thieves' guild and as such would have been expected to sleep in the crowded guild barracks with the rest of the apprentices. Instead, the young man rented a room above a carpenter's workshop in the maze of streets that made up Oizan's Craftsman District.

"Can we discuss this later?" Even when he whispered, Seran's voice had a sharpness. It had taken the pair the better part of the day to work through the list of guild members that had been with Toni during the previous evening's attack. Dael was the next on their list. Given his suspicious living arrangements, Asaege had thought he should have been nearer the top of it. The elder thief had felt differently.

"It is not like Hollis to be out of contact for so long."

"The boy will be fine. He is a survivor." Seran's hushed words sounded casual, but she saw her own concern mirrored in his eyes. "We need to focus on what is directly ahead of us." He indicated the building with a shallow bow of his head. "There are better things than that to have clutched in your fist when we go through that door."

Slipping the loop of leather over her head, Asaege tucked the whisper stone safely into her tunic and drew her sword.

"That is my girl."

She forced down her visceral reaction to Seran's patronizing comment. Given that he was Hollis's only real father figure for much of his youth, she wondered at how the two men could be so different. It was not the first time she found herself presented with that particular paradox.

Leaning in towards her, Seran placed his mouth close to her ear. "Milaes the carpenter should be tucked safely in his bed by now. The stairs to Dael's room lie at the far side of the shop."

As quickly as the question of how the elder thief knew the layout so well occurred to her, he answered it.

"Milaes and I have done business in the past. Follow me and try your damnedest to be quiet. Step where I step." Without waiting for affirmation, the elder thief opened the door and slipped inside.

Asaege caught the closing door before it could slam and stepped in behind him. As she watched him move across the sawdust strewn floor as if he hovered above its surface, she saw that Hollis and his mentor had their similarities as well. Although Seran was older than she by a decade and a half, he moved with a grace she could only aspire to.

Even though she followed in his faint footsteps, the floor crunched beneath each of hers. The sound didn't seem to carry far enough to be noticed by the sleeping carpenter or his family, so Asaege afforded herself some grace. By the time the pair reached the wooden stairs, she was drenched in sweat, feeling as if she had walked twenty miles rather than twenty yards.

Seran turned to her and mouthed the words of his last command. *Step where I step.* Agonizingly slowly, he climbed the steps one at a time. Although it took them more than a minute to reach the top, they did so without coaxing more than a token squeak from the wooden structure.

The elder thief pointed to Asaege and then the door. He held up three fingers in sequence before pantomiming pushing it open. He then tapped himself on the chest and motioned inside. She nodded and waited for him to count to three again. As he held up the third finger, Asaege gave the door a mighty shove. Before it had swung completely open, Seran was inside, his Slazean stiletto held by his side at waist height.

The small room's closed shutters permitted minimal light from the alley beyond to filter through cracks in their surface. It was enough for the pair to make out the simple furnishings within. A large trunk and modest bed dominated the apartment's tight confines. By the time Asaege stepped into the room, the elder thief was half-way to the bed; not so much as a scrape of his boot reached her ears.

Lost in her momentary fascination, she almost forgot to catch the door before it struck the wall. Reaching out quickly, she stopped it before it collided with the daub wall. Her heart beating in her ears, Asaege turned her attention back to the bed to see Seran straddling the struggling figure of Dael. The apprentice's muffled protests filtered past the hand covering his nose and mouth. They quieted immediately as the elder thief laid his dagger beside the man's throat.

"Close the door," Seran whispered, never taking his attention from the prisoner below him. "We are going to require some private time for conversation."

Asaege did as she was bid, gently shutting it with a barely audible click.

Still as a statue, Seran waited for her to come up beside him before leaning closer to Dael's face. "I am going to remove my hand. The only sounds I want to hear from you are answers to my questions. Anything else will be your last. Nod if you understand."

In the months she had known Hollis's mentor, Asaege had witnessed the casual approach he had to violence. She'd heard tales of a multitude of other examples of it. None of it prepared her for the almost complete void of emotion his words carried. Gooseflesh raised at the back of her neck at the casualness of his threat. It was as if Dael's life meant less to him than the motes of dust dancing in the beams of moonlight dribbling through the shutters. The effect was haunting.

The apprentice nodded slowly, careful to avoid the point of the stiletto pressed against his flesh.

Seran lifted his hand from the man's face. "Why did you do it, Dael?"

Asaege frowned, concerned that the elder thief's question wasn't specific enough to get to the root of why they had come.

"S .. S .. Seran," Dael stuttered. "I did not see any harm in it."

Wow, she thought, *That was easy.*

"No harm?" Seran leaned closer to the apprentice's face. "How did you figure that?"

"I grew up in a small fishing village off of the Mantrian coast. My father lost his leg in an accident when I was very young. Most days, drowning his pain and disappointment in the bottom of a mug was more important to him than filling the bellies of his family. When Finnel found me outside the inn begging for drabs from pass-ersby, he offered to take me with him to Oizan."

Asaege thought she could make out the confused expression pasted on Seran's face, although he didn't let it bleed into his voice.

"What did the Finn tell you he wanted at the time?"

She picked up on the purpose of Seran's line of questioning later than she would have liked. Without providing any details of his own, the elder thief allowed Dael's fear and guilty conscience to do it for him. The man didn't so much answer their questions as confess to the sins that weighed upon his heart.

"He had concerns about the direction of the guild, whispers of dissatisfaction among the apprentices and journeymen." Dael's voice became desperate. "After Toni's uprising, he feared his relationship with the former guild master would make him the next target. Finnel moved us all out of the barracks. He said it was to protect us."

"How did that work out for you?"

Dael began sputtering nonsense as he sought words that would delay what he must have seen as his inevitable death.

Seran clapped his hand back over the man's mouth. "Shh," he warned, "I would hate to wake the carpenter and his family. In our profession, witnesses are strongly discouraged."

Asaege took a step forward, the elder thief's implied threat chilling her to the core. He looked up and shook his head quickly before returning his attention to the man beneath him.

"At the moment we are just talking, Dael. I am sure you can imagine what could happen when I am no longer feeling chatty."

Dael nodded again.

"I am going to remove my hand. The next warning you get about extraneous noise will be when I pin your tongue to the roof of your mouth."

Another nod.

Seran lifted his hand. "Tell me what the Finn has asked of you in the past few nights."

The man carefully whispered, "He told me to stay close to Toni's team and report back to him what I saw. I think he is scared. We all are."

"What is he frightened of?"

"The city guard. The templars. The revolution itself. He said …" Dael must have thought better of his confession.

"Now is not the time for secrets. The Finn is not here. I am. As such, I am your immediate problem, boy."

"He said none of it is any of our concern. Toni and …" His eyes locked with Seran's pleadingly. "These are his words, not my own."

"Of course," Seran granted.

"Toni and you spend our lives for your own benefits, not those of the Brotherhood."

"Do you share his concerns?"

"No."

Asaege winced. Even she could hear the lack of conviction in the answer.

"Dael, Dael, Dael, I did not believe that I needed to stress how important it is that you are honest with me. If I cannot trust you, where do you think that leaves us?"

"Not in a good place?"

"Not in a good place," Seran confirmed. "Given the heightened tension of the situation, I am willing to grant you a little grace this one time. Do you share his concerns?"

"A lot of us do. We joined the guild because we wanted better lives for ourselves. We did not want to be soldiers in the war of a prophet none of us have even seen."

The last bit stung Asaege's heart. Her movement had begun as a means to help the people around her. She hadn't realized that others wouldn't feel the same way … or hadn't wanted to.

"That is a fair point." Dael relaxed slightly at Seran's confirmation of his point of view. That tension transferred to Asaege. "However, I am at more of a loss to accept that you and your friends believed spying on your brothers and sisters was the path to change."

"Finnel —" Dael began.

"—Rest assured, the Finn will be dealt with. If I were you, I would be more concerned with your own immediate future and how much of it there actually will be."

Dael arched his back in a futile attempt to put as much distance between his throat and the blade in Seran's hand as possible. "Please do not kill me." Even after his coerced admission of betrayal, the man's pleading tone struck at Asaege's heart.

"Seran," she said softly.

Seemingly ignoring her, Seran tapped the tip of his dagger against the tender flesh of Dael's jaw. "I may hold the blade, boy, but your life is in your own hands. You are going to tell me every-

251

thing about the Finn's little cabal: names, places, anything you can remember."

"And then?"

"And then nothing. You will continue to do as you are told, with the addition of informing me at each step of the way. You wanted to be the architect of your own destiny, Dael. When the Finn's conspiracy is brought to light, you can either be hailed as the hero who exposed it or found face down in a gutter as a victim of it. It is your choice."

Hesitantly, Dael nodded.

Seran extended a hand to Asaege. "I assume you have paper and a quill?" Without waiting for her reply, he turned back to Dael. "As an expression of our renewed understanding, I would expect you to include every detail."

*****

After the chill of the winter evening, the atmosphere inside the Virgin Mermaid felt stifling. A haze of wood smoke hung in the air, creating a shifting miasma over the age-polished wooden tables. Between the bitterness of the night and uncertainly that still lingered within the walls of the Dock District, the common room of Oizan's most popular inn was filled to capacity.

Standing beside Seran, Asaege let her eyes sweep over the crowd. Besides the expected dock workers and foreign sailors, it contained a cross section of the city. Craftsmen sat shoulder to shoulder with laborers and slumming children of wealth. In the corner furthest from the heavy double doors sat a small group of rough looking men. Among them, she recognized the craggy face of Associate Master Finnel, known to friends and enemies alike simply as the Finn.

Asaege laid a hand on her companion's arm. He nodded shallowly and made his way down the wide steps into the common room. Seran whistled softly to himself as he made his way through the crowd with the attitude of drawn steel. A slow dirge-like tune she found strangely appropriate, given their intentions. He was given wide berth by any he approached. She saw Finnel's expression drop as he noticed the people nearest him part, although he drew his mouth into a tight frown in an effort to hide his uncertainty.

The elder thief stopped in front of the table, resting his hands on its surface. "Finn."

"Seran," Finnel purred, "I did not expect to see you this evening."

"I imagine not." He turned a hard glare on the men sharing the table. "Would one of you mind giving up your seat. The Finn and I have some things to discuss."

All three men rose and stumbled over themselves vacating their chairs. As they dissolved into the crowd, Finnel was left alone across from Seran.

Asaege saw his eyes dart from side to side in search of an available escape route. To his credit, he kept his voice even despite his obvious discomfort. "What can I do for you?"

Seran continued to stand, despite the surplus of empty chairs. "I was concerned for your welfare. No one has seen hide nor hair of you since the unpleasantness last night."

"No one was looking hard enough."

Without breaking eye contact, Seran asked, "Asaege, did you see Associate Master Finnel prior to the guard's unannounced entrance?"

"Yes, I did," she confirmed.

"Was he among those who fled through the only available exit?"

"No, he was not."

"Can you see why folks may have been worried?"

"As you can see, I am fine."

"I would so dearly love to hear that story. How did you find your way past a dozen or so guardsmen, not to mention a thaumaturge?"

"I went out a window."

"Asaege?" the elder thief prompted.

"After Lirych set it on fire, the building went up like a tinder box. As the building's only windows faced the alley, I find it hard to believe anyone escaped that way without any of us noticing."

"Asaege finds your story hard to believe."

"The only other exit would have been the way the city guard came in," she dutifully supplied.

"Fuck you, bitch," Finnel snapped.

The elder thief raised an eyebrow, but said nothing.

Finnel leaned forward, his voice softening. "Please tell me you are not going to take her word over mine, Seran."

"How long have we known each other, Finn?"

"More than a decade. She is not—"

Seran held up a hand, cutting him off. "—And in that time, have you ever known me to take anyone's word for anything?"

He shook his head, his eyes growing more wild. Asaege's hand strayed to the hilt of the sword at her waist.

"I am going to ask you again. How did you escape last night's ambush?"

"I —"

"—But, before you say anything, I implore you to think carefully about your answer. It represents a rarefied opportunity. You could either lie to me, perhaps not for the first time tonight, or reinforce the faith you apparently believe I should have in you." Seran drew the slender stiletto from where it was strapped to his right thigh and rested its tip on the stained surface before him.

"This is not what either of us signed up for."

"That is technically not an answer to my question, Finn." The elder thief gestured around himself. "Speaking for myself, this is exactly what I signed up for. I have a strong suspicion that is not what you are referring to, though."

"The Brotherhood of the Night is not a collection of common sell-swords."

The elder thief feigned disappointment. "My dear Finnel, perhaps it would be best to avoid using the word brotherhood when being questioned about your potential betrayal of your fellow guild mates. How did you escape last night's ambush?"

"Between that freak, Toni, the snooty Binders, and the sanctimonious yet unseen prophet, the guild has become nothing more than a tool in someone else's game."

Seran laughed softly before sighing. "Finn, the guild has always served masters other than itself. The revolution is certainly the most obvious example, but essentially it is no different than any other agenda the Brotherhood has served over the years." His eyes narrowed as all emotion drained from his voice. "I am not accustomed to having to ask a question twice, much less three times. I will admit to finding the experience rather vexing, so consider this your last chance. How did you escape last night's ambush?"

"A representative of the Council of Guilds approached me. She recognizes the Brotherhood's usefulness and is willing to forgive the previous actions of any who side with them."

"Markov?" Before Asaege could help herself, the name leapt from her mouth.

Finnel's eyes bore into her, but he didn't respond. "It was the only way I saw for our guild to survive."

"Oh, I see," Seran said, "you actually have no issue with being a tool after all, simply the hands wielding it."

He reiterated, "It is the only way we survive."

Asaege lunged past the elder thief. "Survive? Those that died last night did so by your hand, as surely as if you held the blade

254

yourself!"

Seran held her back with one arm while extending his dagger toward Finnel's chest. "She is not wrong, Finn."

He scoffed. "Is it your plan to kill me in front of all these people?"

The elder thief casually shrugged. "I was certainly entertaining the idea. Once you provide me with the names of rest of your cabal, we can discuss your final disposition."

"What is to stop you from killing me anyway?"

Frowning, Seran spoke slowly as if to a child. "Nothing. However, that result is guaranteed if you are not forthcoming."

Asaege backed up a step. "It is no less than he deserves."

The elder thief's eyes remained locked on the man before him. "That seems to be my prevailing opinion as well, but who knows? When hauling in a net full of fish, a few small ones always seem to wiggle free."

"What makes you think—" Finnel began.

"—That you will betray your comrades?" Seran finished for him. "I have a feeling that as much as you claim your actions serve the guild's greater good, the thing you value above all others is your own skin. If you can trade the lives of others for the thinnest possibility of saving your own, I do not think that you even see that as a choice."

Finnel's shoulders slumped in resignation. "Fine. It started with me, Wilian, Bar—"

His words were drowned out by a great crash as the Virgin Mermaid's double doors were thrown open. Seran's natural reaction to turn towards the sound caused him to take his eyes off the traitor for a split second. It was enough for Finnel to dart past the pair and through the kitchen door.

Three armored templars stood on the landing. A great voice boomed from under the helmet of the closest soldier. "Finnel of the Ash, you are under arrest by order of the Church of Olm!"

"Dumb fucking luck," Asaege cursed under her breath.

The crowd filling the common room parted, opening a clear line of sight to Seran and Asaege as they turned to follow Finnel through the door. "Stop," one of the soldiers called, "in the name of the Ivory Cathedral!"

In a split second, the faces around the pair morphed from informed disinterest into faith-driven civic responsibility. The same patrons who wouldn't have raised a hand to prevent Seran from killing Finnel suddenly latched them around Asaege's arms and torso. In the maelstrom of groping hands and raised voices, she couldn't gather enough of her thoughts to marshal the words echoing in the back of her mind into a coherent spell.

Beside her, the elder thief seemed to be having less of an issue dealing with their reversal of fortunes. The first pair of hands that reached for him found themselves a more pressing task in staunching the flow their owner's blood as Seran drove his dagger into the man's throat. A second weapon appeared in his free hand between heartbeats. He swept the shorter, broad-bladed dagger from side to side before him as he backed toward the kitchen door. His attackers' religious fervor struggled with their unwillingness to join the dying man at the elder thief's feet. In the end, self-preservation seemed to have been the stronger emotion.

Before Asaege could reach for the Talis Fahr at her waist, the pressing crowd had pinned her arms to her side. Over her shoulder, she saw Seran in the open doorway, his eyes darting side to side as he raced to a decision. After a moment's contemplation, she didn't like the one he reached. As the lead templar fastened his gloved hand around her shoulder, the elder thief pivoted and disappeared into the shadowy depths of the kitchen.

Chapter Thirty-One
A Skewed Perspective

Her mind reeling under the weight of the evening's revelations, Jillian hadn't realized her destination until she'd arrived at Church Hill Long Term Care Center. Her latest visit cost her forty dollars, but as she stood in the doorway to Stephen's room, the money seemed trivial compared to the warm feeling in her chest when she laid eyes upon him again. Beneath the subtle differences between Stephen and his reflection, Jillian saw the man she had fallen in love with, despite never having actually met him.

Hovering at the threshold, her imagination made it seem almost a physical barrier. The memory of the overwhelming barrage of otherworldly sensations during her last visit kept her poised at the doorway. *In or out*, she thought. *Eventually, someone is going to come along and choose for you.* There was a good chance that if that happened, Jillian would have more difficulty returning. She mustered her resolve to step into the room, but before she could do so, she felt a hand on her shoulder.

Her mind wildly searching for a plausible excuse for her presence, Jillian turned to find Mateo Albacete on the other end of the gentle grip. "Good Evening, Miss Jillian." His warm brown eyes met hers with an intensity that she didn't remember from their last meeting.

"Chaplain Albacete."

"Mateo," he reminded her with a slight lilt of amusement in his voice.

"Mateo," Jillian corrected. "You're here late."

"The job is rarely nine-to-five. I like to stay as long as I am needed."

She tilted her head. His use of "I am" rather than the more convenient contraction put her on edge. "Are you almost done for the day, then?"

Looking past her and into Stephen's room, Mateo appeared to think about his response for a moment before answering. "I cannot help but feel that I should stay a little while longer."

Glancing over her shoulder into the dimly lit room, Jillian searched for what he found so interesting. "I shouldn't keep you, then. I'm just here to visit my friend again."

He averted his eyes to the watch on his wrist. "Once again, it is past visiting hours. You seem to have begun to develop a habit."

"I'm sorry, it won't happen again."

"Consistency is an admirable trait, Miss Jillian, until it is not. If you value your privacy, it may benefit you to vary your schedule so your visits with the boy are not interrupted."

The boy?

"Anyway, it was nice running into you again. You have my card if you have any further need of assistance."

Feeling off balance, Jillian patted the pockets of her jeans. "I seem to have misplaced it. Do you, by any chance, have another?"

"Of course," he purred, extending what appeared like an empty hand. With a flick of his wrist, a business card appeared. "Enjoy your visit, Miss Jillian." Lifting his hand from her arm, Mateo began to whistle as he walked down the hall away from her.

Something about the haunting, hymn-like tune itched at the back of Jillian's mind. As he disappeared around the corner and the sound of the strangely familiar tune faded into the distance, she turned back to Stephen's open door. The shadows within seemed more ominous than they had moments before. Putting aside the strangeness of her conversation with the chaplain and the trepidation slowly building within her, Jillian drew herself up and crossed the threshold.

Although the dizzying sensation was immediate, its effects were subtle at first. The harsh florescent light seemed to flicker at the edges of her vision, revealing flashes of a different place entirely in her periphery. Breath to breath, the cool touch of the room's over-filtered air alternated with the sensation of the much denser air in Taerh. Putting her disorientation from her mind, Jillian focused on putting one foot in front of the other. Step by step, she unerringly drew nearer to the unmoving figure in the bed.

Unlike during her last visit, the world-bleed grew stronger as she approached. The feeling bore a striking similarity to the haunting influence of adder root, only without the all-encompassing drowsiness that accompanied consuming its leaves. Where adder root softened the world around her until Earth and Taerh blended into one another like two banks of early morning fog, her experience upon entering Stephen's room was more akin to slamming two eggs together in preparation of making an omelette.

Just as she had done when she initially reflected, Jillian had fought the process the first time she had entered Stephen's room. Frightened by the unfamiliar sensation, she had instinctively seen it as a conflict and reacted accordingly. Pushing aside her natural apprehension, Jillian sought to accept the conflicting rush of sights and sounds that barraged her senses. Much like the first faltering steps on a twisted ankle, she found herself unbalanced and aching with the tribulation of the process.

However, the more she acknowledged her discomfort, the easier it became to manage. Jillian's head reeled with the overload of stimulation, but just like hobbling on an injured leg, she slowly began to move forward. Her perception of the room faded to a dull gray as the overpowering, vibrant images of the other world coalesced before her eyes.

*****

Unyielding hands gripped her by the arms, dragging her through a dim corridor. She could feel the rough surface of the rope binding her hands behind her back. A pair of armor-clad templars flanked her, more carrying than leading her along the rough, uneven stone passage. Three paces ahead of her walked a cassocked figure, slim to the point of gauntness. His chin-length black hair was slicked to his skull with sweat and some sort of foul-smelling oil.

"What's going on?" she murmured in English. Besides a curious side-long glance from one of her escorts, her question went unanswered ... at least by her captors. However, memories not quite her own dutifully provided the requested detail. The events of Asaege's evening presented themselves in a rush of images and sensations. The recollection of Seran abandoning her to the not-so-tender mercies of the templars stood out from the others. The sting of his betrayal threatened to eclipse even the fear that pulsed through

her veins.

The cadaverous priest held up a skeletal hand briefly as he searched his robes for a moment. The templars jerked her to a stop, lifting her feet from the ground. After fishing an ancient ring of keys from the depths of the ill-fitting garment, the spindly figure unlocked a thick wooden door and gestured inside.

"This will do." His voice was a raspy hiss, no more substantial than the body beneath his cassock. Rough hands tossed her to the cell's floor. Unable to break her fall with bound hands, the impact rattled her bones. The last thing she heard as the door slammed shut was the mockery of her gaunt jailer. "Welcome home, girl."

*****

Jillian's perception of the hospital room returned in a disorienting rush. Although the stark florescent lighting had replaced the dreary shadows of Asaege's cell, she could still feel the damp chill of the stone floor seeping into her muscles. In her fugue state, Jillian had covered the short distance from door to bedside. Amidst the phantom sensation of cold stone on flesh, one spot of warmth stood out.

Glancing down, she saw her fingers intertwined with Stephen's. The feeling of his hand in hers seemed to hold the numbing influence of Asaege's predicament at bay. Crouching down beside him, Jillian pressed her forehead against the warm skin of his hand. His touch served as an anchor in the sudden turmoil of the unexpected recollections. While they didn't recede, by his side, the taxing voices of Asaege's memories quieted to a more respectful volume.

Without releasing his hand, Jillian tentatively reached out and laid her free one on Stephen's cheek. His face remained placid, but she swore that he leaned into her touch ever-so-slightly.

260

Chapter Thirty-Two
An Unanticipated Visitor

Asaege lay still on the stone floor for a moment, the chill of its touch seeping into muscle and bone. Three months before, she'd found herself in the same situation, but under very different circumstances. The last time she saw the inside of the dungeon beneath the Ivory Cathedral, she's been Plague Man's prisoner, an unwilling playing piece in his shadow-fueled power grab.

She and Jillian put an end to the ancient presence that was his co-conspirator, and Hollis had taken care of the man himself ... or so they thought. Jillian had recently spoken to Plague Man's reflection, something that shouldn't be possible if the assassin had met his fate beneath the city as had been believed. As disturbing as the thought of Plague Man continuing to draw breath was, it wasn't what occupied Asaege's thoughts at that moment.

Whether or not Olm's templars knew her true identity as the Prophet, Asaege was still a known leader of the revolution that had swept the city. As far as most of the Olmites were concerned, it was that same revolution that took the life of the Hand of Light. *The fact that they did not kill me on the spot could only mean the church has other, undoubtedly more painful, plans for me.* There was a good chance that only two things remained in her future: a public sham of a trial and an equally public execution.

Asaege's hand closed around the whisper stone beneath her blouse. If her nights were limited, there was so much she wanted to tell Hollis. *If only the damned thing was not broken*, she thought. *It is just as well. He is at least a week's travel away and could not reach me in time, much less mount any type of rescue.* She looked around the dim confines of her cell, trying her best to shake loose from the self-pity that threatened to overtake her. *Asaege*, she scolded herself, *I guess it is up to you.*

In their haste, her captors had only taken her obvious weapons. The whisper stone wasn't the only tool at her disposal that had been missed. In the chaos of the melee at the Virgin Mermaid, Asaege had been unable to call upon the formulae endlessly repeating themselves in her subconscious. The stillness of her cell presented no such obstacle.

Pushing herself to her knees, she closed her eyes and allowed her mind to become quiet. In the silence of her thoughts, the imprisoned spells' voiceless pleas for freedom were deafening. Carefully separating one from the other, Asaege located the formula she sought. She had used *Trologue's Transmutation* once before and nearly lost control of the powerful spell. If she didn't wish to bring the entire building down on her head, she would need to exercise more caution with her second attempt.

As the words began to form on her tongue, Asaege could feel their weight. Slow and ponderous, each syllable came from deep in her chest, pulling the next behind it. As the echoing sounds hung in the air, she could see the surface of the thick wooden door before her ripple under their force like the surface of a still pond. The steady cadence of *Trologue's Transmutation* dragged Asaege's mind along with it like the current of a mountain stream. As she repeated the words of the formula, they built upon themselves. In the space a few breaths, the gentle stream became a roaring river.

Before Asaege's eyes, the door buckled and sagged in its frame for a second before collapsing to the stone floor in a gelatinous puddle. With the wood reduced to a viscous half-state between solid and liquid, the power of the spell began to affect the stone that had surrounded it. Large blobs of stone dripped from the doorway like cake icing on a warm day.

Asaege tried to clamp her mouth closed, but her lips and jaw worked of their own accord, pushing the spell's arcane syllables into the stone before her. Her heart beat in time with the words pouring from her mouth. She couldn't stop their flow, and wasn't sure she actually wanted to. She could feel it as the bonds of nature itself fell

262

before her power. The addictive sensation carried her along, softening her perception of the world around her. Everything but her spell
and the stone it affected became wrapped in the gauze of apathy.

The door frame collapsed into a pool of stone-made-mud,
spreading into the hallway beyond. Over her words, Asaege heard a
low creaking as the formula began to weaken the ceiling above her.
A small voice in the back of her mind sought to overpower the steady
mantra that filled her senses. *Stop.* In comparison to the thunder of
the spell, it was leaves rustling in the breeze, but annoyingly, every
time she paused for breath, it returned. *Stop.* Each time Asaege
thought she had drowned it out, it pricked her mind like a thorn.
Stop. Irritably, she turned her attention to it with the intention of
smothering it for good.

Pulling her attention from the siren song of the spell, Asaege
saw the devastation wrought by it. Her legs were buried to the shin
in a thick paste of partially liquidated stone. The hallway beyond
her cell was a mess of collapsed stonework and splintered wooden
beams. Mustering all of her strength, she clamped her mouth shut
and let the echoing words of the spell dissipate into the ether.

Asaege pushed the last vestiges of the formula's addictive
effects from her mind as she pulled her feet from the already-hard-
ening stone. She surveyed the damage as she stepped from her cell
into the hallway. Large sections of the ceiling had crumbled onto
the only marginally solid floor, giving everything the appearance of
melted wax. Those doors lining the corridor that hadn't fallen from
their frames hung from them like exhausted children clinging to their
parent's leg.

At the end of the hallway, ten feet beyond the spell's effect,
stood a familiar figure. The sleeves of his silk shirt stained deep
crimson, Seran waved to her with an upraised stiletto. "Did I need to
come? It seems you have things well in hand."

*****

A tense silence hung between the pair as they snuck through
the dimly lit belly of the cathedral. Asaege broke it when it became
apparent to her that her companion wasn't going to.

"You left me." Equal parts angry and hurt, her words were all
accusation.

"Yes," Seran stated simply.

"You left me," she repeated more forcefully.

"I saw no benefit to both of us being captured. That would have
left no one to launch a daring rescue." In counter-point to her tense
tone, his was casual and almost conversational. It didn't improve her

mood. "As it turned out, you did not require one, but I certainly hope you will at least give me credit for the intent."

"Thank you?"

The elder thief's face broke into a smile. "You are quite welcome, my dear Asaege. I am unaccustomed to acts of selflessness and was beginning to wonder at what others saw in them."

"Perish the thought. Are you finding that they suit you?"

"I am reserving judgment." As they approached an intersection, Seran held up a hand to slow her advance. As he put his finger to his lips, Asaege noted again how the sodden crimson sleeve of his shirt clung to his arm. Sinking into a crouch, the elder thief peeked around the corner before motioning her forward.

"Are you alright?" Asaege whispered gesturing to his bloody sleeve.

"None of it is mine. I have always found it fascinating that prisons are far easier to break into than the other way around. Inward-turned eyes rarely look for blades behind them."

"How many?"

Seran squinted at her before answering her question with one of his own. "Does it matter?"

"It does to me."

He shrugged and quickly touched his thumb to his fingers in succession. "Six. The warden should not count, as he had one foot in the grave when I found him." Lifting his hand to his mouth, the elder thief gasped dramatically. "I hope whatever put him in that wretched state was not contagious."

"Something tells me this is not your first experience with communicable diseases."

Smirking behind his fingers, Seran winked at her. "Why, milady, whatever could you mean?"

Despite knowing full well his past actions, Asaege found it difficult to dislike the elder thief. He seemed to want everyone around him to believe his first concern was always himself, but his presence in the dank corridors beneath the Ivory Cathedral spoke of more than self-interest. Seran had fought the shadow-possessed Plague Man almost at the cost of his own life to save Hollis. He did so without hesitation or reservation. She wasn't sure if two good deeds made up for a lifetime of sins, but it constituted a beginning at least.

Impulsively, Asaege placed a hand on his shoulder. He flinched beneath her fingers, but the reaction never reached his smiling face. "Why did you come for me, Seran?"

"I was in the—"

264

She tightened her grip, interrupting his cavalier deflection. "—The real reason."

"You ask a great deal from me, Asaege." Although his tone remained casual, the elder thief's eyes became hard.

"Is a single moment of candor really such a huge request?"

"Yes." His answer was as definitive as it was instantaneous. The mask of casual amicability drained from his face like sand through an hourglass.

"Why?"

"Honesty is habit forming, and it is not one I particularly care to develop."

"How can anyone come to trust you when they cannot believe a word that comes out of your mouth?"

In the same smooth, chilling voice Seran said, "They will not."

A bleak understanding dawned on Asaege with those three words. *He does not want anyone to trust him. Trust breeds affection and affection breeds ... what? Attachment? Vulnerability?* In all the stories Hollis had told her about his youth in the thieves' guild, his time under Seran's mentorship, he had never mentioned any real connection between the two. Every moment shared between them had constituted some sort of life lesson. Each interaction was an opportunity to make Hollis a sharper tool, a better thief, and a more efficient killer. Friendship and love had no role in any of those things, so they had never factored into the relationship between the thief and his mentor.

Sadness pulled at her heart like a puppet tangled in its own strings. Seran's carefully cultivated bearing had been designed to keep others at a distance. Those out of arm's reach could never plant a knife in your back.

Asaege softened her voice. "Surely one frank conversation will not cause an avalanche into sainthood. Consider it a favor to me."

The elder thief raised an eyebrow that said, *Another one?* "The boy would never forgive me if you were to come to harm while he was away."

Her lips turned down in a dubious frown. "Try again."

"I have become accustomed to your presence in his—"

Asaege cleared her throat softly.

"—in our lives. I would find my participation in this little rebellion less enjoyable were you not part of it."

"Was that so painful?"

"Excruciatingly so. If we are through sharing our feelings, I would very much like to be free of the bleak ambiance of our present surroundings." Dropping into a crouch, Seran crept forward to peek around the corner. He sighed softly and allowed his shoulder to slump. Looking over his shoulder, he whispered, "Escape will not be found this way. We are going to have to double back."

Asaege turned to see the telltale glare of approaching torches in the corridor behind them. "That may not be an option either."

Reaching into his boot, Seran pulled free a thin Slazean dagger. "It is not the boy's Uteli blade, but this is going to have to do." After handing the weapon to Asaege hilt first, he turned back to peer around the corner. Without turning from whatever lay down the corridor, the elder thief said, "There are four templars, armored, but sans shields. We are going to move through them. Aim for the gaps: armpit, throat, elbow and knee, but do not let them halt your momentum. Once you are past them, put your head down and run."

"Where will you be?" Guilty images of his intended sacrifice haunted Asaege's thoughts. Seran didn't allow her to operate under those assumptions for long.

"If things go to plan, a half dozen strides ahead of you. I cannot speak for you, but this is not where I intend to die, girl."

She stifled a laugh completely inappropriate for the situation. *I guess that is why they call it gallows humor.*

"One more moment. Let them get a touch closer."

Closer? she thought, panic making her skin tingle.

"Now," Seran hissed and sprang around the corner and out of sight.

Hazarding a quick look over her shoulder at the approaching torches, Asaege followed right behind him.

Seran moved between two soldiers, each struggling to draw their swords. A third lay slumped against the stone wall, a steady flow of blood seeping through his fingers as he clutched at his throat. Between the elder thief and the empty corridor beyond was a figure familiar to both Asaege and her reflection alike.

Pulling back the hood of her crimson cloak, Remahl scowled deeply. "There has been a terrible mistake. Let us not compound it any further. Please do not make me regret my initial impression of you, Asaege."

*****

"Although it comes with nicer linens, this room is no less a prison than your previous accommodations." Seran half-sat, half-leaned against the simple desk that dominated the small chamber. It was no doubt intended for visiting priests, but she couldn't help but agree with his analysis of the situation.

"I had to make a split-second decision." As the hours passed, Asaege was coming to doubt the one she had made.

The elder thief echoed her concerns. "It happened to be the wrong one. With surprise on our side, there was a good chance we could have broken free and made for the surface."

"I was not prepared to take that chance."

He lifted his hand and gestured to the confines of the room in which they found themselves. "Obviously."

"Is it too much to ask for you to trust me?"

His only response was a deep frown.

"Of course it is. I am going to ask it all the same."

"I do not see that I have much of a choice at this point."

Wrapping her left hand around the hilt of the Tallis Fahr at her waist, Asaege said, "The fact that they returned our weapons has to count for something."

The elder thief opened his mouth to respond, but his words were cut short as the door slowly opened. In a smooth motion, he rose to his feet, his fingers closing around his stiletto.

"Now, now, Master Seran, if I had wanted you dead, I certainly would not have come to do the deed myself." Remahl stepped into the room. Over her shoulder, Asaege saw two fully armored templars in the hallway. They remained there as Remahl pulled the chamber's only chair from beneath the desk and sat down. "I am not going to lie to you; there are those among my brothers and sisters who wish to see you punished for the deaths of their comrades. It took some time to convince them of the fact that extenuating circumstances were at play."

"Such as arresting the girl with neither cause nor provocation?"

"Among other things." Remahl turned her attention to Asaege. "It is nice to see you again, Asaege, although I regret the events that preceded it."

"You are not alone. I was beginning to think I may have mis-judged you."

"I assure you it was not by my order that you were captured. I sent men to the Virgin Mermaid in search of a thief by the name of Finnel. One of them recognized you from your last ... stay here and thought to seize what he saw as an opportunity."

"This templar—"

"—Has already paid for his miscalculation." Remahl indicated Seran with a nod of her head. "Your friend extracted more than a fair price from the man during his rescue attempt."

"Why were you looking for the Finn?" Seran asked, clearly

ignoring the obvious accusation.

Turning her attention to the elder thief, Remahl smiled softly. The expression wasn't quite the comforting one Asaege wanted it to be. "Finding himself conflicted by Lady Markov's recent rhetoric, one of the faithful brought his concerns to our attention."

"So much for the sanctity of the confessional," he muttered.

The Crimson Sister elected not to acknowledge his words. "As it turned out, he was privy to a good deal of information about the inner workings of the council. That included details on their response to the revolution."

"Of which Finnel is part," Asaege interjected.

"That is correct. The rebellion has a rat in its walls, and in my experience, for every one you see, there are two others hiding just out of sight."

"Why do you care?" The accusation in Seran's tone was sharp as steel. "When the lines were drawn months ago, the church of Olm stood with the city."

"Things change, Master Seran. I will admit there are plenty within the Ivory Cathedral who place the blame for the Hand's death squarely upon the shoulders of the revolution. Neither I nor the Triad happen to share that opinion, but even our house is not without its share of rodents. Upon my arrival in the city, I made it clear that the Olmites would not take sides in the conflict until we were clear on which side stood in the light and which remained in shadows."

Asaege wasn't sure if Remahl's use of shadows in her analogy was merely coincidence or something more. With the aid of a being of ancient darkness, Plague Man was able to infiltrate the highest halls of power within the church. In doing so, he had almost delivered its faithful—rich and poor alike—into that same darkness. Through steel and ritual, she and Hollis had been able to put an end to the assassin's plan, but Asaege had a sneaking suspicion that those loyal to him still stalked the corridors of the Ivory Cathedral.

"I take it you have found some clarity?" The elder thief's toothy smile reminded Asaege of a shark. "Late is better than never, I suppose."

Remahl turned to Asaege. "Your friend is certainly a charmer."

Still lost in her swirling thoughts, she replied without thinking. "He grows on you."

"So does fungus." Returning her gaze to him, she addressed Seran's comment. "Yes, Master Seran, after some investigation, I believe the church may have been too hasty with its support of the council."

"Brilliant."

She raised an eyebrow but continued. "My personal experience with Lady Markov in the square only strengthened that belief."

"So you will stand beside us?" For the first time in months, Asaege felt hope flare to life in her heart. It was only a brief flash, however.

"I am afraid not. The church can not be seen siding against the city itself. If we did, we would soon find ourselves unwelcome across the Cradle, not simply in Oizan."

"While you fret about your public image, our people are dying for the right to be treated like human beings. If Olm cares not for the fate of his people, what good is he?" Said in anger, Asaege instantly regretted her words. "I did not mean—"

Although her face hardened, Remahl held up a hand. "I understand your anger. The needs of the church and those of the faith do not always align."

"Gods are for suckers," Seran offered.

"You are not helping," Asaege whispered harshly.

"Just because the Ivory Cathedral cannot publicly support your cause at the moment does not mean we cannot still be of assistance. Few in the halls of power will refuse my invitation, where others may fall on deaf ears." Remahl's eyes held a sparkle that Asaege had seen in the memories of her reflection.

"What are you proposing?" Asaege felt a small flicker of hope return.

"You saw as clearly as I the reluctance with which the Nine Families endorsed Lady Markov's bid. Their agreement was more out of fear of the mob than respect for the woman herself."

"I noticed that, but the Families are so removed from the day-to-day realities of the city that they make their choices based more on what brings them peace than what is right."

"And in that apathy lies the key to success. The Nine Families see themselves above the existence of both laborer and craftsman, politician and revolutionary. Your rebellion represents nothing more than an inconvenience to them, but as it continues to infiltrate their gilded gardens, the more it affects their lives. That is not something they can tolerate for long."

"So if the price of renewed tranquility is Markov's downfall —"

"—They are so used to solving problems with silver, they would gladly pay that cost as well."

"How quickly can you set up a meeting?"

269

Chapter Thirty-Three
A Bitter Victory

Aristoi tossed and turned on the fur-strewn floor of the large tent, lost in the midst of troubled slumber. The flickering light provided by the single lantern played across the rippling surface of her back and shoulders. The Songspear's hands were curled tightly against her chest, their fingers coated in a thin sheen of blood from lacerated palms. Whatever went on behind her tightly clenched eyelids caused Aristoi's breath to come in desperate gasps between the bestial growls emanating from deep within her chest.

*****

"As a member of the Songspear, the Elder Council has no right to judge my innocence or guilt. By the old ways, it can only be determined by a member of my order."

Aristoi stood in the center of the street, her mother's spear gripped casually in her left fist. Her empty right hand was held out before her in a sign of peace. Ofin Taloi, his anger seemingly unblunted by her time away, emerged through the gathering crowd. At his side was Junwei, a shining steel songspear clutched in her hands.

"You should have stayed gone, sister." Her voice was hard, almost hiding the tremble of fear beneath its angry tone. "I have recently taken our mother's place among that very same order. If you seek judgment, you need look no further."

Rage rose in Aristoi's throat, almost choking her with its intensity. For a moment, all she could do was stare hatefully at the woman who took from her everything she had loved.

"I find you guilty of matricide. You were foolish to return, but that crime's penalty will pale in comparison to the murder of our mother."

A voice came from behind Aristoi. "That is neither the word nor intent of the ways of our people." It was soft, almost conversational, yet carried to the crowd without issue. She turned to see a tall Kieli man, the hair at his temples gray as the swollen clouds above their heads. An ancient, broad-headed songspear rested in the crook of his elbow. There was no mistaking him for anyone other than the Branded.

A member of the Mouhn, or Heralds, he was one of the most puissant living wielders of magic known to the world. The group was charged with safeguarding Taerh, free of any ties to any one Kingdom or government. Despite his oath to remain free of influence, the Branded had always been a friend to the Kieli people. In addition to his duties as one of the three Heralds, he served as the leader of the Songspear order as well. It was with that authority that he spoke.

Those assembled dropped to a knee before the Branded. He extended a hand and gestured for them to rise. "None should kneel before me. A Herald's place it to counsel, not rule." Again, he motioned to the crowd. "Rise, my friends. Rise."

As the people slowly rose, Aristoi turned suspicious eyes towards the Branded. "I am no murderer."

"I have no reason to not believe you," he responded softly. "But I also have no call to deem Junwei a liar either. That leaves us in an awkward position, do you not agree?"

Glaring at her sister as she approached, Aristoi asked, "Could you not separate truth from deception through your magic?"

The Branded nodded. "I could, but that would violate both my oath as Mouhn and Songspear. I am pledged to advise, not judge. Even if I was willing to decree your innocence or guilt, it would only last as long as I was present."

Junwei stood next to her sister, out of reach. "It is the people of Willow's Ridge that bear the brunt of my mother's murder. It should be they who decide the fate of her killer."

He studied the crowd for a moment before speaking again. "I would need to be a fool to not see the great love this town had for her. While heartwarming that she was so esteemed, it may color their judgment in this matter. As you both are members of the Songspear, a quorum of our order should adjudicate the matter."

"The order has no place in this," Junwei snapped.

"There is another way." Their eyes turned to Aristoi. "In the times before the quorum, when members of the order disagreed, they settled their differences through spear, song or deed. They let the Lady decide their worth."

The Branded laid his hand upon her shoulder. "Are you sure you wish to make a challenge in the old ways?"

Aristoi nodded. "I am."

He turned to Junwei. "As the challenged, it is your privilege to choose the means: spear, song or deed."

Her face tightened. "I choose none of them."

The Branded frowned. "Then you forfeit your claim. Aristoi's name is clear of this accusation." He seized her in an unwavering glare. "I would then suggest that the town council look more deeply into the matter. Perhaps there was a suspect that escaped their notice originally."

Fear flooded into Junwei's face. "Um ..." she stammered. "I choose ..."

As angry as she was, Aristoi cringed. Her sister had always been bigger and stronger than she, but their mother learned early on that her skill with the songs of her people was sorely lacking. That had been the primary reason she had looked past Junwei when seeking to pass on her legacy. Choosing the trial of song would be as good as denying the challenge all together.

There was little doubt in Aristoi's mind that rumor of her Long Walk had reached the town of her birth. She had discovered one of the mythical Wells of Worlds. None in ten generations could claim such a deed. If Junwei decided on the trial of deed, the result would likely be no different. Still six inches taller and twenty pounds heavier than her sister, if Junwei had any chance of victory, she would need to choose ...

"... the spear."

*****

In a field just outside town, a wide circle had been drawn in chalk. Standing just inside it, Junwei was flanked by what seemed to be the entire population of the Willow's Ridge. Aristoi stood alone, the weight of the crowd's anger hanging about her shoulders like an oxen yoke. The expressions of anger and hatred directed at her from across the expanse of dirt nearly broke her heart.

In the back of her mind, a small voice whispered to her. The blood of her blood had betrayed her and driven her from her home,

273

taken that which belonged to her. Now Junwei came to her with fangs bared and eyes raised. She approached as predator rather than prey. That could not be allowed to stand. Aristoi recognized the thoughts as not her own, but that knowledge didn't dull their influence. As she fought against the counsel of the beast within her, she didn't notice a lone figure approaching until he stood beside her.

"Are you sure this is what you want?" the Branded asked. "Even if you succeed, these people will never accept you again. Say the word and we shall leave this place. I am no judge, but my respect among our people will afford you the grace to leave with me."

"I do not want this. I never wanted this. My mother is dead and there is a good chance that when either my sister or I step from the circle, the other will be as well."

"Then come with me."

"You would travel with a murderer?"

"You no more killed your mother than I did." He gestured across the circle. "But look at those people. Do you think they will believe that, even coming from my lips? In their minds, you have to be guilty, or everything they have accepted as fact for the last months is naught but a lie. Their pride cannot allow that."

"So my fate is to be decided by pride and jealousy?"

"Those two things have been responsible for more deaths than a mountain's worth of gold and steel. Leave the past behind, Aristoi. Walk a new path."

Again, the voice whispered to her. She didn't need that man's counsel or friendship. A true predator hunted alone. These people huddled together out of fear, not pride. Just as all prey did, they sought to tear down that which they feared. They were right to fear her; her sister would be an example to them of their place in the world.

Closing her eyes, Aristoi shook her head in an attempt to clear it of the foreign thoughts. Even so, she was unsure of whether her words were her own. "Junwei killed my mother. The moment she did, this was inevitable."

The dark desire within her surged once more. Those around her had to bear witness to what became of those who challenge her. The order of things had to be restored.

A low, bestial growl rumbled deep in Aristoi's chest as she stepped into the circle. Out of the corner of her eye, she saw the Branded's lips turn down in a concerned frown. Before she could think any more about it, Junwei leapt forward, her spear leading the way. Aristoi met her charge, sweeping her sister's spear to the side.

274

The darkness filled her senses for a moment. She could hear Junwei's heart beating in her chest and smell the fear-stench of sweat that coated her skin. Aristoi's jaw ached to sink her teeth into her sister's flesh and taste the sweet blood running across her tongue. A surge of recognition struck her like a wave of cold water. The pain in her jaw was far from figurative. Aristoi had been so lost in the whispers of the foreign presence that she hadn't realized that muscle and bone rippled beneath the skin of her face. In her anger, she had almost given in to the call of the creature within.

Mustering her resolve, she forced the voice into silence. As she did, her vision cleared, and the circle came back into focus again. Her distraction cost her dearly as Junwei lunged forward, the point of her spear aimed for Aristoi's chest. Pivoting quickly, she was able to turn away from the weapon but not avoid it completely. Rather than it piercing her heart, the spear sank into her shoulder, sending tremors through her arm when it impacted bone.

Nearly dropping her own spear, Aristoi back-pedaled away from her sister's furious attack. Although the wound bled freely, she could feel the pain begin to ebb. The next time Junwei extended her weapon, Aristoi's was there to meet it. Forcing the tip of her sister's spear into the dirt, she brought the shaft of her own around. It struck Junwei on the side of the head and the woman dropped to one knee.

Once more, the voice demanded her sister's heart, but Aristoi was prepared for it. She reached out for the sound of her mother's voice. She used to sing to the sisters in the garden on clear nights. Her voice mingled with the smell of gardenias in her memory. Through the comforting remembrances of scent and song, Aristoi was able to drown out the snarling urges.

As Junwei tried to rise, she kicked her hard in the chest, sending her sprawling to the dirt. Aristoi spun her spear above her head and brought it down in an overhand swing. She halted the iron head above her sister's neck, resting it lightly at the base of her skull.

"The challenge is ended. I have proven I am no killer. I will not become one today." Kicking Junwei's spear away, Aristoi turned to the crowd, holding her own weapon aloft. "This is the spear of my mother, and her mother before her. Stolen no longer, it is mine by right of trial." She sought to meet their gaze, but to a person they averted their eyes. "Let none dispute my claim."

Turning on her heel, Aristoi felt a pang of regret dissolve any feeling of accomplishment. There was no returning to Willow's Ridge. For good or for ill, she was a woman without a home.

*****

275

As rough hands grasped her shoulders, Aristoi partially returned to her senses. With half of her mind still entangled in the events of her dreams, she struck out blindly at the figure crouching next to her. Her fist connected solidly with something in the dark. As they rolled away, the Songspear heard their breathy curse.

"—the hell?"

Even in her partial fugue state, she recognized the voice. "Hollis?" She could make out his silhouette in the darkness, a hand raised to rub at his jaw.

"This is the first time I have seen the 'swing first, ask later' side of you, southerner. I am not sure if I am proud or disappointed."

"You surprised me." Emotional wounds, freshly opened by her increasingly vivid dreams, sat upon Aristoi's mind as she tried to shake herself loose from their weight. The hatred that filled her sister's eyes when Junwei had looked at her bored into the Songspear's soul, as if she were in the room with her, not separated by months and leagues.

"Do I even need to ask if the nightmares are getting worse?"

"I can handle it," Aristoi snapped, more hostile than she had intended.

"Of that, I have no doubt. You once told me burdens carried in silence are burdens carried alone." Hollis reached out tentatively to lay his hand on her arm. "You do not need to carry this one alone."

She opened her mouth to argue but settled for, "Thank you, Hollis."

He squeezed her arm gently and stood up. "You would do no less for me. As a matter of fact, you have done a great deal more."

A soft droning had been echoing in Aristoi's ears since her dramatic awakening. One of the few actual gifts of the dark presence inside of her was a sharpening of her senses. Since her initial run in with the gwyllgi almost a year before, she'd had to learn to live with the hushed cacophony that most people heard as silence. The buzzing had slowly become louder, clarifying into the sound of voices.

"Someone approaches," Aristoi warned.

The thief cocked his head, furrowing his brow as he called upon the "Understanding". He nodded grimly and took a few steps away from the tent's entrance just as the flap opened.

"You have been summoned." The rough words from a rougher warrior carried with them an ominous feeling.

Chapter Thirty-Four
A Desperate Challenge

The pair emerged from their tent-turned-prison into the midday sun. Squinting behind his raised hand, Hollis could make out a throng of fur-clad Rangor gathered in the center of the camp. Aristoi stepped out beside him, her own hand shading her eyes from the blinding light of the afternoon. A makeshift wooden structure loomed above the heads of those gathered. Obviously constructed from thick tent poles and rough-cut logs of evergreen, the thief couldn't mistake it for anything other than a gallows.

"Perhaps the Snow Queen has changed her mind." The Songspear tried to keep her tone casual, but Hollis could hear the worry that tainted every word.

"I very much doubt it. Mika is not known for being mercurial." He kept his tone even, but felt a prick of doubt in his gut as the pair approached the crowd.

A strong hand clamped onto his shoulder. Glancing behind him, Hollis saw Ret's lined face. His former comrade seemed to have aged a year since the previous evening. Worry creased the skin beside his eyes and lips. "The gallows is not for you, my friend." Although the warrior's words were terse, his tone held a gentleness Hollis hadn't heard in many years.

"Who is it for, then?"

"If the clans are to be united, none may be allowed to challenge the Snow Queen."

"Mika," the thief corrected. "These people may see her as prophet and queen, Ret, but you and I know she is only Mika."

"There are many who would see that as sacrilege."

"In all the years I have known you, Ret, the Rangor have stood tall in both my imagination and reality. It truly makes me sad to see them so diminished."

"Hollis," Aristoi cautioned. "We are not among friends. Measure your words carefully."

"I just never thought I would see the day where the northern clans would bend the knee so readily."

The thief noticed immediately that he had struck a nerve. Ret's face reddened for a moment, his jaw clenching so tightly Hollis heard his teeth grind. "You would be wise to heed your companion's advice, thief. Wisdom has never been one of your strong points."

"So I have been told."

Ret raised his voice above the murmur of the crowd. "Make way!" The gathered Rangor turned to regard the pair and their captor before parting to allow them free passage.

Mika sat on the crude stairs leading to the gallows. Beside her, lounging on a thick support beam, was the gwyllgi, its half-lidded, rust-colored eyes observing the scene before him. In the daylight, the beast's mottled pelt looked more reddish-brown than the charcoal-gray Hollis has imagined.

"I thought they could only come out at night," he whispered to the Songspear.

"What would make you think that?"

He shrugged. "Monsters belong to the night."

Aristoi swept her gaze over both Snow Queen and gwyllgi. "Not all of them, apparently."

Hollis saw one of the creature's ears twitch in his direction. "Can it hear me?"

"Most likely. Does it matter?"

The thief locked eyes with the creature, a fleeting feeling of dread flowing through him like a winter breeze through a city street. Whatever power those eyes held was no match for the serenity of the Well. "Not really." The surface of the gwyllgi's pelt rippled as it focused its attention on the thief.

Before the situation could escalate further, Mika stepped between Hollis and the creature.

"How nice of you to join us."

"I got the impression it was more of a summons than an invitation."

"You were always a quick learner, Hollis."

"But I'm obviously still a poor judge of people." The thief switched to English smoothly, watching Mika's reaction.

Her entire body tightened as a frown etched itself on her face. It took her a split second to reign in the panicked darting of her eyes. It seemed if for an instant, something within her sought escape. Buried somewhere deep in the Snow Queen was a presence that was not quite under her control.

"How rude of me." Hollis switched back to Trade Tongue. "What were you saying?"

"I feel it is important for you to understand the seriousness of the alliance I have formed here. The Rangor stand united under my leadership." Raising her voice for the benefit of those gathered around her, Mika continued. "No longer will they need to scratch a meager survival out of the frozen dirt of the north. They are warriors and conquerors. It is time that Taerh recognized their worth."

Keeping his voice conversational to contrast her over-the-top theatrics, Hollis said, "They do not need you to define their worth. The clans of the north are a proud people, not objects of wood and steel for you to wield against those you feel have wronged you."

A collective gasp echoed through the crowd. From its depths, a voice called. Although he didn't understand the words, Hollis comprehended their meaning. *How dare you!* The throng surged forward, only to be blocked by Ret's hulking form. The warrior shouted something in a northern dialect, and the crowd receded.

"I think that proves my point." The arrogance of Mika's voice turned the thief's stomach.

"Even the lowest of charlatans have their true believers, but not all of the north is so easy to deceive."

"Strange you should mention that, Hollis. My reasoning for summoning you and your companion here was twofold." Mika turned and mounted the gallows steps in three leaping strides. "Bring forth the traitors!"

Again, the crowd parted to reveal two limping figures wrapped in tattered cloaks herded before a trio of Rangor warriors. As they drew closer, the thief recognized the swollen and blood-stained faces of Valmont and Sagaun.

The Snow Queen called out in a clear voice to those gathered below. "Let their fates serve as a warning to those who seek to poison the destiny of the Rangor people!"

Hollis felt Aristoi's hand on his sleeve. He could not drag his eyes from the beaten bodies of his companions. "I know," he said softly.

"We cannot allow this to happen."

"I know." As Valmont passed him, the thief reached out to touch his shoulder. It was hard to read the appreciation in his swollen eyes, but it was there.

"Please tell me you have a plan."

"Not even close."

"Perhaps the gwyllgi—"

"No." Hollis's tone left no room for argument. "Neither Valmont nor Sagaun would want you to pay such a high price for their freedom." He continued to watch the pair's slow march towards the gallows and their untimely end. "If we could get our hands on some weapons, perhaps we could hold the platform for a short time ..."

Turning the "Understanding" upon the wooden structure, the thief didn't like what he saw. Without question, the Rangor were among the fiercest warriors on Taerh, but as builders, they fell far short of the mark. The gallows would hold the weight of a handful of people, but the hastiness of its construction left it far from structurally sound.

"... until a few well-placed shoves send it crashing down, bringing us with it."

Aristoi's brow furrowed for a moment. "Do you remember the cave outside of Drunmarch? If you give me the space of a dozen heartbeats, I could turn the permafrost into a quagmire. It will not catch more than ten or twelve, but it could give us the lead we need."

Hollis remembered the events with a bittersweet smile. It had been the last time he had fought beside Rhyzzo before his death. Seeming nothing short of miraculous at the time, the Songspear had turned an entire section of sand into a patch of quicksand. Her song had turned a bad situation into their favor. Slowly, he shook his head. "The gwyllgi would catch us before we reached the outskirts of the camp."

Aristoi seized her lower lip between her teeth, her internal struggle plain on her face. "Perhaps we could catch their queen unaware? A hostage might buy us a little distance."

The thief shifted his attention to Mika. For all appearances, her attention seemed to be on the condemned before her. However, Hollis saw that she kept shifting her stance to keep him in her peripheral vision. "She expects us to try something; there will be no taking her by surprise. No one else present will serve as an appropriate hostage.

280

The northerners will carve through them to get to us."

"I am ashamed to admit that I find myself running short of ideas."

Finally tearing his eyes from their doomed comrades, Hollis laid his hand over hers. "You are not alone, my friend." *Think, Hollis*, he scolded himself. Like a bolt of summer lightning, it came to him. "Our companions are to be executed, but I never saw a trial. Did you?"

Aristoi shook her head. "The word of the chieftain is sacrosanct. If she declares them guilty, there is no use in arguing the point. The only thing left to them is—"

The thief's eyebrows shot up as they both reached the same conclusion.

"Trial by combat!" they said simultaneously, their voices raised in their excitement. The crowd turned to them as one, angry sneers painted on their faces.

"What was that?" Mika took a half step towards Hollis.

Aristoi cleared her throat before speaking in a clear voice, her singer's training allowing it to carry to even the furthest ears. "Trial by combat. By the code of the clans, Valmont and Sagaun have the right to prove their innocence through strength of arm."

It was soft at first, but a rumble began to build among the throng.

"Have they been afforded that right, Mika?" Hollis's confident tone indicated he already knew the answer.

"They have already accepted the weight of their sins. No trial was requested."

Valmont lifted his head, the dried blood coating his lips cracking as he spoke. "I request it now. I demand trial by combat."

Sagaun haltingly stepped forward, joining him. "I, too, shall prove my innocence through blood and steel."

Mika let out a loud laugh. "In your conditions, the gallows would be a less cruel end." She drew the stolen sword at her side. "So be it. Someone provide the condemned with a blade. I will judge the woman's worth after I have delivered the Bone Dog's sentence."

Aristoi called out, "A moment, please, Snow Queen."

She turned her attention to the Songspear. "What is it?"

"Now that the challenge has been made and accepted, the code of the clans also provides for the choosing of a champion in the event that the accused is unable to face trial themselves."

"Do you wish to take their place, Southerner?"

Hollis saw the gwyllgi stand slowly, its eyes fixed on the Snow

Queen's back. Soundlessly, it dropped to the ground and approached her, lips pulled back to reveal wickedly sharp, ivory teeth. Ret put himself in the creature's path, his axe clutched in his fist.

"As a matter of fact—" Aristoi began.

"—I will champion Valmont." Hollis stepped past the Songspear. As she turned accusing eyes on him, he mouthed, "Sorry."

"Did you not learn your lesson, boy?" Mika made a show of looking the thief up and down.

"Apparently not."

"If we lock blades again, the result will be no different."

"I guess we're going to have to find out." Again, he switched to English and watched Mika tense as if she fought something deep within her.

Through clenched teeth, she asked, "Are you willing to let your arrogance be responsible for two lives?"

Aristoi gripped his shoulder tightly. "Do not do this, Northerner. It was I who brought you north, my debt that put us in this situation."

He caught her eye out of the corner of his own. "The debt may be yours, but the fight is mine alone." Turning his attention back to Mika, he said, "The challenge has been accepted, and the champion chosen." Speaking in English, he added, "The ball's in your court, Queen of Nothing."

Hollis watched her face flush and her eyes narrow in anger. "I will accept you as champion for both Valmont and Sagaun ... under one condition."

I have a bad feeling about this. The thief pushed down his trepidation. "Name it."

"If you win, you may not only leave with the traitors but your southern companion as well." The gwyllgi lunged forward, only to pull up short as Ret's axe cleaved the air in front of it. "If you lose, however ..." The Snow Queen locked eyes with him, her glare doing credit to her name. "... Valmont and Sagaun pay for their crimes as I have decreed. The Songspear belongs to the beast." She paused dramatically, allowing the significance of the thief's potential failure to settle upon his mind. "And you join me, willingly become my second. You will do great things, Hollis, if I have to drag you to them kicking and screaming."

He glanced over at Aristoi. Her features were set in a determined frown, but her eyes looked at him softly.

"Bargained well and done."

Chapter Thirty-Five
An Uneasy Alliance

As Jillian's eyes flickered open, a brief wave of panic washed through her body. She was not in her apartment's mauve and gray bedroom. It only took a moment to get her bearings and remember the events that led to her staying in Marisol's guest room. The recollection brought with it a measure of relief, but with it came other, more concerning, memories. The worst of them was the thought of working with Hector to find a murderer that he had brought into their lives with his damned logbook.

I'm sorely tempted to let the killer get their hands on him, she thought bitterly, *it would serve him right. Maybe if they find Hector, they'll leave the rest of us alone.* Of course, she had no intention of doing so, but the idea made her feel slightly better.

A soft rapping on her closed door distracted Jillian from her grim line of thought. She emerged from the cozy nest of blankets and padded to the door. When she opened it, a smiling Marisol stood in the hallway, almost vibrating with her excitement. "Come in," Jillian droned before turning on her heel and heading back to the bed.

"Aren't you a ball of sunshine this morning? I don't think I've slept that soundly ... well ... ever."

Jillian chuckled, a smile marring the otherwise grumpy lines of her morning face. For all of its possible negatives, adder root had one advantage that couldn't be denied. Once it was taken, you were guaranteed a good night's sleep. Often plagued with insomnia, she could see how the charm of that wouldn't be lost on Marisol.

Crawling under the blankets, Jillian patted the space beside her. "I've got a lot on my mind."

Marisol bounded across the room and hopped onto the bed. "I'm sorry. Perhaps two heads will be better than one? It might help spread the worry out a little." As hard as she tried to sound earnest, she couldn't hide her contented smile.

"I assume you reflected last night?"

Marisol nodded.

"What do you remember?"

"I was present for your conversation with Remahl about the Nine Families. It was like watching a movie through my own eyes. I could experience everything, but like being a passenger in a speeding car, I had no control."

"That will come with time. There are moments where it is best to observe and remember, and others where more of an active role is required. At least you have the first part down."

"Even now, I can feel a piece of her in the back of my mind. I'm not sure I'll ever get used to that."

"Like I said, everything in time." Jillian debated her next words carefully. "What is your sense of Remahl? Is she sincere?"

"One hundred percent. The whole reflection thing is super overwhelming, but the one thing I am sure of is Remahl's intentions. I don't know how I can be so sure, but I am."

Jillian let out the breath she hadn't known she'd been holding. With the seemingly stark differences between Cyrill and his reflection, she'd been afraid that the Crimson Sister would not share Marisol's character.

"Are you going to go through with her plan?" Marisol's voice was tentative, something Jillian was not accustomed to hearing.

"I'm not sure. No matter how similar we are, in the end, Asaege and I are separate people. I get the sense that working with the Nine Families is one of the only hopes of bringing the revolution to an end."

"It seems dangerous to me. Both of you need to be careful."

Jillian smiled lightly. "I'll pass on the message."

"Good." Marisol studied the closed door for a moment, as if she were debating something.

"Is something else on your mind, Mari?"

She turned her attention back to Jillian, but refused to look her in the eyes. "I'm torn."

"About what?"

"You are my very best friend, Jillian. That being said, there are times when Remahl seems like just another facet of my own personality."

A feeling of dread echoed in the pit of Jillian's stomach. "There is something she is not telling Asaege."

Marisol nodded slowly. "Whether I tell you or keep her confidence, both seem like betrayals."

Jillian yearned to press her friend, to demand to know what Remahl was hiding. She resisted that urge with all of her might. The relationship between reflections was a tenuous one, as she knew from all too personal experience. Asaege and she had fought the bond for some time, allowing jealousy and pride to get in the way of their connection.

"Is it something that will bring harm to Asaege ... or Seran?" She mentioned the elder thief as an afterthought; he was beginning to grow on Jillian as much as he had on her reflection.

Marisol closed her eyes and sighed softly. When she opened them again, something had changed in her gaze. It was somehow more confident, more comfortable in her own skin. "She seeks a child. He was imprisoned by the ..." She searched for a word, her head tilting as if she were listening to a voice just out of earshot. "... Hand of Light." She pronounced the title carefully, as if she were repeating words provided to her.

"A child?" Jillian felt both her own outrage and that of her reflection boil up in her.

Marisol put up both of her hands in a gesture intended to soothe. "Remahl had no idea until she arrived. Neither the Hand's papers nor those of his curate have any record of the child, but one of the templars remembered them being brought into the dungeon."

"What could a child have possibly done to warrant being thrown in a cell?"

"I'm not sure. Remahl has the same question, but they seem to have ... um ... lost them. There was a break in less than a week ago. Three guards were killed, including the prison commander, and the child's cell was found empty."

Jillian's mind was flooded with the memories of her reflection. Asaege clearly remembered when Seran returned with her sword, he had a small boy in tow. "Remahl knows nothing else about the child?"

Marisol shook her head. "They must have been important to

the Hand of Light, but she has no idea why." A deep frown creased her face, as if she heard words only meant for her. "Your friend … Asaege's friend didn't have anything to do with the child's disappearance, did he?"

Fueled in no small part by Asaege's paranoia, Jillian's first instinct was to avoid the question. Marisol, and through her Remahl, had placed their trust in Jillian. How could she, in good conscience, do any less? "I'm not sure. He returned something precious to me, taken during my first visit to the Hand's dungeons. We can look into it." She was unsure if Asaege would keep that promise, but hoped her reflection would see the wisdom of information flowing both ways.

Both women were so focused on the matters before them that when Marisol's phone beeped, they gasped in unison. Pulling the device from her pocket, Marisol unlocked it with a swipe of her finger. An embarrassed smile pasted on her face, she said, "My mother made us breakfast and it's getting cold."

*****

The delectable scent of bacon overwhelmed Jillian's senses as she came down the stairs on Marisol's heels. A large china platter sat steaming in the center of the oak table. Piled high with French toast, scrambled eggs, and, of course, bacon, the sight of it was almost as welcome as Abril Diaz's smiling face.

After wiping her hands on the apron around her waist, Abril gestured to the pair. "Sit down while everything is still warm."

"Mami, you made so much. There's only two of us."

She dismissed her daughter's protest with a wave of her hand. "Your sister and the baby may be stopping by."

"Mariana would need to bring Lucia's entire Mommy and Me class to eat all this food."

Abril wrapped a gentle arm around her daughter's waist, hugging her firmly. "Everyone is welcome, mi amor."

As she approached, Abril released Marisol and reached out to grasp Jillian's hand. "I'm so glad you decided to stay. We're so happy to have you here." The warmth and welcome that Jillian felt in the Diaz home helped her forget the life-and-death struggles that awaited her outside of it. "Sit and have something to eat."

"Thank you, Mrs., Diaz."

Abril snorted. "Jillian …"

"Mami," she corrected.

"That's better." She reached into her apron and pulled out a slim black remote control. She placed it on the table in front of Jillian before walking back into the kitchen. "Put on the TV if you want. The muffins will only take another few minutes."

As Jillian reached for it, she heard Marisol protest. "Muffins? You made more food?"

Abril repeated, "Your sister and the baby may be stopping by."

Shaking her head and chuckling, Jillian thumbed the power button, and the television flared to life.

"… important that we represent the values that this county was founded on." Veronica Moses's face filled the screen. Her attempts at an earnest expression were sabotaged by the self-satisfied smirk she wore on her face. A round of applause blared forth, concealing the words that followed. "… didn't intend for our youth to be corrupted by influences that run counter to those values, influences that lead to drug use, delinquency and loose morals."

The camera pulled back and swept the audience. Not every face that passed wore a glassy-eyed expression, but the majority did. Hands raised above their heads and mouths drawn into slavish grins, their lifeless eyes stared back at Jillian through the screen. The effect was truly haunting. Asaege's memories of the plaza came unbidden to her mind. Each member of the mob possessed the same dead eyes as they called for revolutionary blood.

"Freeholder Fredericks stood against this corruption of our youth, and so will I." More applause rang out, mixed with indistinct shouts of support. "He wanted someone who shared his vision to have his seat." She paused to allow the wave of adulation to roll over her. "I am that person!" The camera cut back to the crowd, stopping on the face of a middle-aged man dressed in a powder-blue polo. His spit-flecked lips were pulled back over clenched teeth as his vacant eyes stared into the distance.

"That is enough of that terrible woman," Abril said as she swept into the dining room and snatched the remote from the table. With a pop, the TV went dark, but the image of that man had already burned itself into Jillian's memory.

*****

Hector was waiting for her in the food court when Jillian arrived. He sat with his back to the wall, huddled in a long olive drab border guard coat. He wore an over-sized hooded sweatshirt beneath it, the hood pulled up over his head. As she approached, the man looked up nervously, only relaxing slightly as she sat down.

"Rough night?" Jillian asked.

He lifted the stub of a cigarette to his lips and took a deep drag before responding. "You could say that. I can't go back to my apartment or the flower shop, so I had to stay in a shelter last night."

"An excellent use of my tax dollars," Jillian remarked. When he frowned at her, she said, "Go on."

"I was up all night worried someone would recognize me. Every time the door opened, I expected to see the big bastard that tried to burn me alive."

"If you don't want to sleep with one eye open for the rest of your life, however long that may be, we need to get to the bottom of what's going on. I suspect it's about more than putting a small-time drug dealer out of business."

"Who are you calling small time?"

She raised an eyebrow. "Why is that the part you choose to focus on?"

Hector shrugged. "My high school guidance counselor told me I was self-centered, but what the fuck did she know?"

Unwilling to be pulled into his post-teen-age angst, Jillian rolled her eyes and steered the conversation back to recent events. "For some reason, I keep coming back to Veronica Moses. I can't put my finger on exactly why."

He smirked knowingly. "I can tell you why."

"It has nothing to do with him."

"If you say so."

Ignoring his leering grin, she continued. "The only connection I can find is Fredericks."

"The freeholder?"

Jillian nodded. "He was killed in the same way as the people in your ledger, but unless you've been holding out on me, he wasn't a customer."

"If I was selling to a politician, I sure as hell would have moved out of that crappy florist shop."

"Given her recent power grab, having Fredericks killed makes sense, but why target the others? Besides showing poor judgment in suppliers, what do a high school athlete, a single mother and Cyrill have in common?"

"I sold them all Dreamtime Dank."

"So theoretically, all of them had reflected."

"It stands to reason. Are you saying the killer is targeting Taerh reflections here?"

"It wouldn't be the first time."

"But why? More importantly, why them specifically?"

"I know Cyrill's reflection is a thaumaturge-for-hire, but he's working for Lady Markov."

"Or is he?"

"What do you mean?"

"I realize you don't like to get your hands dirty, princess, but paranoia runs rampant in the shadows. If Markov is getting close to her endgame, having someone powerful close to her is going to make her uncomfortable. Hollis demonstrated with the Walker that it's easier to deal with a mage here than there."

Jillian found herself amazed at the casual way Hector referred to the death of his former employer. "Okay, I'll give you that for the moment, but what about Lillian Krieger and Erik Gunn?"

He shrugged. "Perhaps we're looking at this all wrong. What if it has less to do with who their reflections are and more to do with the fact that they can reflect at all?"

"I'm listening."

"Adder root has its advantages, in Taerh as well as our own world. It makes both you and your reflection better in both places."

Realization dawned on Jillian. "What if Veronica wants to be the only game in town? If she can't arouse enough outrage among the council, among the voters, it would make sense to go straight to the source."

"It's what I would do." The matter-of-fact way Hector spoke about multiple murders caused a chill to run down her spine. "There is only one problem: I never sold to her."

Jillian's mind went immediately to her experiences at Stephen's bedside. "Are you sure? Could she have sent someone less conspicuous?"

He frowned, his brow furrowing in concentration. "Anything's possible. Besides you, Cyrill and the corpses, I only sold Double D to a few other people."

"Can you remember their names?"

Hector looked up from his thoughts, the left corner of his mouth turning up in a condescending expression. "That's why I had the ledger, so I didn't have to remember."

"How'd that work out for you?"

"I'm starting to rethink my business plan."

"Better late than never."

"What makes you think the Widow Moses is reflecting?"

"Both she and Markov have an unusual way with people."

"You of all people should know there's more to reflection than charisma."

Jillian laughed out loud at the absurdity of the moment. "Their charm is more 'look into my eyes' than 'countrymen, lend me your ears.'"

He seemed lost for a moment, squinting as he digested the words.

"Mind control," she added. "When she speaks, most of the crowd looks like they are under some sort of mind control."

Hector wrinkled his nose, as if he smelled something off. "Most? Not all?"

Jillian thought back to the press conference. Almost every face in the audience stared back at the camera with glassy eyes, but not everyone seemed to have been under her spell. Asaege's memories of the plaza revealed much the same. Neither Remahl nor the representatives of the Nine Families appeared to have been affected, even though the mob itself was firmly under her sway.

"No. It was almost like her words were pass-fail. Either people ate them up or they didn't."

"What was she talking about?"

"The same anti-drug, anti-education rhetoric she's been spouting for a week now. The people that were buying it were drooling and shouting like true believers. The others, they just didn't seem impressed."

"Good."

"How so?"

"Actual mind control would be really hard to beat. What it sounds like is she intensifies thoughts that are already there, magnifying them. But if someone doesn't believe her bullshit, her words have no effect, good or bad."

"You never cease to surprise me, Hector."

A smile appeared on his face, perhaps the first genuine expression she'd seen from him besides anger. "I'm complex."

"Yes, you are. So, where does that leave us?"

"The widow is my prime suspect for the brains behind the operation, but that doesn't put us any closer to figuring out who's actually pulling the trigger ... so to speak. If she can convince like-minded folk to do anything they're inclined towards, it could be anyone."

Jillian thought for a second, allowing silence to fall between them. "But could it? The murderer would still need to know how to go about it in a way so as to not get caught. That would require some familiarity with—"

"—Law enforcement," Hector finished for her. "It's that fat fuck, Blaine."

"Although I would not have used that exact term, I'm not sure I disagree with you. He seemed more interested in why I was at the florist shop than what actually happened."

"That's because he knew what happened, he just wanted to make sure you couldn't identify him."

"Or that he shouldn't add me to his list."

"We have the who —"

"—Or whos—" Jillian corrected.

"—And a compelling why, but not the how. Given what we know of Lady Markov, her reflection is unlikely to trust someone off the street to buy her adder root laced product. Even if she had, it's been almost a week since Blaine put me out of business. Where is she getting her supply?"

Again, Jillian thought of melding of both worlds in Stephen's hospital room. "I think I may have an answer to that."

"I'm all ears."

"I've been to visit Stephen recently."

Hector made a scolding, clicking sound with his tongue. "Shame on you, princess. You shouldn't play with things that don't belong to you."

She felt an uncomfortable heat rise in her cheeks, but continued. "When I stepped into the room, I felt as if I'd just taken adder root, but without the drowsiness that comes with it. I was fully awake, but experienced Taerh through Asaege's eyes as if I were reflecting."

"So he is the key to all of this?" Hector's expression darkened as a cloud of anger passed over his face. "It always comes back to him."

Suddenly remembering why she should have been suspicious of Plague Man's reflection, Jillian leaned forward. "What does?"

He shook his head. "Nothing. We should pay Stephen a visit. If we are going to put an end to dear Mrs. Moses's plans, saving our own lives in the process, we are going to have to find a way to deny her access to Taerh."

The hair raised on the back of Jillian's neck. She desperately hoped that Hector's newfound lack of contractions was simply a coincidence. "How do you intend to do that?" she asked uncertainly.

"I am not sure, but not doing anything assures us both an early grave."

Chapter Thirty-Six
A Tumultuous Visit

Asaege couldn't help gazing around with wonder at the opulence of the foyer that surrounded her. Lady Fremht, the slain councilman's sister, had greeted them personally. Dressed in a midnight blue velvet gown, the noblewoman competed for attention with the marble and gold inlays of the beautifully appointed vestibule. Half a step behind the lady of the house stood a pair of armored guards, their hands resting on the hilts of the swords hanging at their sides.

"Welcome, Remahl of the Falling Water. To what do we owe the unexpected honor of hosting Olm's Grand Inquisitor?" Lady Fremht hid the trembling of her voice admirably beneath the sweetness of her tone, but Asaege could only imagine what thoughts were running through the noblewoman's mind. Even in the civilized society of Oizan, the term inquisitor brought with it a specter of dread.

"Thank you for seeing us on such short notice, milady. It is my understanding that you are able to speak for the other families as well?"

A wave of irritation crossed Fremht's face, but years of etiquette dispersed it almost before Asaege could notice. "Of course. With my brother's death, I inherited his place as representative of the Nine Families until a quorum of my fellows decide otherwise."

"Please accept our sympathies for your loss, Lady Fremht," Asaege offered.

With a curt nod and a flick of her fingers, the noblewoman dismissed her condolences. "My thanks, but I fear that is not why you have come."

Asaege felt her jaw clench of its own accord as a smoldering anger began to build in her gut.

"That is precisely why we asked for this meeting," Remahl said gravely. "Perhaps we could adjourn somewhere with a little more privacy?"

Rubbing at her lips with a gloved hand, Lady Fremht murmured, "Of course. Pardon my lapse in hospitality." There wasn't a trace of remorse in her voice. "If you would care to follow me, I will have refreshments brought to the study."

The noblewoman's false courtesies and calculatingly flippant manner caused Asaege's vision to flash red before her eyes. "We have no need of your refreshments, Fremht," she snapped.

Lady Fremht spun on her, the corner of her mouth twisted in derision. "Perhaps you would like to wait with the servants, then. No doubt you would feel more comfortable among those of your own station."

"As a matter of fact—" Asaege began.

Remahl interrupted her. "None of this is helpful."

Asaege felt dread settle upon her. *Did I ruin our only chance to put a stop to Markov?*

The noblewoman smiled with satisfaction. "I agree, Lady Remahl. Your girl should mind her manners around her betters."

"I was speaking to you, Raelyn Fremht." There was a sharpness to her voice that cut the air like a knife. "We have come to your home on a matter of great import not only to you personally but to all of the Nine Families, only to be insulted and placated. If you claim to speak for your fellows, you serve them poorly indeed."

I should have known better than to think Marisol's reflection would turn on me.

"My sincerest apologies, Lady—"

Asaege didn't see Remahl move, but before her guards could react, she was nose to nose with the lady of the house. "I am no lady. You may call me Sister Remahl … or Inquisitor, if that is easier to remember. While you play at your games of double entendre and false courtesy, the city smolders around you. My associate and I came to the Nine Families with a means to smother the building flames before they blaze out of control." She never raised her voice, but each of her words struck Lady Fremht like a stone from a sling.

Recovering from their surprise, the two guards surged forward with their hands on the hilts of their swords. Asaege stepped up beside Remahl, allowing the words of *Sarcune's Spectral Shield* to surge to her lips. The soldiers could not have recognized the arcane syllables that flowed from her mouth, but the raw fear in their eyes showed that they knew them for thaumaturgy, and they ceased their forward momentum.

Lady Fremht looked upon Asaege with a new appreciation and a fair share of trepidation. "I am truly sorry, honored guests. I meant no disrespect."

Asaege felt the barrier of energy flare into being around her, adding to her confidence. "Yes, you did." Although it was subtle, the spell that encompassed her body added an echoing quality to her voice. "You may not have thought we would be offended, but you meant every ounce of disrespect. In the interest of our ongoing cooperation, the inquisitor and I are willing to let the matter drop."

Like a fast moving summer storm, the steel in Remahl's voice disappeared. "Perhaps we should start again. Good Afternoon, Lady Fremht. Thank you so much for seeing us on such short notice."

The noblewoman's genteel mask was once more in place. "It is my pleasure, Sister Remahl. Won't you come this way?"

*****

"Are you certain Lady Markov killed my brother?" The noblewoman's words had lost their practiced tone and rang of honest emotion. Anger and loss warred for dominance in her voice.

"We are," Asaege confirmed. "She used powerful magic to hide her role in his death, but I was able to untangle its threads to see the truth."

"What proof do you have?" The question implied skepticism, but Lady Fremht's tone was one of pleading.

"You will have to take my word for it."

The noblewoman slumped back in her chair, obviously disappointed. "I am afraid the Nine Families cannot take a stand against a figure of Markov's popularity on your word alone. We wish her gone—and the influence she holds with the people along with her— as badly as you do ... perhaps more, but we cannot, *will* not, act without evidence."

Remahl sat across from Lady Fremht, her legs crossed at the ankles. The only sign of her frustration was her white knuckles as she clutched the arms of the chair. "The Nine Families ... the church ... the revolution, we all want the same thing. Lady Markov and her mob of supporters are dangerous. They pose a risk to each of our interests, as well as the city itself. How can you not see that?"

"We are very aware of how dangerous she is. Lady Markov has been the topic of much debate among my fellows since her speech in the plaza. No matter how much I want to personally, the risk is simply too great to move against her based on hearsay."

Remahl gripped the chair more tightly. "Risk? You speak as if the Nine Families were acting alone."

"We are. The revolution has made its share of enemies, and the church of Olm supported their destruction until a few days ago. If the families were to make a stand, the full force of any opposition would come down upon our heads."

The Crimson Sister snorted sharply, seemingly at a loss for words in the moment.

Asaege felt her frustration acutely. *How can three disparate groups come together when each of them wants vastly different things?* At the back of her mind, Jillian's voice whispered to her. She saw in her mind's eye her reflection's classroom, the rapt faces staring back at her as she taught about the Three Sisters.

"Lady Fremht," she began, "you are sister to a slain brother. I am the second of three sisters as well. If anyone harmed either of my siblings, I would seek vengeance as well. This is not about vengeance, though. It is about a common goal of bettering the city that we call home. Each of us, church, revolution and families, want something different, but that does not mean that those goals need to be ours alone."

"Go on."

"A close friend once told me a story of her homeland. The native population was faced with a problem similar to our own. They needed to plant corn, beans and squash, but each plant had unique needs that required separate solutions. Being tall and narrow, the corn stalks had few broad leaves to shade their soil, allowing it to dry out quickly in the summer sun. While easily planted, beans need something to cling to in order to grow properly. By combining the three crops, they were able to support each other in ways they could not do on their own. The broad leaves of the squash shaded the soil, preserving its moisture. The corn stalks served as a pole to allow the beans to climb to greet the sun. In turn, the beans enriched the soil beneath both of the others, ensuring all three would thrive. They are known in her land as the Three Sisters."

"That is a nice story, but I fail to see the relevance."

"I think I understand," Remahl said. "Just as each of the plants has their own advantages and needs, each of our groups have ours. We are the Three Sisters."

"Exactly." Asaege smiled, silently celebrating her reflection's quick thinking. "The Nine Families will always be outnumbered by the ranks of the guilds, thus have they always been outvoted when important issues came before the council. Those the revolution represents, if given representation, would be willing to grant the families the support they require to keep you in the comfortable lives you have become accustomed to."

Remahl added, "Your house guards are well trained, but sadly few. If it came to open combat, the city guard outnumbers your forces three to one. The church has at its disposal battle-tested templars to make up the difference."

Lady Fremht leaned in, excitement and suspicion coloring her voice in equal measures. "What do the revolution and church get from this arrangement?"

"Without your financial support, the Ivory Cathedral can not afford to arm and feed those same forces. Our reliance on the population of the Common Quarter is self-evident. Without them to swell the ranks of priests and soldiers, the machine that is the church of Olm grinds to a halt."

The noblewoman turned to Asaege. "What about you? What does the revolution gain from this suggested alliance?"

"Representation. These people have been ground under the heels of those around them, if not ignored completely, for too long. Oizan was built with their hands. It continues to be carried on their shoulders to this day. It is time they had a say in its direction."

"Fair enough. I will bring the Alliance of the Three Sisters to the rest of the Nine Families."

Asaege felt a wash of relief flow through her. Lady Fremht's next words swept it away.

"Of course, I will assure them that when the time comes to act on our new found understanding, you will provide the evidence that Lady Markov was responsible for my brother's death."

*****

The door to Remahl's chambers hadn't yet closed before Asaege whirled on her. "How are we going to provide evidence of something that happened on another world?"

"I imagine that will be quite difficult," she said over her shoulder as she strode across the marble floor to an exquisitely crafted dressing table situated between two floor-to-ceiling windows. Opening the lid of a wide jewelry box dominating its surface, Remahl picked up a small oval amulet by its delicate golden chain. "That is why she is going to have to give us a confession."

Asaege rolled her eyes. "Is that all?"

"No. It is quite complicated and most definitely dangerous." Remahl pressed her hand to her mouth, but words kept streaming forth even as she tried to muffle them. "The chance of success is actually very low, and that is assuming you are not killed in the process."

The inquisitor's admission struck Asaege like a barrage of arrows, each one adding to the force of the one before. "Aren't you a ray of sunshine?"

Before she could speak again, Remahl put her hand over Asaege's mouth. Only then did she uncover her own. "Ask me no further questions until I am finished speaking."

Asaege nodded, her brows furrowed in confusion.

Remahl raised the amulet and held it before her eyes. The profile of a beautiful woman was etched into its gleaming platinum surface, her mouth hidden coyly behind a spread fan. Given the circumstance, Asaege shouldn't have been so taken with the charm, but found herself marveling at the intricate details carved upon it. A longing burned white-hot within her to snatch the necklace from her friend's grasp.

"This is known as the Gentle Lady; she is the bane of thieves and liars. While in possession of her, not only can a lie not pass your lips, but the powerful magic woven into the metal itself forces the holder to confess that which weighs heaviest upon their soul." Pausing for a second, Remahl seemed to fight a battle within herself before continuing. "In light of our unique position, the Lady seems our only hope. She must find her way into Markov's hands, and it must be done in the presence of the Nine Families."

Unable to take her eyes from the reflected lantern light glinting from the amulet's surface as it spun, Asaege fought against the urge to reach for it. "A gift perhaps?" As soon as she had said it, an anger began to simmer in her belly. *If she was mine, I could never bring myself to give the Lady away.*

"That is the first obstacle in our path," Remahl explained. "The Gentle Lady cannot be given away, the spell set upon her all but assures that. Her maker intended the Lady to be the perfect trap. She must be taken, and once she comes into your hands, none can give her up willingly."

Asaege's hand rose without her command, hovering near the amulet as it sang its silent siren's song. "If Markov's greed is half as strong as her ambition, tricking her into taking it shouldn't be all that hard."

Remahl took a step back, pulling the Gentle Lady out of Asaege's reach. "It becomes more complicated when you do not want to relinquish it."

"I do not believe even she would be foolish enough to steal from you … at least not in plain sight. If we require witnesses, that may pose a problem."

Remahl's mouth turned down into a frown. "For our plan to work, she must take it from someone whom she believes has no allies."

"Me?"

"I am afraid so. What is more, there can be no revolutionaries nearby to give her pause. She must believe you are alone and at her mercy."

Her throat suddenly dry, Asaege swallowed hard. When she had imagined bringing Markov's reign of terror to an end, it was always with her friends at her side: Toni, Seran, Rudelph. The thought of facing her alone, in the midst of a crazed mob who would tear her to pieces as soon as look at her, filled her with a fear she hadn't felt since she had banished Plague Man's shadowy master beneath the Ivory Cathedral.

Remahl reached out and wrapped her arm around her shoulders, even though she continued to hold the amulet out of her reach. "I wish there were some other way, any other way. I would gladly take your place if I could."

Asaege leaned into her embrace. The inquisitor's words struck her particularly hard, knowing that the amulet she clutched in her fist wouldn't allow her to soothe her with platitudes. "And that is only the first hurdle?"

"The second is doubtlessly the more difficult. While the amulet is in your grasp, you will not be able to deceive her into taking it. Despite wanting with all your heart to hold on to it, you must find a way to convince her to part you from it."

"What you are saying is that I have to talk someone into taking something I do not want to give up, all while speaking nothing but the truth?"

"Pretty much."

Asaege folded her hands before her face, resting her thumbs on the bridge of her nose. She felt as if the air of the room itself had weight to it and it rested upon her shoulders. *It all comes down to this. Success or failure lies with me alone.* The only indication of

Jillian's arrival in her subconscious was the warm touch of serenity she brought with her. In that moment, her burden lightened. *Perhaps not alone after all*, she thought.

Reaching out for the amulet, Asaege said, "I might as well get all the practice I can."

Struggling with the power of the relic, Remahl held it steady. "I can not give it to you. You must take it."

*****

"So, you are saying you're completely incapable of speaking anything but the truth?" The amusement in Hollis's voice should have irritated her, but instead she was filled with relief at hearing it at all, even through the hushed intermediary of the whisper stone. Given his situation in the north, the pair spoke English in the name of keeping their discussion private.

"Don't take advantage. I'll be free of the Lady's influence sooner or later and the charm laid upon her has no effect on my memory."

The thief chuckled softly. "I wouldn't dream of it, Magpie. I wish I could be there with you. In some way, I feel Markov is my—"

"Stop," Asaege hissed. "Just because you were involved with her reflection does not make you responsible for what's happened in the months since."

"I can't help but think that Stephen's death drove her to this."

She bit her lip, the burning demand of the relic welling up into her throat. Before she could redirect its urging, she blurted out, "Stephen is not dead." *Come on, Asaege*, she scolded herself, *you are going to have to do better than that with Markov*. "I didn't want you to find out like this." The silence that hung between them sounded deafening to her ears. "Hollis?"

"How long have you known?" There was a hardness in his whispered words.

"A few days. Jillian has been to see him … um … you. I swear I wasn't keeping it from you. I found out after the whisper stone stopped working."

"Okay."

"Is it?"

Hollis's voice softened. "Of course. We've never been anything but honest with one another, and the only secrets between us have been incidental. With everything going on, I seemed to have forgotten that. I'm sorry."

"It's a shocking revelation. I imagine doubly so for you."

"That's quite the understatement. Depending on how the next few hours go, it may not be an issue."

"I have faith in you, my scoundrel."

Hollis laughed again. It was a welcome sound to her ears, but somehow seemed hollow. "I wish I shared your confidence, Asaege. The truth is that the last time we fought, it wasn't even close. When it comes to swordplay, Mika has always been magnitudes better than me. The Gifts of the Well only increased her advantage."

"You'll have to figure something out, my love. You've always done so in the past." In her practice with the Gentle Lady, Asaege had discovered the relic could be satiated by half truths. Both statements were factually true, but when combined, provided a more optimistic tone than she felt. She hoped her hushed tone concealed the worry that gnawed at her heart.

"You are too kind. Try not to be too concerned. You have bigger things on your plate to worry about."

"That's an unreasonable request, Hollis, and you know it."

"You can't fault an old thief for trying."

"It was one of the million reasons I fell in love with you."

"I love you, Asaege, with all that I am."

"Come back to me, my beloved scoundrel."

"The whole of the north couldn't keep me from your arms, Magpie."

Chapter Thirty-Seven
An Unlikely Hope

Aristoi laid upon the pallet of furs, allowing the gentle scraping of whetstone on steel to soothe her frenzied thoughts. Without opening her eyes, she could picture Hollis stroking the edge of his Dwarven steel blade. The Fair Folk crafted weapon would maintain its edge under more brutal conditions than the thief could ever subject it to. Yet in their time together, the Songspear had noticed that he put stone to steel when otherwise idle hands forced him to focus on unpleasant thoughts.

"I will stay up with you, if you like, Northerner."

"That is not necessary," the thief responded. "I have a feeling no matter how my second go-round with Mika turns out, you are going to need your strength."

"What of yours?"

"I still have some things to work out."

Aristoi was tempted to argue, but instead crossed her arms and tucked her head into her chest. As the stone smoothed the imagined burrs in the steel, so to did it lull the Songspear into slumber by inches.

*****

As Aristoi reached the edge of the village, she found the Branded was waiting for her. Seated on the trunk of a fallen tree, he appeared as if he were before his own hearth. "That was quite a show, Songspear."

"Blood does not pay for blood. Her death would not have been my mother's dying wish."

"Of that, I have no doubt, but it is not what I am referring to. Within that circle, you fought against more than your sister. It is of that victory you should be more proud."

Suddenly, Aristoi felt as if his gaze peered into her soul. Her hand tightened on the shaft of her spear. "I am not sure what you are talking about."

"Your mother was a dear friend, one I will miss very much, but it was not for her I came to Willow's Ridge."

The sound of her heart in her ears warred with his words. "What brought you here then, esteemed Branded?" She added his title in a bid to placate the Herald.

"Why ... you, my dear. Once you ... or more precisely, the curse that rages within you, entered the Verdant Sea, charms that I laid upon the forest itself alerted me to its presence."

Aristoi stepped back, her spear tip snapping up between them.

"Peace, child. Had I wanted you dead, you would not have lived to step into the ritual circle with your sister." The Branded motioned for her to lower the weapon; she wasn't sure she did so of her own volition. "You are not the order's first experience with the gwyllgi. Ironically, it was your mother who slew the first one any of us had seen in person."

"My mother?"

"Yes. She was very young, less than a year after her own mother had passed down to her the very spear you hold in your hands." His eyes became unfocused as they drifted to a time long removed. "I wish you could have seen her in her prime. Deadly with both spear and song, the order had not seen her like in generations. There was a wisdom in her, though, even in her youth." His attention snapped back to Aristoi's face. "You would have made her very proud. It was in her memory that I insisted on coming myself."

"It was not my fault. "

"I know, child. The gwyllgi are more a curse than a species, one from which death itself is no escape. Once their fangs ravage your flesh, their corruption claims your soul."

"I fight its influence with everything within me."

"Have you ever given into the change?" The Branded stood slowly, lifting his ancient spear from where it rested against the fallen trunk.

"No."

"Not even once? In weakness?"

"I am my own master, body and soul."

He squinted at her, looking past the cage of muscle and bone into her very soul. He found something hidden there that caused his eyes to open wide, obviously impressed. "So you are, Songspear. So you are."

"Is there a cure?"

He exhaled through pursed lips. "If there is, I am unaware of it."

Aristoi felt her fear rise into her throat, threatening to overcome her. Beneath it, she felt an alien sense of satisfaction at her dilemma. "There must be some hope?"

"The most ancient songs tell of the founding of our order by a wise warrior known as Haldroi the Swift. Spear-brother and counselor to the Well-Child, Corbane the Singer, Haldroi helped shape Kiel into the kingdom it is to this day. Not everyone was pleased with the thought of the Verdant Sea finding civilization. The gwyllgi, for example, prized it for the hunting it offered."

"The Singer fought against them?"

"Haldroi, and what became the Songspears, drove the beasts from the forest through iron and song. In purging it of their corruption, many brothers and sisters fell beneath the creature's fangs and their corruption. Among them was Haldroi."

"But if he was lost to the gwyllgi's influence before the Songspears became an order, why is it that he is credited with its founding?"

"That is an excellent question. The last of the black dogs were driven from the Verdant Sea when Haldroi was no older than twenty, but there are stories of his work with the Songspears well into his eighties."

"If he found a way to purge himself of their corruption—"

"—There is hope for you. Although, his road to a cure is lost to the ages."

A haunting howl split the night, raising the hair on the back of Aristoi's neck. She could feel the rejoicing of the darkness that clung to her soul like a tick. "You may not have been the only one to have followed me." A second voice joined the first, and then a third.

"I hear them as well." The Branded motioned her towards the road. "There is not much time. I know you have recently returned from your Long Walk, bringing back lore thought lost forever, but you must repeat that miracle. This time it will not be legends you chase, *but your own salvation."*

Again, the baying rose around them, closing in from all sides.

The Branded gripped his spear in both hands and gestured into the distance. "Find the cure. I can not allow you to return until you do. The darkness within you poses too much risk to our people."

Additional voices joined the yowling that hung upon the wind. "What about them?"

"Let me deal with the intruders. Let your footsteps be like the wind, ever forward, ever swift."

The Branded turned to face the first of the gwyllgi as it emerged from the underbrush at a run. The iron tip of his spear impaled it through the chest.

"Run!" he called as two more charged from the shadows.

*****

The Songspear jarred into wakefulness at the sound of her name. The tent was still draped in the shadows of early morning, but Hollis stood over her, her spear held casually at his side. "There is a commotion building outside, my friend. I think our deferment is almost at an end."

Aristoi rolled over and pushed herself to her feet. "There is still time to escape … if that is what you want." She took her weapon from him, swinging it slowly from side to side as she warmed up the muscle of her arms and shoulders.

"I want that more than I could ever say … but it is long past time for this issue to be put to rest."

She stepped close to him, wrapping her free arm around his shoulders. Feeling a tear welling up, she laid her face against his broad chest to hide it from him.

"On a road too often walked alone, you have been my friend. You stood beside me when no one else would. I can never repay you for that."

"No matter what awaits us outside, it has been an honor standing by your side, Hollis."

Over his shoulder, the Songspear saw the tent flap open. Hollis's Rangor friend filled the opening.

"It is time."

Chapter Thirty-Eight

A Final Gesture

Hollis heard Ret's hushed voice behind him. "It is time."

"Do you think I have one more fight left in me, Southerner?" He held Aristoi close, whispering into her braids.

"One or two, at least." The Songspear's voice sounded weary, as if it came from a long distance.

"I hope you are right," the thief muttered as he released her and turned to face the massive Rangor. "Nice of you to come yourself."

"You may not believe it, but I am still your friend, Hollis."

He seized the big man with a skeptical glare. "So you have told me. Actions speak louder than words ever could."

Ret frowned deeply, averting his eyes. "Mika is waiting."

Hollis sheathed the Wallin Fahr. "Well, we certainly cannot have that, can we?" He looped his sword belt over his shoulder and gestured towards the tent's entrance. "Lead the way."

As Ret pulled back the flap, he saw a sea of humanity arrayed between him and the gallows at the camp's center. It seemed that none of Mika's warriors wanted to miss their queen's victory over the arrogant outsider.

The thief felt Aristoi at his shoulder. Without turning, he whispered, "That is not intimidating at all."

"It is obvious she wants to prove a point."

He swallowed hard, the trepidation that had been building all night blossoming into the sharp bite of fear. "Point proven."

The Songspear wrapped her hand around Hollis's wrist and turned him to face her. Not wanting her to see the panic in his eyes, he averted them from her gaze.

"Look at me," she demanded. Slowly, Hollis did as she asked. She gestured at the gathered crowd. "They mean nothing. One witness or a hundred, there are only two people who are important, and both of them will be in that circle. Nothing else, no one else, matters."

He nodded quickly, drawing a lungful of cold morning air in an attempt to calm his nerves.

"I never would have thought the man I met in the Emir's dungeons would have made it this far."

Hollis raised an eyebrow. "Is this supposed to be inspiring?"

"You are no longer that man, if you ever were. At every turn, you have defied those who sought to force you into the mold of their expectations: The Walker, Plague Man, even your own guild."

He opened his mouth to argue, but she cut him off.

"One day, you will meet a challenge that proves your equal, but I do not believe this is that day. You hold three lives in your hands, mine among them, and I could not be more secure in seeing another dawn if I were entering that circle myself."

"Okay ... that was a little inspiring."

Aristoi smiled lightly. "You know what you need to do. Now get in there and find a way to get it done."

*****

As Hollis passed through the crowd, stepping into the wide circle around the gallows, the throng fell into silence. The bound and kneeling figures of Valmont and Sagaun could be seen atop the wooden structure. Standing beside them, Silvermoon's stolen blade held casually at her side, was the Snow Queen herself. "I thought this might save us time afterward." She began to descend the stairs, continuing to speak to him. "I must admit to feeling a sense of excitement to begin our shared endeavor."

Shrugging the sword belt from his shoulder, the thief drew his Dwarven steel blade and cast sheath and belt to the ground. "If we're gonna do this, let's get to it," he called in English.

Her smile disappeared between heartbeats. The rising sun highlighted the slight twitch in her right cheek as she responded in Trade Tongue. "Perhaps you feel the same?" The frozen dirt crunched be-

308

neath her boots as Mika dropped the last few feet to the permafrost.

Hollis wrapped his left hand around the hilt of his Wallin Fahr and extended the point towards her. He filled his lungs with the crisp morning air. He exhaled slowly, focusing on expelling with it the fear and doubt that clung to his heart with bony claws. The familiar warmth of the "Understanding" wrapped him in a cloak of serenity. *It's been a long road.* He clung to English, even in his thoughts. *I've pushed my luck to its limits and beyond too many times to count. It's a lot to ask, but I need it to hold out one more time.*

A Rangor stepped from the crowd, extending a rounded shield to his queen. Drawing her lips into an arrogant sneer, she waved him away. "I do not want you to have any excuses. Once this conversation of blood and steel is concluded, I never wish to have it again." She raised her sword, matching Hollis's form. "Shall we begin?"

The thief responded by shuffling forward, launching a probing thrust as he did so. Mika easily deflected the attack, knocking his weapon to the side. She swung her blade horizontally in a lazy arc, forcing Hollis back on his heels. Gliding across the ground as if her feet barely touched it, Mika pressed her advantage and forced him to continue to backpedal.

"Come now, my friend, you must put up more of a fight than that. Our army will lose respect for someone beaten so easily."

"We've only begun. It's not the first exchange that decides a battle, but the last." The effect of his words, spoken in Stephen's native tongue, was obvious and immediate. Mika cut her advance short, pulling her sword back to a guard position as her face contorted into a mask of anger and confusion. Hollis lashed out quickly, feinting high before switching his sword's direction to strike at her unprotected legs.

Even in her distracted state, the Snow Queen beat aside his attack with little more than a thought. In doing so, she surrendered a measure of the ground she'd claimed a moment before, but not all of it. A short thrust kept Hollis from taking any more, as she snorted sharply to clear her head. "Your tricks may serve you well elsewhere, Hollis, but you find they will come up short today." She leapt forward, bringing her sword down in an overhead chop before he could bring his own up to meet it.

Allowing his legs to collapse beneath him, the thief sank to the ground and desperately parried one-handed while he planted the other on the ground to arrest his fall. He dug his fingers into the permafrost, peeling back the nails on his fore and middle fingers. Along with the pain, he felt the coarse weight of the tundra dirt in his hand.

Mika leaned over him, her sword pulled back against her body in a loose guard. "Call an end to this now, before you or your pride are further injured."

Hollis swung his weapon wildly in a backhanded slash. She stepped back out of range, a condescending smirk painted on her lips. When his free arm came around, aided by the sword's momentum, Mika snapped her own blade up into a guard position. Its steel edge proved itself ineffective against the cloud of dirt and ice that struck her squarely in the face.

Momentarily blinded, the Snow Queen staggered backwards. Her sword wove back and forth in an effort to deter Hollis's follow up attack. The thief sprang to his feet and cautiously approached. Mika desperately rubbed at her eyes with her right hand as she continued her retreat. Hollis danced to the side, swinging his Wallin Fahr in a low arc.

Instinct and the scraping of his footsteps must have warned her of the attack. Mika was able to deflect the blow, but not before it cut deeply into her thigh. What should have been a debilitating wound was turned into an inconvenience instead. Tears streaking her face, Mika focused her attention on him once more. "More tricks?"

"I'll take every advantage I can get. It's rare for a tree to be felled with a single blow. I'm more than willing to take as many whacks as I need." Hollis didn't wait for the disorientation he knew his words would cause. He lashed out again, swinging at her injured leg. No doubt slower than she would have liked, the Snow Queen turned his blow aside, but in the moment of confusion, she allowed him to shorten the distance between them.

The thief lashed out with his left fist, catching her solidly on the jaw. Too close to bring his sword to bear, he drove his knee into her wounded thigh. As she limped backward, he scraped the sole of his boot down her shin.

"Whack, whack, whack," he taunted in English, adding to her consternation.

"Shut up!" she screamed. Her narrowed eyes and bared teeth aptly displayed the fury that boiled within her. Leaping forward in a hitching step, Mika brought her sword down in a vertical strike. Hollis redirected its momentum, but she adjusted her weapon's line with a deft twist of her wrists, opening a painful cut in his side from ribs to armpit. "Shut up!"

Skipping backwards, Hollis narrowly avoided a second, lighting-quick slash meant to disembowel him from gut to groin. Not pausing in her attack, the Snow Queen thrust her sword towards his

310

throat. The thief flinched from its path, but the blow still traced a crimson line along his jaw.

"Shut up!," she growled. Too distracted fending off Mika's pressing assault, Hollis was forced to do as she bid. He worked his blade with every ounce of skill he possessed, but just as in their first confrontation, it was proving to be insufficient for the task. The Snow Queen's attacks became less frenzied, but didn't lose any of their efficacy. Although she dragged her injured leg behind her in a hitching limp, the thief couldn't pull his attention from defending himself long enough to take advantage of it.

I've got to get away from her, find some way to use her lack of mobility in my favor. His eyes swept around the circle, penned on all sides by Mika's warriors. They stopped on the ramshackle gallows. It was just high enough that he could duck beneath it, but in an attempt to stabilize the structure, its builders had crisscrossed the underside with braces seemingly placed at random. *It'll have to do.*

Hopping back, Hollis put some distance between them. When Mika lunged forward, he dashed around her. Putting his head down and running towards the gallows, he heard Mika's mocking tone behind him. "Run all you like, boy; it will not change how this ends."

The thief didn't slow as he reached the stairs. He dropped his hip and slid beneath them in a cloud of dirt. An oddly angled support stopped his momentum, sending a jolt of pain up his leg. He stood as quickly as his throbbing leg would allow and turned an appraising eye to his newly chosen battlefield. The underside of the structure was a claustrophobic mess of oddly placed beams and exposed nails. He was forced to crouch to prevent dragging his scalp across the rough boards above him, only able to stand up straight if he bowed his head. As he experimentally put his full weight onto his aching leg, he found the pain fading to a dull echo of itself. *I can work with this.*

Mika stepped beneath the gallows just as he was turning to face her. A full six inches shorter than Hollis, she didn't need to duck as she joined him beneath the structure. "You are quickly running short of hiding places, Hollis." Stepping over a low, angled support, she approached him carefully.

In the midst of the "Understanding", Hollis felt as if he knew the area beneath the gallows as well as Stephen's childhood bedroom. "I'm done running, Mika. This is an appropriate place to finish what you started a decade ago. You murdered Silvermoon out of sight of prying eyes, it's fitting that you pay for it away from them as well."

311

The Snow Queen shook her head, as if trying to clear undesired thoughts from her mind. "Shut up," she muttered, but it was only due to the acoustics of their confined space that carried the words to his ears.

She's not talking to me. Realization dawned on him. *She never was.* Even Samantha had been unable to completely excise her reflection's influence from her mind. Hollis theorized that Stephen's friend must still remain in Mika's subconscious, no matter how hard the Snow Queen tried to silence her. "Beatrice." The word snapped like a whip from his mouth, causing his opponent to pull up short. "I know you're in there."

"Your appeals fall upon dead ears, Hollis. The wallflower died the night I claimed the power of the Well of Worlds for myself." Her voice was more panicked plea than definitive statement.

Ignoring Mika, Hollis continued to speak to her reflection. "You have to fight her, Beatrice. She thinks you're weak, but we know the truth."

The Snow Queen rushed forward in a limping charge, but Hollis ducked under another crossbeam and stepped back out of range. As she tried to follow him, Mika's leg threatened to give way under her. She was forced to pull up short to remain standing.

"You're stronger than she could ever know, stronger than even you realize."

Mika pressed her right hand to her temple. "Shut up!"

"She killed Jeff. She left Nellie and Mike without a mother. She betrayed everything you believed in for her own selfish desires."

Her eyes shot up to seize his in her glare. "I was wrong to think you could be brought around to see the truth. I should have killed you, too."

Over her shoulder, Hollis saw Ret standing in the morning sun, just outside their wooden battle ground. His thick eyebrows knitted together when he heard Mika's proclamation. Beside him stood Aristoi, her spear once again clutched in her hand. She slowly nodded her approval, although worry clouded her face.

"I wish I could put things back to the way they should've been. If I could have saved your life … Jeff's and George's too, I would have, but that was taken out of both of our hands when Mika decided that power could be bought with betrayal."

She ducked beneath the crossbeam and lunged at Hollis again. He dodged to the side and stepped over a knee high plank nailed between two vertical supports. Even so, her short slash drew a painful line across his right bicep.

"Together, we can make sure she doesn't hurt anyone else."

With a wordless scream, Mika brought her stolen sword down across the wooden obstacle, cleaving it in two. Lunging forward, she swung at Hollis in a series of short chopping slashes. Holding his blade before him, the thief parried each, but her skill, combined with the fury of her attacks, made each successive one harder to deflect.

"Help me, Beatrice," he begged. "Help me stop her once and for all."

Ignoring her injured leg for the moment, the Snow Queen pressed Hollis hard, driving him deeper into the structure. He tried to put beams between himself and his attacker, but she chopped at them with the same fury she directed at him. Around them, the gallows creaked and swayed under its own weight.

Missed in the chaos of the melee, an exposed nail caught the thief in the face, only missing his eye by the width of an eyelash. Recoiling from the unexpected pain, he nearly tripped over a low-slung plank. He kept his balance, but Mika took advantage of his distraction to drive her boot into his gut.

"Beatrice, it's now or never," he gasped with the little air he could draw into his lungs.

Mika raised Silvermoon's sword above her head, prepared to bring its razor-sharp edge down on his head. Hollis twisted away from the oncoming blow, blood streaming into his eye. The gallows shifted again, causing the planks above their heads to sag under the strain. When she tried to bring the weapon down, its tip caught on the straining wood and stuck fast for a second.

"Now!" The word, spoken in English, emerged from Mika's throat in a voice that was not entirely her own. Filled with desperation, it still held a pleading, genuine quality of which the Snow Queen was incapable. "Do it now!" Her expression was a paradox of fear and serenity, each in equal measure. It spoke of the battling polar opposites that no doubt raged between the personalities of Mika and Beatrice.

In the months since discovering the truth behind the deaths of his friends, Hollis had imagined this moment a hundred times. Not a single time did his quest for vengeance end with such circumstances. His mind spun with the possibilities of Beatrice's survival within Mika's consciousness. *If only I could save her*, he thought.

Mika's Beatrice voice begged again. "Do it, please. I don't know how much longer I can hold her." Her straining tone broke his heart. The muscles in her arms twitched as Mika fought for control of her own body.

"Okay," Hollis said, drawing the broad-bladed dagger from his belt. He caught Mika's gaze as her eyes darted back and forth, fighting against Beatrice's influence. Cradling the back of her neck in his palm, he whispered into her ear. "Rest well, my friends." Before he could change his mind and stay his hand, the thief drove the weapon into her heart. The body in his arms spasmed once, fighting its inevitable end, and then went limp. Resting his cheek against hers, Hollis gently lifted Mika into his arms and made his way from beneath the structure.

Chapter Thirty-Nine

A Revealing Truth

Asaege stepped out of the shadows of the surrounding buildings and into the sunlit plaza. Her cloak was wrapped tightly around her, as much to hide her trembling hands as ward off the morning's chill. Just as it had days before, a large crowd filled Guild Square almost to capacity. Every eye in the sea of humanity was turned, focused on Lady Markov as she stood above them at the top of the council building's stone stairs. From that dais, she wordlessly surveyed the throng before her. Arrayed behind her was the remainder of the guild council.

Further back, Asaege could make out nine well-dressed figures she hoped were the representatives of the Nine Families. Each of them was flanked by a trio of soldiers. The early morning sun glinted from breastplate and spear tip as they stood stoic watch over their charges. Not for the first time since entering the Merchant's Quarter, she remembered that none could help her should something go wrong. She had ordered the revolutionary forces to remain within rebel-controlled territory for fear of them standing out among Markov's supporters, and potentially starting a riot. Remahl stood at the head of a small detachment of templars at the edge of the crowd, but if things went awry, they might as well have been a mile away.

An intense feeling of loneliness settled upon her shoulders, but its presence didn't lessen the building fear in her heart. Her only companions were the stiletto strapped to her thigh beneath her dress and the endlessly repeating syllables in the back of her mind. As she pushed her way into the crowd, Asaege felt as if the world closed around her. She turned suddenly as a hand wrapped around her wrist. "Get your—" The words froze on her tongue as a familiar face peered out at her from beneath the hood of a heavy woolen cloak.

Seran pressed his finger to his lips as he winked slyly at her.

She leaned in to whisper in his ear. "I thought I made myself clear. Everyone was to stay behind."

"Following instructions is not one of my strong suits."

Asaege found herself unable to scold him. Wrapping her hand around his on her wrist, she whispered, "Thank you." His only answer was a wry smile as he released her arm and melted into the surrounding mass of people. Even after he disappeared, she could feel the comforting weight of his eyes upon her. Knowing she didn't have to face what lay ahead alone dulled the trepidation that gnawed at her resolve.

As she approached the front of the throng, Lady Markov began to speak. "Good Morning, esteemed men and women of Oizan." In response to the sound of her voice, the jostling bodies around Asaege settled. "Thank you for braving the chill and early hour to join me on the day of my induction to the ranks of the Guild Council."

A rumble began to build near the front of the crowd, rolling backwards towards Asaege in a wave of raucous cheers. The people around her raised their fists into the air, voicing their approval through guttural shouts.

"For too long, we have carried this city on our backs. Those in their gilded mansions look down upon us from the very palaces bought with our sweat and blood." Each of the Families' representatives pulled back closer to their guards. "While they determine Oizan's direction, it is left to us to stagger along towards a destination in which we have no say. That ends now!"

Again, a roar of applause rose from the crowd. The glassy eyed stares of the people around her hung above spit coated lips and bared teeth.

"Unhappy with the opportunities given them out of the kindness of our hearts, the filthy masses of the Common Quarter make demands beyond their station. We allow them to be part of wonders beyond their comprehension, teaching them skills they can bring back to their hovels to better themselves. Rather than the gratitude expected of civilized people, these savages demand to be treated as

316

equals!"

The faces around Asaege contorted into masks of rage. She was buffeted from all sides as the mob surged forward as one, seeking to vent their anger.

"Equals! Does the farmer invite their donkey into their home? To dine beside their children? Does the blacksmith seek the counsel of his anvil?"

As one, the crowd roared, "No!"

"They see the things we have earned through hard work and keen minds, and like the beasts that they are, they turn to violence. That ends now!"

The mob's chants morphed from "No!" to "Now!"

Building on their momentum, Lady Markov continued. "Now ... is the time!"

"Now!"

"We draw the line!" Markov raised her fist in the air in time to the chanting before her.

"Now!" The crowd mirrored her gesture, their cries increasing in volume.

"Is the time!"

"Now!" Asaege could feel the anger of the throng reverberating in her chest in time to their shouts.

"We draw the line!"

"Now!" With each repetition, she could feel her resolve shrinking.

"Is the time!"

Mustering her courage, Asaege elbowed her way forward. As she reached the edge of the crowd, she noticed that a double row of city guards ringed the stone stairs leading to the dais. The eyes staring out from beneath steel helmets seemed no less empty than those of the mob behind her. *Now or never.* "Markov!" she shouted as loud as she could. Her voice was swallowed by that of the crowd. Taking a deep breath, Asaege put everything she had into a scream that felt as if it came from the depths of her soul. "Markov!"

The gazes around Asaege turned on her, unfocused yet still oozing with malign intent.

"You are not these people's solution!" Staggering her words between the chanting of the mob, Asaege yelled towards the woman above her. "You are their problem!"

Lady Markov ceased her intonation and stepped forward. The crowd carried on for a few seconds, but quickly fell into a confused muttering.

317

"The revolution is not about them! The revolution is about you!" Glassy stares turned angry around her. Grasping hands pulled at her from all directions. They tore at Asaege's cloak, seeking to strip it from her. Hooked fingers reached for her hood, searching for face and eyes.

"Guards!" Lady Markov's voice split the building rumble like a peal of thunder. "Bring her to me." Her command was spoken rather than shouted, but her words carried clearly through the cacophony. Absently, Asaege noted the flare of magic as she spoke. "I would speak with the sympathizer."

A pair of guardsmen stepped forward, lashing out at the people closest to Asaege with the butts of their spears. Those struck fell back a few steps, allowing a third soldier to pull her free of the crowd. As she felt arms wrap around her own, Asaege instinctively reached back into her subconscious to release one of the formulae there, bound by chains of her will. Forcing herself to relax both body and mind, she allowed herself to be carried up the stairs to what would, for good or ill, be her endgame.

*****

Thrown down at Lady Markov's feet, Asaege was forced to look up into the face of her opponent. Markov leered down at her, a satisfied smile pasted on her lips. Behind her stood a group of stern-faced men and women, the remainder of the guild council. Asaege would find no friends among them. At the edges of her vision, she saw Lady Fremht among her fellow representatives. The noble-woman's expression was unreadable. Turning her attention back to Markov, Asaege found the woman staring down at her with interest.

"I have seen you before." As if from thin air, Lirych stepped up beside her. He leaned down to whisper into Lady Markov's ear. "Ah, yes, I remember now. You were at the brothel."

Asaege felt her true feelings well up in her throat, a function of the amulet that pressed against the skin of her chest. "You fled so quickly, I am surprised you remember anything but the door." Asaege's retort caused Markov's face to tighten in anger.

"You should not have come," Markov muttered, only loud enough for Asaege to hear. Returning her attention to the crowd, she announced, "Fine people of Oizan, we seem to have captured a revolutionary!" A chorus of jeers rose from the mob. "What ever shall we do with her?"

Yells of "Hang her!" and "Make her an example!" emerged from the storm of voices in the plaza.

Looking down at Asaege, Markov shrugged dramatically. "It

seems you have no friends here. Where is your prophet? Where is your glorious revolution?"

Asaege found herself grateful for her rapid-fire questions, just as she opened her mouth to confess her true identity, the Gentle Lady's charm pushed an answer to Markov's last question from her lips. "Far from you, Markov."

She drove the toe of her boot into Asaege's gut. "Lady Markov."

Asaege narrowed her eyes, scowling up at the councilwoman.

Markov kicked her again and repeated, "You must learn to properly address your betters. Lady Markov. "

Curling into the fetal position, Asaege refused to give her the satisfaction. She slipped her hand into the folds of her dress to pull the Gentle Lady free. When her fingers wrapped around the amulet, a simmering feeling bubbled within her. Warring with the anger boiling in her veins, this new emotion pricked her heart like a thorn. *The relic is mine. If she wants it, Markov will need to pry it from me.* The greedy thoughts that filled her head cooled her anger into a cold rush of fear. She was afraid to be without the amulet.

Lady Markov raised her foot and stomped on Asaege, catching her in the side of the face. She felt her cheek immediately begin to swell. Addressing the crowd, Markov said, "If you need further proof of the character of the filth that rises against us, you need look no further. Like a beast, all she understands is violence." Turning to the guards beside her, she demanded, "Get her up."

Iron grips closed around Asaege's arms and pulled her to her feet. Holding the Gentle Lady balled in her fist, she fought to keep her hand concealed in her dress. The soldier holding her arm pulled it free, snapping the delicate gold chain securing the relic to her throat. Like strands of honey dripping from a broken hive, the broken chain caught the morning light as it hung from Asaege's clenched fist.

Even without laying eyes on the amulet, Markov must have felt its pull. She turned from the mob and focused on the waterfall of gold cascading from Asaege's closed hand. "What is this?"

Asaege was seized by a terror so absolute that her vision began to dim. The single spot of clarity in the twilight of her fear was what she held within her fist. "Lady Markov," she blurted, hoping to placate the woman.

Seemingly oblivious to her words, Markov leaned in. "What does she have?"

"Beware," Lirych warned.

Lady Markov spun on him. "Quiet! When I want your counsel,

I will demand it!" Almost as if she couldn't bear for the relic to be out of sight for long, she turned her back on the thaumaturge and focused on it once more.

Digging her nails into her palms, Asaege strained against the guard's grip in an attempt to pull her hand closer to her body. "Lady Markov," she begged, "please."

Markov's hand wrapped around her forearm, digging bony fingers into Asaege's flesh. "Let me see what is in your hand," she demanded. Digging her thumb into the sensitive area between hand and wrist, she pried Asaege's grip open, revealing the Gentle Lady. "Who did you steal this from, gutter rat?"

Her panic was so intense that Asaege didn't even try to remain silent. "The Crimson Sister. It is mine." An agonizing wail came from somewhere deep inside of her as Markov snatched the amulet from her hand. The utter despondency of losing the Gentle Lady made her feel as if her heart was torn from her chest. And then ... nothing. Once Markov turned away to study her prize, the all-encompassing possessiveness evaporated like rain after a summer storm.

Cradling the relic to her chest, Markov whirled to address the crowd. "These ungrateful wretches would even steal from the coffers of Olm himself. When I control Oizan, they will be chained like livestock when not of service."

The mob erupted once more, but the cries changed as some of the assembled thought about her words. A muted grumbling began to build among the crowd. One of the guards restraining Asaege loosened his grip on her in his apparent surprise.

"Your control," Asaege called. "What happened to the will of the people? How does 'we' become 'I'?"

Markov wheeled on her, lashing out with her empty hand. The sound of the slap echoed through the plaza, but it didn't drown out the councilwoman's voice. "I did not come so far, work so hard, for anyone's good but my own."

More rumbling arose from the plaza, competing with the rabid cheers that still came from glassy-eyed supporters.

The guard still tightly clutching Asaege's left arm moved to cover her mouth. His hand was slapped away by the soldier on her right. "Let her speak."

Encouraged by his change of heart, Asaege pressed her again. "You? I find it hard to believe you would work hard at anything."

Lady Markov's eyes began to dart back and forth as she realized something was wrong. The relic didn't require her active participation to work its charm, however. "It was no mean feat planning

Lord Fremht's murder across worlds. Securing the aid of both Claerius and his reflection took time, effort and money. The timing had to be perfect so he would die while rutting in the Silver Courtesan, placing the blame squarely on the revolution and its sympathizers."

Asaege's gaze shot to where the murdered man's sister stood. Confusion was evident on the noblewoman's face as her mind wrestled with the insinuation of reflection without reference. She had to force Markov to speak more plainly. "So you killed Lord Fremht?"

"I had Freeholder Fredericks killed." Panic began to seize the councilwoman. Asaege was running out of time.

"That is more like it. There is no way you could be responsible for the death of a member of the council."

Markov's jaw clenched, but her confession continued through gritted teeth. "It may not have been my hands around his throat, but I murdered Lord Fremht as surely as if they had been."

Asaege pulled her arms free from the stunned grasp of the guards flanking her and walked towards the cluster of nobility. "Is that going to be sufficient?"

Lady Fremht turned to her fellow representatives; each nodded in turn. "We are convinced." She raised a manicured finger and gestured to where Markov stood with her hand clamped tightly over her mouth. "Seize her."

The condemned woman backpedaled quickly towards the stairs. Behind her, a good portion of the mob still cheered wildly, their empty stares focused on her. Spinning, Markov descended two steps at a time. "Help me," she cried. "They mean to arrest me." Wisely, she kept her pleas short and general.

Across the plaza, Remahl and her templars rushed towards the crowd, but even armed and armored as they were, they wouldn't be able to prevent Markov's escape if she reached the safety of the mob.

I can not stop her from reaching the crowd, Asaege thought, *perhaps there is a way to make it a less attractive sanctuary.*

"Oh, Lady Markov," she called as she approached the edge of the dais overlooking the councilwoman's assembled supporters. "Before these people risk their lives to shield you from justice, perhaps they should know who they are protecting. Why do you not tell them how you really feel about them?"

Before she could cover her mouth, words flowed from Lady Markov's lips like water from a broken vessel. "The people are a convenient means to an end. I care no more for them than they do for the population of the Ash." The faces of the mob's vanguard dropped as they pushed against the line of guardsmen trying to hold them back.

"So why use them, then?" Asaege prompted.

Witnessing with her own eyes the change in what had been her most fanatical partisans, Markov stopped a handful of steps above the plaza. "Their desperate hunger for someone to validate their perceived victimhood, combined with a gullibility free from skepticism or examination, makes them the perfect shock troops in my bid for power."

A smattering of cheers still peppered the air, but they became lost amid the shouts of anger in the crowd.

Walking slowly down the stairs, Asaege continued to question Markov. "And what were your plans for these shock troops once you realized your rise to power?"

She clamped her mouth shut and shook her head vehemently. Her furrowed brow and crimson face betrayed how hard she struggled against the Gentle Lady's influence.

Her voice sharp as a blade, Asaege repeated her question. "What was to become of these people once you ruled Oizan?"

Her resolve spent, Lady Markov blurted out, "Their credulousness would be a liability should someone rise to oppose me. The majority of them would need to be rounded up with the laborers and restricted to the Common Quarter."

The crowd pressed forward again, not a glassy eye among them. Instead of Markov's name on their lips, they wore expressions of fury.

"But didn't you say that the population of the Common Quarter were no better than beasts? What does that make these people?"

Markov began to back up the stairs as the line of soldiers became overwhelmed. Trickles of angry former-supporters pushed their way through the breaks in the line. Regarding Asaege with a look of abject hatred, she announced, "Less than. At least animals have their own minds." A united cry of outrage rose from the mob as even the guardsmen holding it back turned on her. Her face pale, Lady Markov turned and fled back up the steps into the waiting arms of the assembled house guards of the Nine Families. When Asaege reached the dais, she was firmly in their grasp, but Lirych was nowhere to be found.

Chapter Forty

A Deadly Distraction

As Jillian pulled her car into Church Hill's half-empty parking lot, she felt a measure of Asaege's relief. The effects of her last visit to Stephen's bedside were fading but persisted enough for her to still get a general sense of her reflection's emotions. She found herself missing the intimate connection that the waking communion brought with it.

Beside her, Hector pulled a new pack of cigarettes from inside his jacket and peeled away the cellophane. "You're not smoking in here," she warned.

"I wouldn't dream of it." After sweeping his eyes around the car briefly and not finding what he sought, Hector dropped the tattered wrapper on the floor at his feet.

"By all means, put that anywhere."

With a snap of his wrist, he pushed a cigarette to the top of the pack. "You don't have a garbage bag." He gripped it with his lips and pulled it free. "I assumed you didn't care."

Jillian shifted the car into park more violently than she'd intended. "Get out."

He opened the door and stepped into the crisp morning breeze. It mingled with the stale, artificially heated air of the car's interior as he fished in his jeans pocket for his lighter. With a flick of his thumb, a flame sprang to life. Hector cupped his hand around it and lit the cigarette dangling from his lips.

Jillian quickly exited the car as well, favoring him with a withering glare. "The point of smoking outside the car was to not have it smell like an ashtray."

Gripping it between thumb and forefinger, he pulled the cigarette from his mouth. "You should've been more specific, then."

"Close the damned door," she growled.

Hector pasted an insincere smile on his face and did as she asked. "Happy?"

"Ecstatic." Without waiting for him, she began walking towards the building. "Finish your smoke break, then meet me at the fire door around the side. Parading a murder suspect through the lobby is asking for trouble."

He touched his thumb to his forehead in a mocking salute. "Of course, Miss Allen."

*****

Jillian found the rehabilitation center's hallways harder to navigate during the day without attracting attention, making her question Mateo's cryptic advice. It would have been easier without Hector by her side, but the two forged passes she'd created on her computer the night before seemed to survive passing scrutiny. Jillian's heart rose into her throat as they approached Richie's room. Above the persistent hum of the building's aged fluorescent lighting, she heard the bass tones of Officer Parr's voice. Luck was with the pair, however, as Billy's attention was focused on Richie's battered copy of *The Fellowship of the Ring*.

When she and Hector reached Stephen's room, they found it unexpectedly dark. Unlike the rooms surrounding it, the lights were off and the curtains drawn across its only window. More strangely, the overhead curtains had also been pulled around the bed, concealing it from view. Jillian's natural caution was tempered by the promise of waking reflection that awaited her within. Even standing in the doorway, she could feel the layers of distance between her and Asaege begin to fall away.

As Hector took a step to cross the threshold, she lifted her arm to bar his way. "Something's not right," she whispered.

He studied her for a split second. "Do you want to turn back now?"

"We could come back later, when there are fewer witnesses."

"Witnesses go both ways. If someone's gonna try to kill me, I want to make it as hard as possible for him to get away with it."

324

Jillian dropped her arm. "I don't like it."

"Trust me." As soon as Hector stepped into the room, she saw his shoulders tighten. She'd not warned him of the effects proximity to Stephen brought with it. It had been a calculated risk. If he'd had a chance to prepare for it, she had no doubt he could have somehow turned it to his advantage. In the moment, however, Jillian hoped that Hector's disorientation would be enough to interfere with anything Plague Man might attempt.

Jillian took a deep breath, a mixture of trepidation and anticipation boiling within her gut. As soon as she crossed the threshold, her vision swam with visions of a world not her own.

*****

The mass of humanity churned around Asaege as she desperately tried to tell friend from foe. After the Nine Families' representatives fled inside the building with Lady Markov in tow, the mob sought to vent its anger on whatever, whoever, remained. Caught between the Families' house guard and the oncoming tide, she was forced to defend herself from both sides. The mystical protection provided by Sarcune's Spectral Shield *was strained to its limit, battered with fist, club, and steel.*

Regretting her decision to not commit Flynn's Floating Trance *to memory that morning, Asaege quickly took stock of the formulae remaining to her. Having exhausted her supply of simpler spells, she was left with only three.* Killian's Killing Fog *would harm everyone within its reach, no matter their intentions.* Murdael's Murder Flies *would limit its effects to a smaller area, but was still indiscriminate in its targets. Inspired by Lirych's effective use of it, Asaege had tracked down a formula that evoked fear in those around her,* Traefalgor's Instant Terror. *Of the three, it offered her the best chance of escape, if she were not trampled by the stampede it caused.*

Relying on the last vestiges of Sarcune's Spectral Shield *and with her thoughts elsewhere, Asaege didn't notice the figure emerge from the crowd until he was right on top of her. Raising her dagger, she slashed at him to reestablish some breathing room for herself. Her blow was parried aside by an open hand as a lion swats aside the clumsy paw of its cub. It was only then she realized that her attacker's other hand didn't hold a knife or club, but rather her sheathed Talis Fahr.*

Pulling back his hood, Seran frowned at her. "You rely too heavily on your arcane words, and do not pay enough attention to what goes on around you." Tempted to hug him, she elected to take the offered weapon instead. "That is the first wise thing you have done all day, in my opinion."

"Thank you, Seran," she offered.

The elder thief drew a gleaming steel stiletto and turned to face the undulating mob around them. "The boy would never forgive himself if you came to harm while he was in the north, settling scores. I doubt he would be much more forgiving of me if I allowed it to happen."

Asaege drew her blade and looked around. Their plumed helmets just visible from the dais, the templars were working their way up the stairs behind the crowd. "Remahl's lines are ten yards away, if we can make it to them—"

"—There is only one way we do that." A sneering figure stumbled out of the mob, swinging a broken chair leg. Seran stepped into the charging man and ducked under his extended arm. Catching his opponent's arm behind the elbow with a raised forearm, he drove his dagger into his side twice in rapid succession. The dying man's last gasps were drowned out by the surrounding roar of battle. "Innocent or guilty, good or evil, every one of these people stands between you and survival. Put aside your sympathy and live ... or die with a clear conscience."

Steeling herself, Asaege fought back the gorge rising in the back of her throat. "There is another way. Stay near me and brace yourself." She reached into her subconscious and let slip the mental chains holding Traefalgor's Instant Terror *in place.*

*****

By the time Jillian came to her senses, she had covered most of the distance to the curtain-shrouded bed. The queasiness in her stomach mirrored Asaege's aversion in Taerh. Pushing it down as her reflection had done, she pulled back the curtain. Russell Blaine sat beside Stephen's bedside in a frayed chair that had seen much better days.

"I wasn't expecting you so early, but I'm certainly thankful for your timing." Looking past her, he smiled when he laid eyes on Hector. "And you brought a guest. How thoughtful!"

"Why am I not surprise to see you, Detective?"

"Maybe you're smarter than I gave you credit for ..." He stood casually. "... unlike some other people. It solved a lot of my problems when your body wasn't recovered after the fire, Mr. Thompson. You should have stayed gone. This time, I'm going to have to make sure you stay dead."

Hector reached into his jacket, his hand emerging with a hunting knife. "You are going to find that more difficult this time

326

around." The authoritative tone of his voice and lack of contractions told Jillian that both Plague Man and his earthly reflection had adjusted to the waking communion better than she'd hoped.

Blaine picked up the baton that had lain unseen beside the chair. "We'll see about that."

Hector advanced cautiously, the knife held before him in a relaxed grip. The detective moved around the bed towards him. Jillian scanned the room, desperately seeking something to use as a weapon.

"Don't go anywhere, Miss Allen. Once I'm done with the drug dealer, I'm going to have use for you. The Weed Killer will need a final victim to cement his legacy. Tragically, I'll have been too late to stop your murder."

Blaine brought the baton down hard, but Plague Man's reflection sidestepped deftly and closed the distance between them. The knife held at chest height, Hector slashed at the detective's face with a flick of his wrist. The detective recoiled from the blade's path, only suffering a shallow cut along his cheek. Denied the advantage of his longer weapon, Blaine lashed out with a fist. The blow caught his opponent in the side of the head, staggering him.

As he stumbled back, the detective drove the baton into Hector's gut. Abandoning her search, Jillian charged Blaine before he could bring his weapon down across the back of Hector's head. Driving her shoulder into his side, she and the detective fell to the floor in a tangled heap. As Hector fought to catch his breath, the two fought for control of the baton.

The reek of cigars and halitosis stung Jillian's nose as Blaine's breath hit her in the face like a blast furnace. "You're a cop." She could feel the stink of it on her tongue as she asked, "Why kill all those people?"

He drew back and drove his forehead into the bridge of her nose. Instinctively, Jillian raised her hands to her injured face, releasing her hold on his wrist. Through watering eyes, she saw Blaine rise slowly, favoring his side where she'd tackled him.

"I needed the money and Veronica was paying. I suspect Fredericks was politically motivated. As for Ricky Gunn, the druggie single mother ... hell, even Hector over there ... she wanted to keep her husband's parting gift to herself and they were in the way." Just as Lady Markov had stood above Asaege, Blaine towered over the prone Jillian. He kicked her viciously in the ribs before leaning down towards her. "You, though ... you're personal."

Jillian gasped for air. "What'd I do?"

The detective brought the baton down across her ribs. "You

burned my face, bitch. I didn't know it when we first met, but once I came in here to see what all the fuss was about, it all became clear."

Rolling over onto her stomach, Jillian cradled her ribs. She muttered something under her breath; the sound of it didn't even reach her ears.

Blaine leaned down further, mockery in his tone. "What's that, Miss Allen?"

Jillian lashed out with her elbow, putting all the coiled energy in her body behind it. She felt something crack beneath the blow. Blaine lurched backwards, clutching his left eye. Jillian snatched the baton from where it had fallen and scrambled away from him. Through his splayed fingers, she could see that the area around his eye had already begun to swell. The eye itself was quickly turning crimson as it filled with blood.

As Jillian climbed painfully to her feet, Blaine pulled his hand away from his face and fixed his abattoir gaze upon her. "I'm gonna make you hurt for that!"

Hector stepped up beside her, his knife held casually at his side. Plague Man's voice rolled from his lips. "I imagine you are going to find that quite difficult, dead man." Still cradling her ribs, Jillian hefted the baton. Only able to draw enough air to breathe, she had none to spare for witty repartee.

Although his left eye had already swollen shut, the detective's expression brightened as he looked past the pair. A devious smirk formed on his lips. "Help me."

Jillian turned to see Billy Parr standing in the doorway.

"What's going on here?"

"That's Hector Thompson. I liked him for the Weed Killer murders and tailed him here. He pulled a knife on me and his bitch took my nightstick. If you hadn't come along, they were going to kill me."

"Billy," Jillian wheezed. "He's lying. He killed Martin Fredericks, as well as Erik Gunn and Thomas's mother."

"Pull your gun, Officer Parr, and throw me your cuffs."

"With all due respect, Detective, I'm not sure what's happening here. Everyone stays where they are. That includes you, Jillian." Billy pointed to Hector. "Son, put the knife down and take two steps back towards me."

He glanced over at Jillian, a wild look in his eye. When she nodded, he bent down and carefully laid the weapon on the floor. "Whatever you say, officer."

"Now take two steps back. Keep your hands where I can see them."

Hector did as he was told, holding his arms away from his body as he moved backwards.

Blaine moved forward carefully, satisfaction evident in his face. "Put the weapon down, Miss Allen. You're under arrest."

Billy put his hand on the butt of his pistol. "Detective, please remain where you are."

"What are you talking about, Parr?" Blaine said incredulously.

"There are some things here that just don't make sense. If you were following Thompson, where's your backup? Why did you wait to confront him in this room?"

Blaine took another step towards Jillian.

"Detective," Billy snapped. "I'm not going to ask again. Remain where you are."

"This is ridiculous. Arrest these two now, or I'll have you brought up on charges."

Realization dawned on Billy's face. "You didn't follow them here. If you had surprised them, your back would be to the door, not theirs."

Blaine's shoulders slumped. "Well, that sucks. Why couldn't you have just done what you were told, Parr?" With a swift movement, the detective reached into his jacket.

His hand already on his gun, Billy drew it before Blaine could pull his free from his shoulder holster. "Don't do it, Detective!" There was a pleading in the officer's voice that must have given Blaine confidence, because he continued to draw his pistol. The thunderous report of a single shot rang out, deafening all three of them in the confined space of the hospital room. Blaine was beyond such discomfort.

Jillian wrapped her hands around her painfully ringing ears, closing her eyes against the pulsing agony. She pried them open as something brushed by her. Billy knelt beside the motionless form of Detective Russell Blaine, his nostrils flaring as he fought whatever emotions roiled within him. When she tried to approach, Billy held out a hand and said something. Through the clamor echoing in her head, she could barely make out the words. "Stay there."

More than happy to obey, she sank to the floor and focused on drawing slow, deep breaths. She wasn't sure how long she sat there trying to forget the look on Blaine's face as the bullet ripped through his body, but when she opened her eyes, Billy was kneeling beside her.

As if the words were spoken underwater, she heard him say, "It's going to be alright, Jillie. It's over." When she reached out to

329

grasp his hand, he seized hers in a vise-like grip. Jillian tried to pull away from him, but his limp body collapsed on top of her.

Hector stood over them both, a bloody knife clutched in his hand.

Chapter Forty-One
A Dreaded Revelation

Hollis emerged from beneath the gallows into chaos, the coppery scent of blood hanging in the morning air. The assembled Rangor fought for their lives against more than a score of snarling gwyllgi, their muzzles soaked with the blood of those already lying dead on the permafrost. Maintaining a buffer of calm among the turmoil, Ret and a battered Valmont stood back to back fending off a pair of the beasts. Motionless at their feet lay Sagaun.

Out of the corner of his eye, the thief saw Aristoi climbing the gallows steps. Crouched above her was the Hungered. He allowed Mika's body to slide to the ground and mounted the stairs behind her. "I leave you alone for five minutes …"

Stopping just out of claw's reach of the beast, the Songspear said, "If your business with the Snow Queen is at an end, I think I may require your assistance."

The Hungered snarled defiantly. "This is a pack matter, Song-spear. If you send the Child away now, he can leave unmolested."

Hollis tightened his grip on his Wallin Fahr. "That is not going to happen. We are a package deal."

The creature chuffed loudly. "So be it. I will see to it that once you have surrendered to your nature, his will be the first soul you feast upon."

Laying a comforting hand on Aristoi's back, the thief said, "I will be honest, I do not much like the sound of that. Let us try not to let that happen."

"I will do my best," she replied. Gathering her legs under her, Aristoi lunged upward, her spear lashing out before her. The gwyllgi leapt backwards, out of the path of the iron tipped weapon. Before it could block her ascent, she scrambled onto the platform on hands and knees. Before the Hungered could pounce on his prone companion, Hollis dashed up the stairs to stand beside her, blocking its path with Dwarven steel.

The Songspear rose quickly, extending her spear before her. "Your reign of terror ends here, monster."

"Does it, child? The Branded was no match for us. What makes you think you will fare any better?"

"He did not truly understand you, what you were capable of. I do not suffer from the same delusions. This voice has been whispering to me since its curse was laid upon my soul. Its words were designed to break my resolve and pave the path to the destruction of my will. The only thing is, I listened as adamantly as I fought. Without realizing, that voice told me everything I needed to know in order to destroy it, destroy all of you."

Hollis heard the strands of hope woven into the Songspear's declaration, coloring it with equal parts fear and defiance. The beast sank into a crouch, slinking forward with its powerfully muscled legs coiled beneath it. Stepping sideways, away from the edge of the platform, the thief put distance between himself and his companion. The Hungered altered its path accordingly, its rust-colored eyes focused on him.

Although the creature stalked Hollis, it continued to speak to the Songspear. "Against the ancient power of the gwyllgi, knowledge is neither weapon nor armor. All you have learned should only make you more certain of the fruitlessness of resistance."

"Said every dictator, fearing their own mortality ever." The beast narrowed its eyes at the thief's taunt. "What an overblown sense of your own worth you have, Grandma." He knew the reference went above both of their heads, but it made Hollis smile.

"You may have the power of the Well behind you, Child, but that is nothing compared to—"

"Blah blah blah. Do you know who else spouted that same garbage when they realized they were hip deep in shit? The Walker. Her carefully crafted monologue bought her a one-way ticket to Sharroth's cage."

The Hungered bared its teeth in a condescending snarl. Hollis saw the muscles beneath its mottled hide tense a split second before it leapt. As rear paws left the ground, propelling it forward, he rotated his body out of the creature's path, putting his sword between them. The Dwarven steel edge sliced hide and flesh like a razor through honey. Just like the viscous substance, though, the edges of the deep wound flowed together, masking the blade's passage beneath swollen scar tissue. As the creature pivoted, the thief saw that it was the only thing that remained of what should have been a debilitating wound.

"Aristoi," he called. The Songspear closed on the beast from its unprotected flank. "What the hell have I gotten myself into?"

The gwyllgi's ear closest to her twitched. As Aristoi thrust forward, it leapt above the blow and out of range of her weapon. With a mocking chuff, it answered for her. "Taerh will lose two Children of the Well today." Glancing quickly over its shoulder at the melee raging below them, it added, "But I shall add dozens to my own forces when the sun rises tomorrow."

The Songspear regained her balance at the edge of the platform, turning on catlike feet to face the creature once more. "It is not wise to celebrate something you will not live to see."

Rather than responding, the Hungered sank into a crouch and turned its attention to Hollis once more. Seemingly having learned its lesson, rather than leaping, it stalked forward with jaws agape. When the beast's paw lashed out, the thief met it with his Uteli blade. Again, it sliced deep into the creature's flesh. Again, the only evidence of the wound was a thick line of scar tissue.

Its frustrated growl rumbled in Hollis's chest, but the sound quickly built into a soul-wrenching howl. As when they faced Gorm among the barrows, the undulating call's effect was immediate on Rangor forces below. Blooded warriors let weapons slip from nerveless fingers and backed away in terror. The beasts they fought pounced on the frightened northerners, tearing into them with renewed vigor. The baying raised the hair at the back of the thief's neck, but he was insulated from most of its effects by the cloak of serenity wrapped around him.

"No," growled Aristoi. Her song started deep in her chest, playing counter-point to the rolling howl. Within the span of a few breaths, the gwyllgi's call dissipated as the Songspear's magic forced it into silence. The Rangor regained their will to fight almost immediately, but the tide had clearly turned against them.

Despite their recent history, Hollis's eyes searched for Ret among the fallen. He breathed a sigh of relief when he spotted the massive man still fighting beside the slim figure of Valmont. The pair were beset on multiple sides by gwyllgi, but they seemed to be holding their own for the moment. Turning his attention back to events closer at hand, the thief saw that his opponent had retreated a few steps. Having slunk back out of range of his weapon, the Hungered's head was thrown back against the morning sky. Rather than a terror inducing howl, an arcane song emerged, beating a counter point to Aristoi's own. As they built in strength, her voice faded to a dull murmur.

"How dare you!" Although Aristoi's voice was risen in anger, Hollis could barely make out her words through the tapestry of sound woven by the beast.

Lowering his head, it allowed its song to fade into silence. As he did, the ambient noise around them returned full force. "You seem surprised, Songspear. Your mother taught you that song to combat the gwyllgi." Rearing onto its hind legs, the Hungered's muscles rolled beneath its hide.

Thinking to take advantage of the creature's momentary distraction, Hollis leapt forward. He held his sword at waist height in order to drive it home in the gwyllgi's exposed gut. The beast swung its paw almost faster than his eye could follow, driving him to the ground. Its thick, talon tipped toes having already slimmed into long fingers, the thief escaped with his head attached, but it still rang with the power of the blow.

Rolling to his feet quickly to avoid a follow up strike, Hollis saw that in the beast's place stood a powerfully built Kieli, naked as the day he was born.

"Who do you think taught her?"

Aristoi stood slack jawed, the tip of her spear falling to the planks at her feet. "Branded? But how?"

Chapter Forty-Two
A Vehement Denial

The Branded? But how? Standing before Aristoi was her worst nightmare come to life. Believing he had given his life for hers, she had mourned the Herald. The leader of her order and protector of the Kieli people, the Branded represented the best of them. *If he could not resist the pull of the corruption within, what chance do I have?*

As if in answer to her unspoken question, the malicious voice in the back of her mind whispered to her once more. *We are the inevitable end of all things, the scourge that will wipe clean the face of creation so it may begin anew. Like the steady advance of death, no matter how long you resist, the gwyllgi can not be overcome, only accepted.*

"No," she muttered.

"Cast aside the doubt that plagues your existence, Aristoi. Lay down the burden of morality and pain. Once you accept the truth that echoes within your soul, it all disappears. All that remains is an anointed purpose."

Aristoi's mother had told her to set aside a burden, but that had been the weight of anger and vengeance, not kindness and mercy. Conjuring the image of the woman's kindly face to ward off the dark voices threatening to consume her, she felt a measure of peace return

335

to her thoughts.

"No," the Songspear repeated more vehemently.

"Fighting against the instincts within your heart must be exhausting. When they came for me, I had the intention to do the same. The voice of the Destroyer showed me a new path, one of freedom from the chains laid upon us by an uncaring universe."

"This is not you, it can not be."

"I have never been more myself, Songspear. Compared to the power of the pack, the cheap tricks of word and song are as leaves upon the wind."

To her left, she saw Hollis shake his head vigorously to clear the cobwebs that remained from the beast's clubbing blow. *How am I to fight the Branded*, she thought, despair threatening to overcome her. In the wash of it, Aristoi felt the voice grow bolder, stronger. It was almost as if it fed on her doubt. *No, never the Branded again. The creature before me is and shall evermore be only the Hungered.*

"For what you were to my people, my family and to me, I will give you the release you would have wanted before the light of your soul was swallowed by the darkness."

"I had hoped you would come to join our ranks of your own accord, but I am prepared to drag you by the hair if I must."

"I have slain your kind, your pack, before, monster."

Hollis added, "And we have put one Herald in the ground already. I have no issue doing so again."

"Beware, Child of the Well, you are but a mote of dust before the power of my purpose."

Stepping forward to stand beside her friend, Aristoi felt the last of her hesitation disappear as she became resolute in what must be done. "And you are nothing more than a stupid beast who has yet to realize that its leg is caught in a trap."

Chapter Forty-Three
A Predictable Betrayal

"Hector! What are you doing?" Jillian felt Billy's chest pressing against her as he fought for air. His struggles became weaker with every breath.

"He … I warned you what this was, princess. While Detective Blaine was looking to finish what he started, you were an important part of my plans."

"And now?"

"You cannot be so foolish as to believe I have only one. With the immediate threat to my life taken care of, it has become time to keep a promise I made to myself."

Gently pushing Billy off of her, Jillian unbuttoned his uniform shirt. Three gaping stab wounds dominated the officer's side under his left armpit. "What promise is that?" Her eyes searched for something to use to stop the bleeding.

As she tried to stand, Hector chided her. "I'd prefer if you stayed there, if you don't mind." His and Plague Man's consciousness switched places freely, marked by their use of contractions. When she looked up, she was greeted by the muzzle of Billy's service pistol.

"Unless you're planning on killing us both, I need to apply pressure to his wounds. I'd prefer to use something a little cleaner than my bare hand."

Stepping back to Stephen's bedside, Hector pulled at the blanket that covered the comatose man's frail form. Jillian had no idea how frail until it was laid bare. Used to seeing Hollis through Asaege's eyes, she was shocked to see Stephen's sunken skin and bony extremities.

"Use this."

"Does that mean you're not going to kill me?" Folding the blanket as best she could, Jillian placed it over the cluster of wounds on Billy's torso. He groaned feebly as she laid both her hands on the blanket and pressed hard.

"Let us not get ahead of ourselves. I made a promise the night you destroyed the brooch, the night your boyfriend threw me off a cliff."

"It was no less than you deserved."

Hector raised his voice. "That's not—" He took a quick breath and gathered himself. When he spoke again, it was in Plague Man's calm, measured tone. "That is not true. I offered to share power with you. Each of us could have had everything we sought."

"You know I'm not Asaege, right?" While factually true, Jillian could feel her reflection in the back of her mind, a panicked observer to what unfolded.

"What happens to one happens to the other." An angry, impatient glare flashed in his eyes as Hector surged to the fore. "That's something I'm real familiar with. When Hollis dropped my reflection fifty feet to what the thief hoped was his death, Plague Man wasn't the only one affected."

"That's something the two of you should discuss. What's it have to do with me?"

"Everything." He pointed to Stephen's motionless form. "If it wasn't for him, none of this would have happened to me. Walker would have used the Well, and Plague Man and I would have been set for life."

She raised an eyebrow. "All he had to do was let you murder his friends."

Hector sneered. "They died anyway. The only thing he succeeded at was ruining my life."

"History repeats itself, huh?" Jillian saw him wince as his temper flared. "At some point, you have to suspect that the issue lies in the mirror."

"I decided that night, as I lay half-drowned and broken, that I would even the scales. That starts right here." Hector reached into his jacket and pulled free a black leather case a little longer than his palm. "After I recovered, I found someone who shared my disdain for the Child of the Well."

"Another master to serve? When will you learn?"

"I serve no master. My new friend and I have a common goal."

"Why don't we call it what it is? You have spent your entire life looking for mommy and daddy's approval. Kill as many people as you like, but you'll never be more than the scared little boy Hollis should have left to die."

Hector took two quick steps towards her, murder clearly in his eyes. Like a puppet reaching the end of its strings, he pulled up short. He muttered to himself in a voice not meant for any ears but his own. "Fool. You will not screw this up as well." In a timid voice, he responded to his external monologue. "I'm sorry."

Now those are daddy issues on a whole new level. She found herself channeling a measure of Hollis's snarkiness in that moment.

When Hector returned his gaze to Jillian, the fire behind it had cooled to a smoldering hatred. "This is an extract that I found in my benefactor's research."

"Benefactor?"

Ignoring her, he continued. "It took me months to procure the ingredients and a small fortune in lab equipment to synthesize. In a moment, it will be worth all my effort." Hector flipped the case open and revealed a small syringe within. "This, princess, is the cure for what ails your boy-toy." He tapped Stephen's slipper-sock covered foot with the barrel of the gun. "The Well of Worlds consolidates two personalities into one. Normally, the process kills the earthbound reflection, but in rare circumstances, it leaves them an empty shell like Stevie, here."

Jillian felt a cold dread rise in her stomach.

Hector held up the syringe. "This acts like a spiritual magnet. It will draw the part of Hollis that is Stephen's essence back to his body. The Child of the Well will be in two places, and in none."

"Undoing the Well's magic?"

Stepping around the bed, he inserted the syringe into the IV and depressed the plunger. "I wish, but it will only dilute it."

Jillian's mind raced in an effort to figure out her next move. "What good does that do you?"

"My associate wants the Child weakened, but my interest is a little more personal. I want both you and Hollis dead, but first I need to know that you have suffered adequately. Once Stephen's consciousness returns, I plan to kill him before your eyes."

Jillian surged to her feet. "This is between you and me. Leave him out of it."

Hector pointed the gun at her, motioning for her to sit back down. "Oh, do not worry, Princess, I will get to you in due time."

Billy groaned again, his eyes twitching beneath his lids. "Please don't do this, Hector. What do you want from me?"

"I want you to watch him die. That is the image I want you to carry with you until the day I come for you."

Jillian felt someone step up behind her. She let her shoulders slump in defeat, lacking the strength to turn and see what else Hector had planned for her.

A familiar voice came from behind her. "Step away from the boy," Mateo demanded as he moved past her, a scalpel held in his hand.

Chapter Forty-Four

A Fallen Comrade

Aristoi allowed herself a small measure of hope. She and Hollis had fallen into a comfortable rhythm. Each time the gwyllgi would lunge towards one of them, they would give ground, drawing it into range for the other's weapon. The hide covering the creature's heaving flanks was slick with its blood and sweat. Each time iron spear bit into the Hungered's flesh, it left behind a gaping wound. Pale, swollen lines crisscrossed its body where the thief's blade had cut it. Each wound healed quickly but, combined with its fatigue, the effect of the thick ropey scar tissue began to slow the beast's movements.

As the gwyllgi leapt towards Hollis, the Songspear prepared to meet its charge ... but the normally nimble thief stumbled. Staggering backward, he fought to keep his balance as the creature's jaws closed within inches of his extended hand. Lunging forward, Aristoi drove the Hungered back, but her heart sank when she heard the solid thump of her friend's body falling to the platform. She skipped backwards to where his form lay motionless.

Its breath coming like a bellows, the beast growled. "What an ... unfortunate turn of ... events."

The Songspear stood over Hollis's fallen body, daring the gwyllgi to come within range of her spear to claim him.

Chapter Forty-Five

A Welcome Awakening

It took Stephen a few tries to force his eyes open due to the gumminess that coated his eyelashes. When he tried to raise his hand to wipe it away, he found that his muscles didn't obey his commands. He vaguely heard the sound of voices, almost as if they came through a subway speaker. He could barely make them out through the cotton that wrapped his thoughts.

"… once Stephen's … I plan … your eyes."

"… is between … leave him … it."

Even filtered through the blurriness of his vision, the stabbing light of the room hurt Stephen's eyes. Pushing through the agonizing needles of pain that stabbed into his brain, he fought to turn his head toward the voices.

"Oh, do not worry, Princess … to you in due time."

"What do … want?"

Successfully rolling his head to the side, the figures at his bedside came into focus. Hector—or was it Plague Man—stood over him, a pistol clutched in his fist. Just out of reach, her hands held before her imploringly, was Asaege. *But it can't be Asaege. What's she doing in the north?* The fog in Stephen's brain began to lift, revealing patches of clarity beneath. *This isn't the north. Where is Aristoi? Where am I?*

343

"I want you to watch him die. That is the image I want you to carry with you until the day I come for you."

I'm in a hospital. What am I doing in a hospital?

A figure appeared behind Not-Asaege. Although he wore his hair in a conservative style and a clerical collar around his throat, Stephen couldn't mistake the face that came into focus.

"Step away from the boy," the man wearing Seran's face demanded.

Chapter Forty-Six
A Friendly Face

"Step away from the boy."

Jillian turned in shock at the sound of Mateo's voice. Gone was the affable man she'd spoken with in the hallway on her late night visits to Stephen's room. The chaplain wore Seran's hard eyes and vicious sneer like they were tailored to fit him. Before Hector could shift the barrel of his stolen pistol from Jillian to him, Mateo raised his hand and threw the scalpel in one fluid movement.

Thunder filled the room once more as Hector fired a wild shot. Passing between Jillian and Mateo, the bullet sounded like an angry hornet. The scalpel protruding from his bicep caused the gun to drop from Hector's suddenly nerveless fingers. Without slowing his momentum, Mateo dove across Stephen's bedridden form to crash into Plague Man's reflection. The two men dropped out of sight.

As she tried to see what was happening on the floor, Jillian noticed Stephen staring at her through half-opened eyes. His mouth moved, forming words that didn't seem to emerge from his lips. Despite Hector's plan for him, her heart rose in her throat at the sight of Stephen finally awake.

Competing with the welcome sight was a second, ghostly vision. Superimposed over the drab hospital room was an opulent sitting room. The scent of roses and brandy fought against that of antiseptic and blood. Mingling with the sensation of the blood-soaked blanket clutched in her hand was the feeling of a bone china tea-cup. Asaege's thoughts pressed upon her from every direction. Her reflection's worry added to her own, compounded it exponentially. Like a rag doll trapped in a river, Jillian fought to find her balance amid the new, severe emotions that battered her.

Mateo and Hector's scuffle spilled out from behind the bed as the chaplain and the drug dealer rolled around on the white tiled floor. Hector had one arm wrapped around Mateo's neck while his free hand pummeled his ribs mercilessly. He let out a shriek as Seran's reflection reached up to dig a thumb into his eye. Releasing his hold on Mateo, Hector cradled his injured face, allowing the chaplain to put some distance between their bodies. As soon as he had the space, Mateo began driving his elbow into the back of Hector's head.

A raspy gasp from beside her drew Jillian's attention from the turmoil that raged within her mind. Billy's body spasmed as blood bubbled from his lips. As she had done before, she tried to accept Asaege's thoughts and feelings, but they immediately threatened to overtake her. She closed her eyes and focused on the hoarse sound of Billy's breathing and the thick feel of his quickly drying blood on her hands. More slowly than she would have liked, her reflection's influence faded to a whisper, but tenaciously refused to dissipate entirely.

Laying her hands over his wounds, she tried to apply pressure once again, but the pain only caused him to struggle more violently. Putting all her weight on him in an effort to hold him still, she pressed down on the already-sodden blanket. His frantic efforts subsided as his breathing slowed.

The room became silent as sounds of Mateo and Hector's fight abruptly stopped. Jillian looked up to find Mateo staring into the distance, the muscle in his cheek twitching in time with his rapid breathing. Although she'd never seen the expression in a mirror, the woman felt that she knew it well. "Don't fight it, Mateo."

Jillian never got the chance to see if the chaplain followed her advice. Hector hit him in the throat with the edge of his forearm and pushed the older man off of him. Mateo rolled to the side and scrambled away from him on palms and heels. His hand cradling his injured eye, a malicious smirk returned to Hector's face as he slowly rose to his feet.

He spat a blood flecked wad of phlegm in Mateo's direction. "Amateur." Turning back to where Jillian huddled over Billy's body, he taunted, "Where were we?"

I can't just sit here and watch him murder Stephen, she thought, *and rely on his word that he won't kill the rest of us soon after.* She could feel Billy's chest rising and falling beneath her hands. There was nothing more she could do for him. All the pressure in the world would do no good if no aid was on its way … or if they were all dead when it arrived. She stood carefully, trying not to jostle the officer. As she did, her head swam once more with a combination of terror and Asaege's persistent voice in the back of her mind.

Beneath her reflection's forceful thoughts and more potent emotions, a stream of nonsensical syllables repeated themselves insistently. Like an itch at the edge of her perception, the buzzing barrage of meaningless mental sounds served to distract her from the life-and-death struggle before her. Like something seen from the corner of her eye, when she turned her attention towards them, they skittered just out of reach, becoming louder as they did. Their increase in volume did nothing to clarify the words themselves.

"I won't—" Another wave of syllables pushed forward, demanding her attention. "—let you hurt him."

Hector laughed. "I am not sure you can do much about it, Princess."

Asaege's consciousness pushed forward, forcing one thought into Jillian's mind. *Speak the words.*

Chills raised across her thighs and up her back as Jillian recognized the arcane syllables for what they were. Desperate and bereft of other options, she closed her eyes and let the thaumaturgical phrases rush forward. The noises in the hospital room faded into the background as the words echoing in her head overpowered them. Jillian was unsure when her voice joined the chorus, but when she tentatively opened her eyes, she could feel the strength of the formula resonating in her chest.

Hovering before her eyes were a trio of thumb-sized flies, their buzzing drone building with every heartbeat. Jillian had seen the effects of *Murdael's Murder Flies* through Asaege's eyes, but when confronted with them in the flesh, she felt an understandable discomfort. The last time her reflection had cast the spell, it had summoned more than a dozen of the flesh-eating insects, but only three hovered unsteadily before her face.

Hector held his knife poised above Stephen's weakly struggling body, but his attention was firmly fixed on Jillian. Horror etched on his face, he muttered, "No," as if through his denial, he could undo the impossibility that hung in the air between them.

"I'm sorry," she whispered to herself as much as Hector. Putting from her mind the stomach-turning effects of the formula, Jillian extended her hand in his direction. Like a trio of arrows, the insects shot towards him. Their voracious buzzing filled her ears as they struck him in the face; it almost covered the sound of his screams.

Dropping his knife, Hector swatted ineffectually at his blood-soaked face. Jillian's stomach rebelled as he rushed by her, his mind fixed on nothing but escape. Two of the three flies continued to tear dime-sized chunks from his flesh. As he fled the room, she sank to the floor, fighting the retching coughs that shook her body.

Jillian wasn't sure when the nurses arrived with hospital security, but willingly gave herself to their care. As they wrapped her in a blanket, a breathy voice broke her out of her spinning thoughts. "Hello … Jillian. It's … so nice … to finally … meet you."

Chapter Forty-Seven
A Renewed Motivation

Subtle at first, the Songspear's vision began to blur at the edges. She stood her ground, suspecting it to be another trick by the Herald-turned-gwyllgi before her. As the dimming robbed her of peripheral vision, she shifted her head from side to side in an attempt to bring the images forming there into focus. She didn't like what she found.

An alien landscape presented itself, all sharp edges and dull surfaces. Surrounded by strange objects Aristoi guessed to be instruments of some sort, she found herself trapped in a small room. Through a thick pane of glass, she could see a handful of people looking on. A disembodied voice rang in her ears; its demands were made in a language she didn't recognize and were lost on her. Clutched in her hand was some sort of elongated lute. A thick black string ran from its bottom into a series of blocky devices beside her.

Fighting her disorientation, the Songspear found a strange calmness beneath it. Like voices heard through cotton, her anger and fear seemed far away in that moment. Through the washed out vision before her eyes, she could still make out the Hungered's crouched form, seemingly as confused as she.

Movement beneath her snapped her free of the mirage's effects, although the sense of serenity persisted. Hollis stirred between her legs. "Stay down," she muttered, turning her full attention back to the beast.

Obviously misinterpreting the situation, the gwyllgi counseled, "Listen to the voice within yourself. They speak the truth, they speak of what you are and what you can become." He must have assumed that it had been the conflict within her that stayed her hand.

The Songspear knew it to be something completely different. She had heard Hollis talk about Stephen's world before and the side-effects of reflecting there. Somehow, she had experienced a measure of it without the benefit of adder root. "The only voice I care to listen to told me to seek a cure. The man to whom that voice belonged is gone, and a monster wearing his face stands between me and his last request."

"You cannot fight the nature within yourself." The Hungered's sweat-slick skin began to roll and the muscles under it twitched violently. Through clenched teeth, he hissed, "This is your last chance, sister." He fell forward, his body contorting under the stress of the change.

Aristoi lunged forward, lifting her spear over her head. Before she could drive it into the former Herald's exposed back, he leapt away, his transformation complete.

"Do not make me destroy you." The Hungered's voice was more guttural through his thick muzzle and wicked teeth, but once she had recognized the soft lilt of the Branded's within it, the Songspear couldn't divorce herself from the knowledge. She suspected it was the creature's last defense against those who knew him in life. Aristoi couldn't allow her compassion for the man he'd been to prevent her from killing the monster he'd become.

"You are going to have to. Only one of us is going to see the sun set today."

She heard Hollis climb to his feet. "Two of us," he corrected.

"I thought I told you to remain where you were."

As the Songspear spared a glance over her shoulder, the Hungered took advantage of her momentary distraction to charge forward. His claws beat a quick staccato on the hastily built platform, the sound of them hitting her ears like an unfinished musical movement. Aristoi allowed the shaft of her spear to drop to the wooden planks with a solid thump that organically added to the building rhythm. She set her foot against the butt with a satisfying scrape, sinking to one knee to put the point in line with the beast's broad chest.

Its eyes widening in recognition, the Hungered tried to halt his momentum, striking a rapid tap-tap on the boards. Its desperate attempt added to the building symphony in Aristoi's head. The Songspear felt herself becoming lost in the unlikely melody. Fearing that it was another of the creature's tricks, she shook off its hypnotizing effects. As quickly as it had fallen upon her, the inexplicable calm lifted from her heart.

The shock of its loss allowed the Hungered to retreat from her weapon's stinging bite with its life still intact, although not without a price. It held its left foreleg close to its chest as it scrambled backwards on three paws. Still trying to come to grips with her first experience with reflection, Aristoi was slow to follow up on its injury. Hollis stumbled past her, obviously still dealing with his own disorientation.

The thief slashed cautiously at the wounded beast, his Uteli weapon drawing a crimson line across its chest. The wound healed into a bulging pale scar almost immediately, but caused the gwyllgi to pitch forward before tendon and muscle could knit together. Quickly gaining strength, he reversed his sword's momentum and brought it down across its shoulders. The Wallin Fahr bit deeply, the force of its blow knocking the creature to the ground.

The wound healed as soon as Hollis withdrew his blade for another strike, allowing the Hungered to clumsily leap away from it. Landing on three unsteady feet, the creature roared in frustration. Aristoi shook off her confusion and joined her comrade. When the Hungered lunged forward again, it was greeted by both of their weapons. Falling back once more, the beast changed tactics.

The Songspear felt the building power of the song before she heard it. Its ancient words spoke of blistering death delivered by fiery hands. Before she could react, the platform on which they stood began to smolder.

Cursing herself for being caught unaware, Aristoi began to sing as well. Calling upon the might of the northern wind, she directed its fury at the smoking planks at her feet. Like a candle before a sharp breath, the barely birthed flames were extinguished. The Songspear was taken aback. *It should not have been that easy.* She had no time to question any further; The Hungered let its song of fire fade and began another.

Like ink dropped into a slow-moving stream, the clear morning filled with clouds the color of dirty wool. As the first rumble of thunder rolled through the quickly darkening sky, Aristoi understood the beast's intent. Knowing the unlikelihood of evading the deadly touch of lightning, she mirrored the Hungered's song in a vain attempt to lessen his control over the storm. To her surprise, she felt her magic wrench it from his grasp. Knowing she had not suddenly become more powerful than a Herald, even given her brush with reflection, the Songspear came to a startling revelation.

The corruption within the Hungered erodes the puissance of the Branded's magic. Despite its assurances to the contrary, the gwyllgi's power comes with a steep price. Realizing it was outmatched, the creature's voice fell into silence. Changing the tempo of her song, Aristoi called a pounding hail from the heavens.

Around the gallows, Rangor warriors dove for cover beneath the structure. When the gwyllgi attempted to follow them, they found themselves faced with steel. Unable to find shelter from the unyielding assault from above, the beasts fled rather than face the bone-breaking precipitation.

Those on the platform fared a little better. In the eye of the storm, they were spared the worst of the hail, but pea-sized projectiles still fell upon them with bruising force. Aristoi and Hollis pushed forward through the stinging curtain toward the Hungered. The beast stood at the edge of the platform, studying the steep drop to the ground below over its shoulder.

The hail tapered off as the Songspear allowed her song to end. "There is no escape, Hungered. You could jump, but on three legs, the Rangor will tear you to pieces before you could reach your brethren." She could see in the depths of its rust-colored eyes he knew her words to be true. "That is no way for a Songspear and Herald to die."

Bobbing its weary head in agreement, the gwyllgi gathered its feet under it for a final charge. Aristoi's spear met it mid leap, sinking into its chest with the force of its weight. The Hungered's jaws opened and closed a few times ineffectually before its body relaxed like an uncoiled spring.

The Songspear eased the creature to the surface of the platform with a gentle reverence. The beast's body twitched and contorted as it lay upon the hail dented planks, returning to the shape it had held before the gwyllgi's corruption. The man Aristoi had known opened his eyes for the last time, reaching out his hand.

Hollis at her shoulder with bared Dwarven steel, she grasped it between both of her own. "I am here, Branded."

"Thank you, child. The strength you have shown today … every day since the curse took hold of you …" He paused for a moment in an effort to catch his breath. "I have never seen its like … even in myself."

She squeezed his hand tightly. "Rest now, your walk is finished."

He shook his head firmly, continuing. "You are going to need that strength. Haldroi's cure is out there, but I know not where."

"Who would?" It was Hollis's voice.

The Branded turned unfocused eyes on the thief. "Ah ... from the mouths of children." He laughed at his own joke, causing him to break into a wracking cough. When he had caught his breath, he turned his attention back to Aristoi. "The Risen is the oldest of us, but also the closest to true evil. It is with him your hope lies." He closed his eyes, the lines of his face relaxing. Without opening them, the Branded warned, "He has yet to abandon his Herald's oath, but I ... I would not put it past him now that he is the only one of us left. Seek him out ... find out what he knows ... but trust him sparingly."

The Songspear rested her lips on the back of the dying man's hand, uncharacteristically at a loss for words.

"Your people should be proud ... Your mother would be proud ... and I ... I am proud."

"Thank you, honored Branded."

"So very ... very proud." With a last rattling sigh, the Branded was gone, his limp hand slipping from Aristoi's grasp. She struggled to hold back the tears that burned the back of her eyes.

She felt Hollis's hand on her shoulder. Placing hers over his, the Songspear squeezed gently. "He was the best of us."

"No he was not."

Anger flaring in her heart, she looked up at him.

"You are. In his last moments, even he knew that."

Aristoi heard the tentative sound of footsteps on the gallows stairs. "I hope I am able to live up to that."

The thief helped her to her feet as the pair turned to face Valmont and Ret, standing side by side. "You already have."

Part Three:

Shadows of Revelation

"Experience is the only prophecy of wise men."
                    - Alphonse de Lamartine

Chapter Forty-Eight
A Joyous Return

A saege stood at the back of the council chamber, leaning casually against a marble column whose value could have fed an Ash family for a year. *One step at a time*, she thought as the first Oizan Unified Council meeting was called to order. Three oak tables dominated the small room, one for each of the city's voting interests.

As one of the conditions for declaring an end to hostilities with the revolution, The College of Guilds was seated in the center. The stern-faced craftsmen would need time to adjust to their loss of almost complete power over city affairs. All things considered, they had handled the loss-in-all-but-name well. In public, they had claimed a nominal victory and had almost returned to business as usual.

To their right sat the Chamber of Lords. Led by Lady Fremht, the representatives of the Nine Families had delivered on their promise to support the population of the Common Quarter. At first, Asaege figured they would provide only lip service and treat the responsibility of shared governance as nothing more than an idle diversion. After the turmoil they experienced—indirectly, of course—during the rebellion, they seemed to be taking steps to prevent it from happening again.

On the opposite side of the room, the members of the Laborer's Union gathered around the seemingly too small table. It didn't differ from the size of the other two, but between the dock workers, teamsters, servants and numerous other small laborer lodges, there had yet to be a clear understanding of who would represent whom. This had led to each sending their own delegate. It promised to drag proceedings to a halt until it was straightened out, but it annoyed the other two groups to no end. That was enough for Asaege.

True to her own promise, the Prophet hadn't made an appearance since the end of hostilities. When the subject of the council's composition was discussed, she had taken Lady Fremht's sour expression as a suggestion that Asaege should keep a low profile as well. It was all the same to her; she'd had her fill of leadership for a while.

As she pushed away from the column, Asaege found Seran standing next to her, observing the meeting as well. "It is an absurd way to conduct business," he noted. "They are likely to get next to nothing done."

She smiled. "It is one of the growing pains of democracy. One can only hope that what does get accomplished is for the mutual benefit of all."

He mmm'ed noncommittally.

As she playfully scowled at the elder thief, Asaege noticed a tiny hand wrapped around his silk-covered wrist. Peeking around his body, she saw the face of Jillian's student, Thomas, staring back at her. "Who thought it was wise to entrust you with a child?"

"I did practically raise the boy."

"Which led to a lifetime of larceny and bloodshed."

Seran smirked wryly. "I am quite proud of the way he turned out, thank you for noticing."

Asaege shook her head in mock disbelief. "I think some people may be looking for this one." She remembered Remahl's search for a missing prisoner, a young boy.

"Then they should have taken better care of him."

"And if they come looking for him?"

"They will find that I will protect him better than they did."

She chuckled lightly. "Fair enough." The volume in the chamber began to rise sharply. "If you care to stay, feel free, but I sense they are getting ready to start shouting."

"That is why I came."

"Suit yourself. I have delicate sensibilities."

"So I have heard." As she walked by him, Seran caught her

wrist. "Someone is waiting for you outside. Just thought you would like to know."

"Who?"

Wearing a full-blown, cocky smile, the elder thief shrugged and returned his attention to the council floor.

One hand on her sword, Asaege pushed the chamber's door open. Before she could react, she was swept off her feet and spun in a tight circle. As soon as Hollis set her down, she leapt back into his arms.

Chapter Forty-Nine
An Ambitious Plan

Hollis walked into the common room of the Virgin Mermaid, his fingers intertwined with Asaege's. After his time in the north, he savored the heavy air of the tavern. Combined with the unseasonable warmth since their return, the early hour would have allowed them their choice of tables had Aristoi not already chosen one.

Her spear resting in the corner behind her, the Songspear chatted idly with a serving girl. As the pair approached, she smiled softly and rested her hand atop the girl's. "Perhaps we can speak more later, Jaecinda?"

"I would like that," the girl responded, her cheeks colored by more than the heat of the room.

"She did not need to leave on our account," Asaege offered.

Aristoi rose and kissed her lightly on the cheek before gesturing to the empty chairs around the table. "We have much to discuss. I am sure she and I can pick up where we left off at some point." As she resumed her seat, the Songspear said, "I trust the two of you had enough time to get reacquainted."

"You could say that," Hollis purred.

Asaege slapped him playfully on the bicep. "Hollis has told me of your plans."

Aristoi raised an eyebrow. "Has he? I am surprised you two found a moment to discuss it?"

"Barely," the thief interjected.

She hit him again, a little harder. "No one is certain where to find the Tower of Ash. The only thing that can be agreed upon is that the Risen's sanctum can be found somewhere in the center of the Expanse."

"Correct."

"Any journey to the Expanse takes you through Oenigh. If what Hollis tells me is true, it is not exactly friendly to either of you."

"That is also correct." Shifting her eyes to meet the thief's gaze, Aristoi asked, "Did he tell you why we seek the Risen's counsel?"

"No."

"It was not my tale to tell," Hollis added.

The Songspear turned back to Asaege. "And you would aid me, no questions asked?"

Asaege's expression brightened. "Oh, I am going to ask plenty of questions. I just do not believe that any of the answers will change my mind."

"Why?" Aristoi's confusion seemed genuine. "You hardly know me."

"I know you well enough, the content of your character even better. You risked your life to journey into the bowels of the city in order to rescue me. You traveled north with Hollis to put the ghosts of his past to rest, returning him to me safe and sound. What more do I need to know?"

"Let that be your first question," Aristoi said.

"The first of many, I am sure." Hollis's joking tone contradicted the dread that had lingered in his heart since witnessing what dwelled inside his friend.

"It will be the perfect amount, thank you very much."

Sitting back in her chair, the Songspear lowered her voice, so it would not carry beyond their table. "When I found my mother, she was already beyond my aid. Looming so large in life, she seemed so frail in death. ..."

Chapter Fifty
An Overdue Farewell

Even as he lay in the hospital bed, Stephen could feel Hollis's mix of satisfaction and trepidation. The path set before Asaege, Aristoi and the thief was daunting, but he shared his reflection's excitement to be walking it with the two people he loved most in the world. Or perhaps it was his own excitement. Since waking from his adder root induced coma, Stephen had found it hard to tell where Hollis ended and he began.

For him, the two worlds had become so intertwined that traveling to Taerh was as simple as closing his eyes. Sometimes, even that wasn't necessary. Stephen had taken to wearing the hood of his over-sized sweatshirt over his head to minimize the ghostly images that haunted his peripheral vision constantly. He found they could infiltrate his perceptions if he allowed them to linger just out of eyesight for too long. Such was the case at that moment.

"Are you even listening to me?"

Stephen closed his eyes, mustering his willpower. When he opened them again, the comforting interior of the Virgin Mermaid had given way to the sterile, pale green walls of his hospital room. "I'm sorry, Ronni. Please continue."

His ex-wife's cheeks were flushed with rage as she stood at the foot of his bed, arms akimbo. "You can't do this."

He frowned in confusion. "Do what?" He must have missed more than he thought.

"Keep me from seeing you."

"Yes, I can. We're no longer married, correct?"

"Well, yes."

"Didn't you also perpetuate a slanderous accusation, damaging my good name?" He found her silence more incriminating than any answer she could have given. "Maybe it was libel. I can never keep the two straight. Did you write anything down?"

"Stephen, please." Her voice switched from anger to desperation like she had flipped a switch.

"Furthermore, you're responsible for the deaths of no less than four people … and that's just here on Earth. There's no telling how many people paid for your hubris with their lives in Taerh."

"That wasn't me. That was her."

His only reply was a stern look.

Ronni's voice became hard. "Prove it."

"You don't mean that. Either through arrogance or ignorance, you left some loose ends lying around. Do you really want me to start digging into this?"

Her response was a tiny, "No."

"I've given you everything you could have wanted in the divorce: the house, the cars. For heaven's sake, I gave you half of my 401k. What more do you want?"

She averted her eyes.

"You don't have to answer. It was a rhetorical question. After all these years, I finally have something of value to you."

"That's not true—"

"Enough," Stephen snapped. "Mark my words. This is the last time I want to see you. You and your reflection used me to wreak all sorts of havoc in both worlds. People died, Ronni. That will never happen again."

She nodded slowly.

"Tell me you understand."

"I understand."

"Good. Now get out."

Ronni bent down to pick up her purse before turning for the door. Just as she reached it, Jillian arrived, fresh flowers clutched in her hand. Looks of sharpened steel passed between the two women before Ronni looked away and dashed past Asaege's reflection.

A cloud still hung in Jillian's expression, but she smiled warmly. "How are you feeling, Stephen? I brought flowers."

Chapter Fifty-One
An Honest Threat

Mateo was waiting for Ronni outside Stephen's room, the dark specter of his reflection haunting the depths of his mind. The two had reached a delicate detente after the situation in Stephen's room the month before. The more time the chaplain spent with Hollis's reflection, the more he understood his own, but Seran's presence still made him uncomfortable. He braced himself for further discomfort, as the impending conversation was more in the elder thief's wheelhouse than his own.

"Veronica," he called. "A word with you?"

Lips pursed in annoyance, she stopped and slowly turned to face Mateo. But at that moment, it was no longer Mateo.

"For some reason, the boy is hesitant to remove the inconvenience you represent. I am under no such disadvantage."

"Didn't you hear him? He doesn't want to see me again."

In a tone cold as a tundra wind, he said, "I had something more permanent in mind."

Ronni's face paled. "You can't …"

"Oh, I very much can. However, I will not, as long as you honor the boy's wishes."

"Alright."

And now we come to it, he thought. Since his reflection had devised their shared course of action, it hadn't sat right with the chaplain. He understood that it served the good of the greatest number of people, but threats of violence felt at odds with his life's vocation. He wasn't sure if it was Seran's or his own, but one thought went a long way toward assuaging his guilt. *Threats represent merely the possibility, not the action itself. As long as she stays away, it will remain as such.*

As she tried to push past him, Mateo grabbed her by the wrist. "You may be thinking that the police can help you, or perhaps one of the slavering mob that launched you to political success. There is one thing you should remember, my dear. The chaplain does not need to lay an uncalloused finger on you here."

Realization dawned in Ronni's eyes.

Leaning close to her, so his breath warmed her face, Mateo whispered to her. "No doubt the echoes of reflection still linger within your mind. If you close your eyes, I would wager you can feel the cold touch of my blade on Lady Markov's throat … taste the coppery taint of fear on her tongue."

He stepped back and released her arm. "If I see you again, I will pay her another visit. Neither of you will see it coming."

Epilogue
A Malicious Conspiracy

Lirych approached the motionless, desiccated figure on the dais. As he leaned down, as if to whisper to the husk of a creature, its head rose to meet his lips. Paper thin lids opened to reveal eyes the color of aged bone. "Plague Man has returned, milord."

With a sound like wind through a field of dried reeds, the creature spoke. "What news does he bring with him?"

Plague Man stepped forward, the yellow-eyed gaze directed at him causing the flesh to rise at the back of his neck. "I have done as you asked, Risen. The Child's power has been divided."

"And its earthly vessel destroyed?"

"There was a complication."

The tight, leathery flesh of the Risen's face contorted into a snarl, revealing blackened teeth. "Why is it that all I am hearing in recent nights are complications?" He turned his dispassionate, pale-moon gaze on Lirych. "I believe I was quite clear with my instructions." Lirych took a step away from the Herald, bringing a smile to the Risen's corpse-like face. Returning his attention to Plague Man, he hissed, "Tell me of these complications."

"I was able to brew the elixir. However, when I used it, the Prophet's reflection stopped me from killing the vessel."

A sound like dry leaves on cobblestone emerged from the

367

Risen. Plague Man took it for an expression of amusement. "Pray tell, how did she do that? How did an instructor of children best the fearsome Plague Man?"

"She called forth a cloud of demonic insects."

A grating creak echoed through the chamber as the Risen leaned forward. "Thaumaturgy?"

"I can think of no other explanation."

"Interesting. Perhaps some glint of hope can be found in your failure after all."

"Thank you, milord."

"Consider yourself fortunate. Your personal vendetta nearly cost me dearly. I will forgive your transgression this once. I trust I will not need to do so a second time."

"No, Risen."

Slowly climbing to his feet, the last remaining Herald drew himself up straight. "The prophecy is coming to fruition, and sooner than I had anticipated."

Lirych stepped up behind the Risen and draped a deep purple cloak over his skeletal shoulders. "Allowing the Child to remove your fellow Mouhn was a stroke of genius."

He raised a tattered eyebrow. "Allowing?"

"My apologies. What I meant to say was authoring their demise at his hands."

"That is more appropriate. I could not have anticipated that he would also end the Snow Queen's uprising as well."

Lirych smiled. "That was indeed a fortunate coincidence."

His grin disappeared as the Risen regarded him coldly. "While it accelerated our timeline, it also poses a risk to our endeavor."

"How so?" Plague Man began ascending the stairs towards the pair.

"Between the two of them, The Child and his songspear companion have bested two Heralds, as well as a fellow Child of the Well. The Prophet banished a primal force of darkness when better thaumaturges have tried and failed. Together, they could represent a thorn in my side."

"Let me kill the girl for you, milord. I will depart for Oizan first thing tomorrow morning. I will not fail you again."

"Of course, you will not. There is no need for you to leave, however."

A female gwyllgi stepped from the shadows where it had been crouching unnoticed. Before Plague Man's eyes, the creature's body began to contort, its corded muscles rolling beneath the brindle hide that covered them. Rising up to her full height, Junwei lifted an ancient spear from its resting place beside her carefully folded tunic. "My sister and her companions will be coming to us."

About the Author

A child of the 80's, SL Harby grew up playing Dungeons & Dragons and classic video games. An only child, he was bitten early by the reading bug, cutting his teeth on the masters of modern fantasy. His days were spent inside the worlds created by Howard and Lieber, Moorcock and Tolkien.

A perpetual Jersey boy, SL Harby now lives in South Carolina with his wife and muse, Jessica, and their bad ass rescue dog, Tallulah.

Shadows of Betrayal is the third installment in the Well of Shadows tetralogy.

Other Works by SL Harby

Well of Shadows Series

Shadows of a Dream (Available Now)
Shadows of the Heart (Available Now)
Shadows of Betrayal (Available Now)
Shadows of a Promise (Available Winter 2024)

Made in the USA
Middletown, DE
23 October 2023

41272482R00212